Praise for Susanna Kearsley

'A creative tour de force ... Sometimes an author catches lightning in a bottle, and Susanna Kearsley has done just that. Brilliant!'
New York Journal of Books

'A deeply engaging romance and a compelling historical novel ... Susanna Kearsley has written a marvellous book'
Bernard Cornwell, author of *The Last Kingdom*

'Highly reminiscent of Barbara Erskine's *Lady of Hay* and Mary Stewart's works: evocative novels that lift readers straight into another time and place to smell the sea, feel the castle walls, see history and sense every emotion. These are marks of a fantastic storyteller'
RT Book Reviews

'A thrilling, haunting and deeply romantic story'
Rachel Hore, author of *A Beautiful Spy*

'A terrific read, evocative and romantic'
Nicola Cornick, author of *The Scandals of an Innocent*

'Susanna Kearsley's obvious love of history is infectious ... *The Winter Sea* is an acknowledgment that so many of us are haunted by the deeds of our ancestors, perhaps literally'
Gail Anderson-Dargatz, author of *A Recipe for Bees*

'Kearsley's gentle drama and accurate detail are sure to satisfy lovers of historical fiction and romance'

Publishers Weekly

'A beautiful and poignant tale of lost love, haunting and humbling ... Romantic, passionate and bittersweet, this intelligent, tension-laden story will sweep you away'

Historical Novels Review

'Incorporating rich historical details that feel as vivid as the present enables readers to quickly lose sense of time as the author weaves threads from two eras into one dramatic tapestry'

Library Journal

'A sweeping love story that expertly explores both the characters and the turbulent times in which they live'

Sunday Post

'A hugely engrossing book and a complete world created'

Ian Rankin, author of *A Heart Full of Headstones*

'An absolute tour de force of historical storytelling, tender and dramatic, gripping and authentic. Kearsley manages effortlessly to balance the epic sweep of the drama with telling moments of gentle characterization, all delivered in pitch-perfect style'

Jane Johnson, author of *The Salt Road*

SUSANNA KEARSLEY

The VANISHED DAYS

**SIMON &
SCHUSTER**

London · New York · Sydney · Toronto · New Delhi

First published in Great Britain by Simon & Schuster UK Ltd, 2022
This paperback edition first published 2023

Copyright © Susanna Kearsley, 2022

The right of Susanna Kearsley to be identified as author of
this work has been asserted in accordance with the
Copyright, Designs and Patents Act, 1988.

'The Word' by John Masefield is used by permission of the Society of
Authors as the Literary Representative of the Estate of John Masefield.

1 3 5 7 9 10 8 6 4 2

Simon & Schuster UK Ltd
1st Floor
222 Gray's Inn Road
London WC1X 8HB

Simon & Schuster Australia, Sydney
Simon & Schuster India, New Delhi

www.simonandschuster.co.uk
www.simonandschuster.com.au
www.simonandschuster.co.in

A CIP catalogue record for this book
is available from the British Library

Paperback ISBN: 978-1-4711-9604-1
eBook ISBN: 978-1-4711-9603-4
Audio ISBN: 978-1-3985-0155-3

This book is a work of fiction. Names, characters, places and
incidents are either a product of the author's imagination or are
used fictitiously. Any resemblance to actual people living or
dead, events or locales is entirely coincidental.

Typeset in Bembo by M Rules
Printed and Bound in the UK using 100% Renewable
Electricity at CPI Group (UK) Ltd

MIX
Paper | Supporting
responsible forestry
FSC
www.fsc.org
FSC® C171272

For James Graeme and the hundreds – known and nameless – who set sail for Darien, with Scotland's hopes and future in their hands; whose passing left holes in the hearts and lives of those who loved them, and who deserve to be better remembered

My friend, my bonny friend, when we are old,
    And hand in hand go tottering down the hill,
May we be rich in love's refinèd gold,
    May love's gold coin be current with us still.

May love be sweeter for the vanished days,
    And your most perfect beauty still as dear
As when your troubled singer stood at gaze
    In the dear March of a most sacred year.

May what we are be all we might have been,
    And that potential, perfect, O my friend,
And may there still be many sheafs to glean
    In our love's acre, comrade, till the end.

And may we find when ended is the page
Death but a tavern on our pilgrimage.

John Masefield, 'The Word'

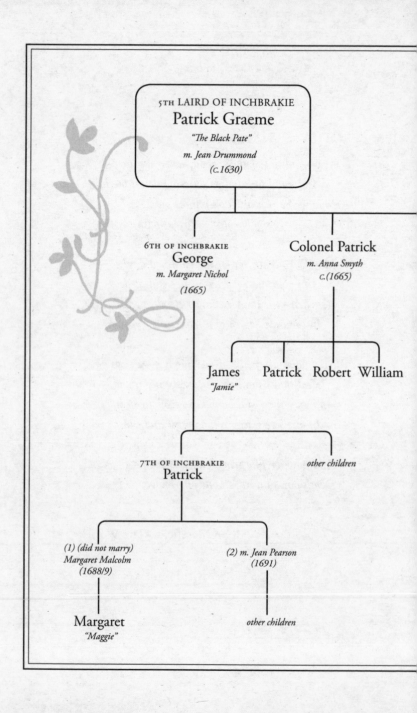

5TH LAIRD OF INCHBRAKIE
Patrick Graeme
"The Black Pate"
m. Jean Drummond
(c.1630)

6TH OF INCHBRAKIE
George
m. Margaret Nichol
(1665)

Colonel Patrick
m. Anna Smyth
c.(1665)

James
"Jamie"

Patrick

Robert

William

7TH OF INCHBRAKIE
Patrick

other children

(1) (did not marry)
Margaret Malcolm
(1688/9)

(2) m. Jean Pearson
(1691)

Margaret
"Maggie"

other children

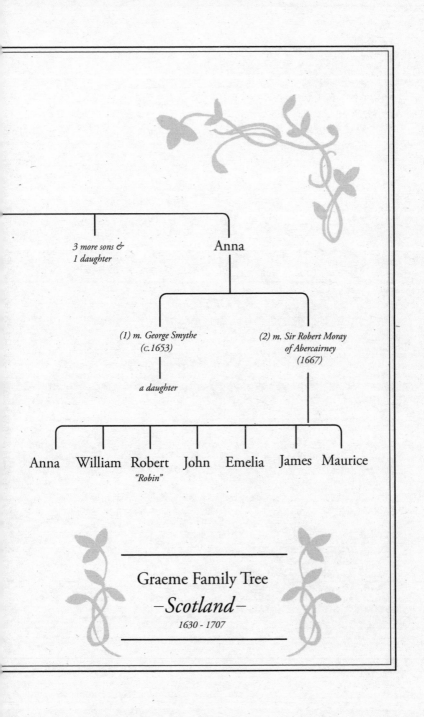

3 more sons &
1 daughter

Anna

(1) m. George Smythe
(c.1653)

(2) m. Sir Robert Moray
of Abercairney
(1667)

a daughter

Anna   William   Robert   John   Emelia   James   Maurice
                   "Robin"

Graeme Family Tree
–Scotland–
1630 - 1707

I

I WAS A YOUNGER MAN when I first met her. I should tell you this in fairness, not because the years have dulled my recollection of that moment, for in truth I could still lead you to the spot where I was standing when she looked in my direction. I've forgotten many things. That is not one of them. I'm telling you because even the wisest man, when young, is ruled by other things than wisdom when he meets with such a woman. And when I met Lily Aitcheson, I knew I was in trouble.

There are many who believe they know what happened, but they do not know the whole of it. The rumours spread, and grow, and take their hold, and so to end them I have been persuaded now to take my pen in hand and tell the story as it should be told – both in the parts that are my own and in those pieces that were hers, as they were told to me by others and as I came to discover them.

You may ask how closely you can trust my narrative, when I have waited until now to set it down, and when those days must surely seem so distant to me, like a magic lantern show of memories played against the coming darkness. I can only reassure you we kept notes from our enquiries – Gilroy's and my own – and I have those beside me here now in my study, for my reference.

As to memory, you may understand this better for yourself, when you are old, but there are some corners of the mind imprinted so indelibly with what we have experienced that, long after the less important things have slipped away and we have lost the simple function of recalling where we last set down our spectacles, those deeper memories yet remain. The slightest thing may make them stir – a wafting scent, a few notes of a song half-sung, the darkness of a passing cloud.

Most evenings in my armchair by the fireside I drift now to those memories and assure you they are every bit as clear as when I lived them.

Me at fourteen in the scorching bright sunlight, the day I was taught how to fire a musket.

A turn, and I'm deep in the jungles of Darien, fighting the Spaniards, and Lieutenant Turnbull, my friend and commander, is urging me onwards in spite of the shot to his shoulder that's just made him fall. 'Go,' he says. 'Do not stop. Go!'

Turn again, and it's several years on and I'm once again following Turnbull's directions, his letter inviting me to come and visit him tucked in my pocket as I climb the worn stones of Edinburgh's High Street in search of his door.

He lived, that year, in Caldow's Land – the term *land* being commonly applied in that town to those great, high tenements in which each floor was, of itself, a separate dwelling, serviced by a common stair. It was a narrow building, and an old one, and the evening I arrived in mid–September under skies that threatened rain it looked unwelcoming. The hollow shadows lying deeply in the arched shop booths at street level, the several looming storeys of dark windows, and the jagged roofline cutting at the sky all seemed to warn me not to stay.

But I was stubborn, I was weary, and I did not heed the warning.

So, for what came next, I've no one but myself to blame.

CHAPTER 1

MONDAY, 22 SEPTEMBER, 1707

M ACDOUGALL WAS WATCHING ME. It was unsettling to waken and find him half-shielded by shadow, an arm's-length away from my bed. For a sick moment I thought I was still in the grip of the trembling fever that had been my curse these past years and that had, as it always did, struck without warning, the same night I'd set foot in Caldow's Land.

Making things worse, my friend, Turnbull, was not even here in town.

Instead, on his threshold, I'd found myself facing his wife, great with child, who had offered apologies. 'But do come in. You can sup with us, surely?'

He'd written to me that he'd married and that they were well matched, but this was my proof – for few women, upon opening their door to find me standing there, a stranger, would have welcomed me inside. And fewer still, when I had shown that night the first signs of my fever, would have brushed aside my protests and insisted that I stay.

I should have protested more strongly. But before I could collect my wits I'd found myself installed within a bedchamber, attended by the Turnbulls' rough-edged and rough-handed manservant, MacDougall.

He was not pleased by my presence.

'It's not right,' he told me one evening. 'Ye should not be here when the master's away.'

I'd have gladly obliged him by leaving, but I had no choice. There was naught to be done for an ague like mine but to faithfully drink my infusion of Jesuits' powder and wait while the hot fevers cycled their course.

At the peak of my delirium, I'd watched MacDougall search the pockets of my coat, remove the letter I had brought from Turnbull, and unfold it. In my outrage, with my lips too dry to form the words, I told him, 'Leave that!'

He'd ignored me. Reading it, he'd held the letter closer to the light to see the signature, refolded it along its seams, and with a frown, replaced it.

What else he'd searched while I was sleeping, I knew not, but from the first, he had determined I was not a man to trust.

This morning, as I woke, he watched me. Setting down my washbasin, he said, 'Terrible things, tertian fevers.'

His tone had a purpose I couldn't unravel, so when there was no need to make a reply I kept silent. What was there to say? The fevers were a nuisance I'd been plagued with now for several years. The first infection, starting in the full heat of the jungle and continuing on shipboard, had been worst of all. Since then the agues cycled round at random, striking when they pleased, and disappearing till the next attack. I'd learned the way to live with them.

MacDougall told me, ''Tis what happens when men muck about in foreign lands. The master, thanks tae God, does have a stronger constitution and brought none of that foul sickness home with him.' He looked at me directly. 'Ye must find it inconvenient, falling ill in other people's houses.'

'I don't make a habit of it.'

'Do ye not?'

I found his open insolence uncommon for a servant, and a contrast to the timid housemaid who kept closely to the kitchen like a shadow and was scarcely ever seen, but my hostess had already warned me that MacDougall was a law unto himself.

'You will forgive him,' she'd apologized. 'He's served my husband's family since he was a lad, as did his father before him, and he considers it a calling. He is overly protective, more so now I am with child, but he does mean well, and is harmless.'

I was not so sure. MacDougall, for his life of service, had the hardened look of one who knew how to do violence.

I preferred to meet him on my feet. I stood, but taking up the gauntlet he'd cast down I said, 'I'm here by invitation. As you know. You've read my letter.'

'Aye. Ye must have telt a sad tale for the master tae have written ye those lines, for him tae offer ye his outstretched hand. He is a giving man, the master. He'd turn out his pockets for ye, let ye use his name and his connections tae advance yerself, and ask for naething. But I'm sure that's not why ye came back.'

He said that last sarcastically, and while I felt my blood heat from the insult, I held back my temper.

I owed this man no explanation. Someone like MacDougall, who had never strayed from Scotland's shores, could never know what drove a man like me. He'd never feel the pull that made a soldier like myself, after the lonely years of hiring my sword to foreign princes under foreign skies, turn homeward once again to seek a face I recognized, a hearth that I could call my own, a wife to build a future with. He'd never understand.

I turned my back, dismissively, and reached for a clean shirt.

MacDougall said, 'The master has troubles enough of his own, without looking tae yours. In the Earl of Mar's regiment, he should by now be a captain commanding a company of his own men, and he's written tae the earl himself saying so, as have the mistress's high-flung relations, but he's held back as a lieutenant while other, more cunning men rise – younger men, with less time in the army.' *Men like you*, he might have said, from the fierce burn of the gaze I knew well that MacDougall had aimed at my back. 'With a wife and a bairn on the way, he's no time tae be burdened with such as yerself. Ye're not even a gentleman.'

I turned then. Met his eyes. 'Then we are equal, you and I.'

There was a moment when I thought he might forget his station altogether and return the challenge in my tone with a strike of his fist. But he did not. Instead, he carefully laid out the towel he had brought, beside the basin.

Looking down, he commented, 'That's three days with no fever.'

'Aye.'

'It's finished, then. Ye're better.'

'Aye.'

'Good,' he said, and turned away. 'Time ye were gone.'

❦

'We must find you a wife while you're here,' Turnbull's wife said, at breakfast. 'No, you may smile, but a bachelor of your age—'

'Of my age? I'm not yet five and thirty. Still a few years younger than your husband, and I hope you will agree he's hardly ancient.'

With a blush she laid a hand upon her rounded belly, in awareness that it proved the man she'd married was yet virile. But her wit would not be bested. 'And my husband was a few years younger than he is now when he met me, so my point stands. What sort of woman do you favour? I have several friends in mind who might do well for you.'

'My dear Mrs Turnbull—'

'Please do call me Helen.'

MacDougall cut in to serve our morning porridge. He gently set Helen's bowl down, but set mine down hard, with a glower.

I'd had time while finishing dressing to think on his words without passion, and now that I knew my friend Turnbull was having his own struggles climbing the ranks, I agreed that my being here would only add to the weight Turnbull carried. I could not do that to my friend.

I replied, 'My dear Helen, then. You're very kind, but I've been in your care these ten days and I cannot impose on you longer, not now that I'm well.' I glanced at MacDougall, who narrowed his eyes as I told Helen lightly, ''Tis time I was gone.'

She looked at me, surprised. 'You will not leave, I hope, until my husband has returned? He'd not forgive me if he learned that you'd been here and gone and he had missed your company.'

No more than I'd miss his, I knew, as I would miss the comforts of this house that I'd been able to explore these past few days since my last fevers had subsided and I had regained my strength.

As stern and forbidding as Caldow's Land might have appeared from the street on the evening that I had arrived, on the inside it was full of life, the floors above taken by an interesting mix of people I had heard about but not yet met, from the former Latin master to the spinster merchant sisters who together kept the shop below.

The Turnbulls' dwelling occupied the whole of the first floor, made warm and charming by its painted walls and ceiling beams. We passed most of the day in this front chamber – the long drawing room, with its row of bright windows along the end wall looking out onto the bustle of the Landmarket.

The merchant sisters were already up and at their business. I'd discovered it was common, when we breakfasted, to hear the daily noises of their trade – the muffled movements as they set their wares in place within the alcoves, and the greetings they exchanged with passing customers – but it was rare to hear a footstep at this hour of morning climb the curved stone forestair leading to the front door of the house, and rarer still to hear those footsteps pause within the common stairwell, at the door of Turnbull's lodgings.

My own attention was then fixed on trying to decide how best to answer Helen, but the footsteps broke my concentration, and the brisk rap at the door that followed made me look, with Helen, at MacDougall, who had crossed now to admit the early caller.

I might not have recognized the gentleman who entered, ducking through the doorway in a practised movement that both saved his high wig from a knock against the lintel while appearing at the same time to be more or less a bow of greeting, but he was no stranger to the others.

Helen stood and dropped so quickly to a curtsey that my first thought was she might have done her unborn child an injury.

Apparently I wasn't alone in that thought. Our visitor hastily moved forward, taking her elbow and guiding her back to her seat. 'Madam, please. I do fear for your health.'

Helen smiled. 'My lord, I am perfectly healthy, I promise you. My doctors assure me it will be at least two months more till I'm brought to bed, and I intend to make use of what liberty I am allowed in that time.' But she stayed in her chair, to appease him, and in a graceful motion of her hand included me. 'May I present my husband's good friend, Sergeant Adam Williamson, who served with him at Toubacanti. Sergeant, may I introduce you to Lord Grange?'

I paid my honours then, bowing so smartly that I drew a glance of sidelong cynicism from MacDougall in his place beside the hearth, to make it plain he thought my actions were for show. Perhaps they were. I'll not deny that when a man like me, with few connections and few prospects, met a Lord of the Justiciary whose brother was the Earl of Mar and rich with friends at Queen Anne's court, then it was worth the effort of a little extra show. But I confess my first thought was that Lord Grange was the brother of the earl within whose regiment Lieutenant Turnbull was now seeking a promotion, and my manners might reflect upon my friend. 'My lord,' I said. 'Your servant.'

Lord Grange was agreeable and pleasant in his manners and his speech. A younger man than me, but I was growing used to the reality that many men I met these days were younger. He could not yet have been thirty.

'I was hoping,' he remarked to Helen, as he took his own seat with us at the table, 'that your husband might be here.'

'No, I regret he's still away, and likely will be for another fortnight.'

'A shame.' Lord Grange seemed genuinely sorry. 'I came to ask a favour of him. Just a minor job, but one that wants discretion, and is urgent. I could think of no one better than Lieutenant Turnbull to perform it, but it cannot wait. I must arrange things now. Today.'

On Helen's face I saw the changing flow of her reactions from dismay to rapid thought to inspiration, so I had a sense of what was coming. 'Adam – Sergeant Williamson – has been my husband's friend for years. He has my husband's trust. He would be eminently qualified to start this work, I'm sure, and then my husband could complete it for you upon his return.'

They looked at me.

I was less sure than Helen I was suited to the task, whatever it might be, but Turnbull had my loyalty. By taking on this job now as his surrogate, I'd hold his place and make sure that it did not go to someone else, for if he won the gratitude of Lord Grange and the Earl of Mar, my friend might also finally win his captaincy.

I felt the weight of all their eyes. MacDougall's coldly disapproving. Those of Lord Grange waiting patiently. And Helen's, holding hope.

'Of course,' I said, 'if I can be of any help at all.'

Lord Grange pronounced this excellent. 'I'll send one of my clerks to you this afternoon, then. Shall we say, at two o'clock? He'll bring the papers you'll need, and explain things.'

He didn't stay long after that.

'I regret,' he told us, 'I must travel up to Alloa tomorrow, and stay awhile on business. I should have been there already, but with circumstances being what they were . . .' He coughed, apologized, and took his leave.

'Poor man,' Helen said, as her hand went once more to the round of her belly. 'His wife fell extremely ill Friday last past, and she miscarried. They are but recently wed. It is said that he would not have married her had she not carried his child, for her family does not have the best reputation. Her father was hanged as a murderer, here at the cross, years ago, and the stain of an act like that cannot be easily washed from a bloodline. Lord Grange's wife, so they say, has a fierce temper. But I am still sorry she lost her child.' She sat a moment in silence, then allowed, 'And that, at least, is one sorrow a bachelor is spared, I suppose.'

'The loss of a child?'

'Yes. Although I do realize a man doesn't need to be married,' she said, 'to have children.'

I said, 'I would need to be.'

'Truly?'

'Yes. I would wish that any child of mine be legitimate, and bear my name.'

'Very honourable.' Fondly, she added, 'I truly must find you a wife while you're here. It's the least I can do in return for this work you've agreed to do, saving my husband's chance to earn the favour of Lord Grange.'

'It seems he does already have it.'

'The favour of such men is often haphazardly given and easily lost if one doesn't stand in the right place,' she explained, with a keenness of insight that put me in mind of the fact she had told me her own father had been a man of the law. 'I'm glad you were standing in my husband's place today.'

I owed him much, so anything that I could do for Turnbull was but feeble payment for the debt I carried. When I told her this, her eyes held pride.

'I do hope,' she said, 'the work itself will not be too unpleasant.'

I was hoping that as well, but I'd resigned myself to anything, so when Lord Grange's clerk appeared at two o'clock precisely with a file of papers underneath one arm, I breathed more easily. The drudgery of paperwork was something I could bear.

The clerk was younger than me, too – a tall man in his later twenties with broad shoulders and a build that seemed more suited to the fields than to an office, but his voice was educated.

Gilroy was his name. 'I will be with you every day,' he promised, 'until we finish the inquiry.'

I tried to sound informed, and failed. 'The inquiry?'

'You've not been told?' His mouth, for just a moment, made a line that I knew well. Mine did the same when I was forced to explain basic things to new recruits. He set the papers on the table by the window, which by now had been cleared of its breakfast things and sat in readiness, with four chairs stationed round it. 'How much do you know of the business of the Commissioners of the Equivalent?'

I knew that since the Acts of Union had been passed

between my own country of Scotland and the English this past spring, dissolving our parliament and creating one united nation, the government of Queen Anne now at Westminster had sent north an enormous sum of money to be managed as a fund designed to offset our assumption of a share of England's debt, and for some other sundry purposes, and that this money was called the Equivalent, and those who had its charge were its commissioners.

I said all this to Gilroy, who seemed satisfied. 'That's fairly it. Except a large part of what those commissioners are doing now is sorting through the claims of those owed money by our African Company, since one promise of the Union was that everyone who lost by that adventure would be compensated out of the Equivalent.'

Helen, who had been all this time in the room with us, spoke up. 'Sergeant Williamson is very well acquainted with the African Company. He is one of our brave men who went to Darien. He fought at Toubacanti, with my husband.'

Gilroy's level grey eyes held a new appreciation. 'Did you? Then you'll not need me to waste my breath on that.'

'No.' I knew all about the Company.

'The people who lost money, and the men still owed their wages, have been publicly invited to apply for payment,' Gilroy said. 'As have the heirs of those who died.'

I worked to smooth the brittle edge from my own tone. 'I should imagine the commissioners are overrun with claims.'

'They are. But this one,' he said, untying the string that bound the file of papers, 'they have passed to us. A woman who has recently come forward with a claim to be the widow of a sailor.'

Helen looked at him. 'You do not think she is?'

'I did not say that.'

'No,' she mused. 'You did not.' Leaning closer, she glanced at the few pages that were topmost in the file. 'So we are meant to ask her questions?'

'Sergeant Williamson is, yes.'

I felt at sea. 'What sort of questions?'

'Ones that will determine whether she was truly married to this sailor, and establish whether she is owed his wages,' Gilroy said, with patience. 'When Lieutenant Turnbull has returned, he will assume the inquiry, but until then you have the lead, sir.'

Not a thought that gave me comfort.

Somebody was coming up the curved steps of the forestair. Gilroy turned towards the sound and said, 'That's probably the lady now. Lord Grange said he would tell her to be here at half past two.'

MacDougall let her in.

She was not tall. She did not have to duck to miss the lintel, but as she entered, she turned her head slightly towards me and I felt the breath leave my lungs.

I'd seen beautiful women. Society women. Their faces would fade from my mind. But the face of this one unremarkable widow, I knew beyond all doubt, I'd always remember.

Our eyes met.

She'd paused just inside the door, hesitant, as though she hadn't expected to see us all waiting there, but when I smiled reassurance, she took a step forward.

Gilroy made the introductions. 'Mistress Aitcheson,' he called her first, then correcting himself, 'Mrs Graeme.'

She offered me her gloved hand and said, 'That is what we're all here to decide, is it not, Mr—?'

Gilroy gave her my name. I was grateful, for I doubt that I could have managed it.

I paid her my honours and felt her hand slip from mine. I missed the touch.

'Well, Sergeant Williamson,' she told me, steadily, 'shall we begin?'

❧

From self-preservation, I gave her the chair to my left at the table, for had she been seated across from me I should have found it impossible not to stare openly, much less to concentrate. Opposite me I sat Helen, whom I'd asked to stay for propriety's sake and to make Mrs Graeme more comfortable, since I could hardly imagine a woman would feel at ease when being questioned alone by two men. Helen, facing me, was at least not a distraction, although she had arguably the more classically beautiful face.

Mrs Graeme had freckles across cheeks and nose, not a porcelain skin, and her face was the shape of a heart, not an oval, the whole framed by hair of plain brown that refused to stay in a smooth style and escaped in small curls from beneath the lace pinner she wore to contain it. A cap, I might have called it in my youth, until the girl I'd lost my heart to in those days had set me straight. 'How did you get to be the age you are and not know what a pinner is?' she'd asked me while removing it and drawing out the hairpins one by one to set her hair loose, and I never had forgotten. It was not the most convenient memory, for my glance at Mrs Graeme's hair, however brief, had left me with a vision of it tumbling loose like that, and to regain my focus I reached for the papers Gilroy spread before me.

He sat at my right hand, which I thought fitting, since he played the role now of my right-hand man with quiet competence.

Much like a schoolmaster setting a lesson, he'd put all the papers in order, so I'd understand. First his summary of all the facts as he felt I should know them, then a declaration from the Commissioners of the Equivalent, and finally two certificates of marriage – one the original she must have given them when she'd applied to them, whenever that had been, and one the copy they'd made from that, both stating clearly the name of her husband – James Graeme – and her full name: Lilias Aitcheson.

The certificate plainly declared they'd been lawfully married at Edinburgh on the second day of January 1698 before the required two witnesses, by a minister whose name was not unfamiliar.

I took time to read through the rest. It allowed me the space to compose myself, and become settled and sure of my footing. Then, taking the marriage certificates, I set the copy aside.

'I can return this to you, now,' I said, and passed her the original. 'I'm sure it's very precious to you.'

'Yes.'

I cleared my throat. 'Mrs Graeme, I'm sure you can appreciate that since the Equivalent money has been brought to Edinburgh, there have been a great many people come forward to lay claim to their share of it, and the commissioners must examine every case with care. Your husband having lost his life while sailing for the African Company would of course be owed his wages, to be paid from the Equivalent directly to his heir. The commissioners must then determine clearly if you are in fact his heir.'

I caught the turn of Gilroy's head towards me, as though he had not expected I'd be able to explain the case so neatly, but while I might not have his education, I was not a fool, and since I had agreed to sit in Turnbull's place, I would not spoil the prospects of my friend through my incompetence.

Of course, I had not counted on the complicating factor of the woman to my left.

She took in what I'd said, and nodded, and she waited, and we all four sat at the table for a moment in our places as though playing at a game of cards, with no one keen to let the others see their hand. And finally it was left to me to say, 'We have a problem.'

In the silence that came after, Gilroy said, to clarify, 'The marriage was irregular.'

By which he meant they'd not been married in the Kirk, and by the parish minister, but in a more clandestine way. The minister they'd chosen was not even Presbyterian. I recognized him by his name as one of those devout Episcopalians who, at the Revolution, had been stripped of their own parishes and had since, with the others of their outcast faith, been barred from leading any form of worship, or from baptizing a newborn bairn – or celebrating marriages.

She touched the edge of the certificate with something like defiance. 'An irregular marriage is still a legal marriage.'

Gilroy allowed this. 'Only this one was never judicially acknowledged.' As though realizing his language might be overly technical, he patiently explained, 'You never went before the Kirk to confess it, so that you could be rebuked and pay the fine and have the marriage properly entered in their records.'

Her nod was cool, as was her tone. 'It was a failing of my husband's that he died before we could confess our marriage to the Kirk.'

'But then it must be proved,' said Gilroy. 'I'm afraid the minister who married you is long since dead. Which normally would leave us with the witnesses, but my initial enquiries would indicate that they, too, are deceased.'

'Again our failing, I suppose, to not choose people who'd outlive us, and to lack the foresight to have filled the room with guests.'

I leaned forward slightly, taking up the space between them in the way one does when sensing friends are in a mood to fight. 'With your permission, Mrs Graeme, that is why we're here. To seek another means of proof.'

She collected her emotions with an effort betrayed only by the slightest setting of her shoulders – something that she likely didn't even know she did, when pressed. But it had the desired effect, for when she spoke, her voice had lost its edge.

'Pray, Sergeant Williamson, if this certificate and my own word are insufficient, then what proof will satisfy the men of your commission?'

'Have you any other documents that bear your husband's signature and name you as his wife? A deed, or backbond, or—'

'We owned no land.'

'His final will and testament?'

'He did not leave one. If he had, I surely would have brought it with me, would I not?'

'A letter, then.' I grasped at any document I could. 'You must have letters that he wrote to you, which might help to establish your relationship.'

She told me, 'I have nothing of my husband's, Sergeant Williamson.'

Others might have missed her faint frown as she turned her face towards the windows. I did not.

It had been years since I'd felt so compelled to help, protect, and care for someone else. The feeling hit me like a hammer blow, and held me silent.

Gilroy said, 'In such a case, the best approach is to attempt to find people who knew you and your husband, when he lived, and who could testify your marriage was a proper one. These witnesses you list on your certificate—'

'—are dead,' she said, 'as you've observed.'

'But were they strangers called in off the street?' he asked. 'I know that's often how it's done, with such clandestine marriages. Or were they people known to you?'

Still looking at the street beyond the windows, she replied, 'They were my friends.'

'I see,' said Gilroy. 'Barbara Malcolm, your first witness named, did she have any family?'

'Barbara Malcolm had a sister, but she died.' She looked at Gilroy. 'Why?'

He made a note upon his papers. 'And this other, Walter Browne?'

'He had brothers, though I don't know what became of them.'

Another note. 'And were these brothers well acquainted with you and your husband?'

'We were very private people.'

'Nonetheless. If you would have us help you, this is how it must be done. We must prepare a list of those who knew you as a married couple, and seek out their testimony.'

'How long will that take?'

'It depends upon the list. Perhaps a fortnight.'

Longer than she'd hoped, apparently, to judge by her expression when she brought her face around again to look at me. Her eyes were blue and shadowed with impatience and, behind that, something deeper and unspoken that looked very much like fear.

It hit me squarely in my gut.

I could not think why such a mundane thing as proving she'd been married to this man would make her frightened, but there were already many things about this 'simple' inquiry I did not understand.

And in that moment I reacted without thinking; without caring what the others in the room might think. I hitched my chair around so that it faced hers more directly, and I told her, 'Mrs Graeme, I realize this is an uncomfortable position for you, sitting here with strangers, being judged. But I can promise, if you'll trust me, I will help you find your way through all of this.' I met her eyes and asked her, 'Will you trust me?'

It might well have been the longest moment I had ever spent.

And then, at last, it ended.

'Yes,' she said.

If I hadn't already known I was in trouble, I would have been sure of it then, when she spoke that one word and attempted a smile and it seemed, for that heartbeat of time, there were only the two of us there in the drawing room, and all the rest of the world fell away.

But we were not alone. There, at my right hand, was Gilroy, his pen in hand, waiting. Across from me, Helen, observing the scene with her clever and curious gaze. And MacDougall, a dark presence who might be standing behind any door, wishing me gone.

If I were to help both my friend Turnbull and Mrs Graeme, I'd have to be careful, conceal what I felt, and be always on guard.

I wanted to smile back at Mrs Graeme, but I held it to myself and merely gave a nod and shifted my chair back into position. 'Good. Let's begin, then, with this list of those who knew you and your husband. What names can you add to it?'

'None,' was her answer. 'At least, none who knew us as adults.'

I looked at her, curious, and she said quietly, 'We met as children.'

And although she owed us no piece of that past, she began, in a soft voice, to speak of it, drawing us back with her words to the girl she had been when she'd first known James Graeme.

CHAPTER 2

SATURDAY, 14 JULY, 1683

He ALWAYS WENT A step ahead.

He'd done that for as long as Lily could remember – since they'd both been set to run together through the fields and woods and rivers of Inchbrakie, the estate in Perthshire where she had been born, in the same cottage where her mother had been raised, within a family that had always served the laird.

'A bit of play will do the lass no harm,' was how her grandmother had silenced any protest. 'Let her keep her childhood.'

As though childhood were a thing that could be taken from you, Lily thought. What foolish things old people said, sometimes.

This summer she was seven and a half. When all her chores were done – the careful sweeping and the dusting and the little bits of mending that her grandmother was starting to allow her – she was free to go outdoors and look for Jamie.

He'd been here three days already, with his brothers and

his mother, come to visit his grandfather, the old laird. And he'd be here for nearly two weeks more, but it was never long enough.

She found him waiting by the gate, as he had promised. He'd been waiting long enough to craft a pair of makeshift swords for them from twigs bound tightly into shape with strips of bark, their handles wrapped with rushes.

They were almost the same age and the same height but he was sturdier, his fair hair as unruly as himself, his cheerful grin a welcome. 'Come on, then,' he said, 'they promised they'd not start without us.'

Lily didn't need to ask who 'they' were. He'd already started off across the long grass of the field, towards the neighbouring estate of Abercairney.

He had cousins there. Their mother was the sister of his father, so the old Laird of Inchbrakie was the grandfather to all of them.

Last winter, with the Abercairney boys away at school in Perth, the two girls – Anna and Emelia – had set up a play school of their own, with Lily as their pupil.

They'd used the room their tutor used for teaching them. They'd taught her how to read, and write, and once Emelia had set her to copy out a chart of all the family of the house of Abercairney.

It had been the family name that had tripped Lily up, at first. She'd copied down the letters carefully: M-o-r-a-y. And she'd frowned. 'But that's not how it's said at all,' she'd pointed out. 'It's "Murray".'

'Aye,' Emelia had agreed, 'but it's the way we've always spelled it. We had ancestors who fought alongside William

Wallace and who walked with kings and they all spelled it that way, too.'

Visual evidence of their ancestral ties to royalty was everywhere within the house. One afternoon with wintry shadows slanting through the windows of the corridors the elder of the two girls, Anna, who was then fourteen and fond of tales of kings and queens and knights and noble romance, led a history lesson solely from the portraits on the walls.

There were dashing men and women of a different time, with eyes that seemed to follow Lily as she walked, but all their names and exploits blended into one dull monologue, until Anna stopped at a portrait of a handsome man with dark hair and dark eyes and a serious face turned towards them, half over his shoulder, as though to say, 'Come, follow me!'

'This,' said Anna, 'is who your friend Jamie is named for. An earlier James.'

Lily read the nameplate on the frame: *James Graham, Marquis of Montrose.*

Even the last names were the same, she thought, though Jamie spelled his 'Graeme'.

Lily's eyes widened. 'Is this Montrose the hero?'

Emelia said, 'Aye, he's the one John always wants to be when we play Covenanters and Montrose.'

'One of the bravest men who ever lived,' said Anna, 'and our grandfather at Inchbrakie was his most trusted friend.'

His own personal history, so Anna explained, was like Scotland's — divided. 'He was himself a Covenanter, at the start, but—'

Lily interrupted her with, 'Why are they called Covenanters?'

'Why, because of their Covenant. D'ye not know what that is?'

Lily shook her head.

Anna explained. 'Well, a long time ago, everybody in Scotland was Catholic. For centuries, they were, and then up came the Presbyterians, led by John Knox. He was fighting with Queen Mary, who was Catholic, and at length he won and the Presbyterians became the new official Kirk. But when Queen Mary's grandson, the first Charles, became king – he was Episcopalian, like us – he stood against the Scottish Presbyterians and then there was rebellion here and rioting in Edinburgh, and in the end the Presbyterians rose up and signed a document that they called their great Covenant – that is a word that means a solemn promise or agreement – that they'd always keep to their own faith. 'Tis said some signed it with their blood. That's why they are called Covenanters.'

'And they went to war against the king,' Emelia added, 'and they caught him, and they cut his head off.'

'That was Cromwell and his parliament, in England,' Anna said. 'They killed the king, although the Covenanters played their part. Grandfather fought them, and he could I'm sure tell many stories if he chose. I wish he would.'

Emelia, sounding wiser than her own nine years, said, 'Father says that men who've truly seen war seldom speak of it.'

Her sister only sighed and said to Lily, 'Anyway, there was a war, and Cromwell occupied our lands, and it was then illegal to keep any but the Covenanting faith, until the king's son – *our* King Charles – returned from exile, claimed his throne again, punished the people who had killed his father, and restored our church.'

Lily was grateful that he had. 'I would not wish to be a Covenanter.'

'Nor would I,' said Anna. 'The laws have rightly turned against them since the king's return, and Presbyterians who try to worship now will lose their land if not their lives, yet they believe theirs is the only true religion, and they'll die before they'll see it altered.'

Emelia, stubborn herself, argued, 'Ours is the true religion, because God does bless and choose the king, and our king is, like us, Episcopalian.'

Her sister smiled. 'And yet his brother is a Catholic, and he will be our king next, so what will be the true religion then?'

Montrose, from his portrait, was still watching them, and Anna drew them back into their proper history lesson.

In that shadowed corridor, she told them stories of the battles Montrose waged for the king's side against the forces led by his relentless enemy, the Earl of Argyll. Every tale was more exciting than the last, and filled with danger. Lily felt every clash of the swords, every galloping horse bearing Montrose to battle.

And when the Covenanters laid a trap for Montrose – sending him a false captain and ship to delay his departure while they closed the snare, setting English ships offshore to choke off all routes of escape – Lily's heart fell.

'But,' said Anna, painting pictures with her words, 'when all seemed black and lost, he did outwit them. He went north, and found a vessel on the coast to carry him to Norway.'

There was something in the triumph of that moment that appealed to Lily – thinking of the great Montrose at sea, far from the reach of wicked Argyll and the Covenanters, sailing towards freedom on the misty shores of Norway.

She was happy to discover he had made the crossing safely, and been welcomed to the castle of a Scotsman there, and so continued on with his adventures.

But it broke her heart when Anna carried on, through his return to Scotland, and his final battle, his betrayal, and his capture, and his brutal execution.

Lily hadn't liked that part at all.

Anna had tried to make it better, telling her, 'They did give him a proper funeral, ten years later. Grandfather was there, and all the grand people of Edinburgh came. They gathered up the pieces of his body and they took his head down from the spike and let him lie in state at Holyrood, and then they had him buried at St Giles' Cathedral, as a hero.'

But that hadn't helped Lily feel better when she looked up at the dark eyes of the Marquis of Montrose that beckoned her to follow from his portrait.

She was thinking of that feeling now, as she tried to keep pace with Jamie through the field of waving summer grass that sang with unseen insects.

Seeing him with his twig sword in hand, striding ahead of her, she heard his cousin Anna's voice repeating in her memory, 'This is who your friend Jamie is named for,' and she frowned.

'Jamie?'

'Aye?'

'You're not to be a soldier. Not for real,' she told him, as he turned round, with a question in his eyes.

'Why's that?'

She could not tell him.

Jamie swung his sword in play, and Lily raised her own to parry his the way she had been taught.

'Your daddie is a soldier,' Jamie said, 'and so is mine.'

'I ken that, but I'd not wish ye to be one.'

'I've no wish to be a soldier,' he admitted, to her great relief.

They found the others waiting for them at the bottom of the gardens of the house at Abercairney, where the river slid by at a languid pace and gave a view of the two islands that divided the calm waters.

Anna was not there – she was fifteen now, and had lately fancied herself grown too old for games, as had her brother William, one year younger, who was similarly absent.

But the other Moray boys were ready with their weapons: Robin, who at thirteen stood the tallest and could win at any argument; the youngest, Maurice, only six, who still kept up as best he could; and in between them John, eleven and a half this summer, and in restless motion.

John's sword was a thing of wonder. Fashioned out of wood, it looked astonishingly real, and had a scabbard he had made for it of leather. What John did, he did with purpose.

Lily knew *he* wished to be a soldier, a dream shared by Jamie's brother Pat, who stepped out now in front of them.

'Ye took your time,' Pat said to Jamie.

'Aye, well, she had work to finish.'

'We've been waiting ages,' Pat complained.

Lily began a quick apology, but Robin Moray, stepping up behind her, placed a reassuring hand upon her shoulder. 'Never mind, you're here now.' Turning to his younger sister, he asked, 'What's the game to be?'

Emelia, with her fair hair loose about her shoulders, stood a moment by the sundial, thinking. She was good at organizing games. Sometimes they'd all be bold adventurers, exploring on the island, or a band of privateers at war with Spain, or questing knights in search of dragons. But today, as if her thoughts had somehow been drawn back into the same current of memory Lily's had, she chose a game they'd not played since last summer: 'Covenanters and Montrose.'

John grinned. He loved this game. 'I'll be Montrose.'

Pat leapt in next. 'And I'll be Grandfather.'

Emelia turned to Robin, but he knew what she was going to ask. He said, 'Shall I be Argyll?'

'Would ye, please?' Emelia gave her older brother a look of pure gratitude.

'Ye mind the rules?' asked Robin, looking at the youngest of the children to make sure. 'When Argyll captures ye, then ye become a Covenanter, and ye have to fight on my side.'

Maurice pointed out, 'John never does.'

'Well, John is an exception,' Robin granted. 'He will never fight against the king, on principle, and so we have to throw him in the dungeon, but that isn't as much fun, I promise.'

Even with the head start he agreed to give them, Lily knew how tricky it would be to hide from Robin. He was clever.

But she thought she knew the perfect place.

'Come on,' she said to Jamie, as she led him back through tangled woods and undergrowth, towards the castle of Inchbrakie.

When they reached the old moat, now a dry and sloping gully, Lily pointed to a spot within the green space it encircled.

'There.'

And Jamie's smile was quick and understanding, for he knew the tales his cousins had been telling her this winter past in their play schoolroom – the same tales that he'd been hearing his whole life. He knew his kinsman, the great Marquis of Montrose, while being chased by Argyll's men, had famously avoided capture by concealing himself in this yew tree Lily was now pointing to: the great Inchbrakie Yew, which had been standing here for centuries, an ancient guard upon the castle.

What better place to hide when playing Covenanters and Montrose?

They broke from cover cautiously and raced across the clearing. Jamie made a stirrup with his hands and boosted her up to the nearest branch the way she'd seen grooms help people mount horses, and then being able to jump higher he scrambled after her.

The tree was imposing, its trunk broader around than her father was tall, and its branches spread out in a thick fall of twisting dark needles that caught at her skirts as she climbed. But it held them securely, the greenery closing around them again like a screen as they settled themselves high enough that they wouldn't be noticed by anyone walking beneath.

From here, although they could not see, they heard the echoes of the shouts and laughter as the game went on, and 'Argyll' claimed his captives one by one and turned them into Covenanters.

Lily held her breath and held her silence.

She and Jamie waited.

Then a flash of motion chased across the clearing. Something rustled through the branches underneath them. And John's head popped unexpectedly up on a level with their own. They all three stared in great surprise a moment at each other, then John grinned and hauled himself onto the same branch where they sat.

In a whisper, Jamie warned, 'Be careful! This is our tree.'

'I'm Montrose,' said John.

'But Lily found this hiding place for us,' said Jamie.

John's face turned more serious. He held a warning finger to his lips.

More movement from the clearing. This time it was obviously Robin and the others, for Emelia's voice declared, 'It *has* to be,' before her older brother hushed her.

Robin called, in a dramatic tone, 'Montrose! We ken you're there. Come out!'

When no reply came, he started walking closer. 'Come, this gallant yew might well have saved ye once, but ye cannot depend upon it now.'

He'd discover them, thought Lily. He was nearly underneath them now. He knew that John was there, and he'd discover her and Jamie too, and then—

John turned beside them on the branch and disappeared from view. She heard his feet drop neatly to the ground. 'Argyll!' he called, and walked into the clearing. 'Here I am, ye devil! Take me as your prisoner.'

Emelia gave a squeal. 'I telt ye! Did I not tell ye he'd be in the tree? John, do join us this one time. There's none left but Jamie and Lily to find, and they're small.'

John said, 'I'll not betray my king.'

Robin reminded him, 'Prisoners go to the dungeon.'

Lily wasn't certain where the 'dungeon' was, she only knew it was a room within the house at Abercairney, chosen by the older brothers as a place no one would wish to be confined in, and she thought John very brave to choose it rather than turn Covenanter.

John said, 'I'll only escape, like I always do.'

'One day ye may not,' said Robin, 'and what then?'

But Lily knew the dungeon wasn't built that could hold John confined. She breathed a little easier when both the boys were gone, and turned to Jamie. 'Should we move, while Robin's gone?'

'There's no need. John won't tell him where we are. This is the perfect hiding place.'

Too perfect, maybe. No one came to look for them.

The afternoon wore on, and Lily's legs grew stiff. 'I'm going down,' she said.

But then, she found she couldn't. Looking down, she found her muscles strangely paralysed. She had climbed trees before, but never one this large, or high.

'It's all right,' Jamie said, 'I'll help ye.'

Only nothing that he did could take away her fear, or make her arms and legs let go their fierce grip on the branch where they were sitting. Lily's eyes burned hot with tears. 'I'm sorry, Jamie.'

'It's all right,' he said again. 'The gardener has a ladder, ye can climb down that. I'll just go fetch it.'

'No!' She grabbed him as he moved, and held his arm more tightly than the branch. 'Don't leave me, Jamie. Please don't leave me here alone.'

She hated to be weak like this, and clinging. But this sudden fear, a thing that she had never felt until this day, was wildly irrational.

He settled back onto the branch. 'It's all right,' said Jamie, for the third time, 'I'll not leave ye.'

'Promise?'

'Promise.'

And he didn't.

Afternoon turned into evening, and the bits of sky that they could see turned sapphire blue, and all around them sounded a great fluttering of wings as gentle wood pigeons moved through the treetops, seeking somewhere they could settle for the night.

He asked, 'Why not a soldier?'

'What?'

'Why did ye say I could not be a soldier?'

'Soldiers die.'

He considered this. 'We all die.'

'Soldiers die afore most other men.'

'So could I be a sailor?'

Lily thought it might be possible. 'And where would ye be sailing to?'

He shrugged and said, 'A land that's not discovered yet. Where else?'

She offered, 'Norway?'

'Norway? Why that? What's in Norway?'

'Montrose sailed there once, to freedom and to safety.'

'Then he should have stayed there.'

'Aye.'

Someone was coming. She could hear the fall of steps across the grass, and something else – a lighter sound of dragging. Closer and closer the steps came, until the low branches beneath them swayed and there was somebody standing below, and a deep voice familiar to both of them said, 'Now, let's see what new birds I have nesting in my tree.'

The old laird himself. Jamie leaned over and called to him.

The Laird of Inchbrakie replied, 'A strange wee bird indeed, that calls me by my name.'

'I'm not a bird,' said Jamie.

'Are ye not? Well then, ye should come down and eat your supper, I suppose.'

He'd brought the ladder, and he set it into place now. Though it did not reach the whole way to the branch that they were on, the sight of those sure, sturdy rungs was all it took to steady Lily's fears and give her confidence enough to ease her way along the branches, finding her way down.

'There, that's the way of it.' The laird reached up to help her. For a man of his age, he was strong. He lifted her the final distance to the ground and held her there to steady her until her legs stopped trembling.

She had always liked the laird.

He'd had an accident when he was a young man, they said, with gunpowder, and it had nearly killed him and had left a mark upon his scalp. And he'd been a soldier and killed countless men with his own hands. But Lily did not find his face so fearful, and his hands to her had always acted gently, and he had kind eyes.

Those eyes were watching hers now, in the swiftly fading light. 'All better, now? Good. Leave that ladder, Jamie,' he advised his grandson, who by now had joined them on the ground. 'The gardener will fetch it in the morning.'

Jamie did as he was told. 'How did ye ken we'd need the ladder?'

'I did not. But I was certain I would need it. It's been many years since I last climbed a tree.'

The night was drawing in more quickly, and with one

child's hand in each of his, the old laird turned and started back across the grass towards the castle, where the light now glowed within the ground-floor windows.

'But,' said Jamie, thinking still, 'how did ye ken that we were up the tree at all?'

'Montrose escaped the dungeon,' said the laird with the solemnity of one who'd been admitted to the play of children and knew to respect it, 'and discovered ye had not returned, so sent word where ye might be found.'

'We won the game, then,' Jamie said.

'Ye did, at that.' The laird's voice held a smile. 'Although ye might have come down earlier, I'm thinking.'

Jamie glanced at Lily in the growing darkness, and said nothing.

But she would not have him get into any trouble for her sake, so she admitted, 'I was feart of climbing down the tree. I could not do it. That's why we stayed up so long.'

The old laird gave her hand a reassuring squeeze. 'I served with men who did not have the bravery to admit their fear,' he told her. 'There's no shame in it. But surely Jamie could have climbed down on his own and come for help.'

'I was feart,' she said again, head dipping low. 'I asked him not to leave me, because I was feart of being up there all alone, and so he stayed.'

The laird was silent for a moment. Then he coughed, and said, 'Well, that's a true friend, that's what that is. Ye are fortunate, the pair of ye. I've had a friend like that myself in life but once, and that same tree did shelter him when he sorely had need of it, and sure I am his arms were there around ye both this evening while we searched for ye.'

Montrose, thought Lily. He was speaking of Montrose, who'd been his greatest friend, the way that Jamie was her own. She held more tightly to the old laird's hand, liking the feel of kinship.

Lily could remember very little else about that evening, only that she had received no punishment. But when she had been tucked into her bed beside her grandmother that night in their small cottage, and been half asleep, her grandmother had stirred and told her, 'Lily, there's a difference between us and them. The Graemes and ourselves. Ye'll mind this better when you're older, but there are some bridges in this life, lass, that ye cannot cross.'

Lily said, 'Aye,' or something like it, since her grandmother was happiest when Lily made a noise like she was listening. But truly, she was tired, and had no real idea what—

'I only say this,' said her grandmother, 'because things will be different for ye when ye are in Edinburgh. Here there is so little true society, that ye and Jamie Graeme and the Moray children can play all ye like and on the level, so to speak, but when you're living down in Edinburgh, it will not be that way anymore, and ye should be prepared.'

Lily's sleepiness had vanished. She lay wide-eyed and awake. 'Has my daddie sent for me?'

'Aye. He has met a woman that he means to make his wife, and he has written I'm to send ye after Lammas Day.'

'To Edinburgh?'

'Aye.'

Lily heard the sadness in that syllable and knew its cause, but she herself could not but be excited at the prospect of a proper home with both her father *and* a brand-new mother and – too much to even dream of, really – Jamie living near to her, each day. And Lammas was but two more weeks away, which meant she had not long to wait.

She hugged close to her grandmother, who kissed her understandingly.

'It will be different, lass, is all I'm saying. When you're down in Edinburgh, Jamie will have other friends to occupy his time, and he might not be there the way ye hope, to keep ye company.'

But that was not a thing to fear, thought Lily, and she said so to her grandmother, and told her why.

'He promised me,' said Lily, with the certainty of innocence, 'that he would never leave me. And he never will.'

II

DEATH WAS A KIND of leaving – irreversible and final.

I felt certain, sitting watching her so closely on that afternoon, that she was also thinking the same thing, because when she had finished speaking she stayed silent a long moment . . .

But here I must pause, for I've been told I need now to explain myself to those among you who are thinking, 'Surely she would not have told her tale that way to strangers, in such detail, as a storyteller sitting of an afternoon might craft an entertainment for her listeners.'

And you are right. She did not tell it to us in that way.

She told it haltingly. We asked her questions, and she answered, and from there the story took its shape. Some details I did not learn till long afterwards, but since my purpose is to write things down for you in all their fullness I have woven everything in place as best I can, that you may have the clearest picture.

I can promise I've invented not a word of any part of this tale that belongs to her – that everything is as she told it, or as it was called to memory by those who were there and lived it with her.

That much I assure you, on my honour.

Whether she was truthful in the telling of it . . . well, that can't be laid to my account.

And that was, after all, the very thing that I was being asked to judge.

CHAPTER 3

MONDAY, 22 SEPTEMBER, 1707

SHE STAYED SILENT A long moment, looking down at her linked hands where they lay resting on the table. All the jewellery she wore was a narrow band of silver on her finger that could not have been worth much in coin, and yet she touched it gently as if it were of great value as she summoned the tight smile that people put up as a shield when seeking not to show emotion before strangers.

'Doubtless you will find it tiresome, hearing of our games,' she said, 'but those, for me, were happy years, and I do have fond memories of them.'

Gilroy said, 'I should imagine that you would. It is not every child could claim the children of the lairds of Abercairney and of Inchbrakie as friends.'

I thought it might have been my ears alone that heard him put the faintest stress on 'claim', as if to say her story was unlikely, but she'd evidently heard it, too.

Her head came up. 'It is the truth.'

Since I was standing in for Turnbull, I was at the head of this inquiry – Gilroy was my junior, and although he worked directly for Lord Grange and was more educated than myself, I reasoned it was better, from the outset, to establish who was in control.

Before he could reply to her I came between them, firmly. 'I am certain my clerk meant no disrespect.'

Gilroy glanced at me. One eyebrow might have lifted slightly higher than the other, but he faced her and said, 'No indeed. They are fine families both, and you were fortunate.' He inked his pen and made a careful note. 'The old Laird of Inchbrakie did have sons, but only one who followed in his footsteps and became a soldier, as you say your husband's father was, so then your husband's father must be . . .'

'Patrick Graeme,' she confirmed, as though she did not wish to let another speak his name. 'Captain of the Edinburgh town guard.'

Helen was too young to have any memory of the late rebellion that had cost King James his crown some twenty years ago, but those of us who'd known this town before that time could well remember Captain Graeme. Even though I'd been a lad myself when last I'd seen him, still his figure rose before me clearly and commandingly.

'Except his rank is colonel now,' said Gilroy, 'since he crossed to France in service of our late king. He does serve the young James now, I'm told.'

'Then he's misguided,' Helen said, 'and I shall pray God turns him from the reckless Jacobites who would divide our country.'

Gilroy sidestepped a reply to that. I did not blame him.

In the years since old King James had been forced from his throne and fled to exile, taking his then infant son along with him, his followers, the Jacobites, had fought for his return, and with his death their focus had turned to the birthright of his son, another James, not yet turned twenty, whom they held to be their rightful king.

Meanwhile old King James's daughter, Queen Anne – being Protestant where he had been a Catholic – held the throne that he had lost, and her supporters were full as determined not to let her half-brother return to take it from her.

I myself took neither side. I'd seen too much of conflict and the lives that it could ruin.

Mrs Graeme smoothly said, 'My husband's father's rank was colonel here in Scotland, also, even when he was the captain of the Edinburgh town guard. He was serving as lieutenant colonel in the forces of the king when he was chosen to be captain of the guard, and that appointment did not then erase the rank which he earned by his honour.'

Gilroy answered with a short nod that appeared to be dismissive, and because I sensed this line of talk might lead us to an argument, I smoothed the waters with, 'I do remember Captain – Colonel – Graeme well. A man most worthy of respect.' A sudden thought occurred to me. 'Did he know of your marriage?'

Mrs Graeme shook her head. 'We kept it secret, for personal reasons. Beyond our two friends and the minister, we shared the news with no one.'

I replied, 'You cannot know that. Not for certain.'

'Do you doubt my word?'

'Of course not. It is only that you cannot answer for your husband's actions,' was my argument. 'The fact you kept your marriage secret does not mean he did the same. It's possible he did confide in any of his friends or near relations, without telling you.'

'I'd think it most unlikely.'

'But it's possible.'

Her eyes were very blue. 'I'll allow you that nothing in life is impossible.'

I counted that as a victory. 'Assuming he did tell someone, whom would he have told?'

She was giving this some thought when Helen cut in with, 'Perhaps his mother?'

Mrs Graeme smiled faintly. 'No. His mother would not have approved.'

Gilroy's tone was certain. 'I believe he would have told his father, if he did respect him.'

'He respected him, but—'

'Then,' said Gilroy, 'it will do no harm to write to Colonel Graeme. I will be discreet,' he promised, 'but if he does know, and will sign a testificate stating you were married, then his word will be believed by the commissioners.'

She shook her head, and Gilroy asked, 'You don't agree?'

'My husband's father is a soldier, fighting on the Continent, and for an exiled king. How will your letter find him?'

'I can promise you,' said Gilroy, 'letters find their way from Scotland to the court of young King James, and back again, with regularity.'

'But it will take too long.'

Everyone seemed to be in a great hurry to see this claim settled. I knew Mrs Graeme might simply have need of the money, but somehow the fear I had glimpsed in her eyes made me feel there was more at the back of her urgency. She looked so defeated now, I sought a way to cheer her. 'There may yet be someone here in Scotland. You knew your late husband best. Who were his nearest friends?'

It was a version of the question I had asked before, but framing it in this way seemed to make her answer easier.

'His elder brother, Patrick, and his cousin, Robin Moray.'

'Well, then—'

'Patrick is a monk,' she said. 'A Capuchin, who lives somewhere in France. I don't remember where. And Robin, last I heard, was also somewhere on the Continent, attending to his private business.'

Gilroy noted all this down, then asked, 'And what of John?'

She looked a question at him, and he said, 'Your husband's cousin John. John Moray.'

Mrs Graeme said, a little cautiously, 'I have not seen John since I was a child. He went to France, and joined the army there.'

'And you've not seen him since? You've no idea where he might be now?'

'No. It's been years since I've spoken to any of that family.'

Helen offered to make use of her connections to enquire.

I said, 'Thank you.'

It was growing late. The sun was not yet down and there was light enough to see by in the street, but it had gained the golden glow that meant we'd stretched the day as long as it was possible and it would soon be coming to its end.

I did not want to let it end. I would have wished for Mrs Graeme to stay longer, but there was no reason for it, nor could I see any reason for her to return here for another meeting until Gilroy and I had made further enquiries on her behalf. She'd told us everything she could, and given us what documents she had. I ran a finger down the edges of my papers so they formed a tidy stack. 'I think we've made a good start, then,' I said, making an effort to mask my own disappointment.

Gilroy agreed. Then surprised me with, 'Is it convenient, Mrs Graeme, for you to return tomorrow morning?'

'Yes,' she said.

I was not about to argue with him, even if I could not fathom what we'd be discussing. Still, since I was meant to be the lead man of this inquiry, I took the lead.

I said, 'Shall we say ten o'clock?'

She gave a nod, and stood.

There was a scrape of chairs as Gilroy and I stood as well. And then it struck me that she would be walking in the street alone, and I had no idea where she lived.

'I'll walk you home,' I said.

The light coming in through the windows was angled directly behind her at that exact moment so I couldn't see her expression as she turned, and paused. 'I do thank you, no. It's a kind offer,' she said, 'but I'll find my own way.'

'Forrester's Wynd,' Gilroy said, at my shoulder.

He'd come to stand next to me at the tall windows that looked to the Landmarket. I had positioned myself at the middle one, from which I had the best view of the length of the street, with its colourful flow of activity and the high, solid bank of lands and tenements opposite, rising from arched shops to uneven rooftops, the windows unshuttered still to catch the last of the light.

When the shifting wheels and carts and people parted I could see the shadowed narrow gaps between the buildings, at street level, giving entry to the wynds and closes that ran back between the Landmarket towards the Cowgate behind.

This time of day called out the thieves and pickpockets, and worse. I cast a keen eye on the young lad with no shoes who watched the ladies passing, and the older 'gentleman' who seemed to take an interest in the stationer's displays.

Another man had settled indolently into the squared opening to Hamilton's Close, his shoulder to the wall, his grey cocked hat and grey coat blending well into the stone.

Forrester's Wynd was not much further beyond that spot, towards St Giles' Church.

Gilroy said, 'That is the address of her lodgings. Or at least, the one she gave to us. She'll not have far to go.'

It wasn't that I did not trust him, but I watched myself as Mrs Graeme walked the distance through the crowd of people in the street, went safely past the man in grey, and took the turning into Forrester's Wynd.

'I think you need not worry for her welfare,' Gilroy said. 'She seems an independent woman.'

Helen pointed out that this was only natural. 'If her husband died at Darien, then she'll have been a widow seven years. That's long enough for any woman to learn independence, of necessity.' Helen had not joined us at the window, staying in the comfort of her chair beside the table, from which she could clearly view the both of us, although her words were meant for Gilroy. 'You do not approve of her.'

He turned. This time the eyebrow was most definitely raised. 'Madam, I honestly have not formed an opinion of her.'

'You spoke brusquely to her.'

'Speaking brusquely is my habit,' he admitted with a shrug. 'I shall rely on Sergeant Williamson to be the one who speaks to her more kindly.' And to me, he added, 'You did very well this afternoon, I must say.'

I could not hold back a smile at his tone. 'Much better than you thought I would?'

'I did not say that.'

'No. You did not.'

Helen laughed, and said to Gilroy, 'You see now, you're a simple man to read.'

He left the window, crossing to the table to return his papers to their former order. 'Am I?'

'Yes,' she told him. 'And I do apologize for teasing you, but it is far too easy. You will stay to supper?'

'No. I thank you, but I am expected elsewhere.'

She accepted this with, 'Then we'll see you tomorrow.'

'About that.' I aimed this at Gilroy, who looked at me.

'Yes?'

'Forgive me, for I have not your experience with matters such as this . . .'

Helen defended me. 'You owe yourself more credit. I am sure my husband could himself have done no better. He'll be very grateful, as am I.'

I thanked her. 'But,' I said, to Gilroy, 'you've invited Mrs Graeme back tomorrow, and I cannot see what we have left to talk about.'

He had a way of smiling that could not entirely be called a smile, as though he held some knowledge closely and in private, as a sharper holds his cards. He said, 'She was mistaken on one point. Her husband's cousin, Robert Moray – she did call him Robin – is no longer on the Continent. He returned home to Scotland in April of this year.'

Helen asked, 'Does he live nearby?'

'His home's near Stirling, at Murrayshall.'

'That's not so far,' she said.

Close enough, I thought, for an express to reach him, and return. 'You mean to ask him if her husband told him of their marriage?'

Gilroy said, 'And to verify our Mrs Graeme is actually Lilias Aitcheson, or at least the proper Lilias Aitcheson. Only a person who knew her and James Graeme both could confirm that. We cannot rely on her word alone.'

I'd not considered this, although I knew he was right – anybody could claim to be somebody else. But I did not like the thought of walking Mrs Graeme into what amounted to an ambush. 'People do change in appearance,' I warned him, 'as they grow from children to adults.'

He glanced at me dryly. 'I'll warrant that someone who knew you when you were a lad would find something to recognize.'

Helen said, 'Then you asked Mrs Graeme to return tomorrow because you intend to write express to Mr Moray and invite him to come here, so they can meet?'

Gilroy confirmed he had hopes of arranging a meeting. 'Though that may be difficult, and having Moray come here,' he said, 'would be impossible.'

It was his habit, I thought, to tell less than he knew, but it did try my patience. I asked, 'Why is that?'

'Because this Saturday last past,' he told us, 'Robert Moray was brought in by night and under close guard to the castle, and is held there now a prisoner.'

CHAPTER 4

TUESDAY, 23 SEPTEMBER, 1707

I FELT COLD PASSING UNDER the portcullis gate.

Mrs Graeme, I think, felt it, too, and her steps faltered slightly, although she recovered her pace so adroitly that none would have thought it was anything but the unevenness of the old cobblestones under her feet that had given her trouble.

The great castle of Edinburgh had been designed to have that effect – built to appear it had grown somehow out of the living rock, solid and strong and unyielding. An army approaching it might as well turn and go home, for they'd never defeat it. A prisoner finding himself locked inside might as well give up hope, for he'd never escape it. And we three who passed underneath the great iron portcullis gate might as well thank the good fortune that put us in neither position, and put ourselves into the hands of the guard who was leading us.

Lord Grange's name had unlocked opportunities. Gilroy had sent a request to the castle's deputy governor, stressing our urgency, and the reply had been quick.

Mrs Graeme had offered no protest to our change in venue,

and if her pale features were wrapped now in worry, it might be put down to the fact she had just learned her childhood friend was in prison.

They were keeping Robert Moray, we were told, in the same tower chamber where they once had held the Earl of Argyll before he'd been taken to his execution.

Not a thing that would inspire confidence, but I suspected confidence was not what they intended to inspire within the hearts and souls of prisoners.

Our guard carried no candle down the winding turnpike stair, and so we followed him with caution in our single file, our footsteps ringing loudly on the stone.

There was a wooden door he had to pause to open at the bottom, where he called out simply, 'Visitors tae see ye!'

Then he ducked aside to let us pass. There were more stone steps – several of them. Mrs Graeme stumbled and I caught her elbow.

'Careful, now,' I said.

But she had already been caught and steadied at her other side by the tall gentleman who'd come across the narrow room to meet us.

There was daylight here, admitted by a single, small, square window set far back within its deep well in the thick wall of the tower. It revealed a room that, while unwelcoming, was neither dungeon nor a pit, but rather a spare room of stone with a high, vaulted ceiling and a plain chair and small, plain table and an even plainer bed of the variety a soldier might have used when on campaign. There was no fire.

Robert Moray – for I guessed it must be him, there being no one else within the chamber – thanked the guard in the reflexive way men do who have been raised with gentlemanly manners, and dismissed him with a nod as though the guard were no more than a servant bringing him expected guests.

The difference in our stations would have been apparent even without that. He was a man of fine appearance. Prisoner or no, he wore a handsome wig of long, brown, curling hair and although his confinement had affected the condition of his clothing it could not disguise its quality. His coat alone would likely have been worth more than three of my own suits, and he wore it well and carelessly.

Not knowing how we'd be received, I had a speech prepared. I started, 'Mr Moray, I do offer my apologies for interrupting—'

'My God,' he said suddenly, still holding Mrs Graeme's elbow. Moving her a step into the light, he looked down at her face as his own slowly creased into a smile of unexpected pleasure. 'Lily!'

Two things struck me, sitting in that prison chamber watching Robert Moray: one, that he had keenly watchful eyes that were forever weighing information and would not miss anything, and two, that he was not nearly as calm and at his ease as he would wish us to believe.

He was the eldest of us, past his middle thirties, and in height likely the tallest of us also, yet he'd felt the need to choose a seat that gave him an advantage. He had given the one chair to Mrs Graeme, and invited Gilroy and myself to sit along the bed's edge, while he half-leaned and half-sat against the corner of the table, facing us, the window to his back. This had the dual effect of making us look up at him, and making it more difficult to read his face against the light.

I'd marked his eyes before he took up that position, when I'd crossed to offer Mrs Graeme my own coat, because the day's warmth could not penetrate that tower's walls, and in the shadows of that room the air had a decided chill.

She'd thanked me, and accepted my help as she put the coat around her shoulders.

Robert Moray during this had watched me, closely. 'Sergeant ... Williamson? Forgive me, but while I've met Gilroy several times, I do not know your face. Have ye worked long for Lord Grange?'

Voices like his, smooth and self-assured, came from a life-time of servants and schooling, though even those had been unable to dislodge the deeper Perthshire accent underlying his more educated tones.

'My employment with Lord Grange,' I'd said, 'is only temporary, and in the place of another.'

He had given me one more look, faintly curious, and that was when he'd leaned against the table. It had seemed a move made casually, although I came to doubt that he did anything at random.

Now he looked at Mrs Graeme. 'I am pleased to find ye well.'

'I thank you, Robin. I do wish I found you likeways.'

Seeming nonchalant, he raised one shoulder in a shrug. ''Tis but a small misunderstanding, which I trust will soon be put to rights. Ye need not be distressed.'

Yet *he* was, I observed. I'd walked too many years upon a

razor's edge myself to miss the telling signs of one who knew his fate was yet uncertain.

He sat a little too straight, making every effort not to let us see the effort that it took. I'd seen men do the same when they kept watch by night and, growing overtired, were determined not to let it show. And while his mind was quick, I did perceive a pause before he spoke, as though he had need of the space to concentrate.

For all his brave appearance, I'd have laid odds Robert Moray was not sleeping well.

It had not dulled his intellect.

He'd clearly had no difficulty following my explanation of why we were here, and his own thoughts had since been travelling on courses of their own. 'I did not know that Lord Grange was appointed a commissioner,' he said, 'to the Equivalent.'

He asked that directly of Gilroy. I let Gilroy answer.

'He's not a commissioner, sir. But he has friends who are, and they have asked him to look into Mrs Graeme's claim.'

A trace of dryness touched the edge of Robert Moray's voice. 'And Lord Grange is obliging to his friends.'

Gilroy had also caught that edge. He said, 'I can assure you, sir, Lord Grange was most displeased to find you have been treated thus, and wishes it were in his power to correct it.'

'Does he? That is very kind. Do thank him for me, and remind him, if ye will, that it *is* within his power, if it pleases him, to send a letter to his brother, who might have more influence.'

Lord Grange's brother was the Earl of Mar, a man with close connections at Queen Anne's court who enjoyed the confidence and private ear of many of the nobles there. As

Gilroy answered back with reassurances, it became clear that Robert Moray's friendship with the earl and, through him, with Lord Grange, had been forged in boyhood when the earl and Moray were at school together.

I found it curious myself that Lord Grange – who'd been roused to come to Turnbull's house in person to arrange an inquiry for Mrs Graeme – seemed to have done little on behalf of his old friend Robert Moray, and had not even come to pay a visit to console or cheer him.

But then, I often found men of the upper classes to be mystifying. These were different men from me, and while we walked through the same city, we might never see each other, for we met in different drawing rooms.

If I were taken up and jailed, I'd have no earl to write to at the court in London – none of noble name to stand and plead my case before Queen Anne, or barter for my life within the crooked halls and corridors of justice.

Nor would I be placed and guarded in a tower cell like this one, which although it had but one small window and lacked warmth was, at the least, a plain and proper room – one made entirely of stone, but with a vaulted ceiling high enough to let the air rise, and a floor that seemed to have been swept not long ago, and walls that were both clean and dry.

Not like the squalor of the Tolbooth, where the prisoners shared spaces little fit for beasts, and suffered from the want of freer air.

Mrs Graeme drew my borrowed coat more closely round her shoulders. Her small action brought my thoughts back to the matter at hand, and reminded me this was a prison – no place for a woman to needlessly linger.

I broke in to the conversation of the other men. 'You'll forgive me, but our time may not be long here, and our visit has a purpose.'

If Gilroy was annoyed with me for interrupting him, he hid it well. He took his pen in hand and waited.

Robert Moray was regarding me with some expression that I couldn't clearly see because the light was angling down behind him from the small barred window, but his voice, when he began to speak, was pleasant. 'I'm afraid that ye will find me of no help to your inquiry.'

I asked him, 'You were unaware that Mrs Graeme and your cousin James were married?'

'Ours is a large family, Sergeant Williamson. 'Tis easy to lose sight of one another. Ye say they wed in January, sixteen ninety-eight? My studies on the Continent were finishing that winter, and I did not see my cousin in that year. That very summer Jamie sailed for Darien, and as ye know, there is no way I could have seen him after.'

There had been so many moments in my life when my survival had depended on my trusting to my instincts that I'd gained a great respect for them, and there was something now, not in the words that Robert Moray said, but in the way he said them, that set all my instincts on alert.

I didn't think that what he'd told me was a lie, but any man could tell the truth and, by omitting details, still deceive.

And instinct warned me he was leaving out a detail, trusting I'd be unobservant and too ignorant to notice.

I asked him, in a tone I hoped was conversational, 'You studied on the Continent? May I ask where?'

'In Holland, at the university of Utrecht.'

I made note of that. 'Do you have family there?'

'I have relations, sir, in many places.'

'How long were you in Utrecht?'

'Three years.'

'And what were you studying?'

'The law.' He said it evenly. 'The civil law, to be exact. Before being sent abroad, I had been bred here at Edinburgh to our Scots law and a knowledge in styles.'

I nodded in a neutral way to mask my irritation. Gilroy surely would have known how Robert Moray made his living, and it put me at a disadvantage, having had no warning I'd be trading words this morning with a lawyer.

With a smile, I matched his tone as nearly as I could. 'Then you'll not need me to explain to you the problem we are facing in this instance, where we have no valid proof of marriage, and no living witnesses. In such a case,' I asked him, 'what procedure would *you* follow?'

'In honesty, I'd probably reject the claim. At least, were it a stranger,' he replied. 'But if Lily says that she was married onto James . . .' He shrugged. 'I'd do the same as ye are doing now: find people who were privy to the marriage and were willing to attest to it, to satisfy the men of the commission.'

'But you cannot help us.'

'No.'

Gilroy put in, 'You do not think your cousin would have told your brother John?'

'Why John, particularly?'

Gilroy paused. He did it for a moment only, but I'd never seen him made to do it in a conversation, so it caught my interest.

Robert Moray said, 'It's only that my cousin was no closer to my brother John than he was to my brother Maurice, or my brother William, come to that, so why are ye concerned with John?'

Gilroy shrugged. 'Would he have any knowledge of the marriage, do you think?'

'I think ye'd have to ask John.'

'Would you know where we could find him?'

Moray changed the angle of his head a fraction, as one does when light strikes something differently, although to me the shadows looked the same. He said to Gilroy, 'On a battlefield in Flanders, I expect. Or on his way to one.'

Accepting he would get no more than this, Gilroy asked, 'And your uncle, Colonel Patrick Graeme, is he still at Saint-Germain?'

'My uncle is a man of action. I would never hazard to presume where he might be at any moment.'

Some men, I reasoned, fought with blades and pistols. Others did their parrying with words, and were as skilled as any swordsman.

Even Gilroy seemed to realize he was never going to get the best of Robert Moray, for at last he turned instead to Mrs Graeme. 'We have concentrated so far on your husband's friends and his relations, Madam, but not on your own.'

Again I saw that very subtle setting of her shoulders, as though she were bracing herself against some inevitable test. 'I have already promised you that no one knew of our marriage.'

'Not even your mother?'

'My mother was dead,' she told Gilroy.

'I see. I am sorry,' he said. 'And your father?'

Robert Moray broke in. 'Is this relevant? Lily has said—'

'It's all right, Robin.' Looking directly at Gilroy, she told him, 'My father was also dead, when I was married. Would you wish to know how he died? Would you wish to know why Jamie's mother would think me unsuitable?'

Moray leaned over and covered her tightly linked hands with his own. I could see her drawing strength from both his gesture and its comfort, and I envied Robert Moray that he had the freedom, in this room, to offer it where I could not.

His voice turned gentle. 'Lily.'

She was resolute. 'No, Robin. I will tell them.'

CHAPTER FIVE

MONDAY, 8 JUNE, 1685

HER GRANDMOTHER'S WORRIES THAT Jamie would no longer have time for Lily when she came to live with her father had not come to pass.

If anything, they'd had the freedom to see one another more frequently these past two years, with her father serving Jamie's in the Edinburgh town guard.

Long before her birth, from the first days her father had been made a soldier, he'd served Jamie's father. That had been what took him north to Perthshire, to the home of Jamie's family at Inchbrakie, where her mother – as her father had admitted once to Lily – stole his breath and heart together, so there'd been no choice left to him but to marry her.

She only knew her mother through those memories of her father's and her grandmother's, and through the stories shared with her by others who remembered. Like the old Laird of Inchbrakie, who one day had looked at Lily in the sunlight near the window in the drawing room, and smiled, and said, 'You have the very colour of her eyes.' And Lily's heart had felt sublimely full.

She could not call to mind a certain image of her mother, having only been three years of age when sudden illness and a fever stilled her mother's heart for ever, leaving but a carved name on a small stone in the churchyard, that gave very little comfort.

Her father had decided.

'She should have a home,' was what he'd told her grandmother, from all accounts, his jaw set tight against his own emotions. It was not his wish to make such an arrangement – and indeed he made his visits when he could, and wrote her letters, and sent little gifts, that she would not forget him – but 'a soldier's life alone is not a settled one, and no life for a bairn, and I would have her know the safety of a home, where she is loved.'

And so she had been. So she was.

There was also love for her in this house with her father and his new wife here in Edinburgh, and there was Jamie every evening, given that his days were taken up now with his studies at the grammar school of Mr Skene.

She met him in the street outside the school, as was their custom. It was only a few minutes after seven, so they'd have an hour at least to make their own, and being early summer, it was bright.

Jamie stretched. He'd grown taller than her by the breadth of a hand and could now look straight over her head, but his fair hair was just as unkempt and his grin was as ready and cheerful as ever.

'You're lucky to be a girl.'

'Why?'

'Mr Skene doesn't teach girls.'

There weren't many schools that did teach girls, and those few that did charged a fee Lily's father could not afford, so she would have to make do with the learning she'd had from the Moray girls at Abercairney. Besides, she had plenty of work at home to keep her occupied. Still, she was envious, sometimes, of Jamie. She'd liked reading, and there were no books at all in her father's house.

Jamie asked, 'What will we do? Will we look for your cat?'

Lily nodded. She'd first spotted the black-and-white kitten three days ago and had been worrying since for its welfare. She had searched for it, but Edinburgh had not been built upon a simple plan — it was a labyrinth of wynds and closes twisting off the broader streets and narrowing to falls of steps that disappeared in shadows, overhung by painted tenements with galleries and watching windows crowding close together overhead.

Although she'd lived here nearly two full years, she'd still not learned the name of every street and winding passage, but her father, who had knowledge of them all, strictly forbad her to take some of them by daylight, and by night they all were barred to her if she was on her own.

'Ye're of an age now where some men will take advantage of ye, Lily, should they catch ye in a corner,' he had warned. Being only nine, she'd felt the need to ask him what it meant to 'take advantage', whereupon her father had, for help, looked to his wife, who'd said, 'They'll try to put a baby in ye,' and since Lily hadn't wanted *that*, she had kept clear of all the places she'd been ordered to avoid.

But having Jamie at her side gave her the freedom to go anywhere, not only because she was not alone, but because everybody knew his father was the captain of the town guard.

They could, if they wanted, go down past the Netherbow, past all the houses of merchants and craftsmen and, further still, past the grand houses and gardens and right to the palace of Holyrood. Or they could walk up the other way, up past the menacing Tolbooth and past the tall spire of St Giles' and on into the Landmarket and up the hill to the castle, where sometimes they'd look for the secret way in through the walls Jamie once overheard someone speaking of.

Today, though, they kept to Carrubber's Close, where Lily had glimpsed the black-and-white kitten this morning.

'She was there,' Lily said, pointing. 'Under the stones.'

Jamie bent to look. 'How d'ye ken it's a she?'

'I just do.'

'Well, she's not there now.'

All down one side of the close they searched, carefully, and up the other, until Lily finally saw two tiny pointed ears poking up over the rim of a bucket. The bucket was, thankfully, empty of water or anything less pleasant, and it held only the kitten, who cowered inside upon Lily's approach.

Jamie said, 'Ye'll get scratched.'

'I will not.' And she didn't. The kitten came easily into her hands, in the end, with a few coaxing words and a gentling touch. There seemed no weight at all to the creature as Lily drew her apron up to wrap the folds of cloth around the kitten.

As she straightened, there were footsteps on the cobblestones behind them and a shadow fell across them all.

The shadow of a man, who said, 'What's this, now? Theft? And with the sun yet up?'

Jamie was unconcerned. He did not bother turning round, but told his father, 'Lily's found a cat.'

Lily did turn. She had no fear of Captain Graeme.

She'd always thought him taller than her father, until recently she'd seen them standing side by side and realized that for all her life her mind had played a trick on her – that it was something in the way the captain moved, or held himself, that made him seem the larger man. She guessed that quality was why they'd put him in command.

She had to tilt her face up, anyway, to tell him, 'It's a kitten.'

'Aye, I see that.' He had eyes like Jamie's, clear and full of thoughts, set in a lean face that she'd seen be hard or charming, as he chose. With a soldier's disregard for current fashion, he wore his own hair curling to his shoulders and a neatly-kept brown beard and, like her father, a town guardsman's coat over his breeks and boots, crossed with his sword belt and with pistols at his waist. He bent to be at Lily's level. 'A wee kitten, surely too young to be taken from its mother.'

Lily said, 'She has no mother.'

Captain Graeme looked at her a moment. 'Does she not?' He touched her shoulder lightly with one hand, as though he understood. 'Well then, it is fortunate indeed she has found you.'

It was not far around to Lily's house in Kinloch's Close, and Captain Graeme walked her home, with Jamie going on a step ahead of them, as usual. Occasionally Jamie, turning back to chide them for not going faster, or to tell them some new thing he had observed at school that day, failed to mind his steps. And so it was that Jamie near collided with the violer who lived within their close, and who reacted with impatience.

Captain Graeme calmed the moment, offered an apology, made Jamie do the same, and all shook hands; but Lily was a little frightened of the violer, and as they passed him by, she looked behind and saw him spit upon the ground where Captain Graeme had been standing.

She was glad to get indoors, into her own house – as she'd come to think of the low room her father rented from the building's owner – where the single-chambered space was always filled with welcome warmth and happiness.

Captain Graeme came, too, standing squarely in the doorway like a guardian, as lightly padding, almost skipping footsteps came to greet them at a childish run.

Little Bessie, not yet two, but already with twice as many words stored in her brain than it seemed able to keep hold of all at once, so they kept tumbling out in speech and song and constant, random questions.

'Whatsat?' she asked Lily, reaching up towards the bundle in the apron. 'What did ye bring home?'

Lily crouched to show her. 'Careful, now. Be gentle.'

Lily's father, who'd been resting on the larger bed set in the corner of the one low-ceilinged chamber, rose with a groan to come and see. 'Oh, God, what is it now?'

Except the wink he sent to Captain Graeme over Lily's head betrayed him. He might have a temper, and she'd witnessed it, but he was never angry with his children.

Jamie, who till now had stood and held his tongue beside the captain in the doorway, answered, 'It's a cat.'

When her father's wife, Jean, set her kitchen work down

with a look of dismay, the captain, in defence of Lily, clarified, 'A kitten. With no mother, so I'm told.'

Her father, in the tone he used to tell her things he knew she would not wish to hear, said, 'Lily, it's a pretty thing, it is, but ye ken Jean already telt ye she cannot abide a creature in the house.'

'She's not a creature, she's a kitten, and she'll help protect the baby,' Lily argued. 'Just this morning ye were saying that the mice ran clear across the baby's blanket. Well, the kitten won't allow that, if she lives with us. And anyway, Jean has a loving heart, it's not so hard. I have no mother, either, and she welcomed me.'

She paused for breath, and looked to see Jean with one hand upon her heart, her dark eyes glistening. And then Jean glanced across at Lily's father, and their eyes met, and Jean shrugged a little helplessly.

'She has ye there,' her father said.

And Lily had her kitten.

Jean tried to protest that she had enough fleas in her household. 'Am I not plagued with them enough from our own bedding, do I need more carried in from out of doors?'

Lily's father said, 'Perhaps our fleas will better like the kitten and leave ye in peace.'

Jean rolled her eyes, and fetched a fine-toothed horn comb that she gave to Lily. 'Comb your kitten well with that,' she said, 'and kill whatever fleas ye find on her. And she'll sleep in a basket on the floor, mind, not in bed with ye and Bessie.'

But her heart, as Lily knew, was not so hard, and she set down a dish of water and of scraps to feed the kitten while the children gathered round it on the floor, then asked the captain, 'Will ye stay to sup?'

'I thank ye, but I cannot. Not this evening. I have company awaiting me. My sister has come down from Abercairney with her second son, young Robin, who is now fifteen and aims to be a lawyer and is seeking education. Not that I am well connected in that area, but where I can assist, I will.'

Jamie, sitting on the floor, said, 'He can have my place at Mr Skene's school, if he likes.'

The captain thanked him very solemnly, but Lily saw the crinkles at the corners of his eyes that meant that he was holding back a smile. 'I doubt that Mr Skene would be the best instructor of Scots law. Although,' he said to Lily, 'I believe that ye could well instruct our Robin in the art of pure persuasion.'

She was not sure what he meant by that, but she liked Robin, and she said so. 'Will he be here long?'

'I do hope not,' said the captain, but again he was not serious. 'I've four lads of my own. What I shall do with five, I can't imagine, and my wife, poor lady, is beside herself at the idea.'

Jean remarked, 'Your sister's brave, to travel such a distance at a time like this.'

'My sister in her life has met too many dangers on her own estate to fear a little travel when the need arises.'

Jean said, '*I* should not stray far from my own hearth when such a monster as the Earl of Argyll is yet loose upon the countryside with his wild, Highland men.'

The captain smiled again, but this time it was with his lips alone, and there were no crinkles beside his eyes. 'Ye'll be confusing Highland men with Campbells,' he told Jean. ''Tis a mistake the earl himself makes all too often in his scheming, but the hearts of our good Highlanders are true, and they will hold fast for King James. We'll have that devil Argyll in our hands afore the month's end.'

Lily stopped combing the kitten to look up at Captain Graeme. 'When ye catch him, what then will ye do with him?'

His smile, for her, was genuine. 'I'll pay him the same wages that his father paid the great Montrose, with interest. Then he'll worry ye no more.'

But it did worry Lily, thinking of the Earl of Argyll.

She was thinking of him when her father came to settle her with Bessie in their little bed built close against the larger one. She asked him, 'Are the rebels in the west, still?'

'Aye.' He smoothed the curling hair back from her forehead so that he could kiss her there. To sweeten her dreams, so he always said. 'Why d'ye ask?'

She'd thought about the rebels much. She knew that things were different, since King Charles had died in February. Now, his brother James was king, and many men were angry because King James was a Catholic, and some did not think a Catholic should be king.

She'd heard the adults talk, these past two weeks. Somewhere in England was a nephew to the king who, while he had no right to sit upon the throne, was making plans to claim it, and the Earl of Argyll – son to that same Argyll who had driven all the games she'd played with Jamie and his cousins – had now landed in the west of Scotland, raising men for a rebellion. While the adults, when they talked, spoke of important-sounding things like freedom and the crown and bishops and the Covenant, one thing alone concerned her: 'Will ye have to go away to fight them?'

'No.' Her father's hand upon her forehead was a reassurance. 'No, I'm not that kind of soldier anymore, I guard this town. My sword stays here.'

'And if the earl comes here?'

'He'll have to get through Captain Graeme and myself afore he does ye any harm, and there's no chance of that,' he promised. 'Get to sleep, now.'

'Daddie?' she asked. 'Why do some men not like Captain Graeme?'

'What men?'

When she told him what she'd seen the violer, their neighbour, do – the way he'd spat upon the ground – her father's eyes flashed darkly with a swift show of his temper, but he held it in and only said, 'Some men are fools.'

But that was not an answer, so she pressed him, and he told her that the town guard in its present form had only been created some three years ago, and that there were still people who resented it, and resented even more the tax collected from them for the wages paid to Captain Graeme's soldiers. And, he said, some wished there were no town guard there at all to keep the peace.

'But those are lawless men, and ye need not concern yourself with what they think,' he told her.

'Cannot ye put the lawless men in prison?'

'Some we can, aye. But there always will be lawless men, the prisons cannot hold them all, so ye must learn to ken them when ye meet them, for it is not by their look alone.'

'How will I ken them, then?' she asked.

'I'll teach ye how. But not tonight.' Bending, he kissed her again on her forehead. 'There, that's to sweeten your dreams.' He kissed Bessie, too, although she was already asleep, nestled warm into Lily's side.

Lily sank drowsily into the blankets and hugged Bessie closer. She liked the soft feel of her sister beside her – the comforting feel of her sister's light breathing against her own neck. Bessie's curls were not brown like her own, they were golden – so fine and so pale they gleamed white in the light of the candle her father set into its place in the wall niche before he extinguished it, and the house fell into darkness.

Jean was nursing the baby – wee James, scarcely two months old. Lily could hear the small baby sounds. Jean humming quietly, soothingly. Ropes on the bigger bed creaked as her father rolled over to settle himself.

Lily treasured this time of night. Treasured the feeling of being a part of a family.

There had been so many times she'd envied Jamie, and envied his cousins the Morays, because they'd had brothers around them, and sisters, to keep them from being alone. And now she had that, also.

It would have been perfect if she'd had her grandmother here with her, too, but the house was not large. Maybe later this summer, when Argyll was captured and travel was safe, she could go north to visit. But not alone, Lily thought. Not alone.

Not anymore.

Something small landed lightly beside her leg, on the bed, making her startle before it curled carefully into the blankets. The kitten.

She dared not reach down for it, lest Jean see that it had

jumped on the bed when it wasn't supposed to, but silently she wished the kitten goodnight.

And she slept.

⤡

When she woke, it was dark. Baby James was in full-throated cry.

From out in the close came the discordant strains of a fiddle, played loudly.

'I'll skelp him,' her father said.

Jean murmured, 'Edward . . .'

He said, 'There are laws against breaking the peace at this hour.'

Lily knew not the hour, but they were not the only ones having their sleep disturbed. She could hear some of their neighbours in Kinloch's Close calling from windows now, bidding the violer, Watson, to stop playing.

Watson ignored them.

Jean tried to soothe baby James, who cried more lustily. And Lily's father swore under his breath as he levered himself from the bed.

Jean said, once again, 'Edward . . .'

But he had his breeks on already. His waistcoat. In darkness, he reached for the sword belt that hung on its peg at his bedside, and buckled the straps of it over his shoulder with fingers that, after so long, knew the motions and needed no light. 'Jeannie, it is my duty,' he told her. 'The town guard is here to keep order and peace, and there's nothing that's peaceful nor orderly happening out there the now.'

Lily heard the firm stride of his boots cross the floor, and the door opened in a swift rush of cool air and then closed with a hard, final slam.

There were voices. She struggled to hear them above all the shouts, and the sound of the fiddle that had not yet stopped, and the cries of the baby.

Her father was using the cold voice she hated to hear, though she did not know what he was saying. The strings of the fiddle played almost as though they were making a human reply. And her father called angrily back to it, moving wherever the violer led.

Although he couldn't hear her, Jean begged, 'Leave it now, Edward. Please, let it go.'

But the fiddle kept taunting him, leading him further away, down the close to the High Street. The music and voices grew fainter, and then came a cry. And then silence.

A terrible silence.

Even baby James stopped wailing, and began to sniffle as though somehow he had sensed the change.

The shouts began as though at a great distance, and the sound of running feet, and of a sudden it seemed the whole town was in their close, with voices rising steadily. A woman keened, and cursed, and called to Jean to come outdoors, but Jean stayed sitting in the bed, the blankets clenched within her fists.

When Lily looked at her, Jean told her, low, 'Lie down, now. Wait until your daddie comes.'

Lily waited.

And at length there came a pounding at their door. Jean hesitated, but she rose and went to answer it. The man who stood outside held up a lanthorn, so that she could see his face and know that he was not a stranger.

'Baillie Spense?' Jean greeted him in some confusion. She was trying to look past him, Lily thought, into the close, but he was standing in her way.

Lily heard metal scrape over the worn stone threshold. 'Ye can hold his sword,' Baillie Spense said. 'He'll be in the Tolbooth.' And he told Jean something, quietly, that made her answer, 'No!' and nearly fall against the door frame so that he was forced to hold her up a moment.

'No,' she said, again.

He said, 'I'm sorry,' and he closed the door, and left them there in darkness.

Lily shivered as the sound of wailing filled the house a second time, but this time it was not the baby crying. It was Jean.

❧

Once, Lily had been taken by a fever that had caught her brain and twisted time till everything was wrong, so sometimes things moved past her in a fog, and sometimes single moments rose up piercingly and sharp, like pins pricked through a silken fabric that was spilling on the ground in bright confusion.

The next few days felt just like that.

She held the kitten on her lap and soothed and sang to Bessie and she held the baby while Jean talked to all the people who came by. Some women came with food, and other women came with gossip – Jean would chase *them* off, or keep them in a corner, talking low, so Lily couldn't hear. Three men came, too, at different times – friends of her father's, from the town guard. One, whose name was Morison, stayed with them some nights, sleeping sitting upright in a chair beside the door. 'To see ye'll not have trouble,' he told Jean.

One morning Captain Graeme came, and he had Robin Moray with him. Robin looked like a young man now, even taller than his uncle. He stood quietly aside and let the others speak, but Lily noticed that his eyes were watchful. He was going to be a student of the law, Lily remembered. He was going to be a lawyer. Maybe then he'd help her father, because from what she was hearing, there were judges and the courts involved.

Jean shook her head. To the captain, she said, 'He was plainly provoked. Watson called him a rascal, and other bad language besides. There are witnesses.'

'Not all the witnesses will take the part of a man of my guard.'

Jean had tears on her face. She wept often, these past few days. 'What will I do? Captain, what will I do with the bairns? I can't—'

'Hush, now.' He folded her into his arms. 'Be brave.'

'I'm not brave.' Jean's voice sounded small, muffled against Captain Graeme's strong shoulder. 'I can't be.'

'Ye must be,' he said. 'For the bairns.'

Bessie tugged at Captain Graeme's leg and asked him, 'Is my daddie well?'

Jean straightened from the captain's arms and wiped her eyes. 'Of course he is,' she answered Bessie. 'And we'll keep him so.'

'Why does he not come home? I want to see him now.'

Jean said, 'We all do wish to see him, but he's where we cannot visit.'

Lily knew that was not true. They'd said her father was now in the Tolbooth, and she knew that people in the Tolbooth, whether prisoners or soldiers, could have others come to visit them, but she knew it was impolite to contradict her elders. She said nothing.

Looking up, she found that Robin was now watching her. 'What is the name of your kitten?' he asked.

'I've not named her yet.'

'It's a boy kitten,' said Robin.

She gave him no answer, because in that curious way, time had twisted, and Robin was gone again, and in his place stood the soldier named Morison, looking out into the close.

Jean said, 'She's a bitter, vengeful woman. Others lose their husbands, and her man was in the wrong.'

'The captain did the best he could with her,' was Morison's reply. 'He offered money – a fair sum, I'm told, if she would let the matter drop, but she was having none of it. I'm sorry, Jean.'

'I'm sorry, too.' Jean rubbed her eyes. 'Is it a good thing that the Earl of Errol now does have the judging of it, do ye think?'

'I cannot say. I ken the captain hopes the earl will be a fairer judge than would the magistrates, but we will see. There's little justice in the world for such as us.' A hard wind gusted through the close, and raised the dust in dancing swirls. 'A good day,' he told Jean, 'to be indoors.'

Lily was kept indoors now every day, and not allowed to

go meet Jamie after school. 'There's too much danger in the streets,' was all that Jean would tell her. Lily looked towards the wall, to where her father's sword hung in its sword belt, waiting on the peg, and thought she understood.

Until he was returned to them, they were not safe. Yet knowing that his sword, at least, was with them still, helped make her feel a little better.

My sword stays here, he had said.

It stayed there all that week, and on the Tuesday evening came another knock – this time from men of the town guard – and Jean said, 'Come now, let's go see your daddie, he's at Captain Graeme's house.'

Lily's heart had leapt with hope and happiness. Her feet had all but danced across the cobbles as they'd walked, for surely this meant things were better now, and all their troubles ended. She could not fathom why the faces of the men around them were so grim, nor why Jean was so quiet, unless it was because they had to walk the town's streets in the nighttime and, as she'd been told so often, streets were not so safe by night.

But she'd have walked through any dangers, then, to see her father.

He'd grown paler, and his face was tightly lined, but his embrace was warm and sure. He gathered Lily in his arms, his head tucked hard against her shoulder, as though somehow the few candles in the drawing room were too bright for his eyes, and he would shield them from the light.

She snuggled close against his chest, and when he told her how he'd missed her and he asked her how she'd been, she answered back with stories of her kitten, and she felt her father's smile.

'He sounds a right wee sodjer,' he said, giving her small kitten the great compliment of calling him a soldier like himself.

'He's growing bigger every day. Ye'll see when ye come home.'

His arms were briefly tighter. 'I'm not coming home the now, my Lily. I've been called away.'

They were sending him to fight the rebels, Lily thought. She shook her head against his chest. 'Ye said ye were no more that kind of soldier, that they would not make ye go.'

His breath fell warm against her neck. 'A soldier does not always get to choose, lass.'

'It's not fair.'

'No.' Pushing back the curls that tumbled hot against her forehead, he half-raised his head to look at her with eyes that held a brightness she had never seen before. 'It is not fair, it's not. But I would have ye smile for me, and wish me a good journey, all the same. Cannot ye do that for me?'

Lily tried. Her smile was trembly, but she tried. She only glimpsed the smile her father gave in answer, for he'd leaned in once again to kiss her forehead.

'That,' he said, 'will keep your dreams sweet while I'm gone.'

Then it was Bessie's turn, and Lily sat with Robin Moray looking through the pictures in the atlas of the world that Captain Graeme kept among his books, while in the other corner of the room her father said farewell to Bessie and to baby James and, finally, to Jean.

'Where would ye sail, if ye were able to sail anywhere?' asked Robin.

'Norway,' Lily answered, certain.

Robin raised his eyebrows. 'Why is that?'

'Because that's where Montrose went when his enemies were after him, so it must be the safest country.'

Robin said, 'That is fair logic, Lily. You should join me in a study of the law. Norway it is, then.' And he turned the page to show her, in the atlas, where the map of that strange country lay, its long and jagged coastline with its ready, waiting harbours.

Jean was at her shoulder, then. 'It's time to go.'

Her father gave a final hug to little Bessie, who wrapped both her arms around his neck and told him, 'Don't cry, Daddie.'

He squeezed his eyes tight shut as though they pained him, and he blinked them, hard, but they were nearly dry when he hugged Lily. 'Be a good girl, mind your prayers, and ye will see me, by and by.'

'I will,' she promised, wishing he were anything at all except a soldier. 'I'll pray every day, for then ye'll come home safe, and will not die.'

His eyes filled brightly once more with the sheen of unshed tears, the line of his mouth turning downward slightly as he sought to hold it steady.

She clung to his hand. 'Daddie.'

'Go, now.'

'But, Daddie . . .'

He looked at Jean. 'Please, take them.'

Gently, Jean took Lily's hand and loosed it from her father's, and said, 'Come, we have to leave him now.'

The walk home was the longest one that Lily could remember. It was also the first time she did not fear the dark.

For nothing waiting in the darkness could hurt her more deeply than the pain of letting go her father's hand.

CHAPTER SIX

WEDNESDAY, 17 JUNE, 1685

LILY HAD NOT SLEPT. At home in bed, with Bessie at her side, she'd tried to raise from memory all her father's words of comfort. He had said them only hours ago at Captain Graeme's house and yet already they were losing force, so Lily brought them to her mind repeatedly, that she would not forget what he had told her: 'Be a good girl, mind your prayers, and ye will see me, by and by.'

And so she prayed, in a small whisper, being careful not to wake the others, that God would watch over him and bring him safely home.

When she'd been very small, he had been called away to fight the Covenanting rebels once, with Jamie's father – back when Jamie's father had been a lieutenant colonel in the army, and not captain of the Edinburgh town guard – and although the fighting had been fierce, both men had been returned from it unharmed.

She had faith the same would happen now, if she did as her father asked – if she was good, and prayed. And yet, she could not lose the sense that something was yet left undone this time, about his leaving.

It worried her all morning, even after she had risen and begun her daily work, but she said not a word to Jean, because it seemed to Lily that Jean also had not slept well and was weary, and Jean's forehead bore the lines that meant her head was aching.

Lily did not wish to be the cause of any trouble. She kept quiet, did her chores, and tried to bury her misgivings.

Then, not long past midday, came their visitors.

The Laird of Abercairney's lady – Robin Moray's mother – was a graceful woman with a slender figure and fine clothes to show it to advantage. Today she wore a gown that Lily had not seen before, of deep blue silk so dark that it was nearly black, her skirts protected by a pretty apron edged with lace. There was lace also on the cap she wore tied over her brown hair that had been artfully arranged in curls that massed around her temples and were elsewhere gathered, leaving one long ringlet, tied with ribbon, hanging past her shoulder.

She was Jamie's father's sister and, from all accounts, the favourite daughter of the old Laird of Inchbrakie, and since Lily did admire both those men, it had been easy to extend that admiration to the Laird of Abercairney's lady, who could reason with the cleverness of Captain Graeme, and had the old laird's kind eyes.

A lady of her quality arriving at their door in Kinloch's Close was an occasion, apparently. Some of their neighbours had gathered to gawk.

As Jean opened the door, Lily spotted the face of the violer's wife and shrank back out of sight. It was very unsettling, the way that the violer's wife looked at all of them. When Lily's father's friends from the town guard had been here these past days helping to watch over them, they'd talked to the violer's wife sometimes; told her to keep away.

But those men weren't here this morning.

The violer's wife called out, loudly, 'May God damn his soul!'

Robin's mother, just crossing the threshold, turned fully to face her, making her elegant body a shield for Jean, Lily, and Bessie and baby James. Calmly, she said, 'There are children here.'

Lily heard the sound of shuffling from the close. And silence.

Robin's mother said, 'Shame on ye all. Go home.' Then turning again, she stepped into their house.

She had brought Robin with her, and a sombre, heavy-featured man whose name went by too quickly in the introductions for Lily to make note of it beyond the fact they'd called him Mr Somebody, and he had brought a Bible with him, carried in his hand with care, which meant he was a minister.

Lily would have wished for Jamie, too, to keep her company, but he felt ill, so she was told. 'We are not any of us feeling well at heart, this day,' was Robin's mother's explanation, making Lily wonder whether Jamie's father had been called to war along with hers, and who would stay and guard the town when all the soldiers were away.

Those worries joined the others in her busy mind.

It was, from the beginning, a perplexing visit. Jean, instead of setting out refreshments for their guests, retreated privately into the further corner with the minister and knelt with him, and prayed. This went on for so long that wee James began to fuss, and Robin's mother took him from the bed and carried him about as if it were quite natural for visitors and bairns to be ignored in such a manner.

Robin had brought games with him – a spinning top, and knucklebones – to Bessie's great delight. But Lily did not join them in their play, and even watching them, her thoughts were turned to other things.

Her kitten, as though he could sense her distraction, presented her with a dead mouse – his first capture and kill.

Lily praised him with her father's words, by saying, 'Ye're a right wee sodjer,' but when she reached out to pet the kitten, he leapt up onto the larger bed, where he was not allowed to be, and she was forced to chase him down again.

And that was when she saw her father's sword, still hanging in its sword belt on the peg upon the wall, beside the bed.

Lily's mind cleared. *That* was what was out of place, she thought. He'd gone from them in such haste he'd forgotten it, but he could not fight Argyll and the rebels if he did not have his sword.

She could not go to Jean, who was still praying with the minister, for it was rude to interrupt a person when at prayer.

Instead she went to Robin's mother.

'If ye please,' she said, 'my daddie needs his sword, if he's been called to fight the rebels. It's just there.' She pointed. 'I can run and take it to him, if ye like, at Captain Graeme's house.'

She did not know why Robin's mother's eyes should fill with sudden tears. 'There is no need, my dear, he is no longer there. But fear not, Mr Cant will see that he is armed with all that he requires, for where he will be going.'

Which made little sense to Lily.

Mr Cant was their own minister, from their own church – Trinity Church, where they went for the service every Sunday, and he'd always seemed a very peaceful man who wished to take no part in war. But Robin's mother was a clever woman, and if she said Mr Cant was giving arms and armour to her father, then it stood to reason he would know the way to get the sword to him, as well.

Lily would have mentioned this, but Robin's mother at that moment noticed the dead mouse, and praised the kitten for such bravery, but, 'Robin, I must get this cleared away. Will ye please take the bairn?'

Wee James did not approve of being passed from Robin's mother to her son, and made his disapproval known in a full-throated cry, and Bessie was not pleased to have her game of knucklebones disturbed, and Robin's mother had her back turned as she swept the mouse into the hearth.

In the confusion, Lily took the sword belt from its peg and slipped out, very quietly.

She could not wear it as he wore it, she was not so tall. She could but sling the belt high over her thin shoulder so the scabbard of the sword hung down her back, its point just knocking at her heels as she ran pell-mell down into the neighbouring, narrow, steep confines of Halkerston's Wynd. At the foot of the wynd, through the old dry stone gate, lay the orchards and gardens of Trinity Church.

She would always remember the scent of those orchards, years afterwards. Always remember the sound of her own breathing mingled with swift-running footsteps some distance behind her, and Robin's voice calling her name.

She'd remember, as well, her first sense of surprise upon seeing the churchyard.

Why, here are the men of the guard, she thought. *This is why they are not watching our house today. They are all here, standing in a formation, and aiming their guns . . .*

Then she saw what it was they were aiming at.

Robin had reached her. His hands quickly caught her and turned her and pressed her against his warm chest and he covered her ears and his head came down low and he said to her, over and over, 'Don't look now, *don't* look, Lily.'

But she had seen.

And for all Robin's efforts, the sound of the musket fire, when it came, struck just as surely through Lily's own heart.

&

Time did not pause for them, nor wait. Just as the sea's waves, having come to shore, were too soon overrun by even stronger waves that followed, so it was that not three days had passed since Lily's father's death when news came Argyll had been captured and would be brought in to Edinburgh a prisoner.

And two days after that his fellow traitor, Colonel Rumbold, was brought in as well, and carried to the castle.

Then it seemed to Lily that her father was forgotten by the world outside their own house, and that none but those who loved him best remembered he had lost his life, for all the town had turned its mind already to coming executions of these more important men.

Rumbold was brought to trial first, within a week of his arrival, and was executed that same day.

'He faced it well enough,' said Corporal Morison – the soldier who'd most often come to guard their door and help Jean with the heavy work around the house since Lily's father had first been imprisoned. 'I will allow,' he said of Rumbold, 'that he spoke with passion, though his words were mostly nonsense. He thinks all of us are equal in our lives, that's what he said – that he believes there is no man born marked of God above another.'

Corporal Morison smiled as though that thought amused him, and Jean smiled, too, and Lily recalled what her grandmother had said about Jamie's family. She'd said: 'There's a difference between us and them. There are some bridges in this life, lass, that ye cannot cross.'

Lily wondered whether God had marked the Graemes differently, so they would be higher than the Aitchesons, and have a nicer house. A better life. A happy family.

Jamie came around each afternoon that week to call for her, but Lily made excuses why she could not see him. Finally Jean, when tucking Lily gently into bed at night, said, 'It's not like ye, to not wish to play with Jamie.'

Lily knew in her own heart that she was not behaving fairly to her friend, but neither was it fair, she thought, that he still had *his* father. She'd lost both her parents, now.

She tried explaining this to Jean, who listened carefully, and bent and placed a kiss on Lily's hair, and told her, quietly, 'Ye still have me.' Jean's hand found Lily's smaller one, and held it. 'Your brother and your sister and myself, we're still your family, as we ever were. Ye'll no more be alone.' Her hand squeezed Lily's, reassuring. 'But ye should never turn your friends away when they've done nothing wrong and ye have need of them. Especially a friend as faithful as your Jamie Graeme.'

Lily nodded, and she promised, 'When he comes the morn, I'll go along with him.'

'No, not the morn. Best wait till Thursday.'

'Why?'

'Because the morn's when Mr Campbell will be served his justice.' Jean refused to call the Earl of Argyll by his title. In her view, he had no claim to such an honour, since he was a traitor to King James, and son besides to that same Argyll who had stood against the great Montrose. 'The streets will not be safe.'

'Why?'

'Because there are many who do think on Mr Campbell as their leader, and who wish that his rebellion had succeeded,' Jean explained. 'While he had his Covenanting army in the field, they were content to bide their time and keep their true hearts hid, like serpents in the grass, but now their cause has come to naught there are some will be boldened by it, who will show their anger freely and make trouble for the good men of this town.'

Lily said, 'But Captain Graeme will not let them.' She had meant that to sound sure, but even she could hear the waver in her voice that made it come out as more of a question, and Jean lightly squeezed her hand again.

'No,' Jean assured her. 'Captain Graeme will not let them. He and Corporal Morison and all the men of the town guard will put themselves between us and all harm. Now, be like

Bessie. She's been sleeping all this time that ye've been worrying, with not a care to stop her dreams. Try that, and I'll
be right here when ye waken.'

Lily rolled obediently, snuggling close to Bessie in the
blankets, trying to recapture that elusive sense of comfort
and security she'd felt when they had been a complete family.

'Lily?' Bessie hadn't been asleep at all. Her warm breath
stirred the hair at Lily's cheek as, in her baby whisper, she said,
edging closer, 'Ye still have me, too.'

Lily couldn't say anything back, for her heart, at that
moment, was filling her throat, but she held to her sister more
tightly than ever and, after a while, she did sink into dreams.

Jean was right. Lily did notice a change in the mood of the
town in the days that came after Argyll's execution.

Like his father, he had been beheaded by the Maiden – that
machine of death with its great, weighted metal blade that,
when the rope was loosed, dropped swiftly down upon the
person who was forced to lay their bare neck on the crossbeam
underneath.

Jean had no sympathy to spare him. 'He stood and he
watched and made merry enough when Montrose was led
by to his own execution, I'm told,' she said. 'I only wish I
could have done the same for Mr Campbell. But I dared not
leave the bairns.'

Corporal Morison touched her arm, offering comfort. 'Ye
did wisely. We may have our own Scottish rebels dispersed,
but their plan from the outset was to act in concert with those

down in England who've risen to follow the king's nephew, that traitor Monmouth, and till his rebellion is ended, there still will be those here who wait and have hope. There'll be danger.'

Jean said, 'There will be more danger when the rebellion is ended, I promise ye that, for there's nothing so dark as a heart that's lost hope.'

She sank heavily into her chair by the hearth as she said that, and fell silent for a while. Then Corporal Morison sat, too, in the tall, rush-backed chair across from her, and reached to take her hand into his own.

Lily's eyes stung because he was sitting in her father's chair, and that was a hard thing to see, so she looked down, and her kitten climbed into her lap and demanded attention, as though understanding.

The kitten had no name yet. Lily had not settled on a name that suited him, though Jean had made suggestions. He had grown a little, and his coat of black and white was filling in most handsomely, and when he caught a mouse he made a habit of presenting it to Jean, who now seemed nearly as attached to him as Lily.

Lily was then unprepared when, two weeks after Argyll's execution, Jean announced they could no longer keep the kitten, but would have to find it a new home.

The tears came instantly. 'Why?'

Jean had turned her back. Her voice was light, but her tone meant there was no room for argument. 'Because we cannot live in this house any longer. And where we'll be living, we are not allowed a cat.'

It was unfair. And Lily said as much. She said it with

a breaking heart, and did not care if all the neighbours heard her.

'Aye,' said Jean, 'it is unfair. But life will be that way, sometimes.' Jean turned, and Lily saw that there were tears in Jean's eyes, too. 'Have ye learned so little of me that ye think I'd wish to hurt ye?' From beneath her skirts and apron, Jean reached deep into her pocket and drew out a scant handful of coins. 'This is what I have left now, Lily. All that I have left, to keep a roof above our heads until the summer's end. I'll not ask Captain Graeme for a penny more, not after all he's done for us. Nor will I ask Jack Morison to put himself in debt for us. I'll find a way, I promise, but I cannot keep this house past Lammas Day, ye ken? Or all of this' – she held the coins out – 'all of this is gone.' She turned away again, as though she could not bear to look at Lily's face. 'I'm sorry, Lily. I am doing all I can, but I do have four mouths to feed, and no silver to do it with, and aye, it is unfair.'

Lily thought long on this, afterwards, and on the following morning she asked for the small, covered basket. 'The one with the handle.'

Jean asked her, 'And what are ye doing with that?'

Lily took a pair of stockings and arranged them in the bottom of the basket, for their softness. 'For my kitten,' she explained. 'When Jamie comes the day, I'll take the kitten to another home, so ye'll not have to worry anymore.'

Jean hugged her, hard, and Lily kissed her, and when Jamie came to fetch her, Lily kissed Jean once again, and also gave a kiss to Bessie, and her baby brother, and went out into the strong midmorning sun.

Robin was there, too. He always came along now when

they played outdoors, for reasons that had not been stated but which Lily gathered had to do with safety. Being Captain Graeme's son had once been Jamie's golden key to go wherever he might like within the town, with none to bother him – now it seemed more a key to hold him prisoner, confined to but a handful of the streets that were less troubled by unrest. The whispers ran beneath the cobbles like the waters of a swiftly-flowing burn that had been deeply buried, hidden everywhere from light, but Lily heard them in the shadows.

They did not appear to bother Jamie, who skipped a small stone across the cobbles before letting her decide the day's adventure. 'Where are we away to?'

'To your house.'

'Why?'

'Has your daddie gone on duty yet?'

'Not till he's had his dinner.'

'Then I need to speak with him.'

'He's not alone,' warned Jamie. 'Mr Cant is with him, visiting.'

She did not think that Mr Cant would mind the interruption. As the minister of their own church, he knew her well. 'Your daddie telt me I could come at any hour I wished to speak with him, and he would always listen, and I ken he'd never say a thing that was not true.'

Robin took her side, with a slight smile at her reasoning. 'No, he would not.'

They found Captain Graeme and Mr Cant in the front drawing room, with the old chess board between them. Both men looked up in some surprise at the sudden invasion, but neither complained.

Mr Cant went so far as to reassure Robin they'd done him a favour. 'You've given my bishop a welcome reprieve, for he's in mortal peril.'

The captain winked. 'Aye, and ye might see your way to remove him from that, Mr Cant. I've spent half of my life now defending the rights of your flesh-and-blood bishops on battlefields, and it would pain me to harm this one.' He turned to Lily. 'What's this, then? Have ye brought me something to eat?'

Smiling encouragement, he nodded at the small basket she carried.

She wanted to tell him that it was her kitten. She wanted to tell him she'd come here to speak with him. No words came. She could do no more than stare at his chair, for it was the same chair where she'd sat with her father, that last evening here in this chamber.

Captain Graeme, somehow, understood. 'Would ye like to sit here, Lily?'

She nodded.

Rising, he pulled up another chair, close to the table, and gallantly waited while she sat before he did likewise.

She felt the smooth curve of the wood of the chair, with its tapestried cushion and woven cane back, and it felt like the warmth of her father enfolding her, giving her strength.

She told Captain Graeme, 'I've come here to serve ye.'

'To serve me?'

'Aye. My mother's family have long served the Graemes,' she said. 'I can work very hard.' She explained all her grandmother had taught her, up at Inchbrakie. 'And I've learned more since, here with Jean. I'll not fail ye.'

'Lass . . .'

'Jean says she'll not take your silver, no more of it, but I ken she'd take my wages if I were to earn them.'

'Lily.' He bent his head, just for a moment, then raised it and met her gaze. 'You're right, our families have been long connected, and I'm greatly honoured ye'd make me this offer. But lass, we've no space for more servants the now.'

'Then,' said Lily, 'my grandmother might take me back again, up at Inchbrakie, so Jean would not have the expense of keeping me.' She said it with reluctance.

While she greatly loved her grandmother, she did not wish to be so far from Bessie and wee James, and from the family she'd been given here in Edinburgh, so she felt some relief when Captain Graeme said, 'Your grandmother's too old now, lass, to care for ye.' He made a study of her face, and something in the upraised angle of her chin made his eyes soften. 'I do ken one family in the Canongate, a family of good character, who need a girl to help within their kitchen. Shall I ask if they would take ye?'

Lily nodded. 'Would they take my kitten, too?' She had the basket at her feet, and pointed now towards it. 'Jean says where we're moving after Lammas day, we cannot bring the kitten.'

Captain Graeme gravely shook his head. 'I'm very sorry, Lily, but ye could not have your kitten in the Canongate. The family is not fond of cats.'

Mr Cant leaned forward with a kindly smile. 'I tell you, Captain Graeme, I have been most plagued of late by mice within my vestry.'

Captain Graeme exchanged glances with the minister, and asked him, 'Have ye, now?'

'I have indeed. I don't suppose you'd wish to sell your kitten to me, Lily? I've a merk here I could pay you.'

If she had not seen the coin that he was holding, Lily would have thought she had not heard him properly.

'Of course,' continued Mr Cant, 'I'd need some time to make the vestry ready. If you keep my kitten for me until Lammas, I will pay two shillings for your trouble and the kitten's care. I'll come and fetch it from you then. Or, if you wish, you can deliver it, and earn a further four pence. Would that suit you?'

Lily could not speak, because her heart had grown too large and risen to her throat. Not only would the kitten's sale bring welcome money she could give to Jean, but if he were to live now at the church, she knew he would be safe. She found her voice, and said, 'Yes, Mr Cant.'

They shook hands, solemnly, and Lily took the merk from him, and at his urging opened up the basket so that he could see the kitten, which immediately settled onto Captain Graeme's lap, to Jamie's great delight. And Robin, having seen the way for Mr Cant to save his bishop on the chess board, made the move himself, making a mirthful ending to the game, with Captain Graeme's king his only piece remaining, stubbornly refusing to stand down.

But after dinner, as the captain walked her home, Lily was still confused about the way the chess game finished, so she asked him, 'How could Mr Cant win when he could not catch your king?'

'It was a stalemate,' Captain Graeme told her. He had changed his clothes and was now in his uniform, and although she still heard the whispers and the murmurs from the shadows round them, she felt safe. 'A stalemate means your king can make no move at all that does not put his life in danger, so he retreats, and his opponent claims the victory, but the king yet lives to fight another day.'

'But he has lost.'

The captain slanted a look down at her, and smiled. 'To lose a single battle does not mean ye lose the war. And to retreat means only that. Surrendering is not within the nature of most kings.' He glanced up at the window of a house they were approaching, where someone had just begun to close the shutters, even though it was midday. 'Nor in my own.'

Lily held more tightly to her coin, and Captain Graeme told her, 'Never fear, lass. It's a good town, this. Good people all around ye, if ye look for them.'

That was the very opposite of what her father had advised, but then her father had not lived to tell her how to know a lawless man, so she asked Captain Graeme now, 'How do ye ken which men are good?'

'Not only men,' he said. 'All people. And ye ken them by their actions, not by what ye might hear said of them. Ye watch what someone does when it will gain him nothing, Lily, and when none but ye is there to see him do it. Then ye'll ken his truest heart.'

She thought about that, after he had handed her to Jean and she had watched him walk away from them with that same sure and even soldier's stride that raised quick memories of her father.

And she thought about it later on that evening, while Jean worked to ready supper and wee James began to fuss, and

Corporal Morison took up the bairn and walked with him, out in the fresh air of the close.

He stayed outside so long that Lily pressed her face against the window, looking for a glimpse of them, and saw the great, tall soldier making silly faces to her baby brother, so the bairn would laugh. There was no one around to see him doing it – or so he thought. There was just Corporal Morison and wee James in the close.

That night, when Lily went to bed, she murmured, 'Jean?'

'Aye?'

'Corporal Morison's a good man.'

Jean said nothing. Only kissed her, very softly, tucked the blankets warm around her, and the small, low-ceilinged chamber that held Lily's family slumbered into darkness.

CHAPTER SEVEN

TUESDAY, 23 SEPTEMBER, 1707

I WAS ALONE WITH ROBERT MORAY.

He had engineered it neatly, asking Gilroy to take Mrs Graeme up into the open air and daylight. 'You can leave me pen and paper, though,' he'd said, 'that I might write my wife, to let her know that I am well. She will be worried.'

Gilroy had complied, and Moray, thanking him, had told him, 'Sergeant Williamson can wait to take the letter.'

So I'd waited.

It was plain that I intrigued him, but he was too much a gentleman to step beyond the common questions. As he inked the pen, he asked me, 'Are ye married?'

'No.'

'I recommend it, though I am not sure my wife would do the same. I fear I rob her of her peaceful sleep, most nights.' He smiled. 'I daresay working every day with Gilroy might have much the same effect upon ye.'

'You have known him long?'

'Let's say I know him well enough to find him most predictable.'

'Yet he surprised you.'

'Did he?' Robert Moray glanced up from his letter. 'When was that?'

'When he asked you about your brother John,' I said, 'and then your uncle. You did seem surprised that he would ask about them. Why?'

He looked at me briefly, the same way he'd looked at Gilroy, then bent once again to his writing and said, 'The more interesting question is, why did the commissioners decide on this inquiry? They could simply have dismissed it outright for a lack of evidence. Why go to all this trouble, and in private? You'll agree it is unusual.'

I caught that ball and held it for a moment, not quite certain what to do with it. 'Perhaps, but surely ... what would anybody stand to gain by it?'

He looked at me. 'At least ye have the wit to ask the question.'

In the pause that followed, I thought he might be about to give me his views on the matter. But he didn't.

Sitting back, he asked, 'How did ye come to be put at the head of this inquiry?'

I couldn't tell if he was questioning my qualifications or simply being curious, but I reacted the same way I'd always done when challenged. Squaring my shoulders, I said, 'Lord Grange employed my friend Lieutenant Turnbull for this post, but the lieutenant's out of town. It was agreed, as a favour, that I should stand in as his surrogate.'

''Tis a favour,' he said, 'ye may come to regret.'

I thought 'regret' was a strong choice of words for a man who chose words with a purpose. It made me uneasy.

Before I could press him about it, he asked, 'I mean no disrespect, but is that your best suit?'

Frowning, I told him, 'I have one better. Why?'

'Ye'll want to keep it brushed and ready. People in high places will begin to take an interest in ye, when they learn ye've talked to me. And if ye have a sword, ye would do well to start to carry it. There's often danger in this dance ye've just been drawn into.'

I'd have asked him what he meant by that, and why he could not speak in words a man could understand, but it was plain that I'd prise nothing more from him. He'd already gone back to his writing. I stood to the side with my thoughts while he finished his letter.

Having no wax for a seal, he made folds so it sealed itself, much like a puzzle.

Rising, he commented, 'You're very quiet, Sergeant. Have ye no more questions?'

I did have one, in fact. 'Where was the place where she was sent?'

'I'm sorry?'

'Mrs Graeme. When your uncle sent her into service as a child.'

'I forget.'

'I don't believe that.' I met his gaze levelly. 'I don't believe men like you forget anything.'

We faced each other a long moment. His mouth curved faintly. Then finally he said, 'Mr Bell, in the Canongate. He was a swordslipper. But surely that has no bearing at all on your inquiry?'

I'd not have wished to face those knowing eyes in a court-room. They gave nothing away, and saw everything.

He didn't need me to answer. He gave me the letter. 'I trust ye to see this delivered,' he said, 'to my wife. Janet Moray, at Murrayshall. And, Sergeant Williamson?'

This time there was no smile.

'If ye let harm come to Lily, I'll not forget that, either.'

He turned away, and our interview came to an end.

III

LOOKING BACK, THAT WAS the afternoon I might have walked away from the affair.

In fact, on writing all this down, I see so many warnings I let pass, so many open doors that I allowed to close behind me, when I could have simply packed my bag and said farewell to Helen and apologized, and let it end.

There would have been regret.

Still, no man is beyond replacing. Gilroy would have carried on his work without me, Helen might have found another of her husband's friends to hold his place, and I've no doubt MacDougall would have cooked them all a feast to mark my leaving.

To them, I was of passing unimportance. But, to her ...

'Why did you stay?' she asked me once, when we were both too far gone past the point of turning back for it to make a difference.

To the uninformed, there was a simple answer: she'd bewitched me.

But the truth was, by that time I could no more have left

her than I could have left my shadow when I walked the lamplit streets each evening.

Even with foreknowledge, I could not have left her then, because my heart, which had for so long been a solitary, hardened thing, had lately just begun to warm and beat and come to life. I liked the feeling. Selfishly, I wished to go on feeling it.

I kept on walking, down into the High Street past St Giles', and back up past Forrester's Wynd, to see that all was well and quiet.

And I did not leave.

CHAPTER EIGHT

TUESDAY, 23 SEPTEMBER, 1707

HELEN EYED ME WITH indulgence as I came in from my evening walk. 'I see you've met our upstairs neighbour.'

'Yes. He looks exactly as a Latin master ought to look.'

'He is retired from teaching,' she reminded me, 'though I'm afraid he still does talk as though he's giving lectures. He kept you on the stair so long I contemplated coming to your rescue.'

I'd enjoyed my talk with the old man, and told her so. 'He's taking some books to the stationer's to sell, and did allow me to relieve him of a couple of them.'

Helen smiled. 'You and my husband share a common weakness. Come then, show me what you've bought.'

One of my new books she approved of – an illustrated study of the plants of the Americas that, while it was in French, was finely bound and large and full of neat, precise engravings. But my other choice, a good-sized volume of Lord Stair's *Institutions of the Laws of Scotland*, she considered a poor bargain. 'It is broken at the binding, with the pages coming loose.'

'It is still readable. Besides, it has good information on the use of witnesses and oaths, which I can use to educate myself.'

Something betrayed me in my tone, because her eyes grew sympathetic. 'A man's worth is not measured, Adam, by his education. What has happened in your inquiry today that you think otherwise?'

I had not spoken of the morning's interview with Helen yet. She had dined out with friends, and had retired to rest on her return, so I had supped alone tonight and gone out for my walk, and this was now the first occasion I had found to tell her what had happened when we'd taken Mrs Graeme to meet Robert Moray in his prison chamber at the castle.

I did not share everything. I did not tell her Mrs Graeme's private history, for as much as I liked Helen I recalled her judgement of Lord Grange's wife, whose father had been hanged for murder. 'The stain of an act like that cannot be easily washed from a bloodline,' so Helen had told me, and while I believed her wrong, I knew she'd alter the way that she viewed Mrs Graeme if she knew the whole of the story. Instead, I described Robert Moray, and how I thought him impressively clever.

Helen's shrug was elegant. 'Cleverness alone is not a mark of virtue. My father was a writer to the signet, and the men he moved among were men of knowledge, some of whom you'd no doubt count as clever – but that did not make them good men.'

I thought of the tale I'd heard that morning – Mrs Graeme as a wee girl asking Captain Graeme how she was to know which men were good, and his reply that she would know them by their actions, if she watched what someone did when it would gain him nothing, and when none was there but her to see him do it. 'Then ye'll ken his truest heart,' the captain had assured her.

And I thought of how she'd later watched the corporal through the window when he did not know she saw him, and how she'd then told her stepmother the corporal was a good man.

Helen asked, 'What is it?'

'Sorry?'

'You seem far away.'

I had been far away, in fact, by many years. 'I was but committing your words to my memory,' I told her, and covered my slip with a smile.

'Oh.' She looked pleased. 'Well, they're true. Robert Moray may have the advantage of his birth and breeding but the defects of his family's faith and politics will always count against him.' To my questioning look she explained, 'They are Episcopalian, and Jacobites, and keep to their own kind.'

I had come to strike a bargain in my life with God, in which He left me fairly to my own devices in return for my assurance I would do my best to keep my feet upon the path He had laid out for me. I'd fought too many men of different faiths to think that men were any different when they bled, or that the God they prayed to at the end was truly different from my own.

But Helen Turnbull, being younger and not having seen what I had seen of life, apparently was stricter in her views, and saw the world divided. I did not dispute with her. I said only, in a light tone, 'You seem very well informed.'

'You and Gilroy have your own investigations. I have

mine.' She smiled. 'After you left this morning, I decided that
I ought to pay a call upon Sir Andrew Hume, my cousin. And
before you tell me I should not be going out in my condition,
you may spare yourself the effort. I've already had a lecture
from MacDougall.'

Her manservant, just entering the room, looked over at the
mention of his name and took the liberty to answer. ''Tis a
risk ye should not take. There are yet tumults in the streets.
Ye might take fright, and then the bairn would bear the mark
of what had frighted ye. Aside from which, ye're vulnerable
to witchcraft at this time.'

If anything was giving her a fright, it was MacDougall. I
could see the smallest waver of uncertainty unsettle Helen's
features, and I sought to lay her doubts to rest.

I teased her, 'Were there any witches at your cousin's home?'

It worked. Her smile returned. 'I don't believe so, although
I did not examine all his servants. I see him but rarely,' she
confessed. 'His father is the Earl of Marchmont, so they move
in social circles higher than my own. But since my cousin also
sits as one of the commissioners in charge of the Equivalent,
I thought it only right that I should thank him for this favour
they have shown us in the case of Mrs Graeme's claim.'

MacDougall, bent at the hearth and busy banking up the
fire with ashes for the night, remarked that Helen could have
thanked her cousin in a letter and thus saved herself the need
to venture out into the streets.

'I have survived my grand adventure, as you see,' she
reassured him.

Learning that her cousin was one of the commissioners for
the Equivalent raised a question that had played within my

mind since Robert Moray had first put it there this morning. 'Did your cousin say why the commission decided to move Mrs Graeme's claim from their hands into ours?'

Helen said, 'No, my cousin was not there, regrettably. I did, though, have a lovely visit with his wife. We dined, and talked. She's well acquainted with the backgrounds of the families of the nobility and gentry, and it was from her I learned the details of your Robert Moray.'

She told me what she'd learned. I had not known he had a young son, though I'd known of course that he was married. I had sent that letter to his wife by an express this evening, and my pocket was a pound Scots lighter for my effort, but I'd reasoned, had I been a prisoner with a wife, I would have wished to put her mind at peace as soon as possible.

I naturally said none of this to Helen.

She'd lost interest in the Morays and was speaking now about her cousin's wife. '. . . a generous woman, and deserving of the happiness she has in life. I don't believe she found such happiness in her first marriage, for her late husband had been married before as a young man, to a Frenchwoman, and half his heart was always held by his first love. Leastways, that's how my cousin's wife felt. As though she could be no more than a substitute, for he'd already found his matching half.' She very kindly caught herself, apparently remembering that I was not as widely read as she was, and explained, 'That comes from Plato. His *Symposium*, in which he claims that every person has one – that we all were made originally whole, then sliced in half like flatfish, so we now must search the world for the one person who completes us.'

A matching half. It was a most romantic notion. My mind

filled with memories of moments when my heart had over-
ruled reason – a night that still lived in my dreams from my
youth with the girl with the tumbling hair, and a day when
I'd truly believed I had seen my own soul mirrored back to
me in a girl's eyes, both of them overlaid now by the steady,
blue gaze of a widow who'd looked at me yesterday morning
and quietly asked of me, 'Shall we begin?'

MacDougall spat into the hearth. 'That's heathen nonsense.'

Helen asked, 'Have you ever been married, MacDougall?'

'I have not.' He said it in a tone that implied that was a
deliverance of sorts, which I privately agreed it was, for the
woman. 'But,' he added, 'if God should send me a woman,
she'd not be mistaking herself for a flatfish.' Straightening, he
faced me with a challenge. 'Were ye going to take your papers
off the table at any time, or will I be serving ye breakfast
tomorrow atop that confusion?'

I had, admittedly, been reading through my few notes after
supper, but had ordered everything as best I could before I'd
gone out for my walk, and would have told him so had Helen
not stepped smoothly in to take my part.

''Tis clear you need a better place to do your work,' she
said, and bade me gather up my papers and my new-bought
books and follow her.

She led me to a room that I'd not yet discovered, being that
it lay behind the kitchen where I very rarely ventured, since
that was the maid's domain. But entering this small room was,
to me, like finding sanctuary.

'I do believe that it was once the scullery,' she said, 'but
when we took these rooms we also took the furniture, and
from this it is obvious the former tenant used this as his

writing chamber, so my husband does the same. I'm sure he would be pleased to have you use it also, while you hold his place in this inquiry.'

'I might not leave a room like this,' I warned her.

Everything had been designed to make a masculine retreat. An ebony-cased eight-day table clock ticked out the hours in comforting measure on top of a walnut-tree bookcase with locking glass doors. Above the open hearth that waited only for a fire, a brave ship sailed forever just before the storm across a seascape in a heavy frame, with candle sconces gleaming from the wall to either side.

The most impressive piece of cabinetry in the room was the scrutore. It was fashioned of walnut-tree also, inlaid with veneers set in circles and starbursts. Fully three feet broad, it stood as tall as me, with drawers below and a fall-front square panel which, when let down upon its hinge, became a level writing surface. Helen unlocked this and let it down now, revealing cleverly made inner drawers and pigeonholes behind and, at their centre, a compartment with its own small door.

She told me, 'There, you see? The perfect place for you to keep your papers. And your books, which I believe will fit just here.'

She pointed to the opening between the banks of small drawers at the back of the writing surface, directly beneath the central compartment with the door. My new-bought books, when laid together on their sides, did fit there perfectly.

She said, 'I am afraid the drawers are very likely full already of my husband's papers, but at least you can leave yours here undisturbed.'

I reached to test the rounded length of moulding at the top edge of the scrutore's row of pigeonholes, and felt it give. 'This drawer is empty,' I confirmed, as it slid open.

Helen looked at me with wonder. 'How on earth did you know that was there? A secret drawer!'

'Not very secret. Every scrutore I have known of this design does have one.' I might have added most had more than one, but we were interrupted by the sound of knocking from the street door, and she turned away from me.

'It is late for a caller,' Helen said, then sighed and added, 'I had better go make certain that MacDougall does not deal too harshly with them.'

She was not gone long. No sooner had I settled in the leather-seated chair, having satisfied myself that the scrutore suited my needs exactly, than Helen was back with the look of a child who'd been given a gift.

'Adam, what do you and Gilroy plan to do tomorrow?'

'Gilroy plans to go to Leith, to search more deeply through the records of the parish for the details of the witnesses to Mrs Graeme's marriage, and since I would only hinder him in that work, I'm to stay here and to meet him in the evening to learn what he has discovered.'

'Good. Because we've just received an invitation,' Helen said, 'to dine tomorrow with the Earl of Seafield.'

I could feel my eyebrows rise. 'The Earl of—?'

'Seafield,' Helen said again. 'The Chancellor. He has a grand house in the Canongate and keeps an interesting table, I am told, although I've never had the fortune before this to be his guest. I don't suppose you have a wig?'

'I do not own one, no.'

'That is a pity. Wigs do make men look more serious. Besides, they are the fashion.'

I'd never liked the feel of wigs – the weight of them, the itch of them, the close, infernal heat of them. I'd had to wear one for a short time as a younger man, and had been glad to leave that 'fashion' far behind, along with the expense. My own hair, while it did not have the tight curls of a wig, could neither be called straight, though I more often wore it combed and neatly tied with a plain black band at the back of my coat collar. 'I'll do my best,' I told her, 'to look serious. But surely ...' Sitting back, I took this in. I had no wish to dampen Helen's joy, but, 'Surely the earl expects your husband to accompany you. He does not mean for his invitation to extend to me.'

She proved me wrong by showing me the paper that had been delivered to her door. 'He asks for you explicitly. You need not fear you'll be unwelcome.'

That was not the thing I feared.

I was hearing Robert Moray's voice, advising me to keep my best suit brushed and ready.

'People in high places will begin to take an interest in ye ...'

Why, I wondered, *would the Earl of Seafield, Chancellor of Scotland, wish to have me at his table? What on earth was I entangled in?*

'There's often danger in this dance ye've just been drawn into,' had been Robert Moray's warning, and I wished now I *had* pressed him further, for while I was poor at any dance, I did far worse when I knew not the music nor the steps.

CHAPTER NINE

WEDNESDAY, 24 SEPTEMBER, 1707

I WAS NOT THE ONLY man at table wearing my own hair. Across from me, a gentleman some years my senior who'd been introduced as Dr Young had also drawn the line at wearing wigs. Twice now he'd regarded me above his wineglass with the private smile of a conspirator.

I put his friendly gesture down to our shared circumstance of finding ourselves sitting at the middle of the table, marking both of us as men of lesser rank and less importance than the guests who had been seated near the Earl of Seafield at the table's foot, or near his lady at the table's head.

Helen held the place of honour at the earl's right hand. The seat at *my* right hand was taken by a less appealing guest – a gentleman who drank too much and talked too much – and on my left the doctor's daughter, who gave her attention to the lady opposite. I feigned an interest in the tennis-games of conversation taking place across the table while I tried to focus on the rules of formal dining.

I'd never eaten in a room so elegant. The Earl of Seafield's dining room was lined with wainscot panelling of quality

I'd never seen. Above the doors and elsewhere there were painted decorations meant to fool the eye and look like ancient sculpture, and the high vaults of the plastered ceiling soared in ornate patterns. I felt I had been trapped within an ivory-lidded box for the amusement of some rich collector.

For relief, I looked towards the windows that provided a view south across the slope of private gardens to the reassuring rise of Arthur's Seat, its weathered crags as sturdy and unyielding on this afternoon as they had been time out of mind.

Dr Young remarked, 'It is a splendid prospect.'

His voice was both cultured and mild and I wasn't entirely sure he was speaking to me until I brought my head around. He'd been looking out of the window also, and now faced me with another of his smiles. I had no gift for social niceties and much preferred to keep apart from shallow talk, but I could not be impolite. I told him truly, 'Yes, it is.'

'And brilliant sunshine for this time of year,' he added, 'although I do fear the evening will bring rain.'

His daughter turned at that. 'Oh, I do hope not! I am tired of dreary weather.'

She said it lightly, not in a complaining way but as a statement. I'd have judged her to be Helen's age or slightly younger, with brown hair nearly the same shade as Mrs Graeme's. Her eyes, like Mrs Graeme's, were blue, and yet her features, while attractive, did not have the same effect upon me. I could admire her as I might admire a painting, and remain unmoved.

Her father looked me over. 'Are you a relation of the Dr Adam Williamson who serves as surgeon in Meredyth's regiment?'

'Not to my knowledge, sir.'

'Where do your Williamsons hail from?'

'New York.'

That surprised them both. 'Where in New York?' asked the doctor.

'Queens County.'

'Long Island? You don't have the accent. And I should know, for I did spend some years in the Americas. My Violet, here, was born at Philadelphia.'

My turn to smile. 'If you'll allow, she does not have the accent, either.'

Dr Young said, 'I should hope not. There is a community of Scots at Philadelphia, and we kept close amongst ourselves, so she was raised with others who spoke properly.' Leaning back to let the servant clear his first-course plate, he asked me, curious, 'Were you born at New York?'

I shook my head. 'Here in Scotland. The Williamsons have long roots in Kirkcaldy.'

'Fifeshire.' He'd been there. 'It has a good harbour, though I cannot fault your parents for believing the Americas would offer them a brighter shore.' He paused, then asked, 'Are they yet living?'

'No.'

Violet Young said, 'I am sorry.'

I thanked her, grateful for the distraction of the second course now being served that let me focus my attention elsewhere for a moment.

Her father asked, 'What did become of their property, then, in Queens County? Did you inherit?'

It was a blunt question. I had to decide how to answer.

'There was little left to inherit, sir. A simple house and barn, and both destroyed.'

'But surely land remains,' he said. As proof, he gestured to the windows and the vista of the gardens with the rise of Arthur's Seat beyond. 'And every house can be rebuilt. What happened to your own?'

'A fire.' I owed him no more details, though because he seemed to wait for more, I did allow, 'I was not there. I was then fighting under Captain Schuyler on his expedition to engage the French in Canada.'

The doctor looked impressed. 'A brave venture. Though I do confess, had you been my son, I'd have hired a servant to fight in your place.'

I noted the lace at his cuffs and the fine cloth that covered his buttons, and called to mind all the men like him I'd known in my life who played carelessly with the lives of those beneath them.

Forcing a tight smile, I answered, 'If I'd been your son, sir, I would have refused such an offer.'

He looked startled, then smiled in return. 'Good man.' Looking to Violet, he said, 'What we have here, my dear, is a man of honour. A rare thing to find these days, in any company.'

On that point I agreed with him, for when the meal was over and the ladies had departed to the drawing room, my own impression was that honour seemed distinctly lacking in the men remaining at the table, who soon turned their cutting talk to politics.

I'd not have trusted any of them, and since I was wary of the reason why I'd been invited, I stayed silent, drank my wine, and used the time to make a study of the Earl of Seafield.

He wore a fair, long wig that would have met with Helen's sure approval, being of the very latest fashion. If I'd had to judge his age, I would have put him ten years older than myself, approaching his mid-forties, with an elegance of dress and movement that belied his friendliness of manner. As a host, he had that quality of setting all his guests at ease and making them feel they were on his level, which undoubtedly some were, but I suspected it was also something he had learned to do throughout his long years in the government. He had survived the Revolution and switched sides to serve King William and now served Queen Anne as Chancellor for Scotland, which position – from my understanding – put him at the head of all our nation's law, above all other officers of State. A man did not accomplish that without becoming skilled at learning how to handle other men.

I watched him do it now with Dr Young, who was complaining of the great disorder in the streets of Edinburgh. 'It's dangerous, with these unruly rascals who seem everywhere these days so that an honest man no more can walk the streets of this town but he feels unsafe. It seems the Union plunged our country into chaos.'

The Earl of Seafield lightly disagreed. 'The current unrest proves in fact how necessary it was we unite with England so her strength would add to our security. There are a multitude of Jacobites here, ready to lay hold of any opportunity to make a disturbance.'

'You have one held within the castle, so I hear,' the doctor said.

'Yes. Robert Moray.' Seafield smiled. 'A prize indeed, although of course we all do wish that it had been his brother John.'

'Why is that?'

'While Robert Moray is without doubt a supporter of his exiled king, his brother John does hold the trust and confidence of all the court of Saint-Germain, and when he's sent to Scotland out of France it is no idle thing. John Moray is an outlaw, and does carry a reward already of five hundred pounds upon his head. A man with such a mark does not step lightly back on Scottish soil. And yet, our spies have told us that for several months he has been here. We know that he is likely in the north, but we do not know where. We know that he is sent here by his king, but we do not know why. These questions, you'll appreciate, are ones we seek to answer.'

A younger, sleekit gentleman remarked, 'It is no mystery why he's in the north. I've heard the Duke of Gordon's men have been buying up horses for going a-hunting in Atholl, or so they would claim. I should think it more likely the Highland nobility calls out its men for to count them and so tell their scheming Pretender the size of the army that he might expect when he lands.'

At my right, the bold man who was fond of his drink stirred to ask, 'So you believe the rumours that there will be an invasion? For my part, I believe that it will prove to be another sham plot.'

Calmly, the young gentleman replied, 'I do believe the Jacobites are planning an invasion, yes. I'll warrant that Lord Seafield does believe it, too, else why would he be holding Robert Moray in the castle?'

Seafield smoothly interjected, 'There are always rumours. I prefer to act upon the facts. Robert Moray, I am certain, could tell more than what he's told us. We examined him some hours, but he kept firmly to his claim that he did go to France upon a private errand. The few papers found upon him tell us very little. He is clever, and one cannot come at clever men directly.'

The sleekit man asked, 'Does he have a wife? She might be used to help him see some sense.'

The man beside me drained another glass of wine. 'Or throw her in the Tolbooth till he tells you what you wish to know,' was his suggestion. 'Failing that, there's always torture. Properly applied, it will shake loose the tongue of any man.'

Seafield said, 'It need not come to that. There are more subtle ways to make men talk.' He turned his head and looked along the table, straight at me. 'You've met him. Tell me, Sergeant Williamson, what would you judge to be Robert Moray's weak side?'

I thought I just might know the answer to that question, even though I'd only passed a brief handful of hours with him, because the stories Mrs Graeme had shared of her childhood had set Robert Moray's character in such a light that I believed I understood him perfectly: his weak side – and the whole strength of his character – was his need to protect.

But I'd be damned if I'd betray that fact to these men, who were strangers and whose attitudes I'd found so far distasteful, so I only said, 'My lord, I'm sure I do not know him well enough to tell you.'

Seafield studied me a moment. In his softly pleasant face, his eyes were shrewd. 'Well, every man does surely have one. I am certain to discover it.'

The eyes of every man around the table were now fixed upon me.

Dr Young asked, 'How did you come to make the acquaintance of a Jacobite?'

Before I could say anything, the Earl of Seafield answered, 'Sergeant Williamson is presently employed on a commission from a member of our high court. The nature of his work is secret, but it did require him to interview the prisoner.'

If he'd meant to put them off asking me questions, he'd chosen the worst way to go about it, for nothing will spur a man to try to prise open a box more strongly than telling him its contents are secret.

The sleekit man viewed me with unconcealed interest. 'I notice you accompanied Lieutenant Turnbull's wife today. Are you related to that family?'

I could easily have played the game and simply told him no, and let him guess again, and for those moments I'd have been for them a curious diversion, but I'd never much liked playing games.

I said, 'I had the honour to serve with Lieutenant Turnbull, sir, at Toubacanti.'

The effect of that statement was swift, though I didn't know why. The sleekit man glanced at the man to my right, who looked in his turn to the earl.

Seafield's gaze sliced sideways from my own, and as if some unseen hand had just turned to a new page in a book, the talk moved on to other things.

～⁂～

'Oh, no, please say you didn't mention Darien.' Helen laid a hand upon my arm as we walked out together from the earl's house into the uncertain sunshine of the fading afternoon.

'They asked me how I knew your husband. Why should I not mention it?'

'Because,' she said, as patiently as if she had been speaking to a child, 'the Earl of Seafield was opposed to the whole venture. He made no secret of the fact, and I remember when the mob here broke his window for it. You must surely . . .' She paused then, as she realized, 'but of course you'd not remember that. It happened when you were yourself in Darien, or else when you were on your way home to New York.'

I had not known her long, but I was learning how to judge the tones of Helen's voice, and from how she dropped the words 'New York' so very casually and left them there the way an angler baits a hook and line, I knew she'd spoken them with purpose. I'd never told her any of the details of my upbringing, and she'd been sitting too far down the table to have heard my conversation with the doctor and his daughter over dinner, so I made a guess and said, 'I see you've talked to Mistress Young.'

'I have indeed. She came to sit beside me in the drawing room, and we had a most pleasant conversation. She asked me if I knew how long you mean to stay in town, and I replied my plan is to persuade you not to leave.' She smiled. 'I do confess, I would not have imagined you were raised in the Americas, from how you speak. Your voice is purely Scottish.'

'I was just shy of my twelfth birthday when I first went to America. I had Scots around me there,' I said, 'and more Scots still at Darien. I've had no chance to lose my way of speaking.'

Helen thought on this. 'Is that where you first met my

husband? At New York, before he went the second time to Darien?'

'Yes.'

'I should like to hear that story. Maybe,' she said, as her eyes turned teasing, 'I should ask your Mistress Young around to dinner one day, so that she can tell it to me.'

I did not take that bait, either, although I did grant her a slight smile. 'There's none who knows that tale except your husband and myself, and he would tell it better.'

Whatever argument she might have made was silenced then by the arrival of two of the earl's men bearing a sedan chair, all enclosed and brightly painted with glass windows at the sides, a half-glassed door, and deeply cushioned seat. The two men set the chair down next to Helen, and the man in front – a tall, broad man whose accent could come only from the Highlands – told her, 'If ye please, the earl says it would not be fitting for a guest of his so big with child to walk when we can carry ye.'

A thoughtful gesture from our host, whose friends had just been urging him to torture Robert Moray's wife or throw her in a dungeon, and who had himself invited me to dinner in the hopes I'd tell him something that might let him place a noose round Moray's neck.

It was a great relief to be outside, away from all of them.

I handed Helen safely up into the chair.

'I feel almost too grand,' she said, settling into the cushions. 'And I'm abandoning you.'

Dryly, I assured her I was capable of finding my way back alone. 'Besides, I'm heading over to the Cross Keys in a while to meet Gilroy.'

'Will you have your supper there?' she asked.

'Most probably.'

She nodded. Then, before they closed the chair's door, she leaned forward one last time. 'I do believe I shall invite your Mistress Young round for a visit. What harm can it do? She is charming and pretty and of the right class . . .'

The first man was closing the door of the chair, but her last words slipped through, resolutely.

'And,' Helen said, 'I did promise to find you a wife.'

⸎

As a young lad, when I'd first been brought into these streets I'd looked at every turning for the mounted guns I felt sure were the reason that this place was called the Canongate. I'd been too ignorant then to know 'canons' was simply another term used for priests in great cathedrals, like those in the king's royal abbey of Holyrood just a short way down the street, where the priests, centuries past, had been granted the right to establish a new burgh between their own abbey and the king's established burgh – Edinburgh.

Visitors could be forgiven for looking on both burghs as one, for a man could begin in the shadow of Edinburgh's castle and easily stroll down the castle hill and through the Landmarket into the High Street and under the turreted, two-storeyed arch of the Netherbow port in an almost straight line that would carry him right the way down to the palace of Holyrood, much as I did every evening, and feel he had not left the town. But in truth, once you'd passed below the Netherbow, you'd entered into the Canongate – the more prestigious suburbs set beyond the limits of the old town walls, where in between the ordinary lands, more moneyed houses – rivalling the Earl of Seafield's with their gates and overhanging galleries and private walls – looked loftily upon the street, or lay concealed from view down quiet closes.

You could smell the gardens.

Common people lived here, too. The Canongate had its own baillies, its own Tolbooth, its own market cross, and its own craftsmen, since the guilds here were kept separate from the guilds above the Netherbow. A baxter from the Canongate was not allowed to sell his baked goods in the town of Edinburgh unless he had the freedom of both burghs, which came by marriage or inheritance or at a fair expense, and so tradesmen kept mostly to their own side of the divide.

Still, one could find whatever one had need of in the Canongate. In the space of a few minutes I passed the street-level shops of a cooper, a glovemaker, potter, and chandler, but it was the next sign I wanted.

I'd seen it before, facing onto the street at the edge of Bell's Close. Today the shutters were drawn back from the front window, and the glint of silver shone through the small panes of glass that cast my own reflection back in pieces.

As I entered the shop, a lad of seventeen or eighteen who I guessed was the apprentice came to greet me and to offer me assistance. Did I have a sword for sharpening? Or did I wish to purchase one? Or had I come instead to buy some cutlery? He showed me several samples, and assured me there was no one in the Canongate whose skill could equal that of Mr Bell.

I could judge that for myself from the display of forks and knives, the gathering of swords that appeared to be awaiting dressing or repair, a scabbard half-assembled on the work-bench in the corner, and the finished hilts that only needed fitting to a blade.

But the apprentice brought a sword to show me anyway – a backsword with a Highland hilt wrought in a cage of silver-inlaid hearts and oak leaves intertwined, to shield the hand that held it in a fight. The blade was a Ferara blade, high quality, with on one side a rising sun and stars inscribed, and on the other side the words: 'Thy king and countrie's cause defend, though on the spot your life should end.'

'It is as fine a sword as I have ever seen,' I said to the apprentice.

He looked pleased, but the reply came not from him. It came instead from the man stepping through the private entry from the rooms behind. An older man, perhaps approaching seventy, perhaps already past it – it was difficult to say. He moved easily enough for one his age, his back was straight, and he reached out to take the sword from his apprentice with the strong, sure hands of someone who still worked with them.

'You honour me,' he told me, 'but this sword was made some years past for a customer who's only brought it back now to be newly dressed and furbished. It is not for sale.' His friendly smile took no offence, forgiving the mistake of his apprentice, to whom he now turned with the request, 'Would you go and ask Marion to bring us in some ale?'

I must have looked more wealthy than I was, from all the care I'd taken dressing for my dinner with the earl, but I did not correct the swordslipper's impression of me, nor refuse his offer of refreshment.

The apprentice nodded and left by the shop's front door, while Mr Bell replaced the Highland-hilted sword among its fellows.

I said, making conversation, 'It would seem that there are many who are sharpening their swords these days.'

'Unsettled times are good for business.'

'Then your business must be always good, for our country is always unsettled.'

He briefly smiled. 'That it is.' As if he sought to divert me from the swords that weren't for sale, he said, 'I have other swords, sir, if you tell me what you are seeking.'

Accustomed as I was to swords, they weren't my favourite weapon. In a battle, I preferred to use a gun, but these streets held a different sort of danger, and I swiftly thought of how I could best arm myself against it, and of what I could afford. 'I am in need,' I told him, 'of a whinger.'

I remembered once attempting to describe a whinger to our blacksmith in New York, who'd never seen one, but had only seen the name writ down on paper. 'No,' I had corrected his attempt to say the word, 'it's not like "ginger" but like "finger". *Whin*-ger. And it's like a Highland dirk, except it's also like a sword. About this long.' I'd held my hands a foot apart. The blacksmith had suggested I should draw it for him, and when I had done that, he'd said, 'So, it is a hunting sword. A hanger.'

I had shrugged. 'It is a whinger. Where I'm from, it's not used much for hunting that I know of. You can use it at the table, though,' I'd told him, 'or for fighting.'

Mr Bell, being a Scotsman and a swordslipper, not only knew exactly what a whinger was, he had a few examples in his shop.

His apprentice, returned now from his errand, fetched three

for me to look at. They were all well made and handsome, but one caught my eye immediately. The hilt was of the simple form that suited me, the woven design of the carved wooden grip repeated on the handles of the smaller matching knife and fork made to slip perfectly into their slots on the smooth leather scabbard, and at the scabbard's back a sturdy mounting that allowed it to be hung from any belt to keep it always at the ready.

Mr Bell approved my taste. 'That is a German blade. You will not find one better.' He drew it from its sheath to show the maker's mark and workmanship, and turned the blade to show me the inscriptions on each side that, although short and clearly marked, were in what I took to be Latin, which I could not read.

'It's perfect,' I said with a nod, as though I'd understood the meaning of those inscribed words. 'I'll have it.'

Thus we struck our bargain and were shaking hands when from the room behind, a woman stepped out bearing on a tray the cups of ale the swordslipper had ordered.

She was near my own age, though her black hair betrayed some early strands of white. Around her eyes and cheekbones she was enough like the swordslipper to make me think she was perhaps his kin, which he confirmed by introducing her as, 'Marion, my daughter.'

When she'd handed round the ale, he turned and offered her a smile. 'You make a very pretty job of wrapping things, my dear. Could you please finish off this purchase for the gentleman?'

Obliging him, she set the tray down, chose a square of soft buff leather from a nearby workbench and began to wrap the whinger, neatly and with care.

Her father raised his glass. 'Your health, sir. I am very glad you chanced upon my shop this day.'

'It was not chance.' I reasoned we'd grown friendly enough now for me to aim at the true purpose of my visit. 'You were recommended to me by a woman who once worked for you, when she was but a girl. Lilias Aitcheson.'

I'd seen things in my life of fighting, and I'd watched the blood drain from a man's face when he felt the crawl of fear.

I watched it happen now, to Mr Bell.

His glass went down. His eyes grew hard. 'What is your game, sir?'

I was genuinely at a loss. 'I do not understand.'

He had turned from me. 'Marion, give him his purchase. Our business is done.'

I'd been so busy watching her father's reaction I'd failed to see hers, but when she pressed the wrapped parcel into my hands, I could feel her own shaking.

She, too, looked as pale as chalk, but when I opened my mouth to apologize, she frowned a warning.

'Not here,' she said, almost inaudibly. 'In the close.'

And with that she turned away from me also, and unsure of what had just happened, I drained my own cup of ale, took up my newly-bought blade, and went out again into the street.

❦

The swordslipper's shop ran the width of his house at its front, and its window and door opened onto the street, but it thankfully had no side window that faced Bell's Close.

In fact, in spite of the houses that crowded and jostled for space in this cul-de-sac, there weren't many windows.

There wouldn't be much light for windows to catch, here. The rooftops leaned too high above the overhanging upper storeys. Shadows waited on the stone steps that descended in steep runs along the walls because there was no place for them to turn within a space so narrow.

It was the sort of place where someone might commit a crime unseen. A place for secret assignations. Like the one that I was keeping now.

Behind the shop, the Bells' house ran back a fair way, with a short flight of steps leading up to a door that had one small, square window set high in the wall at its side.

I'd not been in the close more than five minutes when that door opened and Marion Bell quickly motioned me to come inside. I did, and found myself within a spacious kitchen that appeared to serve a broader function, for an elbow chair and footstool had been drawn up near the hearth, and on the end wall where might once have been a servant's pallet was a proper bedstead with a canopy and hangings.

Beside the hearth, a door that led presumably into the other rooms was firmly bolted and secured with a large lock, and at my entry a brown, mid-sized dog of the mixed breed oft used for fighting half-rose in a challenge till a calm word from its mistress made it settle once more into a deceptive slumber near the chair.

A multitude of thoughts chased through my mind as I was entering that kitchen, but I had no time to sort them.

Marion Bell shut the door to the close at my back and she

bolted that, too. Then she took a step backwards, to put space between us, and came to the point.

'You'll think me very forward and I'm sorry for it, but it can't be helped. I have to know if what you said is true,' she said. 'I have to know – is Lily still alive?'

CHAPTER TEN

WEDNESDAY, 5 AUGUST, 1685

JAMIE WENT FIRST THROUGH the Netherbow.

From the beginning, he'd done that to show her that she had no reason to fear. 'See?' he'd told her the first time, two years ago. 'It's nothing more than a gate.' She hadn't believed him then. She'd thought it looked like a castle.

To her eyes, it still had the look of one, blocking the street with its solid, stone walls rising two storeys high, and round turrets protecting the arched passage that could be closed off at will with an iron portcullis, now winched up and firmly secured. The tall, pointed roofs of the turrets with their crenellations were dwarfed in turn by the square tower that rose like a castle keep over the archway. The tower soared skywards to end in a spire, and contained both a bell and the works of a clock that faced out to the town.

There were guards here, as well.

Lily tried not to look at them as she passed by, since it raised memories of when her father had taken his turn standing guard here. Captain Graeme, as though understanding, offered her his hand, and Lily took it as they walked together underneath the great portcullis.

Jamie had gone through the smaller door off to the side, meant for foot traffic, but Captain Graeme knew Lily was not overfond of small spaces, so he took her under the arch built for wagons and horses and rich men's sedan chairs, and as they came through to the other side, into the Canongate, Jamie was already standing there, waiting.

'Ye'll like Mr Bell,' Jamie promised her. 'And, Lily, his father once made a sword for Montrose. And another for Grandfather.'

'Aye,' said the captain, when Lily looked up at him for confirmation of this. 'Mr Bell's family has been connected to ours a long time, much like yours.'

She was pleased by that.

'And,' Jamie added, 'ye've only to ask him and he'll let ye hold any blade, if ye mind what he says and are careful.'

She already knew that she'd like Mr Bell, for the captain had told her she would, and she trusted the captain. She still worried, though, whether Mr Bell would like her.

On waking that morning she'd scrubbed her face shiny and taken great pains with her clothing and hair, and she'd wished that her sleeves weren't so plain and her skirts weren't so limp, until Jean with a kiss and a smile had said, 'That is my favourite of all of your aprons. The stitching's the very same blue as your eyes.' And then, suddenly, she had felt something like confidence.

She felt it stir for a second time now as they entered the swordslipper's shop and a middle-aged man in a fine-looking suit, having come forward to greet the captain, then smiled at her warmly and said, 'And I see you have brought us our Lily.'

The captain was holding her hand still. He gave it a small, reassuring squeeze. '*Our* Lily, actually, but we will give ye the loan of her for a wee while.'

Mr Bell had a long face and prominent cheekbones and brown eyes edged with deep-set lines that let her know he often smiled. He wore a long wig, like a gentleman – dark, like the king's – and his coat had long rows of brass buttons that gleamed just like gold.

'You couldn't keep her now anyway,' he told the captain. 'I've heard you're headed to London.'

'Aye. Though I'll be back afore ye've had a chance to miss me, if I have my way. My business should not take that long.'

'I wonder that the Privy Council lords would let you go, with all the trouble we have had in town of late.'

The captain admitted there'd been some debate. 'They granted me a furlough only yesterday. I mean to be away afore they reconsider.'

'How is the edge of your sword?'

'Sharp enough.' But the captain unbuckled his sword belt and passed it, with scabbard and all, to the swordslipper, who, after expertly judging the blade, found it wanting, and handed it to his apprentice. 'It will not take long. Now, Jamie, has anything caught your eye?' He asked the question as if Jamie were a true customer.

Jamie drew up to his full height and pointed. 'May I please see that one?'

'Of course.'

He had chosen a broadsword, the shield of its handle inlaid

with bright floral work picked out in silver against a black finish. Mr Bell patiently answered his questions, explaining the blade had been partly blued to resist rust, and that blueing was done by applying heat in the right way, and that he'd made its handle – its hilt – in his shop, but the blade had been made on the Continent. His job was fitting them all into one, and then making the scabbard and mounting, and—

'Is this who made the blade?' Jamie asked, reading aloud the etched letters: 'Andrea Ferara?'

Mr Bell smiled. 'Yes, and no. Andrew Ferara was a gifted bladesmith from Italy, born to a family of armourers. He knew the secret to tempering blades so they were of the very first quality. But he's been dead more than a hundred years now, so his name marked on a sword blade does not mean he forged it personally, only that it was made by his method and, one hopes, by someone approaching his skill. The maker will leave other marks. You see here, this small figure of a running wolf? That shows this is a German blade, from Solingen.'

Jamie leaned in close to look. 'It doesn't look like a wolf.'

Captain Graeme said, 'Aye, well, that's the thing about wolves, lad. They don't always look the way ye would expect them to.'

Mr Bell turned his attention to Lily, who through this discussion had stood back and held her tongue shyly.

'And what about you?' he asked. 'Is there a sword you would wish to see?'

Uncertainly, she glanced around the shop, not wanting to disappoint him. And then she saw it.

He followed her gaze. 'Ah, yes. This one.' He fetched it,

and laid it in front of her, with understanding. 'It looks like your daddie's.'

It wasn't, of course. There were differences in the design of the hilt. But the sure way he'd said those words made Lily look at him. 'You knew my father?'

'I did. I took care of his sword for him.' Mr Bell touched the blade lightly, and coughed, and looked sharply down, but in a moment he lifted his gaze to meet Lily's again, and his eyes held a warm promise. 'And I will take the same care of his daughter.'

❦

The kitchen was familiar ground.

Larger than the one in Kinloch's Close, it was not yet so large as the great kitchen up at Inchbrakie, and any nervous feelings Lily had were calmed by the reminder she'd been taught well by her grandmother.

The Bells had one maidservant, Nanse, who both kept house and cooked and seemed relieved to have an extra pair of hands to help, although she was particular about how things were done. By that first dinnertime, so many rules had been explained to Lily that she didn't think she'd have a hope of keeping them in mind. But Nanse was friendly – an older woman with ruddy cheeks and fading copper-coloured hair beneath her cap – and she sometimes sang while doing work, and Lily liked her.

Nanse was quick to praise. On seeing Lily smooth and spread a washing cloth flat to let it dry, Nanse said, 'Ye are a careful worker, and I'm glad to have ye here. The last lass would not learn so small a thing as that. She aye would leave my washing clouts balled up and damp around the kitchen till they rotted through with holes.'

Lily hadn't known there'd been another girl before her, although of course it did make sense, for there was too much housework here for Nanse alone to do it all, and keep the kitchen, too.

The house had many rooms and passages and stairs to be kept clean. The beds needed airing and making up, everything had to be dusted and swept, and the candles all kept in good order and new ones set in where required. There were linens – bed, body and table – that had to be laundered and dried. The cooking seemed constant, as did the washing up, and any spare moments were filled with spinning and mending.

When evening came, Lily was so weary she wanted no more than to crawl into the low pallet bed she shared with Nanse by the kitchen wall and let the waves of sleep rise and roll over her, dragging her down till they drowned out the ache of her homesickness.

But the day's final chore had to wait for the ten o'clock bell at night, when she and Nanse could haul out the ashes and chamber-pot filth to the street to the appointed place, so overnight the muckmen could collect it in their carts. It was, apparently, a source of pain to Mr Bell that not all of his neighbours in the close abided by the laws, but merely threw their excrement out of their doors and windows under cover of the darkness. Nanse told Lily Mr Bell would sometimes hire the muckmen by himself, with his own money, to come through the close and make it clean.

'He likes things to look pleasing,' Nanse said.

Lily took this to heart. She had but one bodice and petticoat, but she worked always to keep them presentable, and
kept her hair combed and tidy beneath her cap, and tied her
apron with care.

She was not sure Mr Bell had even noticed, for in fairness
she did see him very little. He was busy in his shop all hours,
and Lily so far had not been allowed to clean the shop. She
reasoned this was probably because there were so many things
of value there, and also many things that could be dangerous
if not handled correctly, and Mr Bell preferred to leave it in
the hands of Nanse, a trusted servant with experience.

At mealtimes, Nanse and Lily did not wait upon the family,
merely carried all the food into the dining room, where Mrs
Bell – a tall, spare woman with a gentle voice and manner –
thanked them and dismissed them and attended to the service
of her husband and their daughter by herself.

Nanse greatly valued this, because it gave herself and Lily
time for their own dinner, which she urged the girl to never
take for granted. 'In the first place where I trained, when I
was your age, we had scarcely time to eat at all, and what we
had to eat was scarcely worth the effort. Bread and ale for
breakfast and for supper, same as here, but there the loaf was
always hard and dry, not good and fresh like we get from
our baxter. And for dinner it was always broth, with boiled
beef, or cheese, or herring. Not a bit of green, for health, and
precious little flavour.'

Lily liked broth well enough, but she was glad that here
the servants' meals had more variety, and that even when
there was broth there'd be tasty meat besides, however

scant – perhaps some chicken or a piece of beef or mutton cooked with cauliflower, peas, or onions, followed afterwards by pears. Once Mrs Bell had even shared with them a dish of little gooseberry and cherry tarts, because, 'There are too many of them, just for us. And you've been working hard.'

It was on that same day, when Lily was content and full of cherry tart and humming to herself while she was polishing the wood frame of a picture in the drawing room, that Mr Bell walked past and paid a compliment.

'You've made that shine,' he told her. 'I can fairly see my face in it. Well done.'

Lily wheeled and caught his smile's edge as he carried on and through the door that led directly from the house into his shop, and the warm approval in that smile made her feel tall with pride.

Behind her, a girl's voice said, 'He doesn't praise people often. He likes you.'

Again Lily turned.

Mr Bell's daughter, Marion, was slightly older than Lily. Her hair gleamed a beautiful black, and her eyes had the same rich brown warmth as the swordslipper's. She hadn't spoken to Lily much, but Lily guessed this was less from aloofness than shyness.

The fact that she'd spoken now made this a special occasion, and one that demanded an answer, so Lily replied, 'I am glad my work pleases him.'

'Father is very exacting,' said Marion, taking another step into the room with a tentative smile. 'Mother says he would do very well in the army.' From the pictures and portraits that hung on the drawing-room wall, she singled out one of a very young man in a grey coat, his face set in serious lines, and said, 'My brother is now in the army, and fighting away from us.'

More than shyness, then. Loneliness. Lily knew all about missing the people you loved.

Lily said, 'He looks brave. And his portrait is well placed.'

The other girl asked, 'Why is that?'

Lily pointed out it was between a framed print of the king and a smaller but fine oval portrait of the great Montrose. 'He is in gallant company.'

'Aye,' said Marion, thoughtfully. Then, 'You'll forgive me, but . . . I know the king, of course, but . . . who's Montrose?'

Lily's eyes widened, but she knew better than to say the first thing that came to her mind since it would not be seemly to question her mistress nor forget her place, so instead she retold the whole tale as she'd learned it herself from the Moray girls when they'd played school with her at Abercairney.

Marion's reaction was the same as hers had been. 'I wish that he had stayed where he was safe, in Norway. Why did he return?'

Lily had asked her father that same question, once. She gave his answer now. 'Because he made an oath to see the king restored, and could not then abandon him.'

'But,' countered Marion, 'the king abandoned Montrose. They all did.'

'No, not all. He had one true friend,' Lily said. 'The Laird of Inchbrakie. My grandmother serves him, and he is a good man.'

This pacified Marion. 'It is enough, I suppose, to have one true friend.'

Her smile was small, but hopeful.

Mr Bell feigned confusion. 'I thought I had only one daughter, but here there are two of you.'

Lily looked up from her work and flushed, pleased by his attention. She'd been set to do a very special job for him this morning and was polishing a fine array of cutlery he'd crafted. Nanse had laid it on thick paper on the table in the dining room and given her the polish and the cloth and Lily had been taking extra care and giving the task all her concentration, although Marion had come to keep her company.

These days it was a common thing for Marion to follow Lily while she did her work for some part of the day, and Lily found it comforting, although at first she'd worried it would bring her trouble. She'd confessed to Marion, 'I do like speaking with you, but I'm feart your mother might not like it. I don't wish to be dismissed the way the lass before me was.'

Marion had promised her there was no chance of that. 'I'd not allow it. And besides, you're nothing like her. She was sent away because she was with child.'

Lily had been shocked. 'With child?'

'By the apprentice. Not the one who works for Father now – the one before this. *He* was sent away as well. But my mother will no longer let me spend time in the shop. She says that all apprentices, however nice their manners and their speech, aren't to be trusted.'

Lily, with a frown, had asked, 'How old was she? The lass afore me?'

'Fourteen. I'll be thirteen on my birthday,' Marion had said. 'How old are you?'

She'd felt the gap of age. 'I'm nearly ten.'

'I'd not have guessed. You look ages with me.' And with Marion's cheerful reply, Lily had relaxed.

From that day, they had been often together – so much so that Nanse had remarked she had two helpers now, and not one.

Mrs Bell, being close by and hearing the comment, agreed, but when Nanse looked embarrassed and ducked her head, Mrs Bell said, 'All is well, Nanse. It's good to hear Marion talking so lively. If Lily can still do her work, and both lasses are happy, then it does no harm.'

Mr Bell was apparently of the same mind.

As he leaned over now to inspect Lily's work on the cutlery, he rested one hand on her shoulder as he did on Marion's, as though he would include her in the family. 'That is fine work. From the way you have those shining, we will see if they do not fly off my shelves before the week is out.' Furtively he glanced around, then from his pocket he produced a piece of paper wrapped around some lumps of sugar candy. 'Here, such work deserves reward,' he told them. 'But you're not to tell your mother, Marion. Nor Nanse, else they would lecture me for ruining your teeth.' He winked, and left them.

Lily could not mind the last time she'd had such a treat as sugar candy. Popping one small piece into her mouth, she savoured its dissolving sweetness. She told Marion, 'Your father's kind.'

'He does like giving presents.'

Lily deeply missed her own father.

That night when all the house had fallen silent, and the cinders had been raked upon the kitchen hearth and she was lying in the pallet bed with Nanse asleep beside her, Lily missed her father so intensely that she pressed her fingers to her forehead, as if somehow by that action she might feel his kiss there once again, to make her dreams the sweeter.

She felt the tears squeeze hotly from the corners of her eyes and trace their steady and relentless paths along her temples, dampening her hair, but they would not be held. She was shaking, and not wishing to disturb Nanse, she rose carefully and took a few steps from the bed. She tried to make no noise.

And then she froze, because she heard a sound that was not of her making.

There was only one small window in the kitchen, near the door, and Nanse had fastened it before they went to bed, yet Lily heard the window shifting in its frame as though it had been forced, and then she heard it opening.

At least, she thought that was what she heard, because by then the sound of her own pulsing heartbeat in her ears had risen loud enough to mask all other sounds, and she was rooted to the floorboards by her fear. She could not move.

Someone was coming through the window.

Not a grown man, but a boy. Her eyes, adjusted to the faint light from the near-dead embers of the hearth, could just make out his figure as he clambered through the opening and dropped on cat feet to the floor. He carried something in his hand she thought at first might be a tankard until he unlatched the front and Lily saw it was a dark lantern, designed to shield the candle well within until its light was needed.

In the sudden glow she glimpsed his face. And he saw hers.

From underneath the window, in the close, there came a

muffled cough, and at the same time a rough whisper asked, 'All clear?'

She stared in terror at the boy, who looked not that much older than herself, and he stared back at her, and Lily thought, *He's going to let them in.*

He was not on his own – he'd come with men who meant to rob the shop and house, and he was going to let them in, and then all would be lost. They would hurt her, and hurt Nanse, and . . .

More impatiently now came the whispered, gruff demand, 'All clear?'

She should have screamed. She should have run for aid, or run for safety, or done anything but stand there like a rabbit trying hard not to be seen. Against the candlelight, she held the boy's gaze pleadingly and shook her head.

He closed the lantern, and the light was gone. And then he was, as well. Or very nearly.

He'd gone halfway through the window when she heard one man outside ask, low, 'What is it?'

'There were men awake and talking in the next room,' said the boy.

If he said anything more Lily did not hear it, for she was startled by a shrill scream at her back as Nanse rose from their bed in time to see the boy's feet slipping out of the window.

'Thief!' cried Nanse, and, 'Murder!' as she staggered to the door and wrenched it open and called out into the close after the running figures that had swiftly fled into the shadows of the Canongate.

Upstairs, there was a murmuring of voices and a rush of closing doors and hurried footsteps on the stairs, and Mr Bell and Mrs Bell appeared with Marion behind them in the passage door, still in their nightclothes.

Mr Bell asked, 'What has happened?'

Nanse by this time had recovered herself, closed the kitchen door again and bolted it securely, and had moved to view the window where the boy had entered. 'Thieves, sir. Two men and a lad, that I saw. They sent the lad in through the window to open the door – ye can see where they forced it – but Lily was here, and she frightened him off.'

'Lily?' Mr Bell seemed to take note of her for the first time, standing numbly where she'd stood throughout the ordeal. He crouched close in front of her, and in a gentle voice asked, 'Did he hurt you?'

'He lied.' It was all she could think of to say. She was not sure what had made the boy tell his friends that there were men talking in the next room, but with that lie he had saved her and everyone in this house from being victims of house-breaking, possibly worse.

Mr Bell told her, patiently, 'All thieves do lie, my dear. Don't let it worry you.'

Lily was shaking again, and he felt it.

He said, 'I'm afraid that the child has been frightened by this, and it may not be healthy for Lily to sleep anymore in the kitchen. We ought to prepare her a new place to sleep.'

'She can sleep with me,' Marion said. 'There is room in my chamber.' She looked to her mother and added, 'If Lily can still do her work, as you say, there's no harm.'

With a soft smile, her mother agreed, 'You are right.'

And so it was decided.

Jean shifted baby James high on her hip as she chose two more apples to add to the basket that Lily was carrying. 'Well, I am happier knowing you're sleeping upstairs with the family, but I still do feel I should bring ye away from that place. Are they good to ye?'

'Aye, they are very good. You need not worry.'

'I worry,' said Jean, in a tone that implied doing anything else was unreasonable. 'We scarcely see ye anymore, and when we do, ye look so sad and tired.'

'I'm not sad.' Lily reasoned it would be no sin to stray from the truth this one time, if it helped to set Jean's mind at ease. 'And not so tired today.' She showed a cheerful face to prove it, taking Bessie's hand more firmly in her own as they moved on to the next stall within the greenmarket. 'Will not ye have some plums? They are your favourite.'

'Not this time.' Jean moved along, bought half a pound of nuts instead, and with a single onion added, said to Lily, 'That will do us nicely for the week.'

It was a sorry-looking basket in comparison to those she'd carried in the past, but Lily made no comment, knowing that even with the coins she could give Jean from her own wages, every penny must be stretched as far as possible.

Their new lodgings were more distant from the market-place than their old ones at Kinloch's Close. The walk home took them longer. Bessie dragged her feet, complaining, until finally Lily made a game of trying to guess the secret occupations of the people they were passing.

'See now, he's an outlaw,' Lily said in hushed tones of a

carter standing at his horse's head, his hat pulled low. 'And in the night he rides that horse upon the roads, and robs all wealthy men who cross his path.'

Delighted, Bessie pointed to a merchant in his shop door opposite. 'Who's that?'

'Why, that's the king's own spy, who's sent to catch the outlaw, but at every turn has been outwitted, because some men are not what they do appear to be.'

They'd finally reached the narrow land within the cramped and sunless close where Jean had found them lodgings on the fourth floor. A man had just come down the turnpike stair, and at the bottom turned to call up to a third-floor window where a woman leaned out wearing nothing but her shift, her fair hair tumbled round her shoulders, and waved back to him.

Bessie tugged at Lily's hand and nodded at the woman, wanting still to play the game. 'Who's that?'

'A princess,' Lily said, 'trapped in a tower, by a—'

Jean broke in, and put her foot down. 'No. She's not a princess. She's a common whore.'

Lily had, of course, heard people use that word before. She knew that it was bad to be one, and that it was also bad to call somebody one when they were not, although her knowledge of the meaning of the word itself was vague.

Jean warned, 'Don't look at her or speak to her,' and Lily kept her head down and obeyed, not even glancing upwards when the woman called 'Good morrow' to them in a mocking tone.

But Bessie, who could no more keep from questioning than breathing, barely waited until they were inside their own lodgings before asking, 'What's a whore?'

'A woman who takes money from a man,' said Jean, 'for pleasing him, in ways ye are too young to understand. But it is wrong, and she is wicked. Why our landlord lets her bide here, I will never understand. Were it in my hands, I'd chase her to the gutter where she does belong, and she could take her fancy clothes and false smiles there and try to turn men's heads, and good luck to her. There's no place for whores among us decent folk.'

Lily had questions, but she held them to herself because she'd noticed that beside the bed there was a newly empty place upon the wall. She swallowed down the hurtful words that tried to rise, knowing that Jean was struggling every day to make do with the money she had set aside – 'against hard times, if they should come' had always been Jean's reasoning if anyone had asked why she was saving pennies in days past, and Lily knew times were hard now. But still the empty place would need addressing, so she asked Jean, 'Did ye sell my daddie's sword?'

Jean looked stricken. 'No. I'd never . . .' She looked briefly to the wall, then back at Lily, and when she spoke next her voice had calmed. 'The damp here made it rust, so Corporal Morison has taken it for safekeeping. He knows the way to care for it. Wee James may wish to have it one day, for it still does carry honour.' Coming close, she smoothed the flying strands of Lily's hair that had escaped their pins and curled about her cheek. 'I'll never sell it, Lily. I am not so desperate as all that, not with ye giving me your wages. And the ladies with the red booth in the Landmarket are paying me to knit them stockings they can sell on market days. We will be well.'

But it was now September and the colder days were coming and soon Bessie would be needing shoes, and Lily had these past weeks tried to better learn the price of household things, from clothes to coal. Without her father here, she knew, their winter would be difficult.

The booted footsteps sounding at that instant on the turn-pike stair were so like his it made her heart jump hopefully. She'd turned before she knew she'd made the movement. But of course, it wasn't him, and never would be.

Corporal Morison no longer stood on ceremony. Giving a brief knock, he did not wait for a reply but swung the door wide and ducked through the doorway of their lodgings. He made the room seem warmer with his cheerful ways. Like them, he had been in the market that morning, and carried a large, brown fish half-wrapped in paper.

'I'm not bringing charity,' he said to Jean, when she sent him a look. 'It's a Loch Leven trout. Oh, and these.' From his pocket, he drew out a handful of perfect, ripe plums. 'Ye'd best eat them afore they turn rotten.'

Even had Jean been inclined to argue with him, it would have had no effect because he had already turned to give his full attention to the children. Bessie clambered on him as he sat, and perched upon his knee as if she were a lady riding sidesaddle and he, obligingly, held up a hand to be her reins and jounced and jigged her while reciting the rhyme he'd made up for her:

'*Queen Bess rode north tae Inverness*
Upon her dapple grey.
Her guardsmen all went tae their mess
And fetched the mare her hay.
The mare she liked the hay the best
And tossed the queen away!'

Here Bessie giggled as the corporal tossed her high into the air as though the 'horse' had thrown her off. It had become their favourite game, and Bessie often made him do it over and over, but today the corporal set her gently on the floor and turned to Lily. 'It's good to see ye, lass. They've let ye out the day, I see.'

Jean said, 'But we must have her back by suppertime. I would she had more time to rest, she looks too tired.'

'I'm not tired,' Lily told her, but Jean seemed to take no notice.

With a faint frown, Jean said to the corporal, 'I've half a mind to bring her home again to live with us. The work's too hard for one so young. What do you think?'

Corporal Morison looked steadily at Lily, who looked back at him. He said, 'I think the lass kens her own mind.'

Lily decided that she liked him very much.

He said, 'I did nearly forget, I have good news to tell ye. We captured your thieves in the small hours this morning. Two men and a lad, in the same clothes your housemaid described to our guardsmen, who caught them conducting their business in Hamilton's Close.'

Jean thought it good news indeed. 'It will be difficult for them to do their business from the Tolbooth.'

Corporal Morison agreed. 'And still more difficult, I reckon, from the gallows.'

Lily frowned. She knew it was important to keep order in a town, and she had often heard her father say that laws and justice were things worth defending; but in her heart she could not help but feel that in her father's case, justice had not been fair, which meant that not all men who lost their lives because of it deserved it.

She asked, 'Will all of them be hanged?'

The corporal seemed surprised by both her frown and tone of voice. 'Ye don't agree they should be punished for their crimes?'

She said, 'Not all of them the same. The lad was different.'

Corporal Morison asked, 'How?'

'He did not let them in. The men who sent him through the window,' Lily said. 'He did not let them in.'

'Because Nanse chased him off,' Jean reasoned.

Lily shook her head. 'Nanse was asleep. There was no one but me, and I was too feart to do anything. He could have let the others in, but he chose not to. And he told them he'd heard someone in the next room, but that was not true. I do believe,' she said, because she'd had time now to turn this over in her mind, 'that when he realized Nanse and I were there alone he wished no harm to come to us, and that is why he did not let them in.'

'And *I* believe,' said Jean, 'that ye do have a soft heart that would seek to see the best in everyone. I fear that it will one day lead ye into trouble.'

Lily could not see how it would do so, but Corporal Morison had already come to her defence.

'There's nothing wrong with a soft heart,' he said to Jean. 'Mine's always served me well.'

Jean rolled her eyes. 'That same soft heart that made ye tell me her downstairs looked lonely, and I ought to ask her up to dinner?'

'Aye, well, she *does* look fair lonely, sometimes.'

'Whores don't want for company,' Jean told him. 'But they can't have mine.'

As if in reply, heavy footsteps were heard on the turnpike stair down below, climbing. They stopped at the lodging beneath theirs, and Lily heard a man's voice and woman's loud laughter and then a door closing, and Jean sent the corporal a pained look.

He grinned. 'Ye'll not have to endure it much longer,' he promised. 'Come Martinmas this will all be at the back of ye.'

Lily looked from his face to Jean's in surprise. Martinmas fell on November the 11th, and so was scant weeks away.

Seeing her face, Corporal Morison lifted his eyebrows at Jean. 'Ye've not told her?'

Jean flushed. 'No. I was meaning to, but I was waiting to find the right moment.'

The corporal looked round. 'This would seem like one.'

Jean never liked to be rushed in a task. She came slowly across to them, head down as though she were thinking, and when she looked up Lily saw she was nervous.

Jean said, 'Lily, I need to tell ye . . . that is, we've decided . . . that is, Corporal Morison's asked me . . .' She broke off, and drying her hands on her apron reached out to take Lily's hands lightly in hers.

She smiled. 'How would ye like to come dance at my wedding?'

CHAPTER ELEVEN

THURSDAY, 29 OCTOBER, 1685

WEALTHY PEOPLE, WHEN THEY married, came in coaches to the church in all their finery and gave gifts to the minister and tossed coins to the poor and hosted private celebrations after, at their own expense.

Jean had no coach, and nothing finer than her calico to wear, but she was beautiful in Lily's eyes as she stood in the Tron Kirk with Corporal Morison in his best guardsman's coat and all their friends to bear them witness. And the corporal, though he was not wealthy, still did pay the minister, and coming from the church he stopped to give coins to the beggars who were waiting at the doors.

As for private celebrations, Jean said that the rich could keep them, and leave her a penny wedding.

Penny weddings – where the guests' coins bought the food and drink, and often left the newly-married couple a small profit – could be in or out of doors, depending on the time of year, and sometimes carried on for days. This one, arranged by Captain Graeme, was above a vintner's in a large room with a timber floor that bounced and shook from all the dancing.

People came and went, a laughing, talking swirl and blend of faces, skirts, and shoulders, voices rising and then falling to the music from the fiddle and the drum.

Mrs Graeme had brought her own maid to help care for wee James and for Bessie, which gave Lily freedom to sit on a barrel in the corner next to Jamie, out of everybody's way, and have some time with him alone.

They seldom had this anymore. She missed it terribly, and it was hollowing her heart to find that she would have to learn the way of missing it this winter.

He had scooped a dish of walnuts for them from the table for the guests, and set to work now cracking them with a short pewter nutcracker that had sharp points to help scoop out the meat.

'It is not fair,' he said, with feeling. 'I've no wish to go to school in Perth.'

'The Moray lads did go there. Robin says it is a good place.'

'Ye are *not* to take my mother's side.' He handed her a walnut. 'And my father does not care about the school. I heard them when they argued, Lily. He said he was sending us away because he could no longer do his work and worry for our safety, when the town had grown so dangerous.'

She ate her walnut, looking from their corner at the warm room filled with friendly faces mingling in the shared joy of the day, and she could see no danger, but she knew the captain was a clever man who rarely made a move without good reason.

Lily tried to find something to say that would cheer Jamie. 'At Perth ye will be closer to your grandfather.'

'Aye.' He splintered a walnut. 'But further from you.'

There was no way around that particular truth, and it saddened her, too. 'It will only be backwards, though, from how it used to be, when ye were here and I lived at Inchbrakie. We managed it then.'

'I suppose so.' He didn't look cheered.

Lily tried again. 'Jean says we're faithful friends, Jamie, and so we are, and so we always will be till the end of our days, never matter wherever we bide.'

Jamie considered this. 'It would be better still if we were older, and then I could marry ye.'

'Marry me? What for?'

He cracked her a walnut and shrugged. 'Because then I could bring ye to Perth with me, and there'd be none who could stop us.'

'That isn't why people get married.'

'It's reason enough. Anyway,' Jamie teased her, 'who else would ye have?'

Before she could answer him, a group of dancers swung close to their corner and one of the young men broke off from the others, and when a young woman called out to him, 'Thomas, *do* come back, you'll ruin the line!' he excused himself gallantly, leaving a space that was hastily filled by another dancer who'd been standing by the wall.

The young man named Thomas was not of the guards, but seemed to be a kinsman of Mr Gordon the vintner, and had been several times now up and down the stairs helping supply the guests while also enjoying himself. He was perhaps twenty years old, with blue eyes and a dazzling smile that she had seen him use to good effect on several of the ladies, but now it was aimed straight at Jamie, and quizzically.

'What are ye doing with those?'

Jamie looked at him, equally puzzled. 'With what?'

'My dividers.' He meant the pewter implement that Jamie had been using as a nutcracker, for which he now held out his hand, reclaiming it and giving it a curious inspection.

Jamie said, 'I didn't ken that it was yours. I found it on the table.'

'No, it's my fault. I misplaced them earlier, you're not to blame. In truth, I'm grateful that you've helped me find them, for they are in fact a very useful item, though I do confess I've never thought of using them for walnuts.'

Lily, from her seat atop the barrel, had a clear view of the little tool, hinged at the top with equal pointed sides that could be spread apart or tightly closed to make a whole not quite the length of a man's hand and half as big around as a man's finger. 'Then what are they for?' she asked.

'Dividers? These help me navigate when I'm at sea,' he told them. 'When I have my charts, my maps, these help me measure out my distances, so I know where I am, and where I'm heading.'

Jamie's interest had been captured. 'You can sail a ship?'

'Aye.'

Lily told him, 'Jamie wants to be a sailor.'

Jamie felt the need to add, 'She will not let me be a soldier.'

Thomas nodded with a solemn air. 'Wise lass.' And then he seemed to finally place who Lily was, because he looked from her to Jean and Corporal Morison, top couple in the current dance, and said, 'Congratulations to your family. I do wish you well.'

She thanked him, but there must have been some stray

note in her voice that made him look more closely at her face. He smiled a private understanding. 'Ye weren't needing a new daddie?'

Lily sat more straight and told him, 'Corporal Morison's a good man.'

'Aye, he is. But I do understand, believe me. I lost my mother when I was a bairn and never had the chance to ken her, but she left a hole behind that won't be filled by any other. Too big a hole to be measured with these.' He held up his dividers. 'There's no shame in feeling it.'

Lily felt her own heart thumping heavily in time with every drumbeat of the music as the dancers met and swirled and parted. 'So what do ye do?'

'Well,' Thomas said, 'there's an old saying: we have to live for the living, and not for the dead. And I try to remember that.'

Jamie was ready to talk about other things. 'How do you learn to sail ships?'

'There are different ways. You can apprentice . . .'

Their talk became technical. Lily lost interest, and focused instead on the dancers and Jean who was living her life for the living and finding new happiness, and Lily wanted that, too, only . . . only . . .

'May I have this dance?'

She had not noticed Mr Bell coming in. He wore his best Sunday coat, like a gentleman, and he bowed low to her, offering both hands to help her hop down from the barrel. She did, and then suddenly she was a part of the dance with the rest of them, learning the new steps and gaining in confidence, living her life for the living.

❧

Lily had been warned by Jean to not expect much of the Bells for Hansell Monday, being that it was her first and she was yet so young. 'Mr Bell lives very handsomely, but mind that he's a tradesman and his pockets only go so deep,' said Jean. 'He'll be giving hansell also to the muckmen and the town musicians and how many others who have served him through the year, so take the coin he gifts ye and be grateful for it, even if it's small.'

Small gifts suited Lily, so she did not make complaint. Nor did she tell Jean this would not be her first hansell, since the old Laird of Inchbrakie had been generous with his servants the first Monday of each new year in accordance with tradition, and had always pressed a shiny silver half-merk piece into her hand, stamped on one side with the king's head and on the other with a cross.

It would be too much to hope that Mr Bell would give her such a gift, but Lily still awakened with a feeling of excitement.

She tried to hold it to herself as she helped Marion to dress, an extra task that had been added to her morning chores, though it was one she welcomed for the added time it gave her with her friend.

There, too, she had been warned by Jean, 'Ye can't be friends with those ye serve.'

But Marion had told her, plain, 'We *are* friends, Lily.' And they were.

This morning Marion seemed also near to bursting with anticipation, and too restless to sit still while Lily brushed her hair. Instead, she spun round on her stool and looked at Lily's face intently. 'My father's right. Your eyes are blue. I am so glad,' she said, and with that comment unexplained, they went downstairs.

At breakfast, after Nanse and Lily had brought in the dishes to the family, Mr Bell rose from his chair and bade them wait.

'Nanse, we are grateful for you,' he said, and while Lily could not see the coins he gave the older woman she could hear them clink and knew he'd given more than one. Nanse thanked him, and the swordslipper moved on to Lily, patting at his pockets as though he'd mislaid his purse.

'Now, I had a wee gift for you also, my dear, but I cannot think where . . . ?'

'Here it is, Father!' Marion leapt from her place at the table and, tugging a paper-wrapped package from under his chair, turned to face him beseechingly. 'Do let me give it! You said that I could.'

'Aye.' He smiled at both girls in turn, and stood back.

Lily had not expected an actual gift. In bemusement, she opened the package as carefully as she was able – more carefully when she felt soft velvet under her fingers. And then, when the paper had fallen away and she saw what it was, she stared.

Marion, finally free of the need to keep the secret, blurted, 'It's a hood! Exactly like my own, the one you think is bonny, only mine is crimson because red's my favourite colour and we had the seamstress make yours blue, to match your eyes.' She looked at Lily, waiting. 'Say you like it?'

Lily touched the velvet, cautiously, and still could not believe it. 'It's so beautiful.' Too beautiful for someone of her station, but to tell them that would be ungrateful, and that would be wrong. Besides, she wanted more than anything to have and keep that hood. It took an effort to look up, but she met Marion's expectant eyes and said, 'I like it very much.' And then she looked at Mrs Bell, still seated at the table, and at Mr Bell, who stood to one side watching her, and told them, 'Thank ye. 'Tis a kindness I do not deserve.'

'Of course you do,' said Mr Bell. Coming close, he took the blue hood from the remnants of its wrappings and with sure hands tied it over Lily's head, then held a silver knife up from the table with its flat edge to her so that she could see her own reflection in its polished surface. 'There, you see? That face deserves much kindness. *And* a hood, else you'll be like to lose your ears next time we walk to church, the wind has been that cold of late.'

It was his smile that warmed her more than anything, but Lily gladly wore her new blue hood to keep the wind away, though it was not the wind alone that made the town feel colder.

Increasingly that month, when they were walking back from Sabbath service at the Abbey Church, they met disturbances outside the house of Mr Bruce, the engineer, midway along the Canongate.

It was well known that Mr Bruce and Mistress Bruce were Catholics, and each Sabbath several of their friends – including noble ladies, with their servants – came to celebrate the Catholic service at their house. This had been tolerated well enough before, and they'd been left in peace.

That peace had ended.

The first week Lily and the Bell family had passed the

house of Mr Bruce, there'd been only a few boys who had gathered at the door to jeer and taunt the people leaving after service. Mistress Bruce had chased them off with ease, although the sight and sound had been unpleasant.

The next week there assembled a much larger crowd, more dangerous, some wielding sticks and others flinging ugly words, while redcoat soldiers had stood by encouraging the trouble.

On the final Sabbath of the month, the final day of January, Nanse called Lily early from her work, before the bells had yet begun to ring to summon everyone to service.

'Make haste, now,' said Nanse. 'The mistress would away while all is quiet in the street.'

The street *was* quiet, then, but all through service Lily could not concentrate for worrying what might be taking place outside the Bruces' house.

She could not understand why Catholics were not better liked. After all, as Anna Moray had taught her, 'a long time ago, everybody in Scotland was Catholic.' And now their King James was a Catholic, as was their own Chancellor, and Catholics weren't so different from Episcopalians in how they worshipped and what they believed.

But they *were* different from the outlawed Presbyterians, and to Lily what was happening now in the Canongate seemed like her childhood game turned to terrible true life, with one side ever hunting down its enemies, and ever growing larger, turning all they touched to Covenanters.

When the service ended she was loath to leave the safety of the Abbey Church, and dragged her feet, and fastened on her blue hood as a knight might don his helmet for protection before heading to a yet uncertain battlefield. And it was just as well she did, for coming up the Canongate, they came into a battle.

If last week there had been disorder outside Mr Bruce's house, this afternoon the hatefulness had spread like ink in water, so there were now people tightly crowded along both sides of the street up to the Netherbow.

In such a crush of bodies Lily found it was impossible to know who was a friend and who was someone to be feared.

She saw redcoat soldiers standing to one side and doing nothing, while a guardsman and a grenadier chased down a baxter lad and, having caught him, beat him harshly till he dropped the rolling pin he held and blood showed in a spatter on his baker's apron.

In a rage a woman called out, 'God damn all ye papists and send ye to hell!' and the people around her took up the same cry.

'Stay together,' Mr Bell told Lily as he gathered her close beside Marion and they pressed on through the bystanders.

Lily tried hard not to look. She held tightly to Marion and Mrs Bell and tried keeping her eyes on the toes of her shoes, but she was jostled and losing her balance she glanced up and saw the glass windows of the Bruces' house were smashed through with stones.

'It's all right.' Mr Bell's hand settled steady on her shoulder.

Just in time, for the same young men who had jostled her stepped backwards and bumped into her again, and one called out, 'There is another papist bitch!'

For one heart-stopping second Lily was afraid that he meant *her*, but he and his friends had already focused their aggression on a young maid who was coming from the

Bruces' house. They fell on her and chased her, paying no heed to her shrieks for mercy, grabbing at her clothing till her scarf and hood were torn.

Lily put both hands on her own hood and stopped up her ears as best she could to block the sounds and shouts and cries, and looked fiercely at her toes again and did not lift her gaze until they were indoors and Mr Bell had bolted shut the door and barred the windows.

She discovered she was shaking.

It was Mr Bell who gently lifted Lily's hands down from her ears, untied her hood, and reassured her all was well.

She asked him in a small voice, 'What did happen to the maid? The one they chased?'

'She got away. Somebody opened up their door to her, and let her go inside. She will be safe.'

But nothing outside sounded safe.

When darkness fell, the violence only worsened. She and Nanse dared not take out the muck and ashes as they always did, but tossed them from a window to the street, a thing that was against the law – although as Nanse said, everything about that night was lawless.

All up and down the Canongate came sounds of running feet and shouting voices and rough curses and the clatter of stones striking both the things they had been thrown at and the walls and doors behind.

What frightened Lily most was sitting blindly in the dark with shutters drawn across the windows, being unable to see outside while her imagination wildly conjured every crime she'd ever heard of and convinced her that whatever she was hearing was as wicked.

Upstairs, in the bedchamber she shared with Marion, she cautiously unlatched the shutter, opened it a crack, and peered down on the street.

Marion, behind her in bed, asked, 'What do you see?'

The lanterns that by law were set out on each house to help illuminate the area had not yet been extinguished. The street for a moment looked empty, but then a small group of young men ran past, took a sharp turn into one of the closes, and melted to shadows against the stone walls. Behind them came other men carrying muskets and walking in a measured way Lily knew well. She said, 'I see soldiers of the town guard. And I think that Captain Graeme is among them.'

She could not be sure, not from that distance, but one of the guardsmen gave an order to the others and they raised their muskets to their shoulders and they fired down the close after the fast-retreating shadows.

Lily did not like the sound of musket fire. It clawed the half-healed wound within her heart so that it bled anew, and tore her dreams that night apart with nightmares.

But still, within an hour, the Canongate had fallen silent, and the silence held.

It held next morning all through breakfast, and in the hour afterwards while Lily did her dusting. Mr Bell had gone out, leaving his apprentice to attend the shop, and Lily being mindful of the dangers of apprentices was tiptoeing with caution past the partly open door that led directly to the shop from the room in which she'd been working, when she heard a young man's voice say, 'The devil murder Captain Graeme and his men!'

He said it low, but with such hatred Lily stopped in shock.

She was behind the door, and so could not be seen, but she could hear. The voice did not belong to Mr Bell's apprentice.

'He ordered his soldiers to fire upon us, and if they were better shots I'd be a head shorter, but we did give them the slip and got into a cellar, where we found more of our friends, so we drank to the health of the Trades and the health of our mistresses and to the papists' confusion. And then we made plans.'

'What plans?' *That* was Mr Bell's apprentice.

'First, we'll rescue those two lads they took – the baxter and the other one. Then arm ourselves and rise against the town guard and kill Captain Graeme, and then there'll be none to stop us tearing down the papists' houses and killing them, too.'

Mr Bell's apprentice thought the risk too great. 'I cannot join your rising.'

'You can furnish weapons for the cause. You do not want for blades. I have a friend who has two pistols who has promised he will lend me one of them,' the other said. 'Give me swords as well, and Captain Graeme when he comes tonight will wish himself elsewhere.'

'The swords are not my own to give.'

'Think on it.'

Lily heard the outer shop door slam and quickly backed away into the inner chamber, still on tiptoe, grateful for the solid timber floorboards that did not betray her with a squeak. She felt relief to know that Mr Bell's apprentice was an honest young man. Surely upon Mr Bell's return he'd tell him all, and warn him of the coming danger to the town guard and the Catholics.

In the kitchen, Lily asked Nanse, 'When will Mr Bell be home?'

'I couldnae tell ye. But that pot needs scouring in the meantime.'

Lily scoured the pot, then helped Nanse pluck and breast three moor fowl they'd cook later for the family's dinner, throwing legs and wings and all discarded pieces in the kettle for their own good broth with barley and some well-chopped Flanders onion. It was difficult to focus on her work and not the clock in the next room that counted off the hours and their quarters, but when the clock chimed ten times Lily asked Nanse, 'Did Mr Bell go far?'

'I couldnae tell ye that, and all.' Nanse looked at her. 'Is it important?'

Lily thought of telling Nanse what she had overheard, but Nanse did not approve of people listening at doors. Once when Lily had repeated gossip, Nanse had sternly told her not to scald her mouth with someone else's broth, but to attend to her own business. Lily reassured herself that Mr Bell's apprentice had done nothing wrong, and he was honest. He'd tell Mr Bell, and Mr Bell in his turn would warn Captain Graeme, and all would be well.

Lily was deciding how best to reply to Nanse without telling her a falsehood when a sound of drumming coming from outdoors in the direction of the Netherbow distracted her.

Nanse sighed, and told her, 'That will be the baxter lad, the one they took up yesterday. The council sentenced him to be whipped from the Tolbooth to the Watergate and back again this morning. He lodges with the widow Fleck, who bakes our bread, and she did tell me earlier. Poor lad. But that's what comes,' said Nanse, 'of keeping the wrong company.'

It was an awful punishment to be whipped through the

streets, stripped to the waist, with one official leading you by the same rope that bound your hands while at your back the hangman followed with his knotted whip and drove you on with lashes, like a beast.

At first, Lily was grateful when the shouts and jeers began to rise, because it meant she would not hear the whipping. But the shouting went on growing louder, drowning out the drums, and it became clear something more was going on.

Nanse rose, and crossing to the door opened it just enough to look out on the close. A man passed by, half-running, and she hailed him. 'What has happened?'

'Keep inside,' was his advice. 'A group of the young tradesmen and apprentices just made a bold attack on the town officers and took a soldier's sword, and they did rescue that poor baxter lad and have him hidden somewhere in a house. Ye would do well to bar your door. I fear there will be trouble.'

Nanse closed the door, but did not bar it yet. 'What are they thinking? They've all lost their minds.'

But Lily knew their plan, because she'd heard it laid out plainly: *First, we'll rescue those two lads they took – the baxter and the other one. Then arm ourselves and rise against the town guard and kill Captain Graeme . . .*

And now they'd set their plan in motion, rescuing the baxter lad.

The street fell quiet once again, and Lily helped Nanse serve the dinner. Mr Bell had not returned.

All through the washing up that followed, Lily's worries grew till she could barely keep her thoughts together, and the clock in the next room kept chiming off the quarter hours till she could hardly bear it, for she knew the afternoon was wearing on and it would soon be growing dark. When Nanse went up to tend the fires in the bedchambers, the urgency that Lily felt would no more be ignored, and without bothering to fetch her hood, Lily took her plaid down from the peg and slipped out through the kitchen door and raced on light feet to the Netherbow.

The guardsman she met first was not inclined to let her pass.

'Go home,' he brusquely ordered her. 'Your parents should have more sense than to let ye run about the streets on such a day as this.'

His words stung. Lily raised her chin and told him stubbornly, 'My mother's dead, and ye did kill my daddie.'

He stared down at her. 'I did not. I've killed no man.'

'Aye, ye did, too. Ye shot him in Trinity churchyard,' she said, 'this past summer.'

His face altered then, as when someone remembers. He passed his hand over his eyes, and when he spoke next his voice had also changed – no longer hardened, but bordering on an apology. 'You're Edward Aitcheson's lass.'

Lily nodded.

He told her, 'I'm sorry, I am, but you still shouldn't be out of doors the day. We have our orders, and I'm only trying to protect you. The streets are fair dangerous.'

Lily, more calm now, said, 'I have a message to give Captain Graeme.'

'He'll come by here later. You tell me your message. I'll see that he gets it.'

She shook her head. 'I need to see that he gets it right now. It's important.' And then, because she knew the guardsman could not leave his post while she could go wherever the captain was, she told a small lie. 'I'm meant to deliver it straight to his own hand.'

The guardsman assessed her, but he seemed to have trouble meeting and holding her gaze. In the end he stood, gave a short nod, and said, 'Captain Graeme's up at Patrick Steell's house, at the sign of the Cross Keys. Do you know where that is?'

She nodded.

'Go there, give your message to him, and come straight back down, you hear? I will be watching for you.'

Lily ran the whole way up the High Street to the Cross Keys tavern, her breath making mist in the darkening air that clawed cold at her lungs. At the door of the tavern, a huddle of men stood and talked with their backs to her – men with fine hats and fine wigs and fine cloaks – but among them she recognized one set of sturdier shoulders.

She called, 'Captain Graeme!'

He turned. The man nearest him turned, too, and Lily saw it was the Lord Provost, who had the charge of the town and who'd once said he'd rather be Lord Provost here than the Lord Mayor of London, since both did the same exact work for the same honour, only he was not surrounded by Englishmen.

No Englishmen surrounded the Lord Provost here this afternoon. The other men had Scottish voices. Marshalling them all to move inside the Cross Keys tavern, after Captain Graeme asked a moment's leave to speak to Lily, the Lord Provost said, 'I'll wait for you inside then, with my magistrates. Do not be long – we need you to be with us and in readiness in case this night brings new disorders.'

Left alone outside with Lily, Captain Graeme crouched to her own level and arranged her plaid more snugly round her head and shoulders. 'It is cold,' he told her. 'Now, what brings ye out when there's such trouble in the town?'

It was the trouble, she explained, that brought her out to him. She told him what she'd overheard. He listened to her carefully.

'Ye did not see this other lad? The one who spoke to Mr Bell's apprentice?'

'No. But the apprentice will ken who he is, if ye do ask him.'

'I intend to ask him,' Captain Graeme said, and something in his tone made Lily blink in sudden realization.

'Ye'll not punish him, because of what I telt ye? Please don't punish him.' Her mouth began to tremble. 'He did nothing wrong.'

Captain Graeme hugged her shoulders briefly with his hands, and met her gaze with eyes that seemed to understand her struggles to not lose her faith in justice.

'It's a lesson life does teach us all, in time,' he said. 'Ye cannot always judge a man's heart by the way he looks. Sometimes the people ye best trust may disappoint ye.'

'He is not bad,' Lily told him. 'He is honest.'

'Then I promise ye, if he is as ye say, and tells the truth and takes no part in any rising, he will not be harmed.'

'Ye promise?'

'Aye. And that's a thing ye can take with ye to your grave, the promise of a Graeme.'

Lily was not altogether certain. 'Jamie promised me he would not leave me. And now he is gone.'

The captain's mouth curved faintly at the corner, and he

stood to his full height. 'He had no choice in that decision, I'm the one ye want to blame. Truth is, he would have wished to stay where ye are, and when this unrest is over, he'll be at your side again.' He reached for Lily's hand. 'Come, I'll walk ye back.'

'But the Lord Provost is waiting.'

'I'll not be gone a quarter of an hour,' he said.

She closed her fingers round his hand, as always finding the firm comfort of his grasp and his sure, easy stride a steady reassurance. 'Captain Graeme?'

'Aye?'

'Should ye not have men guarding ye?'

'I will be fine, lass.'

'He said they would kill ye.'

He smiled. 'They can try. But my daddie would tell them the devil's aye kind to his own.'

Lily didn't think that Captain Graeme was acquainted with the devil, but she knew the captain's daddie was the old Laird of Inchbrakie, who'd been a great soldier and survived long years of battling the Covenanters, so perhaps that same good fortune would hold for the captain. She wished for it, regardless, and held tighter to his hand.

As they approached the Netherbow, the guardsmen straightened to attention, and the guard who'd let her pass drew up defensively and told the captain, 'She did claim to have a message for you, sir, of great importance.'

'Aye, and so it was,' said Captain Graeme. 'Very great importance. Ye did right to send her through.'

The guardsman visibly relaxed, and Lily swelled with pride as she passed with the captain through the Netherbow.

The Canongate was quiet yet. Some of the candle lanterns had been lit along the street against the coming darkness, but the windows for the most part were well shuttered as though violence was expected. Lily led the captain up the steps from Bell's Close and into the kitchen, back the way she'd come, surprising Nanse who had not realized she had left the house.

'I thought ye were in the drawing room with Mistress Bell,' she said, one hand pressed to her heart as though to will it to resume its normal pace.

'There's no harm done,' the captain said. 'She only came to give me something I had need of.' Then, before Nanse could enquire what that might be, he asked, 'Has Mr Bell returned from Niddrie?'

Nanse's face cleared. 'Is that where he's gone?'

'That's where he was going when I saw him heading from the town this morn. The Laird of Niddrie called him for a private consultation on the making of some swords.'

Nanse said, 'The laird won't be the only Catholic thinking now to arm himself.'

'Indeed. When Mr Bell comes home, would ye be kind enough to let him know I wish to have a word with his apprentice? He can send the lad to see me at the Tolbooth.' Captain Graeme waited until Nanse had said she'd pass the message on, and then he thanked her.

All this time he had been holding onto Lily's hand, but now he let it go. 'And ye're to bide indoors,' he said to Lily. 'What ye did was brave, and I am grateful that ye did it, but some days it is difficult to do the work I must do and protect those I most care about at the same time. That's why I sent

Jamie to Perth, ye ken? So promise me ye'll bide here till the streets are safe.'

He'd just said he cared for her. Lily said solemnly, 'I promise.'

'Good lass.' He moved to the door.

'Captain Graeme?'

'Aye?'

Lily was thinking of what he had said to her earlier, about how some people weren't all they seemed; how the people you most trusted oft let you down, and she suddenly needed to make sure he knew *she* knew he wasn't one of those people. That he knew she cared for him, too. She said, 'Ye've always had my trust. And ye would not disappoint me.'

His face, in the shifting of shadows and light from the fire on the hearth, showed her little response for a moment while he worked the reference back in his own mind. Then his eyes warmed.

The captain brushed Lily's hair back from her forehead and, bending, kissed her exactly where her father always had kissed her to sweeten her dreams. Quietly he told her, 'God grant I never will.'

And then he stepped through the door and was gone, and the room all at once seemed cold and empty.

CHAPTER TWELVE

THURSDAY, 4 FEBRUARY, 1686

WHEN LILY WENT TO clear breakfast three days later, Mr Bell was at the table alone.

He looked up as she entered the room. 'Lily, give me your counsel.'

'Sir?'

'If you were me, and your wayward apprentice were held in the Tolbooth of Edinburgh under suspicion of being involved in the tumult of Monday night, would you allow him to stay in that prison? Or would you arrange for his bond so that he may be free while awaiting his trial?'

Lily cautiously set down her tray on the table and started to load it with dishes. 'I'd do what I could, sir, to help him. He did nothing wrong.'

'So he says. So you say,' he granted, for Lily had told him what she'd overheard Monday morning. 'But others would claim he took part in the violence.' And the second night had been worse than the first.

Lily said, 'They were probably angry with him for refusing

to join them, and angrier still they've been caught, and they wish their revenge.'

'Fair enough.' Mr Bell stood, and carried his cup to her. 'So you would have me risk fifty pounds Scots on my faith in a lad who may well not deserve it.'

'He does.' Lily looked at him earnestly. 'I'd tell the magistrates so, but I'm too young to swear an oath.'

Mr Bell's eyes softened as he looked down at her uplifted features. 'And I'm an old fool.'

That surprised her. 'Ye're not old.'

The smile lines around his eyes deepened. 'No?'

'No. Ye are . . .' Lily searched hard for a word that would suit him. 'Distinguished.'

'I shall have my wife lend you her spectacles,' he said. But he looked pleased. 'All right, then, since you are so excellent a witness I shall trust you, Lily, and unlike the magistrates I will not take your age into account. How old are you, exactly?'

'I'll be ten on Saturday.'

'This Saturday? The sixth?' His eyebrows lifted when she told him it was so. 'That is a most important birthday, ten years old, for when you've passed it you will no more be a child but a young lady. No, your magistrates themselves would tell you this is true,' he reassured her scepticism. 'Therefore we must celebrate it in a special way.'

Behind them, from the doorway, Marion asked, 'Celebrate what?'

Lily said, 'I am having a birthday, and—'

'We could go skating!' Excitedly, Marion told Mr Bell, 'We have all those skates you made the year before last, and we've not used them once yet this winter, and it has been ages since we've been to Duddingston. Lily, have you ever been? There, you see? We must take her to Duddingston Loch!'

Lily wanted to go, but she tried to explain such a thing was impossible. 'Saturday I have a half day and Jean is expecting me home and my sister will not soon forgive me,' she said, 'if I don't spend my birthday with them.'

Marion posed the solution. 'We'll bring them along with us. Couldn't we, Father?'

Mr Bell looked at both girls with indulgence. 'Of course we could. I'll speak to Corporal Morison. I'm off to find him now, in fact, to see if he'll be witness to a bond for my apprentice, who I'm told did nothing wrong.'

And with a smile and wink at Lily, he went out.

⁓

The day began brightly enough.

It was difficult to fathom that their hired coach could carry them to Duddingston in no more than an hour. It seemed so distant from the town, though Lily only had to gaze up at the high crags rising as a backdrop in their winter shades of mottled green and gold and grey beneath a cobweb cloak of snow, to realize those belonged to Arthur's Seat, which lay within the royal park of Holyrood. Were she to climb it and go down the other side, she'd find the palace and the Abbey Church still standing at the bottom of the Canongate. Another world.

But here, beneath a sky that held few clouds, the sunlight struck the ice upon the frozen surface of the loch and made it sparkle, while around the shore the frost grew thickly on the trees and banks and, catching that same light, turned all to diamonds.

Down the whole length of the loch were countless people skating round and standing still, in groups and pairs and singly, with the rasping of blades carving ice a constant sound beneath the play of cheerful talk and laughter.

Overlooking them, besides the looming hill of Arthur's Seat, there was an old square-towered church, and the thatched roofs of a cluster of small houses Lily took to be the village.

And of course, there were the swans.

Marion told her that when summer came they ruled the loch and sailed its water with their cygnets in regal procession, but the ice had stolen most of their domain now so their kingdom for the winter months was limited to where the ice lay thin enough that they could break a path through with the power of their breasts and keep the water open so that they could feed. They'd opened a small pond of sorts close by the shoreline near the church, and Lily counted five swans swimming tightly pressed together.

Bessie saw them, too. The instant Jean set Bessie down, the little girl became a blur of motion, running straight towards those swans.

A second blur followed her, nearly as fast. Corporal Morison. 'Bessie!'

But the little girl had already gone several steps onto the ice before she heard his voice and turned. Where she stood, the ice would not have borne the corporal's weight. Taking up a tree branch that had fallen near the shore, he edged towards her on his knees and held it out.

Lily, who'd been chasing close behind him, saw the worry on his face but he was careful not to let it touch his voice as he said calmly, 'Lie down, Bessie, on your belly. That's my lass. Now, pull yourself towards me. Come and take a hold of this, and I'll give ye a ride. Aye, that's the way.'

When Bessie grasped the branch, the corporal pulled hard and she slid to him across the ice, away from where the swans were floating on the open water.

Bessie's giggle was a joyous sound. 'I slided!'

'Aye.' The corporal let his breath out in relief. He dropped the branch, and with one arm he swept the small girl up and, holding her securely, took her back to where Jean waited for them, Lily walking alongside.

'Now,' he said, and settled Bessie in the little sledge they'd brought, with wee James bundled on her lap in blankets, 'this is where ye stay while we are on the loch, ye hear? I'll not be losing either one of ye.'

Jean looked at him with meaning, and he caught himself and turned to Lily with a smile. 'Nor ye,' he added.

But the words were said, and she had heard and understood them, and the morning that had started off so brightly had been dulled by them. A slap would have been easier to bear, somehow, than being made an afterthought.

For it was clear to Lily that was what she had become to Jean, the corporal, and her sister and her brother. It was not that they no longer loved her – not so cold as that – but they had formed a family of their own without her, and because she did not share their house and daily lives she had been half-forgotten.

Wee James scarcely knew her, he was not yet a year old,

and Bessie seemed now so besotted with the corporal that she reached for his hand first and not for Lily's as she used to do. And as for Jean, it suited her so well to be a wife again with all the comforts of a home and loving husband Lily could not help but wish her happiness, but even so, to see the four of them together on the loch and laughing, making a new circle that was closed to her and private, caught sharply at her ribcage with a sudden twist of pain.

She bent to tie her skates onto her shoes, being careful of the long, upturned blades, and instantly Marion was there, helping, making sure they were well fastened at her heels and toes, and taking both her hands to guide her first uncertain steps onto the ice.

'No, you glide, like this.' Marion showed her, and Lily tried, feeling off balance and awkward and ready to fall.

After several excruciating minutes of this, Marion's parents came skating past arm in arm in perfect rhythm, and circling round them came back and divided so Mrs Bell at one end took hold of Marion's free hand, and Mr Bell took hold of Lily's free hand at the other, and making a chain of four people across they went skating at speed, pulling Lily along with them, Mr Bell's hand holding strongly to hers so she was not afraid.

It felt like flying.

'See your cheeks!' Jean told her after midday, with a smile. 'They're glowing.'

They were standing near the shore again and Lily thought it possible she might indeed be glowing, for she felt free and alive inside, as one could only feel after long hours of play outside in the fresh, bracing air of winter.

Jean touched her hand to Lily's cheek as though she would draw warmth from it, and glanced behind to where the corporal was already gathering the younger children from the sledge. They could not stay. The corporal had to go on duty soon.

When Jean withdrew her hand, the breeze struck cold. She looked at Lily closely. 'Ye're not sad?'

At Lily's shoulder, Mr Bell replied, 'We'll not allow her to be sad. Don't worry, Mrs Morison, we'll see she has a birthday to remember.'

It was that already, Lily thought, and yet there was still more to come.

With skating done, they climbed the bank and walked the little distance to a large and ancient inn within the village, where they had their dinner – Mr Bell and Mrs Bell and Marion and Lily sitting all together as if they were of one family, and the landlord serving Lily as though she deserved that honour, when in truth it was her daily custom to be in his place, bringing full plates and clearing empty ones away.

The men who sat beside them at the table were a jovial group. The landlord seemed to know them well. Before he served their food he brought to show them, with great ceremony, an elaborate snuff box set into a ram's head trimmed with silver and with jewelled eyes, that a former king had gifted to a former landlord many years ago.

The men did drink a toast to it, and to that king's health and their own, and this led them to talk of the days when King James had come to live a few years since at Holyrood, when he was still the Duke of York and Albany, sent north to manage government affairs.

'I'd never speak ill of our late king,' said one of the men, 'but King James is more a Scotsman than his brother ever was. And he's by far a better athlete. I did see him more than once myself at play at games of curling, right here on this loch.'

'He was more often at Leith Links,' another said, with a quick nod towards a window in the opposite direction to the loch. 'He much preferred the golf.'

A third man countered, 'He preferred Leith Links because it brought him closer by the sea. The king does like his ships.'

Lily could understand the way the king felt. Ships were always on their way to somewhere interesting. Besides, the king had served for years as Lord High Admiral of the navy, so it would be natural for him to favour waves and sails and sky and open shorelines over lochs that, although lovely, held him inland and confined.

With dinner done, there was one more surprise awaiting her when Mr Bell announced, 'It will be dark soon. Shall we take a room, and stay the night?'

Lily had only once before stayed at an inn, when she was coming from Inchbrakie, and she'd been too tired then to have much memory of it, but she knew it had not been like this. The beds had not been soft with feathers, nor the bedsteads finely panelled. There had been no windows over-looking the inn's courtyard where the clopping horses came and went between the side lane and the stables.

Marion and Lily pressed their faces to the window for a while and watched those horses, and they waved to Mr Bell when he passed by below them on his way to take an evening walk around the village before sleeping.

But soon sleep was tugging at them, too, and following the

lead of Mrs Bell they climbed into their own bed in the chamber and, as she had done, drew their bed-hangings round to block the draughts, and that was all that Lily knew until she was awakened by a light touch on her shoulder.

It was dark, save for the moonlight slanting through the window-glass in patterned squares upon the floor, but Mr Bell whispered her name so she'd know it was only him and she should not be afraid. 'I need you to come light me down to the stables.'

Half-wakened, she struggled to sit, trying not to wake Marion. 'I will get dressed.'

'There is no need.' He held her plaid and hood in one hand. 'With these, you'll be warm enough. There will be none to see you in the stables, and we'll not be long.'

She'd kept her stockings on in bed beneath her shift for it was cold, and she was glad of that as she fastened on her shoes and wrapped the plaid warmly around her and tied on her blue hood and followed him.

Outside their chamber in the passage on a hook there hung a candle lantern like the one the robber boy had carried that night in the kitchen, a dark lantern with its metal door full open to let out the light, and a curved handle set into its side so that it could be carried. Mr Bell removed it from the hook and handed it to Lily, and she walked beside him, lighting his way through the inn and out into the courtyard, where he spoke more freely, though his tone stayed hushed.

'I do believe I dropped my shop keys,' he said, 'in the stables, and I will not sleep unless I find them.'

Lily helped him look. The horses lifted lazy heads above their stalls and watched while Mr Bell, with Lily holding up the lantern for him, made a study of the stable floor until he reached a wooden bench and told her, 'Set your lantern down a moment. Let us rest. It's cold.'

He sat, and she sat next to him, and with one arm he drew her close as though to keep her warm, but his hand did not seek her shoulder. It went lower, underneath her plaid, and firmly cupped the small curve of her breast beneath her shift.

She froze in shock, and fear.

Without a word he turned to her and pressed his mouth to hers, lips moist against her own, tongue seeking entry.

Lily could not move.

He raised his head and smiled. 'My bonny Lily, with your bonny hood that makes your eyes so blue. I will be gentle. I—'

But he was interrupted by the clatter of a horse's hooves against the cobbles of the courtyard, and before Lily could fathom what was happening, he'd set her on her feet again and he was standing at her side, respectably.

The man who rode into the stables greeted him as if they were good friends of long acquaintance. 'I did not expect to find you here,' the stranger said, 'but we must wake the landlord, if he is not yet awake, and have him bring us wine and bread, for I have been too long over the water and have many tales to tell.'

'My lass will light us back,' said Mr Bell, and Lily in a kind of stupor took the lantern in her hand again and did so, and when they had reached the inn's door Mr Bell took up her other hand and pressed a coin into her palm and said, 'Now, run back up to bed', and left her standing in the entry.

∾

She did not go back to bed.

She did not afterwards remember how she made her way down to the loch, but there she was, the lantern in her hand and in her other hand the coin that Mr Bell had paid her, feeling now so warm against her skin she thought for certain it would burn her.

Jean said whores took money from a man for giving pleasure to him, and that it was wrong, and they were wicked.

'I'd chase her to the gutter where she does belong, and she could take her fancy clothes and false smiles there to try to turn men's heads,' so Jean had said, and Lily thought of Mr Bell and how he liked her velvet hood, and how he had remarked on it so many times, and how she'd often smiled at him, and how he must have somehow taken all that as an invitation to do what he did. Because why else would he have done it, unless somehow she'd invited him? Unless she were a whore?

The coin – she did not know what kind of coin it was – burned hotter still within her hand, and in a sudden movement Lily threw it out across the ice. The small, metallic clatter raised a movement to her left.

The swans.

They huddled ghostly pale on their unfrozen strip of water not far out from shore. Except one swan had ventured further from the rest, and stealthily the night had closed new ice around it, holding it in place so it could not rejoin the others.

She did not remember setting down the lantern, but she must have done, because it was no longer in her hands. The moonlight was enough to see by, and it showed in front of her the branch that Corporal Morison had used to rescue Bessie, so she picked that up instead and dragged it after her as, keeping low upon the ice, she drew herself across to where the single swan was trapped.

The other swans moved to the further limit of the narrow pool they'd managed to keep open, their reflections all the warning Lily had of where the ice gave way to the black water till her own hand touched the edge by accident and felt a rush of wet that chilled her fingers as the ice depressed beneath her touch.

In haste she snatched her hand back. Pulling off her hood, she dried her fingers before they could freeze, then kept the velvet wrapped around them for protection as she took the branch and struck a blow against the ice that held the swan a prisoner.

By daylight, with her thoughts intact, her life and hopes and dreams intact, she might not have attempted it. She might not have been brave.

But at that moment, nothing mattered more to Lily than to free that one swan.

Cracks were forming on the ice now all around her, yet she did not stop but went on striking with the branch, and all the while the swan observed her with a sideways eye but fearlessly, as if it somehow knew she meant no harm.

The hood had fallen from her hand. She did not care. One final blow, and Lily felt at last a great piece of the ice dislodge and drift away.

'There now,' she told the swan. 'Ye can go home.'

But where was she to go? Not to the inn, where Mr Bell

was surely waiting for her. Nor to the Bells' house in the Canongate, where she would further fall into a life of sin and shame.

And never, ever home again. She would no more be welcome. 'Whores don't want for company,' so Jean had told the corporal, 'but they can't have mine.'

She left the branch upon the ice, and left the lantern on the shore, and climbed the bank and found herself upon the road and walking past the church without a thought of where she might be going.

At the crossroads, as she stood and huddled in her plaid, she heard the voice of Anna Moray telling her the story of the great Montrose: *When all seemed black and lost, he did outwit them. He went north, and found a vessel on the coast to carry him to Norway . . .*

She remembered that at dinner, when the man beside them had been speaking of King James and the Leith Links, he'd nodded in the opposite direction to the loch, so Lily turned in that direction now, and started walking.

Leith was to the north, and on the coast, and there were ships at Leith, and she could go to Norway like Montrose. Except she'd not make his mistake, once she was gone from here and safe.

She never would come back.

IV

Y OU MUST FORGIVE ME if I do not share with you all of
  my thoughts as I stood in the Bells' kitchen that evening,
but remembering the trick of Robin Moray I did keep the
window to my back – the same small window that a thieving lad had climbed through long ago – and let the fading
light do what it could to mask my own reactions to what I
was hearing.

It wasn't all Marion's story to tell.

Some of the parts that weren't hers I learned afterwards,
and some were told me by Lily, and some I did not need to
be told at all – I could see with my own eyes the lock on her
door, and the dog at her side, and the way she had dealt with
her father, and judge for myself what might lie at the back of
such caution.

I knew, as the tale was unfolding, that it had not been an
apprentice who'd ruined the young lass who'd served in that
house before Lily, but then in my life I had known men like
Mr Bell – men who displayed a respectable face to the world
while they preyed on the vulnerable.

Such men were masters of concealment. Carefully selecting those most lonely and in want of love, they set about with patience, stealth, and flattery to win their trust. And then betrayed it.

Rarely were these men suspected, even by their families. They strode freely through all levels of society, emboldened by the knowledge those they injured would stay silent out of shame.

I saw that shame pass over Marion's face.

'When we woke next morning and Lily was not in the chamber with us at the inn, there was a search,' said Marion. 'They found the lantern by the loch, and found her hood beside the broken ice. We thought ... that is, my father said he'd found her sad and walking in the courtyard, pining for her father, and he'd sent her back to bed.'

'And they believed him.'

'Yes, of course. Although I do not think that Captain Graeme did. He argued with my father, and he never gave him custom, after that.'

I wondered whether Captain Graeme guessed the truth, or whether he but felt himself responsible for leaving Lily here so unprotected.

I asked Marion, 'And what did you believe?'

She looked away. 'At first, I could not think it possible. She'd seemed content here. But the summer after that, my mother died ...' A moment's pause. 'I learned then Lily might have had a cause to be unhappy in this house.' She gathered herself bravely and said, 'Still, I did not like to think she would have taken her own life.' And then, remembering, she turned to me. 'But now you tell me she did not.'

The way she said those words will always live with me. I hear them still. I hear their hopefulness.

It is no small thing, hope. Without it, darkness wins. My mother used to set me on my feet again and tell me, 'Were it not for hope, the heart would break,' and she was right. Sometimes, when all seems darkness and despair, hope is the only thing that does remain for us to grasp – a tree branch beating at the ice within a child's hand.

And so we make an opening, and day by day press forward, and we hold that hope.

And therein lies its power.

CHAPTER THIRTEEN

WEDNESDAY, 24 SEPTEMBER, 1707

THE CROSS KEYS HAD for so long stood in one place on the south side of the High Street that its close was called 'Steell's Close' after its landlord, Patrick Steell – a man who seemed as solid and unchanging as the tavern that he kept. He loved good company, good conversation and good music, and would often lead the song himself in hearty voice. He'd placed his tavern well to draw a crowd. The market cross stood all but at his doorstep, and St Giles' Church was his near neighbour, and behind that stood the lofty house of parliament, which would have gone on bringing great men daily past his door had not the Union ended our Scots government in May. In spite of that, so many politicians were his regulars that some would call the Cross Keys 'Pat Steell's Parliament', and from the sounds that spilled onto the darkened street as I drew near the gilded sign this evening, it did seem that parliament was in full session.

In the play of light outside the entry, it was easy to imagine phantoms of another age – a small lass wrapped within her plaid against the cold, her face upturned in earnest conversation with the captain of the old town guard.

I passed them by, and went inside.

Gilroy was waiting for me at a table in the further corner. He was not alone.

The man who sat beside him, of an age to be my father, had a sharply featured face that made a contrast to his friendly manner.

Gilroy made the introductions and said dryly, 'Dr Pitcairn is certain I'm holding some secret and thinks that this claret will loosen my tongue.'

The older man promised, 'It is an exceptional claret.' He called for another pint, and filled a cup for me. 'At least in here we still have our Scots measurements, although the terms of Union soon will take those, too, to please the English. Fools. It takes three English pints to fill a Scots one. The commissioners would do much better to increase the size of English pints than to shrink ours.'

I did not know how long they had been sitting here, but Scots pints notwithstanding, Gilroy seemed to be resisting all attempts to make him drunk. He sat casually, but kept the same expression that he always held.

In level tones he told the doctor, 'Even if I had a secret, I would hardly tell you here. These walls have ears.'

'And all of them connected to His Grace, the Duke of Hamilton. I do agree. But surely, since he is the leader of our side, he would already know the details of the planned invasion, so to him it would not be a secret, therefore you may freely tell me what you know.' Having thus set down his train of logic, Dr Pitcairn settled back and helped himself to bread and cheese from the broad platter set between us.

Gilroy's glance had touched me when the doctor spoke the word 'invasion', but there'd have been no reaction on my face for him to see. I reasoned Dr Pitcairn was referring to the same Jacobite plot I'd heard discussed at dinner earlier today at Lord Seafield's table – a proposed invasion that would bring their young James Stewart, living in his shadow court in exile outside Paris, back to Scotland in an effort to reclaim his throne. I also reasoned that the doctor, and most likely Gilroy, too, were Jacobites, from this exchange.

But it was not my business. Merely something to take note of, nothing more.

I drank my wine. The claret was, in truth, exceptional.

The doctor smiled at Gilroy's stubborn silence. 'I should hope, at least, Lord Grange will stand on the right side of the occasion when the moment comes. He is not like his brother, who stands always where the wind will blow most fair.'

'I do not know the mind of either man,' said Gilroy, 'for I am not paid to know their thoughts.'

'No, just to do their bidding, which I see does keep you far too busy still to take a wife.'

The roll of Gilroy's eyes was almost imperceptible, and yet it made me like him better.

'Not too late, you know,' the doctor told him. 'I was rising five and thirty when my eldest son was born, and even after my first wife died, rest her soul, I found a second wife and went on having children. Men weren't made to live alone.'

We were hardly alone in here, with other men all round us deep in their own drink and conversations, and a haze of pipe smoke hanging in the air. But Gilroy was not answering, and since I had learned something just last night that seemed to suit the talk at hand, I ventured, 'It was Plato, was it not, who said we were created whole then sliced in half like flatfish, and must ever search the world to find our matching half?'

The doctor's face transformed with joy. 'A learned man!' He filled my wine cup. 'See you, Gilroy, here is a romantic soul who speaks of the *Symposium* and seeks his one true love. I shall revive my hopes for you, if you do keep such friends. Come, sirs, a toast to you, and to your matching halves.'

We drank, and Dr Pitcairn's gaze fell on the parcel I had set down at my side, and correctly guessing I had bought a blade of some kind, he enquired if he might see it, so I took the whinger from its wrapping of buff leather and both he and Gilroy looked it over and remarked upon the workmanship.

'The motto is a good one,' said the doctor. 'Very fitting for these times.'

I did not own I could not read the words in Latin. Though I agreed with Helen Turnbull that a man's worth was not measured by his education, I keenly felt the lack of mine and did not like to put that disadvantage on display. Instead I nodded and the doctor slid the blade into its scabbard and returned it to me.

'You'll need it soon enough. And we will need all Scotsmen of good heart to stand together,' he said, 'when the king comes home.'

Having seen someone across the room, he clapped a hand upon my shoulder, gave a nod and wink to Gilroy, took his cup in hand, and went to join another table.

Gilroy met my eyes by way of an apology. 'The doctor is a man of forceful character, who should be more discreet about his politics.'

I broke a piece of bread and shrugged to show I was not bothered. 'He did seem to think that he was in safe company.'

'He is. This is the tavern of the party of the Duke of Hamilton, and half in here are his supporters or his spies. That table there, just by the wall, is where you'll often find the duke himself, when he is here in town in residence at Holyrood. The greatest man in all of Scotland, some will tell you, and it's widely rumoured he does keep a correspondence with the young King James in France and that, should an invasion come, he'd be the first to rise. Of course,' he said, 'it's also rumoured that he seeks the crown himself, because his family by descent can claim it and he thinks his being Protestant would make him more appealing to the people than young James, and to that end he would do all he could to see that an invasion does *not* happen.'

Dr Pitcairn's claret might have had a loosening effect on Gilroy's tongue for all that, since I'd never known him to be so free in his speech.

I looked at him. 'And which rumour is true?'

He shrugged in turn. 'I could not tell you. I'm not paid to know the truth of what I hear.'

'I understood that you were being paid to do exactly that, for our inquiry.'

I had nearly made him smile, but he resisted it. 'That minds me,' he said, taking papers from his pocket and unfolding them between us on the table. 'Let me show you what I learned today at Leith.'

'You're sure you wish to do this here? I thought you said the walls have ears.'

His glance was withering. 'I doubt the Duke of Hamilton will much concern himself with proof of Mrs Graeme's marriage.'

The topmost page was filled from edge to edge with pencilled handwriting, and so I filled my cup again with wine in preparation for the details that would come.

Gilroy began. 'On the certificate, the two witnesses we have are Walter Browne and Barbara Malcolm. When I wrote the first time to the clerk of session for the parish of South Leith, he searched and sent me proof that both were dead. Today I was allowed to search the records for myself, and while I found no more for Barbara Malcolm, in the record of the death for Walter Browne it said he'd died when in his twenty-seventh year and was the son of Archibald, a local notary, so I began there. Twenty-seven years before his death, I found only three lads baptized by the name of Walter. And of those three there was but one,' he said, 'whose sponsor was Archibald Browne. But the child was a foundling. Not Archibald's son, but the son of a woman unknown who had left him exposed in the churchyard.'

I could not help but step in to defend the dead man's honour. 'How is that important? Walter Browne could hardly choose his form of birth, and being born a foundling surely does not make him an invalid witness to the marriage?'

Gilroy granted it did not. 'But there is something larger here that I may have uncovered. In the register of births, there were four foundlings baptized in the space of four years, all lads, all sponsored by this same Archibald Browne.

The clerk of session could not tell me anything about them, since these records dated from the time before the Revolution, when the church was still Episcopalian, so I bid him good day and went to have a conversation with the stabler in the Kirkgate.'

I was unprepared for that. 'The stabler?'

'Aye. He is an old man with a keen, observant eye.'

'And how did you gain his acquaintance?'

Gilroy drank long, and studied me above his cup as though deciding how much of himself to open to my scrutiny. 'My father kept the stables of a rich man who would enter every year a horse or two to run at Leith. I came each spring to help my father and to watch the races, as a lad. It gained me many such acquaintances.' With that established, he went on, 'The stabler did remember when those foundling lads were given to the notary to raise. He also said the minister at South Leith Church in those days was the Reverend Mr Cant. You may remember him.'

'The Mr Cant that Mrs Graeme told us of? The one who bought her kitten?'

'Aye, the very same. They transferred him from Leith up here to Trinity when she was still a bairn, but I do doubt she would have known that. She'd have still been at Inchbrakie then.'

He slid the paper to me with the dates and names, on which I saw the last of the four foundling lads, named Henry Browne, was baptized thirty years ago.

'There were only four,' he said. 'The stabler said that Mr Cant would let no more bairns go to Browne beyond that, and when Mr Cant was transferred out, he did warn the new minister to watch over the lads who were already in Browne's house and see they went to church each Sabbath. I was told that Mr Cant, who was a kindly man, had started having doubts about the morals of the notary.'

I did not ask what sort of doubts, because I knew he'd tell me, and he did.

'There was a woman in the house. That's why Browne was allowed to take the foundlings in the first place, because he did have a wife who was respectable, but I'm told by the stabler that she was in truth a high-class whore for men who knew the proper door to knock upon and who had coin to pay.' He raised his cup and looked at me with steady eyes. 'Her name was Barbara Malcolm.'

I considered this in silence for a moment.

Gilroy said, 'Do not you find it odd that both of Mrs Graeme's witnesses should be from the same house, and that a house of ill repute, and she should not see fit to mention this?'

'We only have the stabler's word it was a house of ill repute,' I pointed out.

'I trust the stabler.'

I could hear the undertone within his voice, and take its meaning. 'And you don't trust Mrs Graeme.'

Gilroy was, if nothing else, the sort of man who did not meet you sideways, but straight on. 'Greed does peculiar things to people. Since the advertisement was first posted for the heirs of those who perished in the service of the Company of Scotland to come forward and claim their share of their loved ones' wages out of the Equivalent, there have been some who have stepped forward falsely, to claim money that does not belong to them.'

My blood rose sharply in reply to that smooth insult but I kept my voice calm as I told him, 'She does stand to gain a little more than fifteen pounds, which is no fortune. And we have established that she is who she does claim to be. She did not lie to us about her friendships with the Morays and the Graemes.'

'Fraud is fraud. And being truthful in some things does not make someone altogether trustworthy.' He took his papers up, although he had not yet shared all their contents, and refolded them into his pocket. 'I find it suggestive that she did not tell us Walter's brother, Henry Browne, still lives in Leith. I think that you and I should go and visit him tomorrow morning. See what he can tell us about Mrs Graeme and her . . . marriage.'

Gilroy's gaze was challenging.

I told him, 'Fine.'

We'd nearly reached the bottom of our jug of claret. As I tipped more out into my cup, I noticed Gilroy looking at the new-bought blade beside me.

'Where did you buy that?' he asked.

I could have told him. Had I wanted to, I could have told him everything I'd learned of Lily's time within the Bell house, her struggles to adapt and settle through that less than settled time, and how she'd been betrayed and presumed drowned that day at Duddingston.

But none of that had any bearing whatsoever on our inquiry. It mattered not to him. *She* mattered not to him.

And so I only glanced towards the whinger and remarked, offhand, 'I bought it in the Canongate, on my way back from dinner at the Earl of Seafield's.'

'And what were you doing there?'

'He did invite me.' Pausing, I weighed how to best frame my words.

There were questions I wanted to ask that had troubled me since Robert Moray had first set me wondering why the committee had bothered itself at all with this inquiry instead of simply dismissing it for lack of evidence. Why, having made the choice to hold an inquiry, had they then passed it to Turnbull – to me – and not led it themselves? Why would the marriage of two ordinary people be of interest to two great men like the Earl of Seafield and Lord Grange? Had I been more sure of Gilroy I'd have talked about these questions with him, for they turned within my mind and I could find no answers.

But while I had no reason to think Gilroy was my enemy, the fact remained I did not know him. He was not my friend.

So in the end I took the middle ground. 'The Earl of Seafield knows of our inquiry.'

'Does he?'

'Aye. I thought it interesting,' I told him. 'When Lord Grange spoke of the matter he said only that it wanted some discretion, I expect since it involves a lady's honour. But the Earl of Seafield told another dinner guest our work was secret.' Looking straight across at Gilroy, I asked in an imitation of his own blunt manner, 'Why would he believe it to be secret?'

As we studied one another and I saw the workings of his mind, there was a fraction of a moment when I thought that he might answer – that the wine or something else had melted part of his reserve.

I was mistaken.

Gilroy said, 'I'm sure I couldn't tell you.'

Which, as answers went, left me completely in the dark.

❦

She kept a candle in her window.

I had marked which window was her own when Gilroy and I had returned her to her lodging after we had come from meeting Robert Moray – had it been but yesterday? It seemed much longer. But then, all the times were lately tumbling in my head and it was difficult to hold them in their place.

The claret, too, had done its work, for I could not have said how many minutes had gone by since I had parted ways with Gilroy at the Cross Keys, but the walk from there back up to Caldow's Land took me past Forrester's Wynd and I found myself standing now near to the wall at the head of the close, looking up at that one window.

The lanterns that hung in the High Street had all been put out now so they were as dark as the shadows that blanketed everything there in the close and concealed me. The only light I could see came from her candle.

Shining out into the darkness, it assured me I was not the only one awake at that hour, lonely with my thoughts. Had I the right, I would have climbed the stair and knocked upon her door. Instead I forced myself to turn my steps again towards the Landmarket.

And as I did so, something else came with me – a tall figure that detached itself in silence from the deeper shadows of the close, and kept a steady pace with me along the street behind.

I did not turn. It was enough that, from the corner of my eye, I'd glimpsed the outline of the man as he'd passed underneath her window, and his footsteps let me know I had him at my back.

But quietly I stripped the wrapping from the whinger I had bought and felt my fist, from instinct, tighten round the weapon's handle, as with even steps I strode the final distance up to Caldow's Land and climbed the curving forestair.

He did not attack me then.

He crossed the street as though that had been his intent the whole time, and passed by without a word, and melted once again into the darkness of the night. But it was some time before I relaxed my hold upon the hilt of my new blade.

Chapter Fourteen

Thursday, 25 September, 1707

I WORE THE WHINGER IN its scabbard at my side when I went down to Leith with Gilroy in the morning, riding one of the two horses we had hired to make the journey quicker. Gilroy rode well. I was not surprised, since by his own account he'd spent his life around the beasts. I kept behind him, and when we had reached Leith's Kirkgate, being not inclined to linger in the stables I dismounted and stood waiting for him just outside the door, my hat pulled low against the rising wind.

Leith had a different character to Edinburgh, although their histories were long intertwined and each depended on the other for its commerce. There was no equality between the towns, since Edinburgh held all the rights and used Leith as its warehouse and its gateway to the sea. The craftsmen of the Leith guilds paid outlandish dues to Edinburgh to keep their right to work, being considered 'unfree men', and that same lack of freedom showed when every year a magistrate from Edinburgh was sent to serve as judge and Baron Bailiff of the town, denying them a choice of government.

Leith was yet a vibrant place, where every day the offshore roads and harbour came alive with sails and hulls of ships from different lands, all bearing merchandise for trade. The long, broad Kirkgate where I stood was one of the main thoroughfares, as was the Shore – another road that ran along the length of the Leith Water by the harbour – and between the two there lay a tangle of connecting streets and wynds and closes filled with houses, shops, and manufactories.

I did not relish the idea of walking into any of them. Leithers were a breed of people who, resourceful to the core, asked little and thought less of their more privileged neighbours, and preferred to keep their own community.

It might not be so easy to get Henry Browne to speak to us.

Gilroy had clearly been thinking the same thing. Having seen our hired horses settled with his friend the stabler, he stepped out to join me in the Kirkgate, tugged his own hat lower, and said, 'I would recommend we take a new approach with Henry Browne.'

'In what way?'

His explanation was pure logic: if there was a fraud intended, and if Walter Browne had been involved, it stood to reason that the other Brownes might be untrustworthy. Asking Henry Browne if he knew Lily had been married to James Graeme would be of no use if he were going to lie. 'We ought to hold our cards with care and not reveal them,' Gilroy said. 'At least, when we begin. In fact, if you have no objections, I should like to ask the questions.'

Even if I'd had objections, I could tell that raising them would not have altered Gilroy's purpose. He was very single-minded.

I said, 'If you like.'

The house we sought was not far off, in Riddell's Close. It was a smaller house, only two floors with a garret above, shouldered in on either side by taller buildings and yet managing to hold its ground. A sign hung near the window read: 'A. Browne, Notary'.

I stood a little to one side as Gilroy knocked upon the door, to let him take the lead.

A voice within bade us be patient. There were dragging footsteps and a thumping sound as of a wooden stave or stick that old men use to help them walk, but when the door creaked open it did not reveal an older man but one a few years younger than myself, who plainly found it most uncomfortable to stand.

His mouth hardened to a tight line as he heavily leaned on the stave and took our measure. 'Aye?'

I'd never seen Gilroy discomfited, but he recovered briskly. 'Henry Browne?'

'That's right.'

'I'd like to ask some questions, if I may, about your brother.'

Henry Browne was a true Leither, through and through. He did not answer straight away, but looked suspiciously from Gilroy's face to mine and back again before he asked, 'Which one?'

Gilroy said, 'Walter.'

'Walter's dead.'

'I know he is, and my condolences. But he did sign a document we're trying to authenticate. We're hoping you can help us.'

I could see that he was going to close the door. I took

a chance, and moving forward said, 'It has to do with Lily Aitcheson.'

He looked at me directly then, and I could see him thinking. 'Best come in,' he said.

He brought us to the room in which the notary received his clients, first along the passage from the front door, with a window letting in what light it could from Riddell's Close and a small hearth that kept things tolerably warm. Two walls were hidden behind cabinets filled with papers and old books, and set against the wall that faced the window was a writing table bearing pens and jars of ink and quairs of paper waiting to be used.

But there were also three good chairs, with broad cane seats and backs, and cushions over those to make them all more comfortable for sitting. One had arms, and Henry Browne chose that, a footstool placed before him to support his left leg as he propped his stave against the hearth and faced us.

Gilroy did not waste his time, but introduced himself and me and took the seat next to the writing table, where he set down his files. 'Would your father mind, do you think, if I were to use one of his pens?'

'He rarely comes by these days,' Henry said. 'I doubt he'd notice. Please yourself.'

His tone was offhand but there was a nervous edge beneath it and I sought to put him at his ease.

I asked, 'You live alone?'

'I take in lodgers, Sergeant Williamson.' No nervousness, but now a different kind of edge. 'And what has that to do with Lily Aitcheson?'

Gilroy resumed control. 'How old was she when she first came to live here?'

I could not have said who was the more surprised – myself or Henry, for we turned to Gilroy at nearly the same time.

He asked Henry, 'Was she a child? Or a young woman?'

'How's it your business?'

'We're trying to help her claim some money,' Gilroy said. 'To do that, we must prove the document she carries is authentic. One of those who signed their name upon that paper as a witness was your brother, Walter, which is why we've come to you. The other was a woman by the name of Barbara Malcolm.' I was watching Henry and I saw how he reacted to that name – not in his face, but by the way his fingers curled to a half fist against his leg. Self-consciously, as though aware that I had noticed, he glanced over at me and relaxed his hand again as Gilroy carried on, 'If you can help us to establish that she knew them, it may well advance her claim.'

Gilroy was lying. He was doing it as expertly and well as he rode horses, and for me it was a revelation to sit there and watch him, and to know that this was how his face appeared when he was twisting truth. Completely calm.

I could not know his mind completely, but I knew that he distrusted Lily, and I gathered he was seeking to learn more about her life within this 'house of ill repute', as he so called it – not to help her, but to help discredit her.

And Henry Browne, God help him, was about to take the bait.

I couldn't warn him, not in words. I'd promised Gilroy I would let him take the lead. Besides, there was a part of me that, having heard the start of Lily's story, wished to have it now continued.

But the wind that struck the window-glass and made it rattle as a coal fell in the fire seemed to set the mood, uneasily, as Henry looked down in the way men do when they're remembering.

And in a voice that, for the first time, held no trace of anger, said, 'She came to us the winter she turned ten.'

Chapter Fifteen

Sunday, 7 February, 1686

THERE LAY THE SHIPS upon the water, their reflections scattering beneath the waning moon, with lanterns hanging from their prows like shining beacons, and yet Lily could not see a way to reach them. She stood shivering upon the Shore of Leith while the sharp wind cut through her stockings and her shift beneath the thin folds of her plaid.

It was still dark. She did not know the hour, nor when it would be dawn. She only knew she had been walking a long time – at first with only fields around her, then with houses closing in, and streets, and following those she had found herself here, at the harbour's edge, where she could see the means of her escape so near, yet out of reach.

Exhausted, Lily sank down on the cold stones of the Shore – the road that ran along the waterline. One light had broken off from all the others in the harbour and with dulled eyes she watched it draw nearer, focused on its swaying and the steady sound of splashing oars that soothed her towards sleep.

Then came the voices. A woman's voice, gentle and kind. 'It's a lass.'

And a man. 'Barbara—'

'Poor wee soul.'

'Captain said I was to see ye got safely home.'

'Then ye'd best carry her for me,' the woman replied, 'for I'll not leave her here.'

Lily could not tell if she were dreaming or awake and since her limbs were halfway frozen she did not resist when she felt herself being lifted.

When her eyes came open she was lying in a bed, and there was daylight coming through a little window close beside her, and across the room there was a woman seated at a table, neatly fixing pins into her hair before an oval looking glass.

The angle of the looking glass allowed a half view of the woman's face, and Lily saw that she was beautiful. She had fine eyebrows and clear skin the colour of fresh cream, and hair so deeply russet red it seemed to glow against the brown cloth of her gown. Her gaze met Lily's in the glass. She smiled, and with the final curl arranged and pinned, she turned and stood and crossed to Lily's bedside. 'Ye've wakened. I am glad.' She smoothed the hair from Lily's face and let her hand lie searchingly on Lily's forehead as though feeling for the signs of fever. Finding none, she drew her hand back and said, 'I am Barbara. What's your name?'

The woman's eyes were brown and lovely, like her gown. And kind. So Lily told her. 'Lily Aitcheson.'

'It is a nice name, Lily. Are ye lost? Where are your minnie and your daddie?'

Lily felt her eyes flood hot with tears. 'My daddie's dead.' She turned her face away against the pillow. 'And my mother, too. I've only Jean, and she won't have me back now because

I'm ...' She could not finish, and the silence that came after was so long that Lily screwed her eyes tight shut, fearing what judgement was to come.

But all that came was one more touch of Barbara's hand upon her forehead, just as gentle as before. 'Well, *I* will have ye.'

Slowly, Lily brought her head around again, eyes opening, not ready to believe yet. 'Truly?'

'Truly. Ye are welcome here. Can ye keep house?'

Lily bit her lip and nodded.

Barbara told her, 'Good, for I've no skill at it, and all my lads will tell ye so.' She smiled. 'Now, let us find ye clean linen, so ye can get washed.'

There was a small adjoining chamber made to be used as a closet, with a washbasin and ewer and the necessary chair. In one corner on the floor there sat a larger basin draped with linens. Bringing heated water in two buckets from the downstairs kitchen, Barbara first had Lily stand within the larger basin in her shift and washed her hair with soap that smelt of roses, then she rinsed it clean and wrapped it in a towel, leaving her in privacy to do the rest.

Lily had never bathed this way before. She did it rapidly, finding the sensation strange, to be naked and standing in a pool of bathwater, her skin warm where she was scrubbing or sluicing and chilled where she wasn't. But when she was done and she'd dried with a clean towel and slipped on the new shift Barbara had laid out for her, she felt almost reborn.

The shift reached to the floor but Barbara rolled it up and pinned it for her. From the chest beneath the window in the larger chamber Barbara lifted out a petticoat and bodice in a sturdy calico with stripes of chestnut brown and ivory. Both looked small enough for Lily.

Barbara said, 'These were mine, when I was small. I kept them in case ... Well, they've been in that box twenty years, so they're long out of fashion, but I have a friend who's fair skilled with her needle and can work them over so that none will notice.'

There were stays as well, and a pair of new stockings still tied with a ribbon. Once her hair was combed and covered by a pinner, Lily could face her reflection in the oval mirror and feel happiness at last begin to rise above the shame.

'There, now,' said Barbara. 'Ye will do.'

Downstairs, a door banged, followed by a thumping rush of footsteps and a tangle of boys' voices, with a man's voice over all, attempting to keep order.

Barbara's gaze again met Lily's in the mirror. '*That* will be my family, back from church, for all the good it did them. Let's go down and introduce ye.'

❧

Henry was the easiest of all the lads to like. Simon, the eldest, who was nearly twelve, was prone to moods and sulks which made him difficult to know, and Walter, although he was Lily's age, shared none of Lily's interests. Henry, though, while he was only nine, was always game for anything, and had a cheerful nature.

It was Henry who had set her straight about the family.

'Archie's not our daddie,' he said, grinning at the thought. 'Well, in a way he is, but not our real one. If ye count the months, ye'll see there's no way we could be true brothers. We were born too close together. We're all foundlings. Archie got us from the church when we were bairns, and every year the elders give him money so he'll keep us. Leastways, that's what Walter says, and Walter kens most things.'

Lily, having never met a foundling, asked why they were called that.

'No one wanted us when we were born, so they just left us at the church when nobody was looking, and the minister did find us there. When ye get found,' he said, 'ye are a foundling.'

That made sense. 'I'm an orphan.'

'Near enough. Ye'll fit right in with us,' he promised.

And she did, adjusting to the rhythm of this newer household as she learned about its people.

At its head was Archie Browne, a thin man who was quick to laugh and rarely raised his voice. He was a notary, a job that Lily only partly understood, but which involved his writing things for other people and sometimes accompanying them to the harbour to bear witness to things that were being done. It kept him very busy.

Then came Barbara, who most often went by her name – Barbara Malcolm – though she also went by Mrs Browne, as she was Archie's wife. One thing Lily had noticed: the lads all called Archie just that, nothing else, but they called Barbara 'Minnie' as though she were truly their mother.

And Barbara plainly adored them all back – even Simon, who shrugged off her hugs and seemed happiest sitting alone. Simon, often unreachable in his dark moods, was the brother that Lily found most unpredictable.

'Simon's all right,' Henry told her. 'He's good with his fists, but ye'll not see him use them much. He isn't Matthew.'

'Who's Matthew?'

She didn't receive a reply, because Henry pretended that he hadn't heard her – a tactic she'd learn he used often, as did they all.

But that was how Lily first found out there was a fourth brother.

She heard him mentioned from time to time, always as if it had slipped in by accident, always as quickly caught, always passed over uncomfortably. From the few pieces she *did* hear, it seemed he had run off not long ago, and that before he'd gone there'd been an argument, and that they hadn't heard anything from him since, so she did not press for details.

He'd been living in the house this past September, because that was the last month with dates marked in his copy book that sat beside those of his brothers on the shelf in Archie's office. Each boy had a copy book, and diligently, every day, they practised writing in those books with pen and ink as if they were at school.

Lily was not privy to those sessions, but she dusted Archie's office and had come across the copy books and seen the one with Matthew's name, unopened since last autumn. He had written with a flowing hand, and formed his letters finely. But to Lily it did seem a waste that he'd left half the copy book unfilled.

She longed to learn. Sometimes when cleaning Archie's office she wished she could take down the books and open them and read them, even those she knew she wouldn't understand. This was her favourite room in all the house. She loved the scents of ageing paper and old leather, and the way the writing table felt beneath her hands while she was dusting it – the smoothly worn imperfections of its wooden surface.

One day when she was putting everything in place again as Archie liked it, Lily let her fingers flutter through the quairs of paper, just to feel them.

From the doorway, Archie asked her, 'Would ye like to learn to write your name?'

She jumped a little at his voice, but Lily did not ever feel uncomfortable with Archie in the room. He always left the doors wide open and he always gave her space, and did not stand too close.

She told him, 'I can write already.'

'Can ye, now?' He was not doubtful, but encouraging. 'Come, show me.' And he chose a pen and inked it for her, setting out a sheet of paper.

Lily wrote her name as Anna and Emelia Moray had once taught her, with a flourish at the finish.

Archie said, 'That's very lovely, Lily. Where did ye learn how to do that?'

She did not wish to spoil this new, unblemished start in life by telling him too much about her former one, but she allowed, 'I used to serve a laird, and his granddaughters taught me how to read and write.'

'To read as well?'

'Aye, sir.'

'I'm not a sir, my dear. I'm only Archie.' He did not ask her to prove that she could read, but took her word, and after thinking for a moment asked, 'How would ye like to join the lads for lessons to improve your writing?'

Lily answered in a rush. 'Yes, please, sir.'

'Archie. Good. I'm sure we'll find an hour or two each day where ye're not doing chores.'

That night was the first time Lily overheard an argument between Barbara and Archie. It was not an argument such as her father had oft had with Jean. There were no voices raised, but Barbara's tone cut through the wall of the next chamber and left no doubt of her feelings.

'Ye did promise to let her alone.'

Archie's answer was equally sharp. 'The lass *wishes* to learn. She is clever.'

'Aye, that's what ye said about Matthew.'

The pause was unpleasant. Then Archie said, 'Matthew was always impatient.'

'And whose fault is that? They are bairns, Archie. Let them be such.'

Barbara didn't slam doors. But the latches clicked firmly as she left the chamber next door and came into their own.

Lily lay in the bed, watching Barbara and thinking of what she'd just said. It made Lily think of her grandmother telling folk up at Inchbrakie, who thought Lily ought to work more and play less, that they ought to let her keep her childhood; and how Lily thought that was silly, because surely no one could take it. Yet hers had been taken that day in the Trinity churchyard. She wasn't a bairn anymore.

Barbara slid into bed.

Lily said, 'Barbara?'

'Aye?'

'I truly do wish to learn to write better.'

The sigh was a small one, admitting defeat. Barbara

turned so her back rested warm against Lily's. 'All right, then,' she said.

❧

Lily paid attention to her lessons and she practised in her copy book, and by the start of the third summer, she was more advanced than all the boys.

'I'm taller than ye, anyway,' said Henry, claiming that small victory, even if he could not match her skills.

Simon was tallest, having shot up to the full height of a man seemingly overnight, though he was but fourteen. Walter, smaller and swift, would provoke him the way someone might bait a bear, stepping lightly to one side when Simon's fists swung.

Barbara told Walter, 'Ye'll do that one time too often and wish that ye hadn't.' To Simon, she added, 'And ye needn't dance to his piping. Ye do have a brain.'

Walter smirked at his brother. 'His brain's not that big.'

Simon's hand moved so fast that they none of them saw it till Walter lay flat on the floor.

'See now, what did I tell ye?' said Barbara, and sighed as she helped Walter stand. 'Shake hands and be done with it, that's right. And try to behave, will ye? I've got a friend coming.'

When Barbara's friends came to visit she saw them alone in the parlour which lay at the back of the house, with its own private door to the yard so that visitors could come and go without having to walk through the front rooms.

The parlour was always kept ready for guests. Chairs sat waiting to welcome them under a framed picture of a perpetual sunrise at sea. Should they wish to stay longer and spend the night, there was a bedstead against the far wall by the fireplace, with curtains drawn around it, but the friends who came to visit Barbara usually stayed no more than an hour or so and then departed. Sometimes they took ale or wine, but Barbara always saw to that herself, just as she always cleaned the parlour without needing Lily's help. 'There are too many things in this room,' she'd said once, 'that are breakable.'

So on this afternoon, when Barbara's guest had but scarcely arrived and there suddenly came from the parlour a loud sound of breaking glass, Lily looked up from her work in surprise.

Being in the kitchen, Lily was already just outside the parlour. Near enough to be in Simon's way as he pushed past her in a running blur, slammed the parlour door fair off its hinges, and dragged out a man by the knot of his cravat.

Lily had witnessed the boys' fights, but those had been brief and had left few real bruises. She'd never seen anyone getting an actual beating.

The man, by the end of it, was on the floor and his cravat was no longer white but stained red from his bleeding as Simon's fists landed relentlessly, blow after sickening blow.

Archie tried to pull Simon away and was elbowed back violently into the wall.

It was Barbara who finally took Simon's face in her two hands and said, 'Stop!' and he did, but the damage was done.

It brought trouble.

The man stayed two days in their parlour, stretched out on the bed. He was senseless at first. Archie sent for the doctor, who said they were fortunate. 'He'll keep that eye, once the swelling goes down, and he's just now begun talking back to me, so I believe he'll recover with rest, though I'd keep him well clear of your lad for a while, else you'll lose that one, too.'

That evening at the table while they ate their supper there was silence.

Archie finished first, refilled his cup with ale, and looked at Barbara, who hadn't been meeting his eyes. He said, 'The man has a job to do, like any other man.'

'Not a good job,' she said. 'Transporting people away from their homes and their families to be sold for ten years of slavery.'

'He only arranges the ships.'

'Doesn't make his hands any the cleaner.' She looked at him then. 'Ye ken what he did.'

'Aye. Ye still should have managed it differently. Because not only did I lose a bottle of wine in this business, but now he will want to be paid, and paid dearly, to keep Simon out of the Tolbooth, or worse. Ye may well hang your head, lad,' he added to Simon. 'You're going to cost me far more than I get from the church for your upkeep. And not just this once, but for years. I'd do better to just let ye swing.'

But his tone held no violence and Barbara looked over the table to tell Simon, 'He doesn't mean that. Not truly.'

'The devil I don't,' Archie said.

❧

'Family,' said the minister that Sabbath as he turned the hourglass to begin his sermon, 'is God's sacred gift to all of us, and one we must let never be divided.'

Archie coughed, and Barbara hushed him.

They went every Sabbath to the South Leith Church. On rare occasions, if one of the lads were ill or someone needed tending in the way that Lily had the day she'd first arrived, Barbara would stay at home to care for them, but otherwise they all went as one family, for the church did not allow parishioners to miss the service without reason, and their searchers went each Sabbath through the streets to find those who defied the rules, so that they could be called to answer and repent, and pay their fines.

Henry always carried Lily's church stool for her, though she carried her own cushion to make sitting through the sermon less uncomfortable. But she did like the church – it had soaring great stone windows that gave her something interesting to look at while the ministers were speaking. They had two ministers, who led the services by turns. The senior one was Mr Kay, who sometimes smiled at Lily when she passed him at the church door, but she did not feel that she could speak to him the way she had to Mr Cant.

He preached well, though.

Today, this final Sabbath of the month of June, he took his sermon from the book of Timothy, and framed it round the verse beginning: 'I exhort, therefore, that, first of all, supplications, prayers, intercessions, and giving of thanks, be made for all men; For kings, and for all that are in authority; that we may lead a quiet and peaceable life . . .'

And this he turned into an impassioned speech of thanksgiving for King James and the queen and their new prince, born earlier this month at London. 'When the king was yet the Duke of York, and his first wife did live, God rest her soul, and their two daughters, Princess Anne and Princess Mary, were but small, the Duke and Duchess did convert their minds and souls unto the Catholic church,' said Mr Kay. 'And yet our late King Charles perceived the danger of his brother's path, and did prevail upon him to allow the princesses to be raised in the Church of England as Episcopalians. And so it was done. And now we see both princesses are grown and happy in their lives and have held to their faith, and King James gave to them his blessing to be wed to princes who are also Protestant, which proves he is no bigot. Let us pray God guide him to do likewise for this newborn prince, Prince James, and raise him not a Catholic but a true Episcopalian. Then will these wars and protests end, and we shall see our nation and our family reunited.'

Archie thought this most unlikely, and he said as much while they walked home after the sermon, under skies that, bright with sunshine, cast long shadows at their feet. 'The Presbyterians hold different views from Mr Kay, and they are over-bold now they've got their own meeting-house.'

At the beginning of last year King James had passed an act that cleared away the old laws persecuting those of other faiths, and allowing Catholics, Quakers, and those Presbyterians who were considered moderate and met not in fanatical field-meetings or conventicles but only in their meeting-houses to practise their own religion. All the old oaths that had touched upon religion were dispensed with, and to hold an office in the country all a person had to do was swear allegiance to the king, so help him God – but how he answered to God was left to his conscience.

''Tis a grave mistake, this freedom of religion,' Archie said.

Walter, who had studiously copied the king's declaration printed up at Edinburgh, summarized its plan. 'The king believes the great divides in our religions these past years are wasting Scotland's harvests, playing havoc with our country's trade, and bringing us to ruin, turning all of us to vengeful, sniping folk who'd rather keep within our factions than live Christian lives or show our neighbours charity. He thinks by giving equal rights to all, he will bring peace.'

Archie dismissed this. 'Presbyterians don't want peace. 'Tis why they hold their greatest meetings in the fields, like nests of adders, and like adders ye may think they've slithered down into their hole and gone away, but mark my words, lad. They've been lying this whole time beneath our feet, and they'll rise up to bite us when they can, and then we'll feel their poison.' He spat, feelingly, upon the stones.

Barbara's hand squeezed Lily's. 'Shall we go and see the ships?'

They often walked down to the Shore on afternoons after the service when the day was fair, the two of them alone, to watch the sails and smaller boats and to imagine where each cargo might be bound. As fond as Lily was of Archie and the lads, she liked it best to be with Barbara.

Walking through the Sheriff Brae they passed the small house where the Presbyterians had lately met – although their congregation had outgrown it and was moving to a larger one. Near the door a little group of people stood, from which an older woman broke away and followed after Barbara and Lily as they passed, and when they came out to the water's edge the woman drew in closer.

'Mrs Browne?'

Barbara turned.

The woman, grey of hair and feature, nervously went on, 'I heard yer lad skelpt Sandy Fearne. I wanted to say thank ye. He . . .' Her pale eyes filled with sudden tears. 'My husband was condemned to the plantations in the Caribbees two winters past, when he refused to swear allegiance to a Catholic king. And Sandy Fearne, he found the ship to carry him. They sent my husband off in shackles like a criminal.' The tears spilled over, and she wiped them angrily away. 'Ye tell your lad he has my thanks.' She half-turned, then turned back again and added, 'And ye tell him I am sorry for his brother.'

Barbara blinked as though the sunlight hurt. 'I will.'

Behind the older woman, a young man, perhaps her son, called out, 'That's enough. I telt ye not to talk to whores.'

The words stung.

Lily's head went down to hide the redness that had started spreading on her cheeks. She tugged hard at Barbara's hand. 'Let's go home.'

Barbara said, 'It's all right, they're gone now. Let's see the ships.'

'Please. I want to go home.'

Barbara looked at her closely, then bent low and, taking the edge of her apron, wiped Lily's face. 'Never let another person have such an effect on ye. Now, lift your chin. This will not be the first time ye will hear me called a whore. 'Tis what I am.' She said it simply, without shame, and there was stubbornness behind her gaze as she met Lily's eyes.

Lily's mind was piecing things together – all the visitors. The men. The times when Barbara was away.

She looked at Barbara silently, and saw how Barbara's face

was set, the way someone might brace themselves against a coming blow.

'D'ye think less of me?' asked Barbara.

Lily shook her head, and without words reached out for Barbara's warm embrace.

'All right, then,' Barbara said, and straightened. 'Let's go see your ships.'

❧

The Catholic King James had fathered three sons by his first wife, and this new prince was his second by Queen Mary. All the others had been taken in their cradle or while young, so Lily prayed hard every evening that the new Prince James would have good health and grow in strength, and live a long and happy life.

But all around the country, as the summer turned to autumn, others prayed for just the opposite.

Among them, it was rumoured, were the king's two daughters – Princess Anne and Princess Mary, who had seen themselves displaced in line to the succession by this new male heir.

Many thought that Princess Mary's stern Dutch husband, William, Prince of Orange, would make a much better and more satisfactory king, being a Protestant. In fact, some whispered he'd been thinking the same thing himself for some time, and had gathered an invasion fleet already this past spring and was waiting only for an invitation from the English parliament to come and seize the throne.

Still others claimed, when all the dust had settled, that

it was the birth of the young prince that was the start of it – that those who were at first unsettled by the new religious freedoms of King James were pushed to breaking point to think this Catholic king might yet be followed by another one.

Whatever the true cause, the match was set alight that summer, and the bitterness and hate that had been building since King James had claimed his throne exploded, leaving only pieces of the world the way it had once been.

Early in November, William landed with his Dutch invasion force of ships and soldiers in the south of England. Many of King James's troops began to join his side, and William steadfastly refused any negotiation for a peace.

Just as his father had been forced to do before him when the Covenanters threatened, King James sent his wife and newborn child across the sea to France to safety, and then followed when he could. But he did not stay long in France.

Three months afterwards, in March, King James had landed with his army on the Irish coast, and raising troops among his loyal subjects there, prepared for battle.

Those men whose sharpest weapons were their words did try to say this was a peaceful revolution, glorious for lack of bloodshed, when the ground in truth would be soaked red with it in days to come.

By May, William and Mary as joint king and queen had accepted the crowns of both England and Scotland, and many rejoiced at their Protestant rule, but there were just as many who did not accept them – who still held James Stewart to be their true king.

Here in Scotland, it fell to a Graham, as always – the bold

Laird of Claverhouse, Viscount Dundee – to gather an army and take to the Highlands and, under the standard of King James, return the fight.

Every day it seemed the streets of Leith were filled with still more soldiers, mustering and heading north, or filing onto ships that waited for a wind to carry them to Ireland and war.

The Edinburgh town guard, too full of men who had been loyal to King James, was now disbanded, by the townspeople's demand.

Lily knew not what Corporal Morison and Jean would do now, but she thought that Captain Graeme, when he could, would do as *his* own father had before him – take his sword and follow the king's standard to the Highlands.

Feeling sure of this, she stayed alert for any mention of the fighting in the north, and she listened always for the captain's name.

But she did not expect to hear it on the day that Barbara's sister came to call.

Barbara had a wide-flung family full of cousins whom she sometimes mentioned, but in all the three years that had passed since Lily came to Leith, this was the first time Lily had met Barbara's sister Margaret.

Margaret blew into the house one windy afternoon towards the end of May, her red hair bright and lovely in disorder. She had laughing eyes and lively ways, a gown the shade of sunshine, and she was so great with child that Archie swore.

'Take care how hard ye laugh,' he warned her, 'else ye'll drop that in my house.'

'Dear Archie,' Margaret said, and settled in the nearest

chair, 'that's what I do intend. I've been tossed out of my lodgings.'

Archie's eyes narrowed. 'And ye think to hide here, is that it? Are ye being searched for?'

'They would have me name the father.'

'Aye, the church is curious, like that,' he told her in a dry tone. 'They're judgemental when it comes to fornication.'

'Even you,' she said, 'can't wish to see me sent to prison.'

'No. But I'd not weep to see you in the place of penitence.'

That was unkind.

It was a shameful punishment within the church when people had to stand or sit upon the wooden stool of penitence in front of the whole congregation while the minister rebuked them for their grievous sins.

But Margaret Malcolm looked at Archie calmly. 'I have faith that ye'll arrange it so that I'm in fear of neither.'

Archie tipped his head to one side. 'Aye. But it will cost ye.'

'I can pay.'

'The father's weighted down with silver, is he?'

Margaret, full of life and mischief in her golden gown, said, 'Aye. 'Tis Patrick Graeme of Inchbrakie.'

Lily had stood quietly aside through all of this, but she was thirteen now – less shy of speaking. She said, 'That's a lie. He'd aye be faithful to his wife.'

All heads within the room turned round to look at her.

Margaret, in astonishment, replied, 'I'm sure he would be if he had one.' And, to Barbara, 'Who is this?'

But Lily answered for herself. 'I'm Lily. I've kent Captain Graeme all my life.'

She saw the change in Margaret's features. 'Captain . . . ?

Oh, ye mean of the town guard? That Patrick Graeme? Faith, lass, he's too old for me. My Patrick is, I do believe, his nephew.'

Lily had a flash of memory from her days, so long ago now, at Inchbrakie – of a younger Patrick, son of Captain Graeme's elder brother George, the old laird's heir. She had not marked him much because in age he'd fallen in between her friends and her friends' parents, but she vaguely minded he'd had both the good looks and good nature of the Graemes. 'I am sorry,' she began. 'I—'

Margaret brushed the matter to one side. 'He would think much of your loyalty. Your captain is a colonel now, ye might be pleased to hear.'

'He always was a colonel,' Lily said, defensively.

Henry, who liked anything that had to do with wars and soldiers, found it truly interesting that Lily knew an officer, and would have pestered her with questions had not Archie brought the conversation round again to where they'd started. 'Leave the fighting to the fools,' said Archie, turning back to Margaret. 'Ye cannot stay here the now, not how ye are. It only takes one searcher from the church to find ye here with ye unmarried and me sheltering ye, and we'll both have trouble. I need time. But I do ken a woman living in the Canongate who'll take ye in, and help ye with the birth, and after that . . .' He shrugged. 'We'll see what your fine man is willing to afford.'

'He will see me cared for, Archie.'

Lily wondered why the younger Patrick Graeme did not simply marry Margaret Malcolm, if she were to have his child. It seemed the simplest and most honourable way to solve the problem.

Later on that night, she said as much to Barbara.

Barbara smiled. 'A man like Patrick Graeme of Inchbrakie does not marry someone like my sister. What would put that in your mind?'

'But Margaret's very beautiful.'

'Fairest flowers soonest fade. And beauty's not enough to gain ye entry to the world of those who live so high above us.'

There's a difference between us and them. The Graemes and ourselves. Lily remembered what her grandmother had said. *There are some bridges in this life, lass, that ye cannot cross.*

And yet, a letter came as Margaret had been sure it would, directing payment for her care and signed by Patrick Graeme, and enclosing for his future bairn a bracelet of small, polished coral beads to ward off any illness.

At the end of June, the bairn was born – a little girl they christened Margaret and called Maggie, fair of hair and face, who waved her tiny fists about as though she would herself do battle with King William's forces.

One month later, at a place called Killiecrankie, Maggie's kinsman the brave Viscount Dundee led his army to their greatest victory. But the winning of it cost his life. He died there on the field, and the commanders who came after him could not reclaim the glory of that battle. Loss followed loss as King William's men chased them north into the Highlands.

In November, Barbara's sister took a sudden fever and was gone, as suddenly as if a wind had carried her, and Lily minded Barbara saying, 'Fairest flowers soonest fade.'

The day after the burial, the woman from the Canongate brought down the bairn, asleep within a basket, and a portmanteau of Margaret's clothes and things, and then departed.

It was Henry who had first opened the door to her, and Henry who stood cradling the bairn when she had gone.

And it was Henry, with the bairn's hand tightly wrapped around his fingers, who decided, 'She's like us, now. One more foundling.'

Archie said, 'We cannot keep a bairn.'

But in that house, as Lily was to learn, all things were possible.

Chapter Sixteen

Thursday, 25 September, 1707

I was watching henry browne. He could not sit in any one position long without it causing pain. While he'd been talking, he'd been restless in his chair, and he was restless now. 'Well, anyway,' he finished. 'That's what I can tell ye.'

Gilroy stood before a cabinet, examining its contents. He asked, 'Are these the copy books?'

I saw the frown that Henry did not bother hiding. 'Aye.'

Gilroy went on, 'Your brother Walter's are among them?'

'I expect so.'

'May I?' Taking Henry's shrug to be permission, Gilroy started searching through the copy books to find one scribed with Walter's name.

Henry asked, 'What good will that do?'

I could answer that, because I had been studying my new-bought book of law. 'By your brother's death, we lost the direct manner of proving he did sign our document, since he's no longer able to attest to it himself. But we can still use the indirect method of matching Walter's signature upon the paper that we hold to something he is known to have signed while he did live.'

Gilroy's eyebrow lifted slightly and he glanced at me, but he did not correct me, and I cannot say I did not take a certain satisfaction from that fact. He only said, to Henry, 'Have you anything that Barbara Malcolm signed?'

'No.'

Up the eyebrow went again. 'No letters?'

Henry stared him down. 'We lived in the same house. Why would she write me letters?'

'But she could write?'

'Aye, of course she could. Are ye implying that my mother was a fool?'

'I am implying nothing,' Gilroy said. He'd found the copy books he wanted. Taking them in hand, he closed the cabinet. 'Tell me, what happened to Simon? Your brother who did nearly kill that man?'

The wind struck hard against the window, and it must have chased a cloud across the sun because the light changed. 'He went south to Bristol. I hear from him now and again.'

'And your father?' asked Gilroy.

'He isn't my father.'

'Archibald Browne, then. You said that he rarely comes by. Does he still live in Leith?'

'Couldn't tell ye.' The fire had burned low and the coals needed stirring but I knew Henry's pride would not welcome my help, so I sat in my chair on my side of the study and watched him lean forward and take up the poker himself. His attention on that, he reminded us he'd told us all he could about his family.

Gilroy said, 'But you seemed very close, in those days.'

Henry's breath escaped through tightened lips. 'Have ye a mother?'

'Aye.'

'And is she living?'

'Aye.'

'Ours died,' said Henry, sitting back into his chair, as if no other answer need be given. But at length he gave one. 'If ye've ever watched a wheelwright at his work, ye ken he does it from the centre out. Well, Archie was our nave, like, at the centre, and the rest of us were spokes, but we had Barbara to encircle us, to bind us all together. Make us function as a unit. When she died' – he made a motion with his hands – 'it was like this, ye ken? It all just came apart.' For that one moment it was possible to see the man he had once been, before the world had made him hard. And then he sniffed and said, 'Mind, we were older then. We had our work.'

There seemed to be no sentiment in Gilroy. He did not say he was sorry for the death of Barbara Malcolm, but instead went straight to facts. 'What work did Walter do?'

'He was a maltman,' Henry said, 'until he grew too fond of drink himself and one night fell into the harbour on his way home from a tavern.'

I had wanted to ask Henry how he had been injured, but till now I had not seen an opening. Now I attempted, casually, 'And what was your trade?'

His eyes were guarded. 'Me? I was a carter, Sergeant Williamson.'

'Hard work.'

'Aye. Even harder when the horse gets spooked and backs

the cart up over ye.' His mouth curved, grimly. 'Doctor said I ought to count my blessings that it didn't break my spine. It broke near every other bone. Leastways it felt like it.'

'I'm sorry.'

He shrugged. 'Why should ye be sorry? Ye weren't here.' To Gilroy he said, 'Leave me a receipt for those. I'll want them back.'

His mind had not been broken by the accident at least. His sharpness showed in how he read the paper Gilroy wrote and handed him, acknowledging that we'd borrowed the copy books and would return them when we'd finished using them. Taking up his wooden stave from where he'd set it by his chair, Henry pushed himself with difficulty to his feet and filed the receipt on the writing table.

I stood, too, and would have been content to leave him then.

But Gilroy had another question. 'You said Lily mentioned knowing Colonel Patrick Graeme, late of the town guard of Edinburgh. Did you ever see him at the house, or any of his family?'

Henry looked at Gilroy as though half-suspecting he was mad. 'No.'

'Never? Think now, very carefully. You never saw his son?'

'Can't say I kent he ever had one.'

'So if someone had claimed that Lily married onto Colonel Graeme's son while she was living here, what would you say to that?'

The answer Henry gave was a surprise. He laughed. A true, deep laugh that changed his features. Made them young. 'I'd say whoever claimed that had been drinking.'

'Why?'

'Because if anybody else had even tried to look at Lily while she lived here,' he said, 'Matthew would have murdered him, that's why.'

I could see Gilroy thinking backwards. 'Matthew . . . that was your lost brother, yes? The one who ran away?'

'Aye, well. He came back when it suited him,' said Henry. 'The point is, once he did, Lily'd have never seen another man. She was Matthew's lass, for then and always.'

Gilroy said, 'I see. And what was Matthew's trade? What did he do?'

The pause stretched long. 'My brother Matthew was whatever ye had need of him to be, except dependable. And if ye have a mind to ask me where *he* is, ye'll waste your time, because I cannot answer ye.' He glanced at me, and something that he saw in my expression must have warned him that what he'd just told us hadn't been of help to Lily Aitcheson, because he frowned and told us both, 'Don't let me keep ye, gentlemen. I've blethered on enough, and there's naught else that I can tell ye.'

It had not been the most gracious nor most comfortable of interviews, but still I felt a sense of loss when we had been dismissed from what small warmth remained within that house, and stood instead upon the stones of Riddell's Close at the full mercy of the bitter wind.

I was grateful for that wind. We could not talk above it, so we rode in silence back to Edinburgh and I was spared the need to hide the way those words of Henry's had affected me, when he'd revealed that Lily had been Matthew's lass.

For then and always, he had said. There was no way that Henry could have known Lily's mind, nor yet her heart. The fact that she'd once loved his brother did not mean she had not loved James Graeme, too, and married him. And I, of course, had no right to feel jealousy. No right at all.

And yet, it had affected me.

For Gilroy, it would only be more reason to suspect her of attempting to deceive us, even though she'd plainly told us she and James had kept their marriage secret from most people. Henry very well might not have known.

It was true she had not told us anything of Matthew Browne, but then we had not asked her, and the act of leaving spaces in one's narrative is not the same as telling lies.

Or so I told myself.

It was already after two o'clock when we returned our hired horses and began the short walk up to Caldow's Land together. Helen had insisted I bring Gilroy back to dinner with me.

He hadn't argued, having no doubt reached the realization, as had I, that there was little point resisting Helen. And while MacDougall's table service might be rough, the Turnbulls' housemaid – who on most days flitted like a wraith unseen within her kitchen – was a cook of rare skill and ability.

The meal, at least, was bound to be a better one than anything he'd eat alone.

I steeled myself, while starting up the forestair, for the conversation that would come. I knew Helen would ask about our morning and expect some answer, so I briefly ran through some responses in my mind and settled on one that would make a good beginning. It was always best, I knew, to be prepared.

But I was not prepared for what met me inside.

Gilroy was smoother in his own reaction. Entering ahead of me, he'd already removed his hat and bent his head to pay his honours while I was still standing just inside the door and fighting not to let my face betray my thoughts – a battle I did win, but barely.

Helen smiled. 'You took an age! Adam, you'll remember Mistress Young, of course, from yesterday. I told you I would ask her up to dinner, and she's graciously accepted. Mistress Young, may I present our dear friend, Gilroy. And of course,' she said, to Gilroy and myself, 'you already know Mrs Graeme.'

I looked at the three women's faces, upturned to me – Helen's triumphant at having arranged this, and Violet Young's eager, and Lily's composed.

'Yes,' I said, and as Gilroy had, took off my hat and bent, paying my honours.

MacDougall, his manners improved somewhat with Violet Young in the house, took our hats and our cloaks, and advised us he'd set out a basin of fresh water – which was, for him, a restrained and polite way to say we still smelt of the horses we'd lately been riding, and should wash our hands.

But his eyes, when I told him that I'd keep my sword belt, still let me know he would have happily drawn my new blade from its scabbard and stabbed me.

And in truth, had he chosen to do so at that precise moment, and had I died there on the spot and not had to go through with that dinner, I might not have actually minded.

⤜✦⤛

Helen, as the hostess, took the top seat at the table. She placed Violet next to me, and Gilroy next to Lily, but this meant that Lily was directly facing me, and that became a problem. As I'd known she would be since the first day we'd sat in this room together, when I had arranged the seating differently on purpose, she became a great distraction.

It was nothing that she did. And it was everything.

I found her smallest movements, even when she held her silence, so compelling that I could not keep my eyes from her, and then I grew self-conscious of that fact and tried to mask it by deliberately not looking at her, which in its own way was very likely just as telling.

Gilroy noticed. Or at least his gaze brushed me in that impassive way of his a few more times than made me comfortable.

It was Gilroy's fault that Lily was here to begin with. She had only come by to deliver the original certificate again, which he apparently had asked her for by letter, telling her that we had need of it for some reason or other. But when she'd arrived and found us out, and Helen here with Violet Young, and would have left the document and gone, Helen refused to hear of anything but that she stay and join us all for dinner.

I suspect that the offer came partly from Helen's own kindness, and partly because, like any good flower arranger, she doubtless believed Violet's beauty and charms would show better displayed against some plainer blossom.

She'd miscalculated. While she had been noticing whose gown was of the newest fashion or the finest quality, whose teeth were the most even, and the other superficial ways of measuring one woman against another, Helen had forgotten the most simple fact of all: in most bouquets, a single lily could outshine a violet.

Not that Violet didn't try. She laughed, and talked, and lightly touched my arm to draw me back to her if my attention wavered, but in spite of that I twice lost track of what was being said around the table and I had to force myself to follow everything more closely.

I gathered they were finishing some anecdote that featured Violet's father, Dr Young.

'Men are great fools when they're in love,' said Helen, fondly.

Gilroy, without looking up from his plate, replied, 'My mother says we are fools the best part of the time, whether in love or no.'

Helen's smile was delighted. 'I cannot imagine you having a mother. In fact, I'd have wagered you sprang into being exactly as you are now – full grown and serious.'

''Tis a fair wager,' he told her, 'but one you'd have lost, for in truth I'm the youngest of eight.'

Which explained, in part, why he so stoically endured her teasing. He must be used to it, being the youngest of such a large family.

'Eight!' Helen found this intriguing. 'Pray, are your parents saints?'

'My parents are inseparable,' he said, 'and wish for nothing more than to die at the same moment, like that couple in the Greek myth who were turned to trees.'

'Baucis and Philemon?' Helen looked at Gilroy with the joy of someone making a discovery. 'You come from romantic stock.'

'I do, I'll not deny it,' he said. 'But I'm not a fool.'

MacDougall, taking up our empty first-course plates, sniffed loudly. 'Who would wish tae be turned tae a tree?'

Violet agreed she would not. 'I should find it tedious to be for ever planted in one spot. Would not you, Mrs Graeme?'

Lily said, 'If I were planted somewhere with a view that let me look on something beautiful each day, I might be happy. I suppose it would depend upon what sort of tree.'

'Perhaps one,' I suggested, 'like the yew tree at Inchbrakie. It did seem to lead an interesting life.'

The smile she sent across the table stole my breath.

She said, 'Exactly that.'

I smiled back at her, and earned myself another glance from Gilroy, who said idly, 'We did meet an old acquaintance of yours, Mrs Graeme, down at Leith this morning. Henry Browne. He sends you his regards.' Another lie, for Henry had sent nothing of the sort, but if Gilroy had hoped to provoke some kind of reaction from that comment, he was disappointed.

Lily said, 'I do return them. How is Henry?'

I assured her, 'Well. He did seem well.'

'I am glad.'

She said no more, but Helen, ever curious, asked, 'Was it a productive visit?'

Gilroy answered, 'It amounted to reliving the late Revolution, for the most part.'

Violet bemoaned being too young to now recall anything of those times. 'Besides, we were still living then at Philadelphia, so all our news came afterwards. I did read some parts later, though. The siege of your great castle here in Edinburgh, when the Jacobite duke refused to surrender it, did sound a very great adventure. So romantic.'

Gilroy said, 'It was a great deal less adventurous and romantic to live through.'

Violet laughed, and turned to me. 'Surely you don't agree? But no, of course you'd not have been here either, would you? You were in New York then, fighting on a different field.'

MacDougall served our second courses, but that failed to save me from becoming the new focus of attention.

Gilroy asked, 'What's this?'

Violet replied, 'Yes, he was born in Kirkcaldy, but like me, he was raised in America. In New York province.' She said that with a light stamp of possession, as though by that shared experience she had more right to claim me by that bond, and though she did not look at Lily while she said it, I could hear the gauntlet dropping.

Gilroy said, 'Indeed.' And then, to me, 'When were you in New York?'

Even Lily's blue eyes showed a light of interest.

I was torn. I did not like to talk about those days. One of the young Moray girls who'd played at teaching Lily had once told her that their father had said men who'd truly seen war seldom spoke of it, and that had been my truth. I rarely spoke of what I'd witnessed. What I'd done.

I *could* talk of my comrades. I'd had those – one, in particular. And I had to talk of something, for with both Violet and Helen asking questions of me, it would have been rude to answer nothing.

Even so, I answered carefully.

When once you've faced a beast and overcome it, and you've put it at your back and barred the gate, you'd be a fool to let the latch swing open.

V

I'M FREQUENTLY TOLD, WHILE I'm writing this down, that I need to be more clear when setting my narrative.

Henry, I'm firmly reminded, would never have said anything within earshot of Gilroy about Barbara being a whore – which is true. Yet, the way I have written it, someone apparently might think he had, even though the one mention of Barbara's profession took place between Barbara and Lily alone, at a time Henry had not observed, meaning therefore that detail must then have been told to me later by Lily and added in afterwards.

Time is a fluid thing, and when you're weaving the memories of witnesses into a single tale, it does ask much of the reader – I realize this.

But the one narrative I have control of, completely, is mine.

So if you will permit me the digression, I will share with you, in summary, what I told everyone at dinner on that day at Caldow's Land – not because I think that you, like Violet, wish to hear my history, but because there are in life some people who do cross our paths and change our course for ever, and they ought to be remembered.

Lily had her Colonel Graeme.

I had Jacob Wilde.

In the year I met him, sixteen ninety, we lived on a small farm carved out of the woods on the north shore of Long Island in the Province of New York. Our nearest town was called Cross Harbor, though in those days it was not a true town but a mere handful of houses, with a church and store close by the harbour, from which you could see across the narrow span of water to the white house on the eastern shore of Messaquamik Bay.

That house, the white one, had been built by Wilde – an Englishman who'd emigrated to Long Island several years before. Some said he'd come across to the Americas because he'd killed his brother and was fleeing justice, and when his house was struck by lightning and burnt to the ground they called it God's own vengeance. But he rebuilt on the same spot, and his white house stood there as a beacon for the small ships that sailed frequently into the bay with cargoes from the greater harbours of New London and New York.

I met him for the first time that same spring, in sixteen ninety, when our town raised its militia for the war against the French, who with their native allies had just led a raid upon Schenectady, on our frontier.

There had long been skirmishes and raids and even battles, but this new fighting grew from the much larger conflict begun on the Continent when the French king threw his own support behind James Stewart – who, after all, was his cousin. King William declared war on France and soon that war, inevitably, bled across the sea to both their colonies.

At length, Cross Harbor received word to furnish our

quota of soldiers to send north to strengthen Albany, and I reported to the town's officials.

Our colonial militias operated very much like the trained bands in Scotland – able-bodied men above the age of sixteen were required to meet for training every year, and muster when their officers did call them to, and make themselves available to watch and ward and guard the town and countryside if enemies did threaten.

Some people were exempt. Enslaved men did not serve in the militias, nor did servants, and there were certain professions, such as schoolmasters, who also were not obligated, but most other men in the community stood with me on the field that day.

Among them was a barrel-chested, fair-haired man who stood at least a head above the rest of us, and stepped up to be counted when the captain called out, 'Wilde?'

The captain had not been long in Cross Harbor, and knew few of us. In fact, there'd been a change all through our town the past few months. We'd not escaped the Revolution – when the word had reached us that King James was overthrown, there'd been rebellion here as well. The governor was seized at Boston and imprisoned, and in New York City the mob rioted and took the fort and overturned the government, while all across the province countless ministers and magistrates and military officers were turned out and replaced with those whose loyalty lay firmly with King William and Queen Mary.

Our new captain, from his Dutch last name, was likely to be overjoyed to see a Dutch prince crowned the king of England, which would safeguard the religion and prestige of all his countrymen still living in this province they'd once held as their own colony, before the English took it from them.

The captain, seated at a campaign table that was set upon the field with a full list of all our names upon it, looked a long way up at Jacob Wilde, who with the broad strap of his bandolier slung over his broad chest and shoulder looked more like a pirate than a soldier.

'That's an ancient-looking musket,' said the captain.

'It did serve my father well enough at Braddock Down. I reckon it will serve me now.'

The captain looked at him more narrowly. 'At Braddock Down? I've read about that battle. Tell me, did your father fight for Cromwell's parliament, or for the Stewart king who lost his head?'

Wilde was too clever to be led into revealing his own family's leanings in these troubled times. He only said, 'My father fought for what was right.'

The captain had to be content with that, and having run through the remainder of the questions, made a mark beside Wilde's name and let him pass, and called me. 'Williamson?' As I stepped up, he looked down at his list and frowned. 'Would you be Adam Williamson, or Peter?'

Before I could answer, his lieutenant leaned in with a look of quick apology at me. 'That's Adam, sir. You see this note here, in the margin? Peter Williamson, the father, he donated a new flag to our militia company and earned himself the right to be exempt from service.'

'Ah.' The captain's tone implied he found this an annoyance. He asked the lieutenant, 'And there are no other men of age within their household?'

'Just a servant, who's also exempt.'

'I see.' The captain seemed at least to find my gun – a newer carbine with a shorter muzzle that made it more useful in the woods – more to his satisfaction. Having made sure that I also had the necessary number of flints for it, together with powder and paper and bullets for cartridges, and having made a close inspection of the leather cartridge case I wore strapped to my belt, he made a mark beside my name as well, and motioned me aside.

'And now the tedium begins,' said Jacob Wilde as I came near where he was standing. 'Counter-marchings, wheelings, doublings, all the drill, and none of it of any use at all once we get north of here, into the swamp and forest. Bloody waste of time.' He grinned, and stretched his hand out. 'Jacob Wilde.'

And with that handshake he became my friend.

He was older than me. In that year he'd have been in his early thirties, whereas I'd not yet turned seventeen, but sometimes you meet somebody with whom that doesn't matter. In the way of small communities we each knew much about the other without ever having met. Leastways, we thought we did.

Despite the rumours that he had done murder, he was quick to offer kindness.

He said, 'It is a shame the air in the Barbadoes did not heal your mother's lungs. Let's hope our bracing air will see her soon recovered.'

The air was not so very bracing by the time we headed north to Albany.

For those who've not endured midsummer in the Province of New York, the fields in afternoon become alive with insects humming in the heat. The air grows heavy and the wind brings no relief, but only gathers clouds that chase their shadows swiftly overland or turn to sudden, violent thunderstorms. There are fair days as well, but with the heat comes sickness, and that summer while our New York forces waited up at Albany for more men from Connecticut to join us, we were struck by smallpox.

Wilde and I were fortunate. We passed our days, while waiting, in the company of Albany's Dutch volunteers – a group of men with whom Wilde got on well. He spoke their language near enough, and might have passed for one of them with his light hair and build, and on the Sabbath he would sit with them and listen to their chaplain, which did please them.

The first time he returned from such a service, I said, 'I thought you were an Episcopalian.'

'I am. But I trust God will find me anywhere I choose to pray.'

He did believe that. He had little time or patience for divisions among men.

I watched him shake his head when, in the last days of July, the major general from Connecticut arrived with his own troops and everyone fell into argument.

'See, this is the problem with our colonies. We brought these disagreements from our old land to our new one. Faith, my daughters have more courtesy with one another,' he told me, 'and they've but barely left the cradle.'

The Connecticut troops did not like our New York ones. The feeling was mutual. Nor did the Dutch volunteers care to serve under any authority but that of Albany's mayor or his brother. The major general disdained the entire arrangement – our lack of supplies and our sickness were only the start of his list of complaints.

But we gathered our forces and marched, notwithstanding, a hundred miles up through the wilderness, to the place called Wood Creek near the lake that the French called Champlain.

Here the major general called a war council together with the mayor of Albany and the leaders of those men of the Five Nations who had come to join us – Mohawks and Oneidas – who advised us to continue on our way towards Quebec, where even now our fleet from Boston might be starting their assault.

But one week passed, and we were still encamped at Wood Creek while the major general sent out scouts, awaited word from Albany, held more councils, and weighed his options.

Wilde and I sat one night with our backs against the trunks of tall white pine trees, watching yet another war council.

'You see now,' Wilde said, 'here you have two very different men, and it's a lesson for you. On the one hand, you have Captain Schuyler, there' – he nodded to the younger brother of the mayor of Albany – 'who clearly thinks we're wasting time with all this talk, and should move on and fight. And on the other, you've our major general, who wants nothing more than to break camp and leave.'

I studied both men, trying to be generous to the major general. 'It might just be caution. After all, not much has gone to plan.'

'You cannot take the measure of a man when things are working well,' said Wilde, as though it were a truth I ought to know. 'It's only when the plan goes badly wrong and everything is broken that you'll see what he is made of – if he breaks, too, or builds something from the pieces that remain.'

Of the things I learned that summer, those few words perhaps have stayed with me the longest. I did take them to my
heart, there on that evening underneath the pines, and they
proved to be true.

The major general did break camp, with his excuses that
it was now too late in the season, and too many of our men
had fallen ill, and there were too few of us, and the men of
the Seneca nation had not come to join us as promised, and
all was poorly planned from the beginning, and, at any rate,
this was the will of God, and not his fault.

But before heading back to Albany, he granted Captain
Schuyler leave to lead a force of volunteers in an assault against
the French of La Prairie.

The volunteers were meant to only be the Dutch together
with their native allies, I believe, but then of course when
Schuyler asked for men, Wilde stood.

I thought of what he'd said about the measure of a man,
and it mattered to me suddenly to try to show this man that I
was made of more than what I might appear, so I stood, too.

So the others left and our force carried on in our canoes,
sometimes by night, always by stealth, building a new plan
from the one that had been broken.

Of the battle that came after, if it can be honourably called
that, there are men who've written histories of it, and I'll
leave the telling of that part to them. They were not there, of
course, which makes it easier to praise or judge, depending on
their point of view, but La Prairie was my first battle, and I did
emerge from it more hardened in my mind, and with a stab
wound in my shoulder from a blade that caught me unawares.

It had seemed clean enough when we had left the field, but

on the march back down again it festered. By the time we came to Albany I was too ill to travel any further, and was put into the hospital.

I stayed there through that autumn.

Then one day I woke and Jacob Wilde was sitting in a chair beside my bed.

'I have some news to tell you,' he began. And that was how I heard.

He travelled back with me, and in Cross Harbor I was met with sympathy. A lawyer gave me documents to sign, and Wilde and our militia captain bore their witness to my signature, the captain making some speech about hardships and endurance.

It was Wilde alone who walked out with me to the farm, and stood beside me as I looked at what had been the house, and now was only blackened ruins.

I knew what had happened. He'd told me in Albany.

'The committee of safety, or so they do call it, that serves our new lieutenant governor, came to believe that Long Island was harbouring Jacobites, so they did send over soldiers in boats who went round the north coast, into all the bays, searching. They broke open houses. They broke open mine,' he said. 'Frightened my wife and the children. I was in the orchard, at work, or I might have done what your father did. When they reached your house, your father came out with his musket, and so did your hired lad behind him. Your mother apparently stepped in between. And that's all we can tell you, for certain. I'm sorry.'

They'd all died. All shot, for a small piece of ground and the disagreements we'd transplanted from our old land to our new one.

How the fire started was a mystery, but it had done its work. Little remained of the house where I'd lived, that had looked to the water.

Wilde stood with me there, gazing down at the ships sailing out through the Sound to the wider sea.

He said, 'Our town intends to write a protest to the secretary of Their Majesties. You may get compensation. When that comes, you'll build another house.'

The measure of a man.

I drew myself up straighter, still with my eyes fixed upon those sails, and gave a nod and answered, 'Aye. All things can be rebuilt.'

CHAPTER SEVENTEEN

THURSDAY, 25 SEPTEMBER, 1707

VIOLET'S FATHER SENT HIS chairmen to collect her after dinner, and because I knew it was my duty, since I was the reason Helen had invited her to Caldow's Land, I fetched my hat and walked her down the forestair to the street.

I had no doubt she looked decorative against my arm. She would make a splendid wife for some man who would then gain, by her father's social standing, all the comfort and respect a man could ask of life. But I was not that man.

I'd been handed what I'd thought I wanted – what I had come home to find – and found it did not suit me after all.

She thanked me prettily, and held my hand a little longer than she needed to as I helped her up into the chair, and sent me a departing smile that raised a sigh from the two spinster sisters who kept shop beneath the Turnbulls' lodgings, and who had been standing sheltered in the portico behind me.

When I smiled at them and bowed, they laughed and called me rogue and disappeared again into their shop. Amused, I turned back to the street.

Violet's chair had moved off, giving me a view across the

Landmarket. Inside the entrance to Hamilton's Close, the man in the grey coat was leaning against the stone wall, with his hat pulled low.

That changed my mood.

Behind me, a door opened and then shut again, and I heard steps descend the forestair. Turning, I saw Gilroy coming down with Lily.

Gilroy's explanation was dispassionate. 'Apparently there was some unrest in the street this morning. Mrs Turnbull asked if I'd see Mrs Graeme home.'

I was not surprised he'd volunteer for that, since it gave him a chance to ask her questions that seemed innocent without her knowing he suspected her of fraud. But it surprised me Mrs Graeme had agreed to have an escort, since she'd turned me down the day that I had offered. It could not be because she favoured Gilroy's company – she stood apart from him, and looked uncomfortable.

But when she glanced across the street as though in search of somebody, I thought I understood.

I said, 'I'll walk with you.'

I don't know if she genuinely stumbled on the street as we were crossing it, or whether it was by design, but either way she seemed to lose her balance for a moment and her hand reached, very naturally, to take my arm. It stayed there, small and sure and warm. I tucked my arm more tightly to my side to anchor it and keep it well protected.

I had the strong impression there were things she might have said to me had Gilroy not been there. Instead she only asked, 'What happened to your farm, in the Americas?'

'It's still mine, although I have not seen it in some years.

The pastureland is rented to a neighbour who does keep his horses there.'

'And have you yet rebuilt the house?'

I looked at her. 'I've never had a reason to.'

We were passing the entrance to Hamilton's Close. It was empty. The man in the grey coat and hat had gone back to the shadows, but I made sure I was the one walking closest to where he'd been, just to be safe.

Gilroy's mind was on other things. 'If you had no house, then where did you live?'

'With the Wildes, that first winter. And then Mrs Wilde's uncle, who kept warehouses near New York's harbour, needed a new clerk, so I went there and started working for him.'

Lily asked, 'To New York City?'

'Aye.'

'That must have been a change, after your years of farming.'

'Aye, well. Sometimes change is for the good.' Our walk had been too short. We'd already come to the corner where she had her lodging, in the house at the head of Forrester's Wynd.

I stood a moment looking down at her, because I sensed again she might have something that she wished to say, but in the end she only thanked me, and withdrew her hand. I felt the loss of it, and did not like the feeling.

When I turned back, having watched her enter safely in the turnpike stair, I found Gilroy observing me.

He said, in his blunt way, 'You should be careful.'

'Why is that?'

'I think you know why.'

I could feel my jaw begin to set. 'I can I assure you, I—'

'We are conducting an inquiry. She's our subject. You're attracted to her. She may try to use that,' Gilroy said, 'to sway your judgement.'

No denial would have stood against those level eyes, so I did not deny it. But I did say, trying to hold back my irritation, 'I don't know what has made you so determined to assume the worst of Mrs Graeme's character.'

'I have my reasons.'

'Pray, what are they?'

For a moment, in the street, he faced me down in silence. Then he exhaled, hard.

And told me.

&

I must have been frowning, still, when I returned to the Turnbulls' a short while later and stood at the windows, my back to the drawing room, looking down over the Landmarket, because Helen asked, 'Is something wrong?'

I lied. 'No.'

The man in the grey coat was back in his place at the entrance to Hamilton's Close. No longer watching Lily now, but me. Or maybe, watching both of us.

Aiming for an idle tone, I asked, 'What was the unrest in the street this morning?'

'A minor scuffle, but it blew up very quickly. It's the Jacobites,' she said, 'and all this talk of an invasion. It puts everyone on edge.'

'The Union has not helped.'

In surprise she asked, 'You're not against the Union?'

'I have no opinion of it. I'm a soldier. I do merely what I'm told, and take no part of politics.'

'That's quite the safest course.' A pause, and then, 'You're sure there's nothing wrong?'

I turned from the window. 'No, all is well.'

'Good.' Her eyes were expectant. 'And what did you think of my dinner?'

'Most pleasant.'

'She'd make a good match for you.'

I knew she meant Violet Young, so I made as noncommittal a sound in reply as I possibly could, then changed the topic to something more important. 'Didn't you say Mrs Graeme came by because Gilroy had asked her to bring us her certificate of marriage?'

'Yes, that's right. He said you had misplaced your copy, so you needed the original. I put it in the writing chamber,' Helen told me, 'with the little books he brought from Leith.'

The copy books.

I glanced around. 'Where is MacDougall?'

'I sent him out,' she said. 'He is delivering a letter for me, to Sir Andrew Hume, my cousin.'

It took me a moment before I could place the name, given that two days had passed since she'd told me about him. 'Your cousin who sits on the Commission of the Equivalent?'

'Yes. I thought it was best that I thank him directly for all of the trust the commission has put in my husband to lead this inquiry. With your help, of course. I did mention the same to his wife when I saw her on Tuesday, but one cannot always depend on a wife to pass on what was said, and MacDougall did tell me I could have as easily written a letter.' She shrugged. 'It can do no harm.'

'No.' I was glad she had done it, not for the advancement it might offer Turnbull, but because it meant that MacDougall was not here and putting his nose into things that were none of his business. He did like to pry.

If he'd read the certificate, that would mean nothing. He'd learn little by it that he'd not have already learned from eavesdropping on our conversations. But knowing that he had been thumbing through Walter Browne's copy book – I'd have disliked that. I would have felt I'd broken faith with the dead.

Even when I did it, carefully, sitting alone at the scrutore, it still seemed like an intrusion. I saw nothing in the pages of the copy book that struck me as unusual. I set it to the side.

The second copy book had not belonged to Walter. It was Lily's.

This, I opened with some reverence, marking how the hand had altered from a childish scrawl to one more sure and strong. Sometimes when her attention wavered from her lessons, she had drawn small pictures in the margins – little houses, little birds, a ship with sails. And on a page towards the end, beneath a row of practised flourishes, she'd drawn a tiny heart, crowned like the ones sold in the Luckenbooths, and signed her name above: *Lilias Aitcheson*. And in another hand below the heart was written: *Matthew Browne*.

I looked a long time at that heart, and felt my frown return as I remembered what Gilroy had told me in the street outside her lodgings.

'Henry Browne did tell us much this morning,' he'd said, 'but he did not tell us all. He told us that his brother

Simon went to Bristol, which was true enough. But Simon only went to Bristol because he did have no choice. Eight years ago he was brought up before the council of the lords for forging a false bond, and was banished out of Edinburgh and the three Lothians, never to return on pain of death or transportation to the colonies. I'm not relying only on my friend the stabler's knowledge,' he'd assured me. 'I did verify this earlier this morning, before we went down to Leith. Which is how I also know the reason Henry has not seen his father for so long is because there's a warrant out for the arrest of Archibald Browne, for assisting a small group of people trying to claim money falsely out of the Equivalent. Apparently, he forged a will.'

My jaw had tightened then, but I'd said nothing, for I'd sensed where this was leading.

'Forgery,' said Gilroy, 'was the family business. And the one who did it best of all the family – so the stabler told me – was the girl.'

CHAPTER EIGHTEEN

FRIDAY, 26 SEPTEMBER, 1707

I BURNED MUCH COAL AND candle through the night in place of sleep, but when Gilroy arrived to start work in the morning, I was well prepared.

Bringing him through into the writing chamber, I set an extra chair for him at the scrutore, where I'd laid out all the papers ready.

There was still a thread of tension stretched between us, but I knew if we were going to be working closely for the next few days, we'd have to clear the air. I started simply, 'Helen told me Mrs Graeme brought us her original certificate of marriage because you said we'd lost the copy.' Wordlessly, I took the copy from its place and set it, for a moment, on the top of all the other papers.

Gilroy said, 'I thought that was the simplest way to ask for it, without arousing her suspicion.'

'And I gather, from our conversation yesterday, that the reason you didn't want to arouse her suspicion – and the reason you wanted this original certificate back to inspect – is because you believe it's a forgery.'

I didn't even need him to answer that. His eyes told me all I needed to know.

I cleared my throat. 'The law sets out all the objections you can raise against a document if you believe it might be forged. I've studied those objections, and I've found no evidence to render this certificate incompetent. Nothing has been added to the margins or between the lines to change the meaning of the text. There are no places where the letters have been scraped or altered or erased and overwritten, nor any blanks that could have been filled in at some later time. And you can plainly see the body of the document is written in a different hand than all the signatures beneath.'

I glanced up, to make sure he'd followed all that, but Gilroy was not looking at the certificate. His gaze was fixed on me, the telltale eyebrow raised.

Hiding my satisfaction, I carried on, 'Furthermore, if you look at Walter Browne's signature, here, it's an exact match to the way he forms his letters in his copy book. I've marked some samples for you.' I slid the open copy book across the writing surface, so that he could make a close comparison if he so chose. 'And the same with Mrs Graeme's.'

Sitting back, I watched while he leaned forward and inspected the certificate and signatures himself.

I said, 'I think you're wrong. I think it's genuine.'

He lifted one shoulder. 'At best, all you've proven is that it was signed by two people who came from a house of known criminals.' Still, he studied the copy books carefully. 'I will allow that, if she *did* forge Walter Browne's signature, she is indeed very talented. It is, as you say, exact.'

Had I known him better, I'd have sworn aloud, but as it

was I kept the swearing silent and said only, 'Are you always this pig-headed?'

'When I'm right, aye. I've an instinct about Mrs Graeme. Do you never have instincts about people?'

'Sometimes.' I dragged my gaze from his before my current instinct led me to an action I'd regret.

Gilroy cocked his head. 'Did you hear something?'

'It's probably MacDougall. He does like to listen at the door. He is convinced that I am trying to advance myself at the expense of my friend Turnbull.'

There was a short pause, then, 'This is a most impressive cabinet,' Gilroy said. He meant the scrutore. Standing, he reached for the edge of the long strip of moulding that ran across the top of the cabinet above the pigeonholes, exposing the same 'secret' drawer that I'd pulled out for Helen when she had first shown me this chamber.

'More than meets the eye,' said Gilroy. 'Like many people.'

I could not tell if he intended that to provoke or to pacify. I waited.

He asked, 'Is the book of law Turnbull's, or yours?'

My chin lifted a fraction. 'Mine.'

He nodded but said nothing for a moment. Then he said, 'I will admit my friend the stabler only said the girl was the best forger, but he did not say which girl, and there were two who lived within that house. We never did ask Henry Browne what happened to the bairn who came to live with them.'

Colonel Graeme's nephew's daughter. Little Maggie Graeme, who'd been born the summer that the Jacobites had won their bitter victory at Killiecrankie, and whose mother – Barbara's sister – had been dead before that winter's end.

Gilroy told me, 'Perhaps you could follow up on that, when you return the copy books.'

I looked at him. 'When *I* return them?'

'Aye. I'll not be here the next few days. My niece is being wed up in Dundee.'

I frowned. 'I thought there was an urgency to our inquiry.'

'We are waiting still for answers from the Continent. You have your book of law. Besides, I would have thought you'd welcome time without me at your side.'

I would indeed. But, even so, I asked, 'You've made Lord Grange aware?'

'Of course.'

'And when will you be back?'

'On Tuesday, I expect. I'll not stay long. But family's family,' Gilroy said, 'and my niece will not soon forgive me if I am not there. I am her favourite uncle.'

He said it convincingly, and with a clear and steady gaze, but then, that was the thing with Gilroy. Whether he was telling you the truth or not, you couldn't tell the difference. You were only left to wonder, when he'd gone, what purpose he'd have had in telling you a lie.

⤨

On Saturday, the little house in Riddell's Close looked even more unwelcoming than it had looked two days before, and Henry Browne looked even less inclined to let me in. He eyed the bottle in my hand and asked, 'Whose cellar did ye steal that from?'

I'd known men who from bitterness or anger tried to goad

me to a fight, and I had learned to let it go, so I did not rise to his sarcasm. I answered mildly, 'From a vintner's near the castle in the town. It was expensive.'

Henry's gaze stayed level on my own a moment, and I saw him weighing his decision. 'Then ye'd better bring it in afore it spoils.'

There was less wind today, and yet the sky was overcast and made the front room darker. As we entered, Henry asked me without turning, 'Where's your friend?'

'Gone north for a few days, on family business.'

'He seems a cheerful sort,' said Henry, meaning just the opposite.

Remarkably, to me at least, I found myself defending Gilroy, in his own words. 'Speaking brusquely is his habit.'

Henry wouldn't let me help. He tucked his stave beneath one arm and took the glasses from the corner cabinet by himself, then motioned I should set the bottle down on the small table near the hearth. I did so, taking a respectful step back while he used his pocket knife to prise the stopper out.

He asked me, 'Sent ye here for information, did he?'

'To bring back the copy books, actually.' I eased them out of the leather case I'd used to carry them as I'd walked down today, so they'd be safe from the weather.

'Then put them back,' Henry advised me. 'Ye ken where they go.' He had opened the wine and was starting to pour. 'But if I judged your friend right, he sent ye for something more. What are ye meant to be asking me?'

I was crossing to the cabinet with the copy books. 'Gilroy did remind me we forgot to ask you what became of Maggie Graeme.'

'Aye. Ye did.'

It was a simple thing to find the place for Walter's book among its fellows on the shelf, but standing there I found myself reluctant to do likeways with the book that had belonged to Lily.

Once more, just once more, I turned the pages to where she had drawn that small crowned heart in ink, and signed her name above it, and where Matthew Browne had written his beneath.

Behind me, I could feel the silence.

Turning, I faced Henry with the feeling that his watching eyes saw more than I would care to have them see.

'Why are ye really here?' he asked.

CHAPTER NINETEEN

TUESDAY, 15 MARCH, 1692

SOMETIMES, LILY THOUGHT, LIFE gave you back the things you'd lost. Or very nearly.

Holding Maggie close against her shoulder in the dark hours of the morning while she softly paced the carpet of the downstairs front room, back and forth and back again, reminded her of holding Bessie, who'd been nearly this same age – the warm weight of that little golden head tucked trustingly against her neck; the lightly rapid breathing, and the small hands holding on to her as though they'd never let her go.

If life had divided Lily from her sister, it had brought her this wee lass whose blood was bound to Jamie's, and she took this as a comfort.

In the room, the fire had died down to a faint glow that could barely cast reflections on the window-glass. The others were a-bed, and she was trying not to wake them. She moved quietly, the swishing of her skirts the only sound, save for the gentle creaking of the floorboards.

So when Barbara whispered from the doorway just behind her, it caught Lily unawares.

'She's still awake, the poor wee thing,' said Barbara, stroking one hand over Maggie's soft cheek. 'Chaft teeth are a misery.'

Lily knew little of chaft teeth, except that in the English anatomy book Archie kept on his shelf they were labelled as 'molars' and looked too large for Maggie's mouth, and had given the little girl no end of pain these past weeks as they tried to break through. Nothing else would soothe Maggie but being held closely, and walked back and forth in this room, where she could see the books in the cabinets and look at the fire with her head resting on Lily's shoulder.

Barbara asked her, 'Did ye mean to have that window open?'

'Aye. She felt very warm, and the fire was not helping. When I let the air in, she went calm.'

'All right, then,' Barbara said. 'I'll get ye a fresh towel.' The one lying over Lily's shoulder was wet through and crumpled now from Maggie's chewing, but Lily paid it no more heed than she did her appearance. She'd not yet undressed for bed, and was still in her day clothes, though she had undone her hair and let it fall free of its pins so Maggie could play with it as she liked, because it helped to keep the little girl distracted.

'Thank ye,' Lily said, and 'Thank ye,' Maggie echoed, as she had been taught, and Barbara smiled and kissed them both and tiptoed from the room.

The quiet of the sleeping house descended on them once again, and Lily went on walking, holding Maggie and remembering how much she'd always loved these hours of peace, and the feeling of being a part of a family.

She might have dreamed the voices.

Colonel Graeme's, strong and so familiar. 'Jamie, wait, lad.'

And a man's voice overlaid atop the voice of her beloved friend, assuring him, 'This way is quicker. They will have ye in the prison if ye're not aboard at dawn.'

'I think 'tis my own son who's eager to be rid of me.' That was said in jest, and met with mild impatience.

'Must ye stroll?'

The laugh that answered him was Colonel Graeme's laugh, Lily was sure of it. She moved into the passage, where she shifted Maggie on her shoulder just enough to free one hand so that she could unbolt the door and open it. The close, in both directions that she looked, was dark and empty. There was no one to be seen.

She didn't know what she'd have said to them, if they'd been truly there, but still the disappointment hit her deeply, and her eyes filled with swift tears. She closed the door against the chill air, bolting it securely.

Maggie's small hand reached for Lily's hair and clung, and Lily wrapped her arms around the little girl for reassurance, starting back into the rhythm of their walking as she entered once more into Archie's work room. It ought to have been soothing, in the dim light with the fading fire, but Lily had gone only a few steps before she realized they were no longer alone.

He must have come in through the window, for he stood there now beside it.

Lily found, just as she had that night those years ago in the Bells' kitchen, she could neither move nor speak nor call out – only stand and stare while the intruder stared at her. It was, in some ways, as if time had barely moved at all – the fire so low, the window, and the tears upon her face. But this was not a boy. This was a full-grown man who faced her, and her mind and body were reacting to the danger of that when she heard a cry behind her – not of fear, but happiness.

And Barbara, rushing past her, flung her arms around the young man who had entered through the window, nearly knocking him off balance. But he stood against the onslaught, and embraced her, too, with tenderness, because she'd started sobbing.

'Matthew,' Barbara said against his shoulder, and no more than that.

But Lily understood.

Sometimes life gave you back the things you'd lost.

❧

Families were curious constructions. Like a child's house of wooden blocks, you took one piece away and all fell down, or added one and all the others settled into a new shape, creating something different.

All the time that Lily had been living here, it had been Simon who'd been eldest of the boys, but Matthew being nearly a year older at eighteen had now resumed that place with ease, and it changed all their interactions.

Henry wept. It was the first time Lily saw him do that. Even Simon showed emotion, hugging Matthew hard and sitting close beside him that first morning as though unconvinced his brother would not vanish just as suddenly as he'd appeared. And Walter, who was rarely one to sit through conversations, sat with patience, uncomplaining.

Lily, watching how they laughed and talked together,

found it fascinating. She had only ever seen the way the family functioned with that one block missing. Seeing it replaced now was a revelation.

She could not say whether Jean and Bessie felt the loss of her so keenly, having had her with them such a little while, but she knew she would always be a missing piece to them as well, and she was sorry for that knowledge. Two years earlier, when Lily had been fourteen and began her monthly bleeding, Barbara had sat down and talked to her of men and having bairns, and in that evening a great weight had been removed from Lily's life. She'd learned that what had happened between her and Mr Bell did not make her a whore, nor had it been her fault, and one day shortly afterwards she'd summoned all her courage and walked up to Edinburgh to knock upon Jean's door. But it was opened by a stranger.

No one in those lodgings knew where Corporal Morison had gone, not since the town guard was disbanded and the Revolution had called fighting men to battle. They knew only that his family had gone with him.

Time moved onwards, Lily knew, and there were few things from the past she could repair.

Which made her doubly glad to witness Matthew's homecoming, and all the happy changes as the pieces of the Browne family fell back into their places. It appeared that only Archie had been pushed out of alignment.

Outwardly, he seemed as pleased as all of them to have his son returned, but when he looked at Matthew something showed beneath the surface Lily did not understand – a deep discomfort, and a wariness.

She did not wish to know what showed on her face when

she looked at Matthew, for she knew she looked at him too often, and not only because she thought him more handsome than his brothers. With the other Browne lads, Lily almost could pretend they were *her* brothers, too, although they were not true relations. But with Matthew, she knew that would be impossible.

His smile did unfair things to her insides.

He was as tall as Simon, and as broad across the shoulders, and his hair was also brown, but Matthew's hair curled slightly with a darkly golden undertone that gave it greater life.

Maggie seemed mesmerized by Matthew's hair as well, and by the buttons of his waistcoat. For the past half hour the little girl had sat upon his knee and concentrated fiercely on the way those buttons fitted into their holes, and he had gone on talking through this, unconcerned. And now, when Maggie showed an interest in the hat he'd set beside him, Matthew simply gave it to her, to her great delight, and earned a dry warning from Archie.

'Ye'll regret that. She's been chewing everything in sight.'

'It's a hat,' said Matthew, in a quiet tone that held a challenge. 'A thing, an object, easily replaced, that will not ever have the value of a child.'

Between them, Maggie took the hat in her two hands and pulled it down over her head so that she fairly disappeared in it, announcing, 'Hat!'

It eased the tension. Matthew lifted up the brim as though to see that she was still inside. 'Where did you get your bonny hair?' he asked, and then, to Barbara, 'She's your sister's child, you said. Did not your sister have red hair like you?'

'She did. But Maggie's father was a Graeme.'

'Was? Is he no longer living?'

'Aye, he lives,' said Barbara. 'I will tell ye later how it is, when there are no small ears to overhear.'

The life of Maggie's father, young Patrick Graeme of Inchbrakie, had grown complicated. Last year he had married onto a young lady of good birth, but shortly afterwards he'd fought a man and killed him, and although the family of the man he'd killed had not brought charges yet, it was suspected that in time they would, being so firmly for King William when those of the house of Inchbrakie were Jacobites.

'That minds me,' Archie said, and turned to Lily, 'your friend Colonel Graeme is aboard a ship, here in our harbour.'

Lily stared. The voices . . . 'Are ye certain?'

Archie gave her the look that meant he was insulted she would ask. 'On Saturday he came to Edinburgh with General Buchan and Brigadier Cannon and others who'd been granted passes to go beyond seas. I don't doubt their intent was to stay in town until their ship was made ready, but they were too well received. Your colonel, I'm told, could scarce walk in the street without meeting a friend or admirer, and there is nothing the government does distrust more than a popular Graham. So now they've been all ordered onto the ship, even though it's not ready to sail.'

Henry asked, 'Why were they given passes by the king, and not made prisoner?'

Archie had been told it had to do with the arrangement made between King William and the Highland forces last year, when they'd ceased their fighting, as a way to keep the peace.

Walter said, 'Aye, we've all seen how well the Prince of

Orange does intend to keep the peace. Did not he show us at Glencoe?'

There was a silence then. The news from Glencoe had just lately reached them, and reports were yet confused, but what they'd heard had left them horrified.

When the fighting in the Highlands had come to an end last summer, King William had offered terms of peace to all the clans if they would swear oaths of allegiance to him. That had been, as Walter had explained to Lily at the time, dishonest. 'He expects them to refuse,' Walter had said, 'because the Highlanders are Jacobites. No doubt he has signed letters of fire and sword and holds them ready so his troops can move against the Highland men the first of January, when the limit of their time expires.'

But all the Highland clans had sworn the oaths. The rumour was they'd written for permission to James Stewart at his court across the sea, and he had given it because he knew their hearts yet lay with him, and he would rather that they swallow a false oath and save their land and lives. And so King William's plans to seek revenge upon the Highland clans appeared to falter.

But the chief of clan MacDonald, though arriving at the place and time to swear the oath, had found no one to hear it, and been forced to journey on some extra days, so the king's men did use this as a reason to say he had sworn too late.

And in his valley of Glencoe there was quartered a detachment of the soldiers of the Earl of Argyll – grandson to the Argyll who had been Montrose's enemy, and son of the Argyll who'd lost his head for treason in the summer Lily's father died. All these soldiers, who till then had peaceably enjoyed the hospitality of the MacDonalds, then received their secret, wicked orders and rose early in the morning and began a slaughter of their hosts, within their homes.

Henry looked at Walter. 'So it's "Prince of Orange" now, and not King William? Are ye turning to a Jacobite?'

'A crown will never make a king,' said Walter. 'There were women at Glencoe. And children. I will call him what I please.'

Archie said, 'Aye, within this house, but mind your tongue when ye step out that door. They hang men here for less.'

'I'm not afraid,' said Walter.

Archie looked across at him a moment. 'Are ye not?' His voice was calm, and yet beneath there was an undercurrent Lily had not heard before, and one that left her cold.

Matthew said, 'Let him be.'

He said it quietly, and without any movement, but again there was that challenge and the sense that there had been a shift within the household.

Archie smiled, and turned his gaze on Matthew. 'Ye'll be turning me out of my bed now, will ye?'

'No. I'll take lodgings. I'm out of the business.'

'Oh, aye? And what else can ye do, then?'

A shrug. 'There'll be plenty of work at the harbour.'

That didn't suit Barbara. 'They've had gangs at work, taking lads from the taverns and off the Shore, pressing them onto the English ships,' she said. 'The king said he'd stop it if we gave them one thousand men out of Scotland to serve in the navy, but it hasn't stopped. It's not safe, being there on your own.'

'Don't you worry for me,' Matthew said. He was talking

to Barbara but looking at Archie when he answered, evenly, 'I can take care of myself.'

‸

The past days had brought storms, but now the skies had cleared and Lily took heart from the fact that Colonel Graeme's ship had not yet sailed. She might have time.

She knew she could not go to him in person, it would hardly be allowed, but there were always boatmen in the harbour who, if paid enough, would carry letters to the larger ships. All Lily wanted was to let him know that she yet lived, and where she was, and that he and his family rarely left her thoughts, and that she wished both he and Jamie well, and hoped that time would one day bring their lives together once again.

With care, she wrote that on the finest paper Archie kept within his work room, and was sealing it with red wax when she heard the voices in the passage. She'd been concentrating so completely that she had not heard the door, but here was Matthew, coming through into the work room beside Henry.

Lily kept her head down, waiting for the flush to leave her cheeks, and slipped the letter underneath her apron as she stood.

He wished her a good afternoon, then turned again to Henry. 'Not till supper?'

'No, they've both gone out, and Walter with them. No one told me where.'

'And Simon?'

'Taken Maggie for a walk upon the Links.'

That earned a smile from Matthew. 'Simon?'

'Aye. He goes all soft, with Maggie.'

'Well, there's none will dare to harm her,' Matthew said. He leaned past Lily, sending all her senses spinning. 'Where have all the inks gone?'

Henry showed him. 'Which one were ye after?'

'One that matches this.' He'd brought a letter of his own, on heavy paper. Smoothing out the folds, he laid it on the writing table as he settled in the chair that Lily had just left. 'They'll not admit me as a carter unless someone recommends me, so I reckon this will satisfy them.'

Henry thought it possible. 'And where did ye get that?'

'Not telling. But the "William Rowan" mentioned here needs little effort to be turned to Matthew Browne.'

Tying a corner of her apron round the letter she had written, Lily put her hand out to stop Matthew when he would have chosen the wrong ink. 'No, that's too dark. It's this you want.'

His head turned, not in doubt or disbelief but simply in surprise, and Henry told him, 'Lily kens more than the rest of us.'

'Is that a fact?'

He was fair skilled as well, when it came to the craft. Lily watched as he expertly razed out the letters or parts of the letters he did not want, using the edge of his penknife, then mixed a solution of chalk and glue to build the scraped places level again before carefully lettering over them. Only in one spot did she see him hesitate.

Henry asked, 'What?'

Matthew frowned. 'Nothing. Only there's no room for error.'

'Then let Lily do it. I'm serious,' he said, as Matthew glanced up. 'She is better than all of us.'

Matthew met Lily's eyes. His were a beautiful brown. 'Can you?'

She nodded.

He stood and she sat. She bent her head over her work. Willed her hand to keep steady. She wanted to do her best, wanted to prove herself so he would be impressed.

'Perfect,' said Matthew.

She felt she could live on that smile.

It made her brave enough to ask him, 'Ye have lodgings near the harbour, do ye not?'

'Aye.'

'Could ye . . . that is, if I gave ye a letter, could ye find a boatman to carry it out to a ship there? They'll not cheat a man the way they will a woman,' she said. 'I've saved some coins from what Archie allows me, to pay for it.'

Matthew looked down at her, quizzical. 'If you mean the ship that your Colonel Graeme's on, it sailed already this morning, as soon as the wind turned fair.'

'Oh,' Lily said. 'Oh, I see.'

She did not know why it suddenly pained her so deeply, when she had not seen Colonel Graeme nor Jamie these past six years, but there was something incredibly cruel about having them brought here so close and then taken away again without her once being able to contact them, and it broke something in Lily.

Her eyes were stinging as she stood. 'I see,' she said again, although increasingly she could not see, because the tears were swimming in her eyes. Then they spilled over.

She'd have turned away and run then, to her room and private sorrow, only Matthew caught her hand and drew her close and held her, unexpectedly.

'It's all right,' he said, although of course he had no way of knowing what was wrong, or how it could be fixed. But she believed him. Matthew's chin came down and rested on her head and Lily rested in his arms like that and felt secure, and for a moment all the things that worried her felt small and far away.

❧

Barbara saw before anyone else did.

She told Lily, 'Best not let Archie see that ye like Matthew.'

They were in the kitchen and Lily was glad of the heat from the hearth since it gave an excuse for the warmth that rose instantly into her cheeks. 'Ye're seeing things.'

'Aye, I ken fine what I'm seeing. Ye might as well hand him your heart and be done with it.'

Lily knew there was no point in denying it. 'If I did, he wouldn't take it,' she said, certain. 'He doesn't look at me in the same way.'

Barbara reached to touch Lily's cheek. 'I see the way that he looks at ye.'

Lily stopped work for a moment and, turning her head, looked at Barbara, who told her, 'They put Matthew into my arms when he was but a few days old, and I can tell when there's something he wants – sometimes even before he has reasoned it out for himself. Give him time. Matthew doesn't trust easily. And he'll be trying to keep ye from harm.

Which is why, as I say, ye should guard how ye're feeling from Archie.'

Lily was very aware of the tension that stretched between Archie and Matthew when they were together, but hearing this warning from Barbara now made her take notice. Barbara did not make such comments lightly.

Taking a firmer grip on her knife, Lily went back to her chopping. 'Why? What would Archie do?'

She had become accustomed to the pattern of their talks and knew that pauses were to be expected, but when she had finished with the carrot and an onion and scraped both into the broth that simmered on the hearth, and still no answer came, she turned again in puzzlement.

Barbara seemed to be thinking, her gaze fixed on the fire while with an absent touch she twisted the plain, narrow band of silver that she wore upon her finger as a wedding ring.

Suddenly she said to Lily, 'Leave that now, and come with me.'

The lovely back parlour was Barbara's domain, and with the door closed behind them nobody would dare intrude. They could speak privately.

The bedstead lay concealed behind its curtains. Barbara drew the chairs around to make a cosy pairing so they faced each other close before the fireplace and the painting of the sea at sunrise.

Barbara breathed deeply. 'When I was sixteen, as ye are now, I met a young man who was ... well, ye might say he was my Matthew. In all my life I had never met anyone like him, ye ken? Just a mariner. Nobody grand or important,' she said, 'but to me, he was everything.' This pause was shorter, as she gazed up at the painting. 'I was in love, and I was careless, and I fell with child. I was so frightened, Lily, I can feel it still, here like a fist around my heart. I had no parents, they were gone, and I felt certain that my mariner would leave and find another lass. But no, he wished to marry me.' Her faint smile was a window, briefly opened, to her younger self, when life was full of promise. Barbara turned her hand to show the silver ring. 'He gave me this, to seal his pledge, and promised we'd be married when he did return from his next voyage. But his ship . . . well, he did not return. There was a storm, ye see.' The breath she drew this time was less than steady, and it held regret. 'So there I was, alone and with a bairn inside me, and ye ken what the church does when they discover that.'

Lily said, 'Aye.' She'd seen enough young women made to stand in misery upon the place of penitence, to be shamed there in public by the minister in front of all the congregation.

Barbara said, 'Then Archie comes along and says that he can fix it all, and make my problem go away. And, God forgive me, I agreed upon his terms.'

Archie, she told Lily, had been as good as his word. He'd sent her to a woman in the Canongate – the same woman who'd later cared for Barbara's sister Margaret when it had come time for her confinement – and she'd stayed there till the bairn was born. 'Then I came down with all the proper documents to say that I'd been married onto Archie up at Edinburgh, and our bairn baptized, and we presented all of this to Mr Cant and did receive his blessing.'

Lily was not sure she'd heard right. 'Mr Cant?'

'Aye. He was minister at South Leith then. He moved on to the Trinity Church up in town, but not afore he gave me my four boys.'

Lily, in memory, saw the smiling face of Mr Cant, and minded how he'd been so kind that day at Colonel Graeme's when he'd bought her kitten. Strange how life wove threads among the people that you met, and bound them into unforeseen designs.

She looked at Barbara. 'What did happen to your bairn?'

'She didn't live past her first month.' An old pain, spoken flatly.

'I am sorry.'

'Aye, well. Bairns are fragile things. And it was coming on to winter. 'Tis a time of sickness. But then two weeks later Mr Cant did give me Matthew.' Barbara smiled. 'Ye think he's bonny now, ye should have seen him then. And it was in his nature from the start to always be exploring, never still. But he was good. I'd not have traded him for gold, and Archie kent it.'

Lily watched as Barbara's smile straightened into an expression of more purpose, and the older woman sat more upright in her chair.

'The thing with Archie,' Barbara said, 'is that he aye looks for a person's weak side. He can't help it, it's the way that he was made. He might not ever have a call to use that knowledge, but he looks for it, and once he's found it out, he keeps it close, just like a book upon his shelf, ye ken? And if he does have need of it, well, there it is and open for him.'

Lily was trying to follow, to take this all in. It was like overpainting a portrait and adding new colour and depth to a face so it still was the person she knew, and yet seemed in some lights unfamiliar. She guessed, 'And Matthew was your weak side?'

'All my lads are, and of course now ye and Maggie. I do love ye all, and I could never pick a favourite,' Barbara said, 'but Matthew was the first, and I let Archie see, and it did cost us. It may never be put right. He's not a demon, Archie. He does have a soul, and I did make him swear upon it that he'd not harm ye nor Maggie. Neither one of ye will wind up in that old house in the Paunchmarket.'

'What house is that?' asked Lily.

'All the truth shouldn't be told. The point is, Archie gave his word, and I don't doubt he'll keep it. He does care for me, in his way.' Barbara lightly touched the silver ring and twisted it again around her finger. 'It may not be what I dreamed of, yet the law would still consider ours a marriage after nearly twenty years, for all we've never had the words said over us in church.'

Lily softly remarked, 'But ye still wear your mariner's ring.'

'Aye. I wear this,' said Barbara, 'to mind me of what was once real, even if it could not last. To mind myself that I was loved, and loved truly, for that is a thing I would hold and remember when I have grown old.'

It was difficult thinking of Barbara as old. She was so very beautiful. Trying to picture the way she'd have looked when she was Lily's age, when the world lay in front of her, hurt Lily's eyes, and she blinked a few times.

Barbara said, 'I'm not meaning to frighten ye, Lily, nor make ye sad. But it's good ye should learn something from my mistakes, so ye'll not show your whole heart to Archie.'

To show she understood, Lily said, 'Because ye think Matthew might be my weak side.'

'No.' Barbara smiled, fondly. 'Because I think that ye're his.'

CHAPTER TWENTY

TUESDAY, 10 MAY, 1692

ALL THE TALK WAS of invasion.

King James was out of Ireland now and had been back in France awhile, and it was claimed the Jacobites who had but lately gone across to join him were assembling in their ships to make a bold return, with the support of the French fleet.

The waters off Leith's harbour teemed with English ships preparing to take back on board the soldiers of the regiments who had been quartered in the town, to carry them to stand against this newly rising threat.

And now all men between the ages of sixteen and sixty were called out and mustered to do training for defence.

Only Henry, being but fifteen, was left behind at Riddell's Close to keep the women company. Then Barbara left for an appointment with a friend, and it was time for Maggie's nap, and Lily took advantage of the time to clean the downstairs rooms, and Henry became restless. In the mid-afternoon, when Maggie wakened, Henry brought her down to Lily and said, 'Let's go see the ships.'

The English fleet was setting sail, which proved a great diversion for the little girl and, privately, for Lily also. She'd not lost her childish love of everything to do with ships – the setting of the rigging and the scrambling of the crew on deck, and most of all the sight and sound of canvas being hoisted up the tall masts, and the shiver that chased over all the sails as they first felt the wind, and then the wondrous moment when they caught it, came alive with it, and slowly brought their vessels round to face the open water of the firth.

Lily found the sight this afternoon so all-absorbing that she did not notice anyone approaching until Maggie gave a happy cry, tugged free of Henry's hand, and took off running back along the pier.

'Mind how you go,' was Matthew's warning, 'else you'll end up in the water, and I'll have to borrow someone's net to fish you out again.'

Maggie ignored him and stretched up both hands and asked him for his hat.

'Na, na,' he said, 'you'll not be wanting it the day. I've made it dirty.' But he gave her both his gloves, which made her satisfied, and holding her hands high she toddled proudly back to Henry.

Henry asked his brother, 'Are the rest of them gone home?'

'Aye. And you'd do well to stay out here awhile longer, till their tempers cool. Our Walter proved himself to be a better shot than Simon, and it may end in a greater war than what these fools are sailing to.' He nodded at the English ships, and pulled his hat brim lower as a shield against the sunlight. 'The word today was that King James's men have landed already in England.'

Lily knew that, if they had, then Colonel Graeme was among those forces. Looking up at Matthew she asked, 'Do ye think it's true?'

He shrugged. 'The story changes day to day. But I will grant he never seems to rest, King James. No matter how much parliament would wish to say that he gave up his crown, they cannot say he's ever given up the fight to claim it back.'

Lily said, a shade defensively, 'Why should he?'

Matthew turned his head, and angled a look down at her that seemed intrigued. 'He may do what he likes. But in my view he'd have done better to have stayed in Scotland and fought here, not run away to France.'

Lily, in disagreement with his view of how King James had managed things, remembered Colonel Graeme's teachings and applied them now in trying to explain. 'He did not run away. 'Twas like a stalemate in a game of chess – he'd reached the end of play upon this board and saw no move that he could make that would not harm his people, so he did retreat and his opponent claimed the victory, but King James did lose a battle, not the war. Retreat means only that,' she said, 'and he is yet alive.'

She watched while Matthew's eyes warmed with a light she'd never seen before. He said, 'You are a strategist.'

She could not hold that look for long. A breath, a blink, and then its force was broken and once more her gaze was focused on the moving sails. 'I did have a good teacher.'

'And I think you're secretly a Jacobite,' he said. 'Like Walter.'

She did not confess to it, but held her silence, which seemed only to intrigue him more. He gave a quiet laugh, and Lily was the only one to hear it, because Henry had moved off with Maggie down the pier.

'What other secrets are you keeping?' Matthew asked.

She turned her head again at that, and braved those brown eyes. 'Not as many as the rest of ye.'

'What are you on about?'

Lily asked, 'Where is the house in the Paunchmarket?'

Whatever he'd been expecting, it wasn't that. 'How did you hear about—?'

'Barbara. But she wouldn't go into details. And none of your brothers will, either.' She looked at him levelly. 'I'm not so feeble that I'll faint. I'd rather folk were honest.'

Matthew studied her a heartbeat longer, then he called to Henry, 'We'll not be a minute. I'm just taking Lily for a walk.'

He slowed his long steps to her shorter ones and kept himself between her and the water.

Lily noticed. Having spent a lifetime walking in the company of boys and young men, first up at Inchbrakie and now here, she had grown used to trailing after them or hurrying her pace. Not that she minded, but she found she liked this touch of grown-up chivalry.

The Paunchmarket curved from the Shore up to Tolbooth Wynd, holding a mix of old, elegant mansions and rougher new houses that rose tall against the late-afternoon sky. Here at its mouth, where it emptied out into the Shore, it was broad, but a short distance in it grew narrow and curved out of sight.

Matthew did not lead her into it. From where they stood upon the Shore, he nodded. 'There,' he told her. 'Third along, with the green door.'

It was not what she'd envisioned. 'It looks like an ordinary house.'

'So does the one you're now living in.'

Lily accepted that as a fair point. She asked, 'How many women are in there?'

He didn't know. 'At one time I think there were five or six. Might still be. None of my business.'

'And where do they come from?'

A shrug. 'There's never any shortage in a place like this.'

Lily felt indignant on behalf of all the women who, like Barbara, had been given little choice in life. 'Ye think so little of them?'

Matthew's head turned at her tone of voice. He lightly put one hand within the hollow of her back to steer her down again towards the pier, and started walking with her as though he did not wish to stand too long in that place where someone might be watching them. 'Ye ken nothing about me.'

'I ken much about your mother, though,' said Lily. 'She's the reason I was spared that life, the reason I'm not in that house, so I'd think ye might at least find some respect for—'

'I'm a foundling.' Matthew cut across her speech. His voice was even, but there was an edge of steel beneath. 'They reckon I was only hours old when I was left within the church porch by the woman who gave birth to me. But I was wrapped well in a blanket, with a note that begged them please to see me cared for. I was wanted, but could not be kept. That's what happens,' he told Lily, 'when you have a church that blames the woman for her weakness when she trusts a man who promises her much and treats her ill. One thing our mother taught us – and she taught us much – was we should never judge the women who gave birth to us. I never have. I never would.' He glanced at Lily, and his jaw was set in such a hard, defensive line, she wanted to take back what she had said and tell him she was sorry, but she knew he wasn't looking for apologies. He said, 'Nor would any of us leave a woman we had loved alone to face the punishment for what we'd done, but there are many men who would. And when they do, there's Archie, waiting with his promises.'

Again, she thought of Barbara, and the silver ring she wore upon her finger, and the life that Barbara might have had that never came to pass.

They walked a short while without speaking, and then Matthew said, without the bitterness, 'It's not that I think little of them. Never that. I'm sorry for the lasses who do enter in that house, because I ken what they've not learned.' His face, when he looked at her, showed her a flash of the boy he'd been once. 'With Archie,' he told her, 'there's always a price.'

CHAPTER TWENTY-ONE

THURSDAY, 22 DECEMBER, 1692

Lily understood why Matthew kept his distance from the house in Riddell's Close, although he did join them for the services in church each Sabbath.

While King James's brave invasion plan had come to naught, his ships cut off by England's fleet and never come to shore, here in their church at South Leith, Mr Kay, their minister, had waged a longer battle. He'd refused to give the church up to the Presbyterians, who claimed that, since the government had changed, it should be theirs by rights.

All over Scotland, ministers who failed to give allegiance to King William and Queen Mary and say prayers for them had lost their livings, and the Presbyterians were taking over from Episcopalians.

'The wheel is turning,' Archie said. 'Best make sure that ye keep to the right side of it.'

But Mr Kay cared only for his conscience. He'd continued to appeal to higher church courts while he held the keys to both the church and session house.

In August there'd been mayhem – magistrates had come

from Edinburgh, without a warrant but with armed guards, who surrounded by a crowd demanded Mr Kay give up the keys. When he again refused, they forcibly broke the church door and replaced the locks, and so the Presbyterians had gained possession of the church.

But they'd taken ground by violence, and could not expect a peace. So Matthew said, and he was right.

There had been more appeals, and Mr Kay had been allowed to preach on Sabbath afternoons and every other Thursday while he waited for a final judgement, and his elders went on meeting in the Cantore – the small room above the church porch, where they'd once imprisoned sinners, and to which he still retained the key.

This stretched on into the autumn, then past Michaelmas, and not two weeks ago Mr Kay had sent someone to their door to ask for Archie, asking would he come at once.

'What was it?' Barbara asked, when Archie had returned.

'They needed me to write an instrument to say the Presbyterians had barred them from the Cantore, when it's where they always meet, and that a new lock had been put upon the door without their knowledge or consent.' Archie had set down his papers. Passed a hand across his eyes.

'So they're shut out?'

'Not anymore. They broke back in, and put their own lock on again, and held their meeting. Stubborn fool,' said Archie, meaning Mr Kay. 'A man should ken when he's been beaten.'

Barbara had asked, 'Would ye ken it, d'ye think?'

Now, some two weeks later, Lily found herself relating that exchange in full to Matthew.

They were at the harbour as before, but this time Maggie

had been left at home and only Henry stood with them along-side Matthew's horse and cart while waiting for the boat to land his next cargo to haul.

It was a raw day, and the late December wind swirled down the Shore in gusts that twisted Lily's skirts and tore her misting breath away, but Matthew kept his body angled so his shoulders blocked the worst of it.

'And what did Archie say to that?' he asked her.

'Nothing.' It was not uncommon, Lily knew, for Archie to let Barbara get the best of him in conversations, and she said as much to Matthew.

'Aye, well, she still wants to watch her step.'

'She thinks he will not harm her.'

'I think she's too trusting,' Matthew told her. 'Like yourself.'

'I'm not.'

'There's some would see you standing here with me and Henry,' he said, 'and think otherwise.'

That brought a grin from Henry. 'Me? I'm harmless. And I'm hungry. D'ye wish anything from the pieman?'

They didn't, and Henry went off on his own up the short way to the stall where the pieman was selling his wares. He'd been doing a brisk business earlier, given the number of soldiers and seamen about, getting ready to ship off to Flanders, but now it was nearly dusk. There were but few red coats clustered about, and the smaller boats carrying men and provisions between the large ships and the Shore weren't so thick on the water. This would be the last cargo Matthew need carry before he could end his day's work and return cart and horse for the night to the Kirkgate.

The horse, growing weary from standing so long in the cold, raised a protest, and Matthew moved round to the animal's head, speaking low words of calm reassurance.

'She's bonny,' said Lily, as she came to join him. She offered her hand and the mare nuzzled into it, blowing warm breath. 'What's her name?'

'Lennet.'

Lily thought that inadequate, given the mare's glossy bay coat and soulful eyes. 'Surely they could have done better than name her for one of the plainest of birds.'

Matthew scratched the mare's neck. 'Nothing plain about a lennet.'

'It's a small, brown bird.'

'Aye, maybe so.' He looked at Lily, and he seemed too close. 'But when it sings, its song strikes to your heart.'

He held her gaze a moment, then he smiled and looked away.

She thought of Barbara saying, 'Give him time', and wondered how much time she ought to give him – whether it was time to speak and tell him of her feelings, or if she should simply wait, or . . .

'Stay here,' Matthew said. His voice had changed and grown more wary. 'Watch the mare.'

His own eyes were on Henry. At the pieman's stall, two soldiers had approached him and were talking to him. Matthew started walking up towards them.

Then one soldier grabbed at Henry's arm and held it fast, and Matthew started running.

By the time he reached the stall, the pieman had come round to try to intervene, to no avail. At first it seemed that Matthew only meant to talk. He stood with outward calm and sought to set himself between the soldiers and his brother. But the soldier holding Henry would not let him go, and then the other took a swing at Matthew, and it came to blows.

What Lily saw next left her shaken. It was swift and it was brutal. Pushing Henry safely to the side, Matthew flashed over into someone she had never seen – a ruthless man. A man of violence. Neither soldier saw it coming. Both of them regretted it.

One stumbled past her with a bleeding face and one arm hanging strangely. His companion took a while to stand at all.

When he did, although a few red-coated soldiers had come to assist him, they found themselves confronting not just Matthew on his own, but a fierce gathering of Leithers – mostly Matthew's fellow carters, but some mariners as well – who'd seen the fighting and were slowly filing in to form a line along his back.

Lily watched while Matthew squared his shoulders, and she watched his bloodied hands form once more into fists.

And when the soldiers turned away, although she let her breath out in relief, she could not help but think that Matthew's face looked disappointed.

Archie showed his disappointment, too, at having been deprived of any chance to use his influence in setting things to rights.

'I could have saved him,' said Archie. 'The players at the

table might have changed, but they do like their silver just as well as in the former government.'

Barbara said he should be glad he got to keep his silver this time, and he grudgingly agreed. But Lily knew it galled him, losing the advantage over Matthew that he might have gained by paying to settle his troubles.

With Archie, so Matthew had told her, *there's always a price.*

Walter pointed out, 'He didn't need saving. No point arresting a man when half the town was there to witness that your soldier struck him first, and that what followed was no more than self-defence. I'm told the soldiers had been ordered only to recruit men from their regiments to go to fight in Flanders, not to press our local lads into forced service. And besides,' he added, 'Henry is not yet of age for them to take. So they were three times in the wrong, and could do naught else but let Matthew walk a free man.'

Simon dryly said he doubted that the soldiers would have left the Shore alive if they'd done otherwise. 'I hear the crowd was not a very friendly one.'

'Well,' Barbara said, 'how many of our lads have they now pressed, when they've been telt to stop? And I did hear they killed two men who did resist them. I thank God for putting Matthew where he was so that he could save Henry.'

Afterwards, as they were scouring pots together in the kitchen, Barbara studied Lily's downturned face. 'It frightened ye to see that in him, didn't it?'

Lily hesitated. Then she nodded. 'It was like that day with Simon.'

Barbara understood. 'It's a thing that lies within them both.

The difference is,' she said, 'that Matthew kens the way to put it in his pocket and control it. He'd not harm ye.'

Lily was not sure.

Her heart still wanted him, and when he was close by her eyes still followed him, but now her mind put up a small, protective wall that made her more reserved. If Matthew noticed, he said nothing. He was busy with his work, and rarely came to Riddell's Close. Nor did he often come to church.

The battle for their South Leith Church had ended very bitterly, with Mr Kay denied his last appeals, and final judgement coming down from his superiors in Edinburgh that he would have to yield his living to the Presbyterians, who now possessed the only legal church in Leith.

So now, in this new year, they found their roles again reversed, as they'd once been in the old Covenanting days – Episcopalians cast out, and Presbyterians triumphant.

It was not a pleasant change. Every Sabbath now, the searchers went throughout the parish with a zeal that none had seen before. They leapt back fences, entered houses when they did not get an answer to their knocking, searched in every nook and hiding place, to seek out those who were not at the service, or those who would break the Sabbath in unsanctioned ways by doing work.

Maggie started having nightmares.

Walter, for his conscience, now refused to go to church, and joined the Leithers who did walk upon the Links instead each Sabbath, and because his strength lay in his mind and not his arm, his elder brothers walked the Links beside him to protect him. Some weeks Simon went, and some weeks Matthew, and some both together.

Archie had no great regard for Presbyterians and only went to church himself to stay on their right side so he could keep his business flourishing, but by midsummer he was losing patience. 'Walter's costing me a fortune in his fines,' he said to Barbara. 'Simon, too. I should just send him to the Bass if he's a mind to be a Jacobite.'

Barbara laughed. She had a way of smoothing over Archie's temper. 'Ye'll not send him to the Bass, don't talk so foolish. There's no profit in it.'

The Bass rock lay not far around the headland of the firth – a small and stony island with a castle fortress that for long years had proved useful as a prison. At the Revolution, King William's forces had made the fatal error of imprisoning four Jacobites within the castle, and when a supply ship came and all the soldiers were distracted, those four prisoners, in one gallant effort, seized the castle for themselves and sent the soldiers off the Bass in the supply ship.

Word had spread throughout the country, and to France. More men had joined the four, and through these past few years, the Bass – the final piece of Scotland where King James's men still held out undefeated – had weathered a blockade by English ships sent by King William who could not abide to see them so defiant. Yet supplies crept through, with help from those on shore. Lily suspected there were several cellars here in Leith from which provisions for the Bass were loaded under cover of the night into small boats that could be rowed across beneath the notice of the English ships – a risky venture, and with very little profit to be made, as Barbara pointed out.

But although Archie's temper calmed, Lily knew Walter

would have gladly gone himself to join the men who held the Bass for King James.

Through the months that followed, it became a focus for all Walter's thoughts and hopes, and Lily watched his spirits rise and fall together with that outpost's fortunes.

Some of the Jacobites were captured on a foray while ashore, taken to Edinburgh, and there imprisoned in the Tolbooth to await their trials. Supply ships came, or did not come. The trials went poorly, and by spring of the next year the prisoners had been condemned to death for treason. One was even hanged. And then the men remaining on the Bass arranged for a surrender.

Having fooled their enemy into believing they had a much larger fighting force, they had been granted generous terms – they kept their arms, they kept their freedom, those who'd given aid to them were left unpunished, those who'd been imprisoned were released, and they were left to sail to France or take their homes again.

But it was a deep wound to Walter, watching this last stronghold yield.

Lily understood, because it stole something from her heart, too, that she could not explain.

When Sabbath came, the grey skies matched her mood, and she was frowning as she fastened Maggie into her best petticoat. Maggie was nearly five now, but she had not learned the art of keeping still. Lily had trouble with the ties. 'Maggie, *please* will ye stand quietly,' she begged, as Barbara put her head around the door.

'You're burning daylight,' Barbara said. 'The men did get so tired of waiting for us, they've gone on ahead.'

Rushing, Lily finished dressing Maggie, tied on both their pairs of shoes, and hurried down the stairs, but when they came out to the close, she could not do it.

Something snapped within her in rebellion, and she could not bring herself to go and sit within that church among the same folk who had cheered for the surrender of the Bass.

In the corner of her apron she had tied the coins meant for the poor box. Handing them to Barbara, she said, 'Ye will have to pay the fine for me today, as well.'

She half expected there'd be argument, but Barbara only looked at her and said, 'All right, then,' and took Maggie's hand and walked away towards the church.

Lily felt a moment's freedom that was quickly doused by her awareness of the quiet of the close and of the windows looking down on her, behind which might be any number of reproving eyes. She briskly began walking towards Tolbooth Wynd. She had not gone far when a familiar voice asked, 'Where are you away to?'

Lily jumped a little, startled.

Matthew had been leaning in the narrow arching entrance to a passage between two of the old houses just across the close. She might have walked straight past him if he had not spoken.

'To the Links, to look for Walter,' she said. 'What are ye doing lurking there?'

'Not lurking,' he corrected her. 'And Walter isn't at the Links. He's gone to Mr Kay's house, for the private sermon there.'

'I see.' She did not wish to go to any sermon. Not today. But it would not be safe to walk alone. 'Is Simon with him?'

'Aye.' He straightened from the wall. 'But I can take you to the Links, if you are not afraid of me.'

She meant to tell him in a calm, collected tone, that she was not afraid, but when she met his eyes it all got jumbled somehow, and the words came out as they had done when she had been a child up at Inchbrakie: 'I'm no feart.'

She'd missed his smile. She'd missed the way he lightly touched her back when they began to walk. Now, she got both.

Chapter Twenty-Two

Sunday, 29 April 1694

THE LINKS WERE FAIRLY empty, since no one could play the golf upon the Sabbath and the only people here were those who, like themselves, were not at church. The searchers could not catch them all, out here. The space was simply too broad, stretching for a mile or more with ample hills to hide behind and access to the town and sea.

She was, for once, glad of the care she had taken in dressing. She wore one of Barbara's old gowns, Lily's favourite – the same gown that Barbara had worn on the day Lily first came to live here, the brown one – made over to fit her, the sleeves turned up over her elbows to show the white ruffles of her linen shift underneath. She'd also, because she was hurrying, taken up Barbara's old hat from the peg by the door in the place of her own, and not realized it until she'd settled it over her lace pinner and seen the edge of an ivory plume over the straw brim. It was a grand hat. Lily liked it immensely, though she hoped the plume would survive the strong winds that were rising this morning, out here on the Links.

It was one with her mood, that wind, wildly unsettled. The

gulls sought to ride it in high, soaring circles, but even they wobbled and gave up the effort and aimed their flight over the sea. And however the sun might be trying to shine, the wind chased clouds in front of it so that the sky was a blanket of grey, dull and surly.

Matthew told her, 'You're quiet, the day. Not yourself.'

'Am I not?'

'No,' he said. 'Something's happened.'

Lily realized he was only prying from concern. She said, 'The Bass surrendered.'

Matthew's face relaxed. 'Aye. But I reckon they had only reached a stalemate in their play, as I was taught by a wise strategist. They have but lost one battle,' he said, looking down at Lily, 'and their king yet lives.'

That made her feel irrationally better. 'You should tell the same to Walter. It might cheer him.'

'Walter needs to sit a few days with his melancholy before he'll be ready to be cheered. I ken the nature of my brothers.'

'Just as Archie kens our weak sides?' Lily teased him.

'In a way. Though weak sides are not hard to see in people, once you learn the way of it,' said Matthew. 'Take Henry, now. Henry would like to believe we're an ordinary family. He wishes for that more than anything, and he'll do anything if it will help him to keep that illusion. Our Walter, he's hopeful that Archie will send him beyond seas to study. To Amsterdam, maybe. Or Paris. Won't happen, but Walter keeps hoping if he does good work, maybe next year. The year after.' His voice held the same tone it had on the day they had talked of the women who lived in the house in the Paunchmarket. 'Simon's more difficult, but I think he feels he somehow owes Archie.'

Lily said, 'He does owe Archie.' She told him about the day Simon had beaten the man half to death in their house. 'It cost Archie a great deal of money to settle that so Mr Fearne wouldn't bring charges. We were all terrified Simon would hang, or be transported off to the plantations in one of Mr Fearne's ships, for at first he refused Archie's money, but Barbara persuaded him.'

Lily stopped then, having realized that Matthew was no longer walking beside her. A few paces back, he had planted his feet. Now he turned from her, looking out over the water that stretched out this morning as grey as a blade to the opposite shore of the firth.

Retracing her steps, she came close to him. 'I didn't ken that nobody had telt ye.'

'How bad was the beating?'

She said, 'Mr Fearne nearly died. Simon said he deserved it.' She stood there a moment and looked at the water, too, thinking, then asked him, 'What's Archie's weak side?'

Matthew's half-smile was grim. 'Greed.'

'As simple as that?'

'Aye. There's nothing and no one he'll not sell for silver. Just mind that.'

She promised she would. Lily paused. 'And what's mine?'

Matthew's head turned, and the look he angled down at her was warm. 'You always wish to see the best in people.' In his quiet voice, it sounded like an accusation.

Lily knew he spoke the truth, for Jean had told her the same thing when she was younger, but it made her feel exposed to think that Matthew had seen with such keen eyes to her heart.

She said, 'Ye ken nothing about me.'

He did not back down, but held her gaze. In truth it seemed he came a little nearer. 'I ken everything about you.'

Lily looked at him and could not breathe.

And then the sky tore open and the rain came, in a sudden, unrelenting downpour. Everywhere around them people scattered from the Links and sought the shelter of the town, and Matthew laughed and grabbed her hand and Lily ran with him.

There was nobody else at home at Riddell's Close. He came with her upstairs and said, 'You'll catch your death unless you get dry clothes on.'

His own coat was soaked, but once he'd shrugged it off, the shirt and waistcoat underneath were not much more than damp, and his broad hat had better caught the water and deflected it than her poor straw one.

Matthew opened up the box beneath the window. There was some discussion over what clothes she would need, but in the end he passed her towels, and said, 'Here, take these. And this. And this.' A shift was added to the pile, together with a petticoat and bodice in a print of orange flowers and green vines. 'You can take these to the closet. I'll wait here, in case the searchers come.'

Another man, she knew, might take advantage.

They were in this house alone, the two of them, with none to hear her if she raised a protest. And he surely had to know by now, from how she did not try to guard her feelings when they were in private, that she'd not protest.

Lily had never felt so nervous as she felt when she stepped back into the chamber from the closet, in the orange-flowered gown, her damp hair loose about her shoulders.

Matthew stood, his back towards her, at the little table with the oval mirror set on top of it. He'd set out a new pinner for her and was now arranging all the pins in almost military order, in a neat and perfect line.

The silence must have somehow warned him. Glancing up, he met her gaze within the mirror.

Lily's breath caught, hard.

She told him, softly, 'You're a good man.'

Matthew turned, and came towards her. 'No, I'm not.' He stopped too close. He was all she could see when she tilted her head up. 'I'm not a good man at all.' Smoothing her hair back, he rested one hand at the nape of her neck and said, 'You would do better to run from me, Lily. As far and as fast as you can.'

Lily shook her head, steadily holding that brown gaze that suddenly seemed her whole world. In a voice that was barely a voice, she assured him, 'I'm no feart.'

She saw the quick flash of his smile, then he lowered his head and he kissed her and Lily saw nothing at all, for her eyes were closed and she was drifting on feeling.

A sound from the passage below brought them instantly arm's length apart.

It was no more than Simon and Walter, returning from Mr Kay's illegal church service at his own house in the Yardheads. When one of them started upstairs, Matthew moved. He was casually standing just inside the door of the chamber when Simon appeared on the landing.

'Still raining?' he asked, noting Simon's wet coat.

Simon stopped for a moment, his eyes moving past Matthew's shoulder to Lily and back again. 'Aye.'

'We were out on the Links,' Matthew said.

Lily held her breath, wondering what Simon thought of her, but he said only, ''Tis none of my business,' and would have walked on but he caught himself. Glanced back at Matthew. 'Ye staying for dinner?'

Lily had never seen Simon when he was a child. He'd already left childhood behind when she'd met him, and now he was twenty. A man.

But there was something almost boyish in the way he faced his brother. Something almost hopeful.

Matthew must have seen it, too.

'Aye,' Matthew said. 'I think I will.'

Barbara reckoned it a fair exchange – her old hat's ivory plume, which had been lost out on the Links in that hard rain, in trade for Matthew coming round more often. She stitched a broad, brown ribbon on the hat instead, and said to Lily, 'Mind, now, what I telt ye. The mistakes I made when I was young. Ye would not wish to find yourself in trouble.'

There was no chance of that. Lily might have lost her heart to Matthew, but she was determined that was all she'd lose. For Matthew's part, the manner of his birth had made him equally determined not to bring another bairn into the world in the same circumstances.

He was every inch the gentleman. And they took care to be discreet.

Matthew's brothers helped by closing ranks around them, screening them from Archie's watchful eyes so he'd not guess the truth.

The late November evening when the family gathered all together in the front room, with the shutters closing out the weather, keeping in the warmth and light, it would have seemed to anyone that Matthew's whole attention was on Maggie.

He was sitting near the hearth and she had climbed onto his knee as she loved best to do whenever he was near, for although Maggie did love all of her adopted brothers it was plain to everyone that Matthew was her favourite. She'd turned five on her last birthday and was just the right size now to rest her head in the strong curve of his shoulder while he read to her.

At the small, square table by the window Barbara and the other brothers played a lively and good-natured game of cards, made all the livelier by the sure knowledge that they all were cheating at their play, while Archie sat beside them in his own chair, alternately reading from his papers and observing.

Only Lily was at work, having a will that needed altering for one of Archie's clients by the morning. It was not a complicated task – a name razed out, another substituted, and the changing of a number. She did not allow herself to think who might be injured in the process. She preferred instead to twist it in her mind and think that she perhaps was helping someone who had been unjustly barred from an inheritance that they were rightly owed. That made it easier.

The first time she had realized that the documents she wrote and changed for Archie were not done in play, but real, and had real consequences, she had gone in tears to Barbara. 'It is wrong,' she'd said. 'It is a sin, like stealing, and I will be punished for it.'

Barbara had held her, and dried her eyes. 'My work's a sin as well, but it is only work, and it is what we need do to put bread on our table. Ye think that the men in high places, the men in our government who make the laws, never break them? They cloak it in righteousness, but aye, they murder and steal, and their sins are far blacker than yours,' Barbara promised her. 'God kens your heart, Lily. Give Him your prayers and be good in all other ways. He will forgive ye.'

Lily knew He'd have much to forgive.

By the time she had finished her work on the will, Matthew was nearing the end of his chapter.

He and Maggie were reading their way through *The History of the Most Renowned Don Quixote of La Mancha: And His Trusty Squire Sancho Panza* – a newer English edition that was richly illustrated with engravings.

As he finished reading, Maggie sighed, her eyes upon the picture. 'But she wasn't a real princess, she was just a maid.'

'He fought for her, regardless,' Matthew said.

'I still wish she had been a princess.'

Matthew smiled. 'Perhaps she was, in secret.'

Maggie brightened. 'Truly?'

'Aye. In life,' he told her, 'nothing is impossible.' He closed their book and gave it to her. 'Here, you put that back, and fetch the red one from the shelf beside it. No, the taller red one. That's my lass. Now, what date was that published?'

Maggie turned the pages. 'It's in funny numbers.'

'Roman numerals,' Matthew said. 'And you can read them, don't pretend you can't. I taught you.' Patiently, he waited while she worked them through.

She told him, 'Sixteen eighty-eight.'

'And what year were you born, then?'

'Sixteen eighty-nine.'

'Right.' Matthew took the red book from the little girl and in an expert motion tore out one of the blank end pages. 'So now you have a paper of the proper age,' he said to Maggie. 'Some papers have marks on if you hold them to the light, so you can't use one that was made after the date you're needing. Now you only need to add the writing.'

Archie commented, 'And what now would ye have me do when someone else does need that page?'

But Barbara looked up from her cards and told him dryly, 'I doubt ye'll have many clients who are ages with our Maggie.'

Matthew passed the little girl the page. 'Take that to Lily. She'll make you a princess.'

They all partly had a hand in it, for Lily wrote the body of the document, but Simon aged the edges of it, Walter bore it witness, as did Barbara, and Henry – who did special work with wax – designed a seal fit for the kingdom of their Princess Maggie's birth.

Even Archie grudgingly agreed the end result was something beautiful. He petted Maggie's head and said, 'Now off with ye to bed and keep it safe. And all the rest of ye, stop wasting my supplies.'

Not all the documents they worked upon were fraudulent or false.

Archie was a notary, and as such he served those who were respectable as well, and performed duties that were legal.

Late in February, a new client turned up on their doorstep. Walter showed him in, since Archie had gone out with Simon on another errand.

Lily had been helping Maggie with her writing lessons in the front room, but she stood when Walter and the visitor came in.

She recognized him straight away. He had changed little in the ten years since she'd seen him at Jean's wedding.

Thomas Gordon would now be just shy of thirty, she decided, and his features had grown firmer in their contours, but his eyes were just as blue as she recalled them being, and his smile was just as quick to charm.

He did not know her. Even when they had been briefly introduced and he had bowed, his gaze passed over her to Maggie and she realized she had not made an impression when they'd met. And she had changed. She was no more the little girl who'd sat with Jamie on the barrel at the penny wedding, cracking walnuts with the tool that Gordon used for his ship's navigation while he told her life was for the living.

'That's a bonny name,' he said to Maggie. 'One of my best ships is named the *Margaret*.'

Maggie's eyes became too large for Lily's liking. Lily did not trust men who showed such attention to young girls. She said, 'Ye will excuse us.'

Firmly taking Maggie's hand, she left the men to settle their affairs.

Later, when Gordon was gone, she went down to the front room to study the papers that Walter had set on the work table. 'This is for him?' she asked.

'Aye. He needs two copies made by Wednesday.'

Plain, straightforward work. It was only a pass that was issued in France giving Gordon permission to sail to that kingdom. She'd copied passes in French before and had gained some of the sense of that language. 'It says that his ship and his crew are Dutch.'

Matthew, that evening, disputed this. Working so long at the harbour, he was well acquainted with some of the skippers. He'd crossed paths with Gordon a few times. He'd heard things.

'His family, I think, comes from near Aberdeen, though he does have a kinsman in Camphere, in Holland, and he himself was made a citizen there. He's well kent here in Leith. He just now came in with a loading of brandy and salt brought from Rotterdam, and aye, his crew was Dutch then when he came, but they've left him now, and he's been taking on Scotsmen.'

It seemed strange to Lily. 'He kens we're at war with France?'

Matthew said, 'I suspect that's why he asked for the pass.'

'He's still risking much.'

'More risk, more profit, as Archie would say.' Matthew turned thoughtful. 'When did he say he was coming again to collect these?'

'You'd have to ask Walter. Why?'

He gave her no reason then, but the following Wednesday when Gordon came by, Matthew was at the house, too, and naturally where Matthew was, there Maggie was as well.

'Good morrow, Margaret,' Gordon greeted her. He'd brought a parcel with him that was roughly the same length as Maggie's arm and twice as broad, wrapped in bright paper. 'I have a great favour to ask you. My ship is too weighted with cargo, and we must find some way to lighten her, so I am hoping that you will take this off my hands. It would be a great kindness.'

Maggie took the parcel from him, and would have done only that, but Matthew said, 'I think you're meant to open it.'

She did. Inside, there was a wooden doll, whose jointed legs were hidden underneath a yellow linen gown topped with an apron edged in red. She had a matching cap that framed her pretty, smiling face with rosy cheeks. Her hands were carved so finely she had fingers. Maggie stared, and could not speak for a long moment, then she hugged the doll and looked at Gordon. 'Thank ye.'

Lily looked at Gordon also, fighting down the stirring of her deep suspicion. ''Tis a generous gift.'

He shrugged. 'I met her in the window of a shop last month in Rotterdam, and thought she looked fair lonely. My own daughter is but newly born and far too young to keep her proper company, but I believe that Margaret might be able to.' He smiled at Maggie. 'And have you a name for her?'

'Dolly.'

'A perfect name.' Turning to Matthew, he said, 'And I've met you before, surely?'

'Aye, you have.' Matthew reminded him of their encounters before at the harbour. 'I'm wondering if you're still taking on crew for your voyage?'

It would have been difficult to tell who was the more surprised – Lily, or Gordon.

As Lily's heart fell, Gordon said, 'I am. Have you experience?'

'None as a mariner. But where you're going, you'll need someone who can guard your back. And that,' said Matthew, 'I can do.'

CHAPTER TWENTY-THREE

WEDNESDAY, 28 FEBRUARY, 1695

'I'LL NOT BE AWAY long,' he promised. 'I'd not leave at all if I didn't ken Simon would keep you safe. It's only ...' Matthew looked away from her, as though in search of words he could not find.

'Ye might have warned me,' Lily said.

'It's been coming on awhile, this feeling. Like it's me that's fastened in the traces of that cart and not the horse, and pulling every day that weight around behind me for no purpose.'

Lily took those words as though they were a slap, and looked away herself, and Matthew cursed himself and said, 'You're not a part of that. You're not. You *give* me purpose. But the rest of it ...' He still could not explain it.

Barbara did a better job that evening, while she worked alone with Lily in the kitchen. 'Since he was a bairn,' she said, 'he's aye been on the move. Our Walter, if he had a book, he'd stay in one chair all the day if ye would let him, happy as ye please, but never Matthew. Some days I'd put Matthew down and turn my back and he'd be off so fast ...' She smiled, remembering. 'These past years he's been working at a job that holds him tightly to one place. He needs the space to run.'

Lily could accept that. Even understand that. But she did not like to see him leave.

Matthew kissed her deeply, as the proof his feelings had not changed. 'I will be back afore you have a chance to miss me.'

But that was impossible.

She could not help but think of Barbara's mariner, who'd promised to return and then been stolen by the sea.

The weeks stretched with no word, and when word finally came in June it left her desolate. Captain Gordon's ship was captured by a privateer from France, and ship and crew were now held in that kingdom at the port of Brest awaiting judgement from their admiralty.

There was more waiting. Maggie's nightmares worsened, and the little girl held tightly to her doll and feared the darkness and though Lily tried to comfort her by keeping up the readings from the *History of Don Quixote*, it did little but make Maggie mind the part where Don Quixote freed the galley slaves, which only made her fear the more for Matthew and the captain, for she knew that France had galleys.

Henry held his worries in so deeply he fell ill, and when he was recovered and could move about the house again he pushed his chair back from the table one morning and said to Maggie and to Lily, 'Let's go see the ships.'

And that was how they happened to be at the Shore the day Matthew returned.

Maggie saw him first. She ran the whole length of the pier, with Dolly flying like a yellow flag behind her. Matthew caught her up and swung her round and held her tightly, but his head stayed up, his gaze fixed over all the crowd of people, straight along the Shore to Lily.

Somehow she could not make her legs move, and it took him an age to reach them. Henry nearly knocked him over in a fierce embrace, and Lily might have done the same had Matthew's eyes not warned her in the instant before Archie's voice said lightly, just behind her, 'So ye're back then.'

She would later learn Archie had been at the house in the Paunchmarket, not far from where they stood, but at that moment it did seem to her that he had sprung from nowhere.

Archie looked at all of them, his features showing nothing of his thoughts, though Lily felt he gave her face a closer study than the others. Nervously she met his eyes, and Archie smiled and looked away, and said to Matthew, 'Ye had us fair worried, lad. Your mother will be pleased to see ye home.'

❧

Simon kept to Matthew's side as he and Lily walked upon the Links the Sabbath following. Although his eyes were fixed protectively on Walter, walking just ahead of them, his thoughts were fixed upon their problem.

Simon said, 'Ye cannot yet be certain Archie kens.'

Matthew accepted this. 'But if he does, he'll hold it for the moment he can twist it to his use.'

'Ye're past his reach now, surely. Unlike some of us.' The half-smile was a rarity for Simon. 'No, it's fine, I'm not complaining. I'm not bothered that he moved me to the Paunchmarket. 'Tis better work than most. The lasses need someone to keep them safe, and we all ken my hands weren't made for forging. Anyway, Archie could hardly put Walter in charge of that house, could he? Walter has eyes for the one little black-haired lass, he'd never get any work done at all.'

Walter heard that, and turned at their laughter. Ignoring his brothers, he told Lily, 'I've only been there to deliver account books, that's all, so ye needn't be giving me that look.' But still, he was red in the face.

Matthew told him he ought to be careful. 'If Simon has seen how you look at the black-haired lass, Archie will doubtless have noticed it, too.'

Which brought them back to where they had begun, with their first problem.

Matthew frowned. 'If Archie does ken I'm with Lily, I'm not worried for myself. I'm worried what he'll do to Lily.'

Lily asked him, 'Why should he do anything to me?'

'Because he kens that it would let him have a handle to me, and then he could turn me to his will.'

She was his weak side. Lily shook her head and told him, 'Archie isn't going to harm me.'

'How d'ye ken that?' asked Matthew.

Lily said, 'He promised Barbara he would not, and he has kept that promise these ten years. I doubt he'd break it now.'

Matthew didn't share her faith in Archie's promises. 'I have a different history with them,' he said, with a sideways glance. 'I'd sleep better if we found a way for you to let me know each night that you were safe.'

It was Walter who finally proposed that she do what a heroine had done in one of the poems he'd read – set a candle each night in her window, to signal that everything inside the house was well.

Matthew agreed that might work. 'But you can't leave it burning all night, that's impractical.'

'No, but I could light it when it gets dark, and then leave it a couple of hours,' she suggested. 'If anyone asks, I could tell them the dark frightens Maggie. It would be no lie. And Archie won't mind the cost of the candles so much if he thinks it's for Maggie's sake.'

Simon offered, 'I can get ye all the candles ye have need of.'

Lily told him, 'Aye, because that's just the way to see that Matthew sleeps at night. For ye to get caught thieving and to end up in the Tolbooth. Could we please have one thing in the house that's bought and paid for in the ordinary way, not lifted out through someone's window?'

Walter grinned. 'Henry would like that.'

'He would, aye,' said Matthew. 'He's long wanted us to be something we're not.'

Walter's grin faded, and he faced Matthew with something approaching defiance. 'Nothing wrong with a man wanting better from life. Maybe Henry should come with me next year when I go to study in Utrecht.'

Matthew asked, 'Archie's letting ye go, is he?'

Walter said, 'He'd have done it this year, only things were so unsettled.'

Lily knew he meant politically. There had been growing arguments in parliament and elsewhere that, Queen Mary having died last autumn of the smallpox, and King William having only gained his right to rule at all through her, that he should step aside in favour of her sister, Princess Anne, or even let King James come back again.

King William was a hard man and unpopular with many people, and moreover, he was Dutch.

'The Stewarts have their faults, but they are easier to like. They're our own kind,' was how Barbara had reasoned things. But politics were rarely based on reason.

Walter said to Matthew now, 'I'd rather go to Paris, to be honest, and I will if this war ends soon, but Utrecht's close enough.'

Simon said, 'Tell the truth, now. If ye go to Paris, ye would travel on to Saint-Germain and we'd no more have sight of ye.'

He said it as a joke, but Walter's answer was half serious. ''Tis possible. Especially now Matthew's helped to fill the chest to pay my future wages.'

Matthew looked at him. 'How's that?'

'Well, by agreement with the king of France, King James receives a portion of each captured prize and cargo that's brought into a French harbour. When your ship was seized, a tenth of what was taken went directly to King James.'

Lily turned this knowledge over in her mind, and afterwards, when Walter walked ahead with Simon, she asked Matthew, 'Are ye certain Captain Gordon didn't let himself be taken by that privateer?'

'So that King James could claim ten per cent profit of what we were carrying? There would be easier ways of supplying your king,' he said, 'were you a Jacobite.'

Lily was not so sure. Since the retreat of the soldiers from Ireland and Scotland to France, King James now had a court to provide for and no nation he could raise revenue from in the usual manner, through taxes and excise, so any small profits that he could lay claim to would likely be welcome.

She asked, 'There were none of your crew who left ye and went overland, perhaps to Saint-Germain?'

She'd amused him now. 'I thought you favoured the Jacobite cause.'

'I do.'

'Then why are you so distrustful of Gordon, whatever his politics?'

There simply was no way to tell him unless she revealed what had happened to her as a child that had left her so wary of men who gave gifts to young girls, and although she knew she bore no fault for that incident, she felt the shame of it still, and did not wish to speak of it, nor to speak Mr Bell's name.

Matthew glanced at her, neither taking her silence for lack of an answer nor dismissing her concern, but simply offering her reassurance. 'I've spent much time with Gordon these past months, and he has my trust.'

She knew he did not give that lightly. Lily frowned.

'Don't worry,' said Matthew. 'I like him. I'd follow him anywhere.'

'Aye,' she said. 'That's what I fear.'

The second time he went to France with Captain Gordon, Lily saw it coming – saw the restlessness beginning to take hold in Matthew weeks beforehand, so when Gordon brought his pass this time to have it copied, she expected what would come.

She did not fear it any less, but Matthew understood her fears and tried his best to make it easier. He showed her on the map the gate they'd enter by at Flanders on their journey overland to Paris.

Walter had been wounded Matthew would see Paris before he would, but he hid it well. He was still hopeful he would make it to Utrecht, although it was becoming clear this would not be the season. 'Archie says I might have travelled in the spring,' he told them, 'but for the invasion.'

Henry answered, 'There is always an invasion.' Which was truly how it seemed.

This one, like those before it, had begun with a brave gathering of Jacobites in France – this time at Calais, and supported by a great conspiracy at London aimed, so it was said, at an assassination of King William. And like those before it, this invasion failed.

'Be careful,' Lily said to Matthew, 'that ye do not find yourself at Saint-Germain, instead of Paris.'

Matthew smiled, and kissed her. 'You're the one who must be careful.'

He asked Simon to step in for him while he was gone and keep watch on the house. And this time, he was not away so long.

When he returned, Lily had news for him. 'Walter is married.'

They were on the Shore. Matthew stopped walking. 'Married?'

'Aye.' She had struggled over how much she should tell him of the truth, in part to spare his brother, and in part to spare the lass involved, but Matthew was no fool and Lily knew he'd learn the truth himself in time, so in the end she shared the whole of what she'd witnessed and been told.

Matthew listened, and his mouth made a hard line. 'The black-haired lass from the Paunchmarket. Aye, well, it would be, wouldn't it? Didn't I tell him to mind how he went down that road?'

'Simon believes she was with child already, before she and Walter . . . that is, Simon thinks Archie might have been solving two problems at once: getting rid of a lass who was of no more use to him, and keeping Walter in Leith.' Of course, Walter wouldn't believe that, but it had been plain to the rest of them from the way Archie had managed the affair, first finding reasons to send Walter to the Paunchmarket on errands, and then sending Simon elsewhere long enough to let the lass play out the part of her seduction.

Archie knew his foundlings well. It mattered not to Walter whether he had proof he *was* the father, only that he *might* have been the father, for then he could not stand by and let the bairn be named a bastard, and its mother made to suffer.

'I wish them well,' said Matthew, but he knew as well as Lily did what Archie had accomplished.

There was no more talk of school for Walter. He made no more plans for travel. Archie smoothed the way for him to join the maltman's trade and settle into lodgings with his new wife. In December, sadly, she did lose the unborn bairn inside her and they all did mourn the loss, but Lily did not think that Walter's grief was for the bairn alone.

All through that winter and the spring and summer that came after, Lily set the candle in her window every evening.

'What's it for?' asked Maggie sleepily one night. Lily did not tell her that it was a signal meant for Matthew, in case Archie prised that information from the child. Instead she said, 'To keep away the dark.'

She knew that Matthew came by every night to see that light, although she did not always hear his footsteps passing by. Once, looking out of the window, she by chance had seen him standing sheltered in the same arched entrance to the passage opposite between the houses, where he'd stood the first day they'd gone walking on the Links.

Even when he'd seen her candle, he had stood awhile there in the shadows as though guarding her, and Lily had felt safer simply knowing he was there.

She felt less comfortable within the house with Archie.

In the work room now, she was always aware when he was watching her, and had to ask him not to do it, for she could not concentrate.

So on that late November day in 1697, when she felt the prickling crawl begin along the bent nape of her neck, she said, not turning from the writing table, 'Archie, please, I've telt ye. I can't do this when ye are behind me.'

Matthew said, 'I thought you did no longer use your copy book.'

She spun, and smiled, and reached to put her arms around his neck and draw him down to her. 'Why do ye never use the door?'

'Who says I didn't?'

Lily let that pass. 'As to the copy book, I'm practising my flourishes.' She showed him.

'Here's a flourish for you.' Taking up her pen, he signed his name, then set a small, bright, open brooch of silver on the page above the place where he had signed.

She blinked. 'What's this?'

'My heart, if you will have it.'

It was indeed a heart – a tiny one, and crowned, and fashioned beautifully of smaller hearts and roses. 'Matthew.' Reaching up her hand again, she touched his hair. He leaned down lower still behind her so his jaw was at her temple, and his voice was quiet, just for her to hear.

'I did not lift that out through someone's window, if you're wondering. I bought it with my wages, in the ordinary way.'

'I was not thinking—' she began, but she had turned her head to say it, and he kissed her and did not allow her to complete the thought.

And then, in fairness, she had difficulty thinking anything at all.

'Marry me,' he said. He drew back just enough so she could see his eyes, and know that he was serious. 'I love you, Lily Aitcheson. I wish to love you always. Take this heart to be my pledge, and say you'll marry me.'

She could not mind when her own heart had ever felt so full. There was no world but Matthew's eyes, and in them she could see her own hopes, her own happiness reflected. What other answer could she give?

She took his heart, and told him, 'Aye.'

CHAPTER TWENTY-FOUR

SATURDAY, 27 SEPTEMBER, 1707

HENRY DIDN'T KNOW WHAT happened after that.

He only knew that by the week's end, Matthew Browne had gone from Leith, and Lily would not speak of it.

'Fair broke her heart,' he said, and settled back into his chair beside the fire within the front room of the house in Riddell's Close.

We'd finished with the wine I'd brought, and moved on to a bottle of fine brandy he had found within the cabinet in the corner.

I leaned over to refill our glasses, knowing I was frowning as I asked, 'She told you nothing?'

'Nothing. She did speak to Captain Gordon, though. It might be he could tell ye more.'

Sitting there, the room seemed filled with ghosts. I saw them clearly – Lily sitting at the writing table, little Maggie wrapt within the tales of Don Quixote, Thomas Gordon standing framed within the door. I thought it possible that Henry saw them, too, or felt their presence, because when a coal fell from the fire to the hearthstone he paid it no heed, and it was left to me to take the poker up and push it back again, and stir the fire to its former warmth.

I asked, 'And where would I find Captain Gordon?'

Henry shrugged. 'He was given a commission some years past with our Scots navy to patrol this coast. Ye'll find him here with regularity. And when he is in Leith, he aye will stop and spend an hour with me.' His tone turned wry. 'He still likes bringing gifts. He brought that brandy.' Henry nodded to the bottle in between us. 'Our merchant fleet is overdue, and Gordon will be guarding them. He should be here afore too long.'

'All the talk in town is that there will be an invasion by the Jacobites. Perhaps that's what's delayed him.'

Henry rolled his eyes and said, 'There's always an invasion. How many times did old King James try to reclaim his crown and have it come to nothing?'

I admitted that was so. 'But this is his son, and the country does seem ripe for some sort of mischief, so maybe this younger James Stewart will do what his father could not.'

'I tell ye what,' said Henry dryly. 'Next time Captain Gordon comes, I'll send him up to tell ye his opinion of the matter, shall I? Me, I take no part of politics. It's all a game to them, these great men and their wars, and we're the pieces they discard when they are done their play. They claim the glory, and we pay the price.'

I was not altogether sure that I agreed with him on every count, for even great men fell in battle, and I knew that Robert Moray sat in prison now in danger of his life while I sat here in comfort, drinking brandy. But I knew what Henry meant.

His mention of the paying of a price turned my thoughts back to Archie Browne, who twisted everything he touched in one way or another, seeking payment.

I'd been sent down here by Gilroy to enquire about one person, and it was the same person whose weak side had not yet been mentioned.

'What happened to Maggie?' I asked.

It was, admittedly, an abrupt shift in the conversation, and Henry looked at me narrowly over the rim of his glass. 'No idea. She left here with Lily. I've not seen her since.'

'And when was that? When did they leave, exactly?'

'In the spring of ninety-nine.'

A year after the date on the certificate of marriage. 'You're certain of the year?'

He said, 'I'm not like to forget it, am I? Not that year. First Walter's wife and wee lad died of fever, then our mother died, and then Maggie and Lily left . . .'

It seemed as though he might have added something else beyond that, but he only took a deep drink from his glass and said, 'It was an evil year.'

I took him at his word. 'You've not seen Lily since then, either, I'd imagine?'

There was evidently something in my tone that made him wary.

'She's in trouble,' he said. 'Isn't she?'

Like Gilroy, I had instincts. It was plain both Henry and myself were on the same side when it came to Lily's welfare. 'Yes, I think she is.'

'What has she telt ye?'

'I haven't been able to speak to her privately.'

'I could,' he offered. 'Where is she?'

'I'm not sure that would be a good idea. She is being watched.' I told him of the man in grey, and while I spoke I saw that he was coming to the same opinion I had come to of that man's identity, because when I had finished, Henry sat in thoughtful silence with his drink.

I asked him, 'If he has come back, do you know where he would be staying?'

'Couldn't say.' He sniffed. 'To tell the truth, I might not even recognize him, after all this time.'

I wasn't having that. 'You might not recognize your brother?'

Henry met my gaze with stout defiance. 'People change.'

Except they didn't, really.

Any man might put on armour for a while, like Don Quixote in that book which little Maggie Graeme had so loved to read, but you could yet glimpse him when he raised his helmet's visor, and beneath the armour he remained the man he'd always been inside.

As I drank my brandy, I imagined that the shade of young Matthew Browne moved past me now and bent to Lily at the writing table, and she turned her head to him and smiled, and I knew one thing sure.

She'd always be his weak side.

VI

I BELIEVE THAT, IN MY heart, I'd known exactly who the man in grey was from the moment I'd stepped from the shelter of the wall when I'd been looking at the candle in her window, and he'd followed from the shadows.

I'd have had to be a fool, with all I knew, not to suspect it, and the more I turned it over in my mind as I walked back alone to Edinburgh that evening after leaving Henry, the more deeply I felt sure.

I have a certain memory of that night, held in the way one holds a seashell gathered on the shore – time dulls its brightness, and wears down its sharper edges, yet we only have to hold it to our ear and we can once more hear the singing of the sea. And so it is with memory.

I remember that the moon was nearly full, and there was music spilling out into the street from Pat Steell's tavern as I passed his door, and near the shuttered Luckenbooths a little cat lay curled and sleeping, putting me in mind of Lily's kitten.

All these things I do remember, just as clearly as the

moment when I glanced up at the window of her lodgings and saw not only the candle, but her standing close beside it, looking down into the street.

She saw me. I touched one hand to my hat and went on walking, knowing well that mine were not the only eyes that would be out there in the darkness, watching Lily's window. It felt wrong to turn my back to her.

I thought of all the times in life she'd had to stand and watch men walk away. I heard her saying to her grandmother, 'He promised me that he would never leave me . . .'

She'd been speaking of James Graeme then, and on that night I felt a bond of kinship with him, thinking that if he had lived, he would at least have understood the nature of my jealousy.

As I walked up the final way to Caldow's Land, I thought, I don't know why, of Helen's cousin's wife – the one who in her former marriage had been sad because half of her husband's heart was always held by his first love.

It made me wonder just how much of Lily's heart was held by Matthew, and if she'd have any left to give another man.

CHAPTER TWENTY-FIVE

SUNDAY, 28 SEPTEMBER, 1707

I ALWAYS BECAME THOUGHTFUL WHEN I sat in great cathedrals. I suspect that was the point. Most had been built by ancient bishops with a single purpose – to make those of us who entered them feel small and insignificant within the sight of God.

St Giles' had that effect upon me.

Like my country, St Giles' had been passed like a child's plaything, hand to hand, down through the long wars of religion – from the Catholics to John Knox, who'd held the pulpit here with fiery sermons, to Episcopalians who'd sought the restoration of their bishops and been met with riots, back to Presbyterians who'd cheered the killing of a king, restored once more to the Episcopalians who'd seen their power falter when King James had fled to France, and now again to Presbyterians, who since the Revolution had maintained it with a firm, unyielding hand.

It was in the divided days of John Knox, a hundred and fifty or more years ago, that the inside of St Giles' had first been divided as well with partitions, a practice that carried on through the last century so that now this one great building, although it was still whole on the outside, had been carved within to form four separate churches, each one having its own minister and congregation.

It was done, so I'd been told, to better serve the population of the growing town.

The central section of St Giles' became the Old Kirk, while the western end was split into the Haddo's-hold and Tolbooth Kirks, which left this eastern end – the soaring choir – to be the High Kirk, where the queen's pew lay and where the lords of session and a good many important men had seats.

Outwardly, it was a practical arrangement, but as I sat paying no heed whatsoever to the raging sermon of the minister this morning, I engaged myself in study of the columns that were meant to lead my eyes up to the intricately vaulted ceiling high above my head. I was thinking, not of heaven, as I was supposed to, but of how wondrous the effect would be if all the space inside that great cathedral could be opened and restored. And I was thinking of the things that had been lost by its division.

In that way, too, St Giles' was much like Scotland.

'Amen,' said the minister.

Helen was in no great hurry to leave. She had spotted her cousin – the one who sat on the commission – and wanted to linger and thank him in person, being somewhat puzzled she'd had no reply yet to her letter, but he was in deep conversation with two other men, so she was waiting.

After some minutes, she glanced at my face. I'd been trying to not let my restlessness show. Evidently I'd done a poor job of it.

Helen smiled. 'Why don't you step out and get some air while I am waiting?'

'I'd not leave you on your own.'

'Why not? And if you tell me that it is because of my condition, I can't promise I won't poison you at dinner,' Helen warned. 'I had enough of that this morning, with the fuss MacDougall made about me coming here. 'Tis only the beginning of my seventh month. I'm not so very large,' she asked me, 'am I?'

I could not help smiling. 'No.'

'Then go and have a walk,' she told me. 'I will sit exactly here until my cousin's free to speak.'

I knew when I was being sent away. 'I'll not be long,' I told her.

Helen said, 'Take all the time you like.' And then, more casually, 'I do believe that I saw Violet Young leaving just now. You might still overtake her.'

With a sideways look I said to Helen, 'I will not go far. You'll find me with the Regent Murray if you need me.'

Since she had been raised here, I knew she would understand that reference, and her nod and smile assured me that she did.

The Regent Murray, long ago, had schemed against his own half-sister, Mary, Queen of Scots, joining with John Knox to raise the citizens of Edinburgh against her. When Queen Mary abdicated, chased to exile and captivity in England, Murray was created regent for her infant son, the young king, but he'd not held power long. He'd been assassinated shortly after by a man he'd wronged, so it was only fitting that his final resting place was where men came to settle their accounts.

His tomb was in the southern transept of St Giles', and being in an aisle of the church left always open, with an access to Parliament Close – where the parliament sat and the lords of the council and session did business – the Regent Murray's tomb had been used for some generations as a meeting place, where messages were passed, and deals were struck, and debts were paid.

This morning there were several people strolling round the space, together and apart.

I noticed only one.

She wore a simple brown silk gown – most probably the same brown gown that once belonged to Barbara Malcolm, carefully reworked to suit more recent fashions, for I'd learned that Lily did not much like to discard things. She was sentimental.

She looked to be waiting there for somebody, and we were not alone, but I was not about to lose the opportunity to speak to her. I made my bow and wished her a good morrow, and because I feared to compliment the wrong thing, said, 'I like your hat.'

She smiled. 'It is an old one.'

'I do like it, notwithstanding. I confess I did not see you at the service.'

'I expect we were in different churches,' she said. 'I was in the Haddo's-hold. The houses on the south side of the High Street and the Landmarket belong to different parishes than those upon the north.'

'I see.' A couple moved behind us, arm in arm. I stood aside to let them pass, then said, undiplomatically, 'I thought your family was Episcopalian.'

She looked at me with patient eyes. ''Tis not as though one has a choice of churches in these times.'

'That's not entirely true. There are still outed ministers who do hold services in private meeting rooms, if you know where to find them.'

Lily glanced around as if amused that I had said as much aloud. 'I thank you, no. I do have more than enough troubles.'

It made the perfect opening. I was about to ask her what those troubles were, exactly, when a cultured voice addressed me. 'Sergeant Williamson?'

The Earl of Seafield, in his Sabbath finery, made heads turn in the transept, and the firm tap of his heels as he approached was like the rapping of a gavel.

'Mrs Turnbull said I'd find you here.' He looked from me to Lily, and I made the introductions. If he recognized her as the woman our inquiry was about, he did not say so. All he said was, 'I see you've been spending time with Regent Murray.' Tipping back his head in admiration he remarked, 'It truly is a most impressive monument. I've always found these figures on the brass plaque very moving – Justice, with her weapons lost, and Faith deprived of her defender.'

Justice, to my eyes, looked lost herself, despondent in her chair, her broken sceptre, scales, and sword upon the floor. Faith bore her cross, of course, but she at least was doing something, seated at a desk and writing in an open book. I did not think that Faith had wholly given up the fight.

The earl went on, 'I do but hope that I'm remembered with a monument that's half as grand, when I am gone.'

In her straightforward manner, Lily said, 'Perhaps they'll raise one like it one day for Montrose.'

'Montrose? You mean the first marquis?' The earl looked at her in surprise. 'He's buried in this church, you know. Just over there.' He pointed to the aisle, not visible from where we stood but not far distant.

'Yes, I know. I've seen the place,' said Lily. 'It is plainer than he does deserve.'

The earl observed her, curious. 'Are you a Graeme by your birth, or by your marriage?' When she told him, he replied, 'Then I commend you, Mrs Graeme, on your fierce attachment to your husband's family. I would that my wife would defend the Ogilvys as bravely.'

She returned his smile, but this time absently. From how her gaze was drawn off for a moment in distraction it appeared she'd spotted somebody outside the transept door.

I looked, too. It was not the man I'd thought to see. This man was older. Thinner. With a lean, sharp face.

'You will excuse me,' Lily said, and curtseyed prettily to Seafield, and we made our bows. I watched her walk away to join the older man, and went on watching until they were gone from view.

Seafield was talking, but I only caught the end of what he said. ' . . . And naturally the challenge is to find the means by which we may be let into the secret.'

I could feel that I was frowning, but with any luck he'd take it as a sign of concentration, not confusion.

He went on, 'We know that Robert Moray deals with the Pretender's court at Saint-Germain, and he has only luck to thank for keeping him alive so long. But luck cannot be counted on for ever.' From his pocket, Seafield drew a thin, sealed letter, and a second paper, folded but not sealed. 'Someone must remind him of that fact, for his own good.'

I shook my head, not wishing to be part of any scheme. 'We are not friends. He met me once. He does not know me.'

'You're an honest man. He will admire that. He will trust you.' Seafield handed me the letter and the paper, which, unfolded, I could see now was a pass to gain me entry to the castle. 'You're expected in the morning. I believe the guard said ten o'clock would be the time best suited.'

I did not like being used, but when you stood against a man of such position, with such power, there was never any doubt who would prevail.

I did, though, meet his gaze. 'I wish to know the substance of what's in the letter, if I am to carry it.'

The earl could very easily have brushed off my request. Instead he said, 'It simply does inform him that we know he has not told us all, but if he does deal plainly with us now and answers all our questions, then whatever he asks will be granted him, and so he has an opportunity, if he is wise, to make his fortune.'

I knew now that it would be a waste of time, to give that message to a man like Robert Moray. More than that, it would insult him. From the little I had seen I did not think he was the sort of man to sell his secrets or his friends for money. When I said as much to Seafield, he was unconcerned.

'Then as the letter does assure him, he will walk a harder road. We'll have the story from him either way,' the earl said, very certain. 'If he will not sell it to us, we will draw it from his lips with all the torture that our gaolers can devise.'

His smile was chillingly polite.

I felt the cold of it when he had gone, and had to turn a moment to the monument again, to school my face. I looked again at those brass figures on the plaque, and felt a quick surge of impatience with the sadly drooping Justice. *Pick your sword up off the floor*, I felt like telling her. *A broken sword still has an edge, and you're not yet defeated.*

I stood straighter, and had tucked the letter and the pass both safely in my pocket by the time that Helen came to find me.

'Do you know,' she told me as she took my arm, 'I had the most extraordinary conversation with my cousin.'

I found a normal smile to show her, feigning interest. 'Did you?'

'Yes. He said he did receive my letter – you recall the one I wrote, asking if he would thank the men of the commission for the honour of assigning us this inquiry.'

'And did he thank them?'

'That's the thing,' said Helen. 'He had no idea what I meant by it. He asked the other men who sit on the commission, and they were of no more help, since neither Mrs Graeme nor her claim had ever come before them.'

While I grappled with the implications of this, Helen seemed to give up any effort to make sense of it.

She said, 'Lord Grange must simply have been misinformed. It doesn't matter. As my cousin says, it's still a claim that wants investigating, and it's one less claim that the commission needs to do, for which they're grateful, and we'll still have gained the favour of Lord Grange when we've completed it.'

She put it thus behind her.

I could not. My mind turned back to the beginning of this week, when Lord Grange had arrived at Caldow's Land. Now that I thought of it, he'd never actually said that the claim had been passed on from the Commissioners of the Equivalent. It had been Gilroy who'd first told us that.

Gilroy might be lying. I had seen him do it expertly. Or he might be repeating what Lord Grange had told him, in which case Lord Grange was lying – or repeating something *he'd* been told, by . . . whom?

And why? Why such deception, for a case of such a passing insignificance? Who possibly could benefit?

Within my mind the voice of Robert Moray dryly made reply, *At least ye have the wit to ask the question.*

Chapter Twenty-Six

Monday, 29 September, 1707

The guard might have expected me, but it was clear that no one had warned Robert Moray he would have a visitor. He took it in his stride.

Nearly a week had passed since I had seen him, and he'd spent a few days beyond that now in this high-vaulted room without a fire, and with the small, barred window letting in uncertain light. He moved more stiffly, and his features showed the strain. If he had been questioned roughly I could see no outward sign of it, but I knew not all ill use left a mark, and he was not the sort of man who would complain. He was too proud.

He'd been standing at the table when the guard had let me in, midway through washing at the small basin of water they had brought him for that purpose. He was wearing neither wig nor coat, his closely-clipped brown hair yet rumpled from his sleep, his Holland shirt well creased and wrinkled, but he still retained an air of calm command, dismissed the guard, and bade me take a seat upon the low, campaign-style bed as though he were at home and in his private chamber and had asked me round to talk over some business matter at his morning audience.

I waited. Gave him time to fit his wig upon his head, shrug on his coat, and face me with his armour well intact. 'Ye will forgive the beard,' he said. 'They seem to think that if I have a razor I will cut their throats, and I've no faith their barber won't cut mine.'

It was a fair dilemma. Briefly, I returned his smile. 'I'd offer you my knife, but I'm afraid your guard took all my weapons.' He had not done so the first time I'd come to visit, but today the guard had made me turn my pockets out and kept possession of my sword belt with the whinger. I had thought he might not give me back my pen and ink and papers either, but he did. Among them was the letter Seafield sent me to deliver, which the guard had not disturbed.

Moray said, 'Yes, he's been diligent of late.' From inside his coat he drew a letter that fell open easily along its folds as if it had been often read. 'I should imagine this is why. I did receive this from my wife, who mentions she received my own last Wednesday morning, for which I'm in your debt. Ye could not possibly have got it there so quickly had ye used the Stirling carrier.'

'No,' I said. 'I reasoned an express was safer. And I thought your wife should not be made to wait.'

'Ye will be reimbursed. I'll see to it when I'm released.'

'That won't be needed. I am only happy that your wife and son are well.'

He studied me. 'You're well informed. How did ye know I had a son?'

'My friend's wife, Mrs Turnbull,' I explained, 'is well connected in society.'

'I'm flattered that she would apply her connections to learn about me,' he said lightly.

I felt moved to defend her. 'She was trying, in her way, to help our inquiry. Her husband's the one who is meant to be leading it.'

'I see. And she considers it relevant, does she, that I have a son?' He'd not altered his tone, but I knew I had struck his protective nerve and should continue with caution. I also knew this was my chance to come sideways at something I'd wondered about.

I said, 'She thinks you are a Jacobite, because you did not name your son for your wife's father or your own, but called him James.' It was an indirect way of asking the question, and he obliged with an indirect answer.

'I had a brother James, whom I did love, and who died young. And, as you know, I had a cousin James. I loved him also, and he too is dead. I might have named my son for either of them. But,' he added, looking half-annoyed and half-amused, 'my son was baptized on the birthday of our young King James, and is named James Francis Edward, like the king, so your friend's wife may have a point.' He turned the challenge back on me. 'And what of ye? Do ye drink to the health of Queen Anne when at table, or pass your glass over the water to honour the king who now lives beyond sea?'

I tried the same approach as Henry Browne, and said, 'I take no part of politics.'

'A politician's answer. But to take no part of politics is, in itself, to take a part. Let no man tell ye otherwise.' He did not lean against the table as he had the first day, only drew the single chair around to face me as he sat, so once again the window was behind him. 'I wondered how long it would take them to send ye back.'

'What do you mean?'

'My wife's letter. It came to me opened, of course, meaning they had all read it and knew what it said – knew I'd managed to write her a letter from here and find someone to see it delivered. My guard appears to be above suspicion,' Moray said, 'and I've not had many visitors. They'd never imagine that Gilroy would do it. He is, as I told ye, predictable, and he'd not venture his neck for another man. But ye are unknown.' He gave a nod towards my pen and papers. 'They'll have sent ye as a test, and when ye leave they'll have ye searched.' He paused, then added, 'They are confident I'll try to write my wife another letter, since in hers she told me we're to have another bairn, and any man who'd not reply to that is heartless.'

I heard the fine edge of frustration undercutting his calm words. I gave him my congratulations, all the same.

'Thank ye. No doubt she believed the news would give me hope,' he said.

I gathered, from his tone, it had the opposite effect. It was a helpless feeling to have those we loved beyond our reach where we could ill defend them, and I knew this word of an unborn bairn would have added to the weight he carried while his wife and child were left unguarded.

I said, 'I'm sure your wife has everything in hand.'

'Yes, she is rare,' he said, 'and I do not deserve her, and I know it. The men among my family do not seem to choose the easy road too often, and we owe a great debt to the women who consent to tangle up their lives with ours. My road would be a lonely one without her.'

I had walked so long alone I could say nothing useful in reply.

Moray read my silence with his keen perception. 'Not every man is meant to settle in his youth. I did not marry till five years ago, when I was two and thirty. I had met my wife when I was younger, but her father did not hold me in great favour then. He wished to see his daughters married onto men of consequence and wealth.'

He stood so obviously higher than myself in social ranking that I know my face revealed my thoughts on just how likely it would be that any father would reject him as a suitor.

'What?' he asked.

'You are the son of Abercairney.'

'That title does belong now to my brother William, since my father died.'

I said, 'I'm sorry.'

'There's no need. But great estates are not so easily divided. They are passed to the firstborn son,' Moray said, 'and all the rest of us carry our own fortunes under our hats.' He tapped his forehead, as if I did not already know he carried more wealth of intelligence beneath his hat than most men. 'Or else seek them on battlefields.'

I could not see his face with any clarity because the light was at his back, and yet I knew that he was speaking of his brother John, and from the tightness of his tone I realized that his wife and child were not the only people he was trying to protect.

I thought things over, but it did not take me long. There were some situations where the right decision was not difficult to make.

I said, 'I heard the Earl of Seafield say he wished they'd caught your brother John, not you. He knows your brother has been in the north on business from the court of Saint-Germain, but the earl does not know what that business is, nor where your brother might be now.'

Moray was watching me. 'Where did ye hear these things?'

'I dined on Wednesday last at the earl's house,' I said, 'by invitation. I can't say I much enjoyed the company. But I believe you have a right to know what they discussed, in case they try to tell you something false while questioning you here, to make you think your brother is in greater peril.'

'I am in your debt,' he said again.

'There also was a mention made that it might help you talk more freely if your wife were taken up,' I said, 'and put in prison.'

This silence felt more dangerous. 'And what did Seafield say to that?'

'He thought it was unnecessary. He said there were subtler ways.' The letter I'd received from Seafield had been sitting like a burning coal within my pocket, and I took it now and passed it to him. 'I expect that this is what he meant. I am ashamed to be the bearer of it.'

'They would have sent someone,' he said, unconcerned. He broke the seal. 'Have ye read this?'

'No, but I was told of its essence.'

He took several minutes to study it. I knew its contents would come as an insult, but its wording must have been worse, because I had the sense he was trying to hold in his temper.

When he finally spoke, his voice was evenly controlled. 'Money's never been my master, Sergeant. And while I suspect that, since the Union, torture is worn out of fashion, I'll admit I'm liable to the weaknesses of any other man of flesh and blood, and am not absolutely certain how I would conduct myself if it did come to that. But I would hope – and ye may tell this to the Earl of Seafield,' he said, his tone hardening, 'I would hope that nothing would prevail with me to part with my integrity. And ye may tell him also that, as I was born a gentleman, so I do hope that by God's grace I would behave as such. There is no sum of money, no amount of pain, that could make me forget my honour, or my loyal friends, and if I ever did, I trust they'd turn me from their presence for a villain and a rogue.'

He'd grown more heated as he spoke. 'Ye tell the Earl of Seafield all of that,' said Moray, then revised the thought. 'No, give me paper and your pen, I'll write it for myself, for I would have the words my own.'

It was the second time that I had waited while he wrote a letter, watched him fold it so it sealed itself, and took it from his hand.

He said, 'I also have a message for my wife, but this one I'll not trust to paper. Tell her I love her. That her words did bring me warmth in this cold place, as did her news about the bairn, but she must write to me no more. Tell her to take our son and go now to her father's house where they'll be better guarded. What is coming will be dangerous.'

He coughed, and from his smallest finger took a gold ring

that had been inscribed inside with writing, and said, 'Send this with it, so she'll know the message comes from me.'

I gave a short nod, and I stood, and slid the ring onto my finger, thinking that the guard would be less likely to take note of it if he believed it to be mine. I tried to frame my next words carefully. 'The last time I was here, you asked why the Commissioners of the Equivalent would bother with the inquiry at all, when they could have dismissed it and saved themselves the effort.'

'It's a fair question.'

'I've found out the answer,' I said. 'The commissioners were unaware of Lily's claim. They weren't the ones who did arrange for the inquiry.' I told him about Helen's cousin, and what she had learned from him.

'I see,' said Moray. 'That is interesting.'

'The Earl of Seafield knows about the inquiry. He mentioned it at dinner, though he said that it was secret, and that it was being done at the direction of a member of the high court. I assume he meant Lord Grange.' Here I paused and looked to Moray, who confirmed that Lord Grange was in fact a member of the High Court of Justiciary. As with anyone who'd ever faced a complex lock, I knew I'd have to spring each pin in proper order before it would open. 'Gilroy is the only person who has mentioned the commission. You know both men – Gilroy and Lord Grange. What can you tell me of their character?'

Moray had stayed seated, which in any other conversation would have meant that I had the advantage, but in this case he was clearly in command. He took his time deciding how to answer. 'Anything I tell ye will be of less use than your own observations. Do I know them? I know what they let me see of them, and whether that is what they truly are, I cannot say. Gilroy does seem to be a man who follows orders and is loyal, though he lies as coldly as a politician when he's called upon to do it. As for Lord Grange, I have known him long, yet know him very little. 'Tis his brother who's my friend.'

'Do you trust them?'

'No, but there are few men I trust in these times.'

I had to ask. 'And yet you trust me with your messages. Why? You know nothing of me.'

He said, 'I know all I need. I saw the way ye looked at Lily. More than that, I saw the way she looked at you. That tells me much about the measure of a man.'

I took *his* measure for a moment. 'Gilroy does not trust her. He believes I'm being played.'

'By Lily? Never. She's not capable of such a thing.' He sounded certain. 'I agree you're being played, but not by her.'

I waited for his further explanation, and when none came I remarked, 'That isn't helpful, as a warning.'

'It's the only warning I can give.' He did stand then, and turned a fraction so the light no longer fell behind him. Robert Moray never did a thing without a purpose. It was his intent that I should see his eyes. They were determined. 'There is more at stake,' he said, 'than ye can possibly imagine, Sergeant Williamson. Ye'll have to find your own way through.'

❧

I was searched, as Robert Moray said I would be, when I left his cell. The guard seized Moray's letter with such satisfaction that I found it comical to watch his face change when he saw to whom it was addressed. He kept it anyway.

'I'll see this is delivered to the Earl of Seafield,' said the guard, which suited me, since I had no great wish to see the earl again.

The guard, for all his searching, missed the gold ring on my finger. Finding nothing else that he had cause to confiscate, he gave me back my sword belt with the whinger and permitted me to leave.

I hadn't realized, till I passed through the portcullis gate and put that castle tower at my back, how being in that place affected me – but leaving it, I felt as though an iron chain had fallen from my chest. All men must feel the same when they're set loose from prison. Free air is a precious thing to breathe.

I breathed it deeply, trying not to think of Moray left in that stone room with little comfort but his honour, and in hazard of his life.

The wind had changed. It drove the dark clouds on before it, and I caught the long-familiar scent of threatened rain. As I came down into the Landmarket I was already lengthening my stride so I'd outpace the coming storm.

Approaching Caldow's Land, I met our neighbour from upstairs, the Latin master, who'd been hurrying home up the street from the other direction. He stopped to greet me, and we stepped into the shelter of the portico outside the merchant sisters' shop, and he asked how I liked the books that I had bought from him, and whether they had been of use.

I told him that they had. And then I thought of something I had meant to ask him.

'Oh, that's very fine work, yes,' he told me, as I handed him the whinger I had bought from Mr Bell.

'But the inscriptions are in Latin, and I cannot read them,' I confessed.

'Ah. Well, this one is simple. *Ne quid nimis*. It means "Nothing in excess", which is but good advice.' He turned the blade, to read the motto Dr Pitcairn had pronounced as being fitting for our times. 'And this one, *Fide sed cui vide*, is more of a warning.' He handed it back. 'It means "Trust, but beware in whom".'

CHAPTER TWENTY-SEVEN

THURSDAY, 2 OCTOBER, 1707

MEN WERE SENTIMENTAL CREATURES, though we did our best to keep it hidden.

In the scrutore in the writing chamber I had found a secret drawer within a drawer that held a single rose, picked long ago, pressed flat with care, and faded now to shades of subtle pink and parchment – yet the faint ghost of its fragrance lingered. Whether it had been concealed there by my friend Lieutenant Turnbull, or by some forgotten owner of the scrutore, I knew not. But I knew it had been given to a man because it lay upon a paper label on which had been written in a careful hand: *Whenever this red rose you see, remember her that best loves thee.*

I left it undisturbed.

The entire scrutore was a cabinet of curiosities. The pigeonholes were crammed with pots of ink and sticks of sealing wax, old pens, cast–off buttons, scraps of notes tucked here and there, and stubs of candles. And on opening the square door to the main compartment that was centrally positioned at my eye level above the writing surface, I discovered a neat row of several shark's teeth. Those, I knew, were Turnbull's. I'd been with him on the day when he and others of the ship's crew had gone fishing for that shark. Beside the teeth, a small brass dish of coins from different countries sat as witness to the travels of my friend, and at their centre sat a blue glass bead of unknown origin.

It might be argued that as grown men we'd not come so very far from the small lads we'd been when we had gathered stones that caught our eye, or chestnuts from the fields in autumn, or a piece of bark or twig, and carried all home in our pockets.

We were magpies still, collecting treasures.

I'd been very conscious of the value of the ring I'd held from Robert Moray, when I had enclosed it in the letter I had written to his wife on his behalf. That ring had likely been a gift from her to him, from the inscription that was scribed around its inner surface, where none else would see. 'Hearts truly tied none can divide,' it said.

And with his message Moray meant to send that promise back to her, that she might hold it bravely through her fears for what might happen to him. I'd wrapped the ring in paper and enclosed it in the letter and sealed both securely, and I'd placed them in the hands of the same man I'd hired last week to carry the express to Stirling. All of this I'd done on Monday morning, within half an hour of my arrival back at Caldow's Land from seeing Moray, for I'd known I would not rest until I knew his message to his wife was on the road.

It cost me more this time. The man I hired had looked at me and nodded to the sky. 'You see a storm is coming.'

'Aye,' I'd said. 'I know.'

The rain and wind had started shortly after, and since then the weather had stayed foul.

It had held Gilroy in the north. He'd sent us word of his delay, with his apologies – or what, for Gilroy, passed for an apology, and was no more than his brusque statement he'd be with us when he could. And so I waited.

I had work to keep me occupied, but there was only so much I could do alone, and once I'd written all the notes I felt I needed, I grew restless.

At least on the first two nights, although the wind stayed fierce, there'd been enough breaks in the weather that I had been able to get out to take my evening walk, but last night it had rained so hard that Helen had been horrified to see me take my hat and cloak and move towards the door.

'You're never going out tonight in *that*,' she'd said. 'You'll have your fever back.'

I knew she was not wrong so I relented, but MacDougall had not missed the opportunity to say, 'Ye'd think spending all the day locked up with books would give ye better judgement.'

All this week, MacDougall had been prodding at my patience. Helen had informed him he was not to interrupt me in the writing chamber when I was at work, and this had left him irritated.

'Next ye'll be wanting a key tae the lock on the door, will ye?' he'd asked me caustically.

'Is there one?' I'd countered, and since this exchange had taken place in front of Helen there'd been nothing he could do but own the fact that yes, there was, and fetch it for me, meaning I'd been able to do all my work in privacy.

The lock was a strong, French one, and while I doubted MacDougall, with all his rough ways, had much skill as a picklock, I still secured all the papers away in the scrutore each day to be doubly safe. Some family secrets weren't meant to be shared, and the notes I'd compiled for Gilroy were meant for his eyes alone.

I had taken care with what I wrote, and yet this morning Helen had, across the breakfast table, said, 'My husband gets that same look when there's something he has left undone.'

I'd pondered that this past hour.

Now, I took the illustrated book I'd bought of plants of the Americas, and gathered up a file of paper with a pen and ink, locked up the scrutore and the writing chamber, and went off to fetch my cloak and hat.

This time, when I passed Helen in the drawing room, I assured her I'd be in no danger. 'There's no rain this morning, only wind.'

She looked at me with open curiosity. 'Where are you going?'

'You were right. I need to follow up on something more with Mrs Graeme.' Gilroy, after all, had asked me to ask Henry what became of the child Maggie, and from Henry I had learned that Maggie went from Leith with Lily. 'I will not be long.'

'I'm coming with you,' Helen said.

'What?'

'Adam. You cannot simply turn up at a woman's door and think that she will let you in. No decent woman would, for you would compromise her virtue.'

Social rules exhausted me. 'And yet when I first came here,'

I reminded her, 'you let me in, and you have let me stay, and I would count you very virtuous.'

She thanked me. 'But I have MacDougall and the maid, while Mrs Graeme is not of the class to keep a servant. No,' she said, 'I will come with you.'

Helen, when she set her mind to something, always had her way.

MacDougall grumbled, but he could do little more than glare accusingly at me and remind us both how foolhardy it was for Helen to be out of doors at all. 'If ye take fright, your bairn will bear the mark of it,' he told her.

As I helped her down the forestair, I bent low against the wind and said, 'I do already pity your wee bairn before it's born.'

'Why?'

'Because it must already be marked in several places with MacDougall's face.'

She laughed. ''Tis very possible. He means well, for his fierceness. What's that book?'

I showed her. 'Mrs Graeme asked about my time in the Americas. I thought she might find this of interest.'

Helen seemed to find my face of interest for a moment, but a passing couple soon distracted her attention. There weren't many other people in the street to watch – the weather had kept most of them indoors, and there was no one lounging in the entrance to Hamilton's Close when we walked by.

The house at the corner of Forrester's Wynd was an older one that had been altered and much improved over the years. As with Caldow's Land, there was a shop at ground level – in this case a candlemaker's – and above that, overhanging galleries leaned out into the street and wynd, with multi-paned sash windows framed in stone. There were three floors above the shop, although the uppermost, considering the steeply angled roofline, could be no more than a garret.

Lily had her lodgings just below that, on the second floor above the shop, which meant our climb was one floor more than Helen was accustomed to, and even though I helped her up the covered turnpike stair the effort stole her wind a little. Whatever surprise Lily might have had on opening her door to us was quickly damped by her concern for Helen's health and comfort.

All the years Lily had spent in service made her an efficient lady's maid, and I knew better than to interfere. While she was seeing Helen settled in a chair with cushions, I looked round the room, for it was only that – a single room. The plastered walls were washed in white, but otherwise undecorated, and the ceiling beams had not been painted like the ones at Caldow's Land, but it was not a cheerless space. There was some colour in the weaving of the blanket on the bed against the far wall, and more colour in the cushions of the chair where Helen sat. The fireplace, while not a large one, was sufficient still for cooking and a pot of broth was simmering upon the hook that hung above the coals. And while the day outside was grey, the room drew light from the two windows that faced to the High Street, and a third that overlooked the wynd.

On the broad ledge of this third window I saw a short brass candlestick that had been fitted with a brand new candle, yet unburnt.

'I wonder, Sergeant Williamson, if I might have your help.'

I turned, and meeting Lily's eyes directly felt off balance though I covered it with confidence. 'Of course. Just tell me how.'

'If we could bring this table close to Mrs Turnbull . . .'

Moving furniture was something I could do that made me feel I had a purpose. There was a second, plainer chair that had no cushions but a seat of woven cane. I brought that, too, and found a third chair in the further corner that was partly broken and had one leg shorter than the rest but did consent to bear my weight if I sat very carefully.

While I was taking care of this, I set my book and papers on one corner of the table. By the time I'd finished, Lily had spread out an offering of cheese and bread and cups of ale, with bowls of nuts and raisins.

Helen had recovered. 'I apologize. I did not think I was so weak.'

'It is not weakness,' Lily told her. 'You've a bairn that's stealing space beneath your ribs and leaving you no room to breathe when climbing, that is all. I'll wager even the sergeant would find stairs a struggle if he were in your condition.'

Helen smiled at that. 'You're very kind.'

I stole a handful of the raisins and remarked that, if I *were* in her condition, I would not be climbing stairs. 'I would be sitting with my feet up, letting people wait upon me at my leisure.'

'Liar,' Helen called me. 'You've been like a caged bear all this week, unable to get out of doors. You'd never make it through confinement.'

Lily asked her, 'Will you stay in town when your time comes?'

'No, my husband's family home is in the Borders, near to Minto. He would like me to go there, for it is sure to be quieter. And safer,' Helen added, 'if the Jacobites continue to cause trouble.' She looked at me. 'We'll have to bring you with us, when we go. For company. The country is a pretty place but there's no true society, and one can only take so many turns about the garden before going altogether mad.'

My mouthful of raisins prevented me from answering, but Lily said that taking turns about a garden sounded lovely.

'There was a garden where I lately lived,' she said, 'and spending time in it was truly close to my idea of heaven. Anyway, you'll have your bairn to keep you company this time, so you've small chance of being bored. Is it a lad or lass you're wishing for?'

I saw how her smile disarmed Helen.

Helen smiled back. 'I know that men are always hoping for a son to be their firstborn, but in truth, I privately am wishing for a daughter. I do not understand the mind of boys. I don't believe that I would know the way to raise one.'

I could feel my grin, I couldn't help it. 'We're not so mysterious,' I promised her. 'We may play more roughly, and lead with our fists when words would do, but I assure you that our feelings are the same as yours and run as deep.'

Both women looked at me with softened eyes, and Helen asked me, 'Truly?'

'Aye.' Deliberately I pulled my gaze from Lily's and told Helen, 'If you had a son, you'd no doubt find him a devoted one.'

'You give me hope,' she said. 'If I could know they would all be like you, then I would happily have only sons.'

Lily smiled. 'My husband's mother had all boys, and was content.'

I saw my opening. 'You also said your husband had a cousin, Margaret Graeme. What became of her?'

It was a gamble. Lily would be well aware she'd never mentioned Maggie to us during the inquiry – I could see her searching backwards through her memory now, confirming this – which would have made her wonder why I'd asked the question in that way. I only hoped she'd realize I had phrased it so that she could speak of Maggie without having to reveal, in front of Helen, any details of her life in Leith. She need not mention Barbara Malcolm, nor the house in Riddell's Close, nor any of the—

'You mean Maggie.' Lily met my gaze with level eyes that knew exactly what my game was, but her light tone betrayed nothing of the kind. 'She teaches music at a school nearby for daughters of good families.'

That surprised me. 'Music?'

'Yes. She is accomplished on the virginals, and also sings most sweetly.'

I was trying to imagine where young Maggie Graeme, with her background, would have learned such arts as those, but I could think of no way to ask Lily without being indiscreet.

Helen said, 'I have always wished that I could play as well as others do, but I have not the patience nor the ear for it, I fear.'

Lily commiserated, 'Nor do I. But Maggie always loved to sing, and we did live for several years near Greenock with a kind woman who saw Maggie's love of music and arranged for her to take her lessons at the great house there.'

I asked her, 'Was that also where they had the garden?'

'Yes. It was an old one, and there were so many trees.' She said that with a wistfulness that puzzled me until I called to mind she'd spent her early years at play within the woods of Abercairney and Inchbrakie up in Perthshire, and as glad as she had been to come down here to join her father and the Graemes, trading open skies for ones framed always by a crowded line of rooftops would be difficult. It must have been a loss to leave the landscape of her childhood.

'It was a happy place,' she said. 'But sadly, my employer died in March. It was not unexpected. She'd been ill for some time. And she'd very kindly written to a friend of hers who kept a school here, recommending Maggie as a teacher, so ...' She spread her hands, a gesture that was all at once resigned and grateful. 'It's not been a terrible transition.'

I glanced round the single room and asked, 'Your husband's cousin lives here with you?'

'No, she has her own room at the school and does board there, but every Monday is her own, so she comes here to visit then.'

It sounded like a lonely life for Lily. I think Helen must have thought so, too, for she asked, 'And have you searched out many of your friends, from when you used to live here?'

Lily, by my reckoning, was only one and thirty – not much older by her years than Helen. But her life had made her older by experience, and it showed in her eyes now when she looked across the table. 'Time makes changes, Mrs Turnbull. We are none of us the people we once were.'

I knew the truth of that. I said, 'My mother used to tell me that you can't take a step forward if you're holding to the past.'

Lily told me, 'Your mother was wise.'

'Aye, she was.' I missed my mother every day, and knew I had been fortunate to have her, but like many men I did not put those feelings into words. I only coughed and said to Helen, 'Do you see? I stand as proof how great the bond can be between a mother and a son.'

'You have convinced me,' Helen said. 'I shall have *only* sons.' She tipped her head a little as though listening. 'This is a quiet house. Are there no other tenants?'

Lily shook her head. 'The candlemakers who do keep the shop live elsewhere, and the floor below me is the private lodging of my landlords, who make use of it but rarely when they are in town. They have not come of late, and may not come again. The husband died in August, and 'tis only by the kindness of his widow that I am allowed to stay here while the family settles the estate.'

I did not like to think of her alone here and unguarded in the night. It left her vulnerable. Nor did I like to know that she might soon be forced to find another place to live. I tried to push both thoughts aside so they would not be a distraction. Taking up my pen and ink, I asked, 'Where is the school at which your husband's cousin teaches?'

Lily's frown was slight. 'Why? She was a child when I was married. Even if she had a memory of that time, which I do doubt, her testimony cannot be of use.'

'I don't expect we'll need to speak to her,' I said, 'but Gilroy did ask me to learn where she had gone. He likes his notes to be complete.'

'I see.' She gave the address of the school. 'But I would thank you not to interview her there. The school does pride itself on having several students from fine families of the first quality, and any teacher who desires to stay there must then guard her reputation.'

'You do have my word,' I told her. 'If we need to talk to her, we'll do it here, where she will be more comfortable. You said she comes on Mondays?'

'Yes, it's her day off.'

'I will tell Gilroy that.' I made another note. 'And in the meantime, I thought this might help you pass the hours.' I slid the book I'd brought across the table to her.

It was very satisfying watching her receive it. Lily handled books with quiet reverence, as though they were made of gold.

I said, 'It shows some of the plants of the Americas, although the author leans a little heavily towards the islands, and I fear the text is all in French. But the illustrations are well done. The ferns, especially.'

She thanked me, and the look she sent me as she promised she would take good care of that book blotted out all other, lesser images within my mind. My concentration foundered.

We were halfway home when Helen asked me, 'Where's your pen?'

'I must have left it there.'

'Your ink as well?'

'It does not matter. It was old ink, and your husband has a trove of ink stashed in the scrutore.' With a smile, I told her, 'I've no doubt that Mrs Graeme will return them with the book.'

Helen granted it was very likely. 'She does seem a very thoughtful woman.'

'Aye.'

'I quite enjoyed our visit with her.'

I was pleased to hear it. It would suit me well if Helen, in her efforts to find me a wife, were to notice Lily as a prospect. I said, 'I enjoyed it, too.'

'For someone of her class, she carries herself well. It is a shame I've not the funds to hire another maid, just now.' Her smile, so bright and careless, did not know the cut it made.

There's a difference between us and them . . .

Helen Turnbull had been raised in softer circumstances, in a family that could boast of loftier connections than my own or Lily's. I knew she had meant no insult by her comment. And that somehow made it worse.

Helen said, 'I do believe she'd make good company.'

The wind blew very hard and cold between us down the High Street, but I found the voice to answer, 'Aye. I daresay that she would.'

CHAPTER TWENTY-EIGHT

FRIDAY, 3 OCTOBER, 1707

BEING RAISED BESIDE THE sea, I'd learned the superstitions of the men who made their living by her. Steer your boat clockwise to follow the way of the sun when you're first coming out of the harbour. Don't whistle into the wind. Never speak the words 'rabbit' or 'rat', among others. And if you should meet with a minister on your way down to your boat, go straight home and start over again, else you'll meet with bad luck on your voyage.

I took all these things as the customs of men who were trying to manage a hard force of nature the best way they could, and I gave them respect, though I'd never believed in them.

But there was one superstition the fishermen held to that always came true – you could count on a change in the weather come Friday.

This morning the wind had turned. Blowing more lightly and steadily out of the west, it had scattered the clouds out to sea, leaving space for the sun in a clear sky. The Landmarket filled with its normal flow of people, and when I stood at the window of the drawing room I could just make out the long edge of a grey coat showing at the limit of the shadows deep within the entrance to Hamilton's Close.

I found ways to curb my impatience while waiting for Gilroy. Turnbull's bookshelves in the writing chamber held a copy of Addison's *Remarks on several parts of Italy*, which allowed my mind freedom to travel if the rest of me could not. And after dinner I taught Helen how to play at cards the game of Quinze – a diverting, fair, and simple game that wanted no more of its players than that they could count as far as fifteen.

Scandalized, MacDougall told her, "'Tis not seemly, for a lady to be gambling.'

Helen reassured him that her soul was in no peril. 'We are wagering for buttons, not for coins. Besides, even the queen does gamble.'

'The queen,' he said, 'is not a Presbyterian.'

I privately imagined she was glad of that, but I said nothing, only dealt a card to Helen who, in triumph, claimed, 'Fifteen!'

MacDougall left us with a look of disapproval.

We were well into our third game when a knock interrupted us. MacDougall being elsewhere, I rose from my chair and crossed the few steps to the door.

I expected it was Gilroy.

It wasn't.

The man who stood facing me wore a blue naval officer's coat trimmed in gold braid with bright buttons, his long wig set in the tight curls of the fashion, but he had the firm, upright stance of a man who did not run from action, and his gaze, level with mine, was unaffected and good-natured.

'Captain Thomas Gordon,' he said, looking past my shoulder to Helen, to include her in the introduction. 'At your service.'

In the time it took me to collect my thoughts, he'd stepped into the room, and seeing our cards on the table flashed a charming smile at Helen. 'Madam, I apologize. I see I've interrupted you at play. What is the game?'

Whether from the force of Captain Gordon's smile or from his handsome face, she seemed to have forgotten.

I supplied the answer. 'Quinze.'

'A good game.' Although Helen had not spoken, he still aimed his words at her. 'I'll wait until you're done. Then, with your leave, I'll borrow Sergeant Williamson.' He turned to me. 'You spoke to Henry Browne. He said you needed information from me. I'm expected shortly at Pat Steell's. Come with me and we'll sup and talk. Assuming,' he said, once again to Helen, 'you don't mind.'

She found her voice this time. 'Of course not. Adam, go. Our game was nearly finished, and it is not as important as the captain's time.'

The captain smiled at her a second time, with nearly as great an effect. 'You honour me.' He took her hand in his and, bowing low above it, touched it to his lips, then as he straightened said, 'I'll try to see he's not debauched. We are a fairly sober crowd, but we've been known to keep our conversations going into the next morning, so if I don't have him back by midnight, don't be too alarmed.'

She promised not to be. 'I trust you'll take good care of him.'

Why she would believe that, having only met the man, I

wasn't sure, but Captain Gordon had the sort of presence that persuaded people he was someone they could trust.

He looked at me with eyes that told me little, and said, 'Get your hat.'

⟡

Steell's tavern was crowded, and Gordon attracted attention. So many men turned from their talking to greet him or shake his hand that it took us some few minutes to press our way through to the back, where Pat Steell himself looked up with pleasure from drying a jug. 'Why, Captain Gordon! It did take ye long enough to come this little distance up the road from Leith. How many days now since the *Royal William* came to anchor?'

'I arrived on Monday, but the wind made it impossible to come to shore,' said Gordon, leaning over to make himself heard above the noise of nearby conversation. 'And my ship's not named the *Royal William* any longer, Pat, not since the Union, just as I'm no longer commodore of our Scots navy, for we have no navy anymore. Our ships are now joined with the English into one great British navy, and the English did already have a *Royal William*, so my own ship is renamed the *Edinburgh*, and flies a Union Jack in place of our old Scottish flag.' His face showed his opinion of the change.

'Aye, well,' said Steell, ''tis just a name.'

''Tis just our independence,' Gordon countered, but he stopped short of an argument. Instead he drew a paper from the pocket of his coat and passed it to the tavern owner. 'Can you post this up for me? I'm having placards printed but they'll not be ready till tomorrow morning, and there may be men in here tonight who take an interest.'

I could see it was a notice, lettered in a neat hand, that invited sailors to come serve Her Majesty at Leith aboard the *Edinburgh*.

Steell said, 'Then it's true? I heard this afternoon ye had some trouble, but I swore I'd not believe it. Never Captain Gordon's men, that's what I said – they'd never mutiny.'

Gordon grinned. 'I thank you for your confidence, but aye, not too long after I did come ashore today, one hundred of my men escaped the ship in boats and are run off. It will take time to round them up, if we can even find them. In the meantime, we can search for men to take their place.'

Steell took the paper, promising to post it up straight away, and asked the captain, 'Will ye take a room tonight?'

'Aye. Thank you. And, if you please, some supper for the sergeant and myself.'

The room, a floor above and at the far end of the house, was vastly quieter. The noise of talk was muted to a constant, raucous murmuring that rose and fell beneath our feet.

Steell knew his clientele. The room was made for men. The walls were lined with dark wood panels, warmly lit by plain brass candle sconces. At the window, simple draperies of striped fabric matched the hangings on the tester bed that dominated the back wall, and by the modest hearth two elbow chairs faced one another over a square table, ready for a meal or conversation or, in our case, both.

The supper sent up to us was a good and simple one – cold chicken and a dish of peas, with bread and butter and a quart of wine to share.

I studied Gordon while I poured my wine. 'A shame about your sailors and the mutiny.'

'Aye. Although they're not entirely to blame. They somehow got it in their heads that we'd be bound for the West Indies next, and that did frighten them.'

'I wonder who began that rumour?'

'I cannot imagine.' He said it with such innocence I knew it had been him.

I told him, 'Now you'll have to spend a week or longer rounding those men up again, and hiring new ones.'

'Definitely longer than a week. I'd be surprised if we were heading north before the middle of the month.'

'And while you wait, our eastern coast sits unprotected,' I said, 'at the very moment young King James and his French allies are reportedly preparing their invasion force.'

'Are they?' Gordon raised his eyebrows as he poured his own wine. 'That, then, is unfortunate in terms of timing.' With a smile he lifted up his glass and made a toast. 'To absent friends. May we be reunited soon.'

I drank, and would have eased into the conversation but he cut straight to the heart of it with, 'Tell me about this inquiry of yours.'

While we ate, I summarized, and Gordon nodded.

Then he studied me in turn. 'I understood from Henry that you had an interest in one talk I had with Lily Aitcheson.'

'Aye.'

'That you wish to know what we discussed.'

'Aye.'

With another nod, he pushed his plate aside. 'In life, you understand, we always say things that we later would take back – a careless insult, or a sharp word thrown in anger. We are none of us immune.' He took his glass in hand and told me, 'But in all my life, there are no words I wish to take back more than those I spoke to Lily on that morning.' When his eyes met mine, they held a deep regret. 'They caused more harm than I will ever know.'

CHAPTER TWENTY-NINE

TUESDAY, 30 NOVEMBER, 1697

MAGGIE LOOKED ACROSS THE water of the firth towards the further shore, her forehead furrowing the way it always did when she felt Lily's explanations made no sense. 'But it looks nothing like a road.'

The day was sunny but the wind was brisk, and Maggie leaned back into Lily, seeking shelter. Now that Maggie had turned eight, the top of her fair head exactly reached the height of Lily's heart.

The symbolism of that was not lost on Lily. With her arms wrapped closely round the little girl, she said, 'Ye asked me where the Road of Leith was, and I've shown ye. It is no more than a stretch of water near the shore where ships may safely lie at anchor.'

From behind them, Captain Gordon said approvingly, 'That is an excellent description.'

Maggie wriggled free of Lily's arms and danced around to greet the captain, holding up her doll to show the new blue cloak that Barbara had made for her.

'Very bonny,' Captain Gordon said, 'and perfect for St

Andrew's Day.' He looked around them at the crowds of
people who were gathering and strolling past, awaiting the
festivities. 'Is Mrs Browne not with you?'

Lily shook her head. 'She said since red hair brings bad luck
to ships, and a woman brings more, then a redheaded woman
is bound to be very unwelcome today.'

Maggie told him, 'They are giving a ship a new name.'

'Aye, so I did hear.'

'It's over there,' said Maggie, pointing out the ship
anchored across the firth at Burntisland. 'Ye see? The second
one, with all the blue and gold. It's twice the size of yours.'

'A little more than twice, I think. But ships are built for
different things,' the captain said. 'My ship, like many others
in the harbour here, is owned by merchants who employ
me as its skipper. Now and then I may have sailed as far
as Spain or Italy, but generally we sail no further than to
Holland or to France and home again, and she needs only to
be large enough to hold her cargo and my men. 'Tis better
she be slight and swift than lumbering and large, in case
we're forced to run from privateers. And sixteen guns are
all I need to make someone think twice about pursuing us.'
He nodded at another larger ship that was familiar to them
all. 'Now, something like the *Royal William* is completely
different. She belongs to our Scots navy and the crown,
and has a duty to patrol our coast and give an escort to the
smaller merchant ships, like mine, when we are travelling
in convoy. That's why she's a larger ship with thirty-two
guns, and can carry troops of soldiers if she's called upon
to keep us safe.'

Maggie pointed out that, if he were the captain of the

Royal William, he could wear a fine blue coat. 'Ye would be very handsome.'

'Thank you. But then I'd be bound to sail wherever the king told me to, and nowhere else. So while I do agree it would be fine to have a ship so grand, I'll steer the course I have a while longer, if it's all the same to you, and bide my time till we've a Stewart on the throne again.'

Lily said, 'You may be waiting a long time, considering the terms of peace.' The ink was barely dry upon the treaties lately signed to end the war with France, and one of the conditions that had been agreed to was that the French king should recognize King William as the rightful British monarch, and deny King James. This had come as a great blow to the Jacobites, and must have been an insult to King James as well, considering the French king was his cousin.

Gordon shrugged. 'Peace rarely lasts, and treaties are but words on paper. King William is not well liked and has no children, so I'll wager before long the throne will pass to Princess Anne,' he said. 'And she's a Stewart.'

Maggie was not interested in politics. 'Ye did forget the two new ships at Burntisland.' She'd been obsessed with those ships since the first of them, the *Caledonia*, had slipped in upon the tide last week, resplendent in her show of red and gold and blue, the wind filling the sails on her three tall masts as she fired the forward-mounted cannon in her bow to hail the townspeople. When she had first been spotted in the firth, the word had spread, so there'd been time enough for Lily to bring Maggie to the pier to watch the great ship gliding past, and to hear that cannon, and to hear it answered by the booming guns of Edinburgh's great castle, high atop its rock.

The second of the ships, arriving yesterday, might well have been the first one's twin.

'Why are they both so big?' asked Maggie.

'Well,' said Captain Gordon, 'those belong to our own African Company.'

'What's that?'

'Well, in full it's called "The Company of Scotland Trading to Africa and the Indies", but that's far too long to say in conversation, would you not agree? Aye, so would I. So then, our African Company is a brave new venture with an aim to raise our country to the level of the English and the Dutch – both of those countries have rich companies that trade to the East Indies and to even further shores where there are markets for their goods. And,' he told Maggie, 'they have colonies.'

She asked him, 'What's a colony?'

He had to think about the definition. 'It's a small piece of your own country that you plant in a far-off land,' was what he finally settled on. 'You build up towns, and farms, and roads, and people go to live there.'

'What if someone's living there already?'

'If you have enough men, you could always take the land by force. That's what the Dutch did at Batavia and their other colonies in the East Indies.'

Maggie disapproved. 'That is not nice.'

'No, you're right, it's not.' The captain half-smiled in the way men do when a child's simple honesty reminds them of their conscience. 'And our African Company agrees with you, which is why they plan to found a colony for Scotland on land that no other European nation has yet claimed, and if our settlers do find natives there, we must get their consent before we build.'

That suited Maggie better. 'Where is the new colony to be?'

'Nobody knows. It is a secret.'

'Why?'

'Because,' he said, 'the English and the Dutch do have their companies that sail to the East Indies, as I said, and they are jealous of our own, and do not wish to share the seas, and if they knew where we did mean to plant our colony, they might make trouble.'

Lily knew King William had been making trouble, too. Although he'd given his consent to the formation of the African Company and its aims, he'd since done all he could to prevent its success. It was by King William's order that no English or Dutch investors had subscribed to the Company, and the English merchants who had at first been so enthusiastically involved in the venture had withdrawn their support for fear of losing the king's favour, leaving Scotland alone to carry the financial burden of raising enough capital.

But the people of Scotland, across all social ranks and religions, had risen to the challenge and subscribed their names into the company's book, and the beautiful ships now anchored in the firth were a testament to what could be achieved when Scots looked past the things that did divide them and pursued a common dream.

Captain Gordon said to Maggie, 'That is why those ships are larger. Because they must travel very far. They need more sail, and must be big enough to carry all the things they'll need to trade, and build the towns, and transport the first people who will live there. And because they're going to an unknown place, with unknown dangers, they must have more guns. I have not counted yet how many these ships have, but—'

'Fifty-six,' said Maggie. 'I did count them when the *Instauration* came in yesterday.'

'Did you indeed?' The captain grinned. 'I think, when you are grown, my first mate will need to be careful, lest I hire you instead. That is a big word for a small lass – *Instauration*. Do you know its meaning? No? It means the restoration of a thing that has been cast aside to fall into a state of disrepair, like our poor country, or our pride, which both do need to be renewed.'

'But they are changing it,' said Maggie.

'Aye. To the *St Andrew*, which is also a fine name for a ship of Scotland, and on this day above all others.'

Maggie nodded her agreement, for she knew about the patron saint of Scotland, and she'd always liked the festive nature of his feast day. 'I'm wearing my saltire today,' she told the captain, showing him the diagonal X-shaped St Andrew's cross pinned to her plaid. 'And so is Dolly, only hers is made of wire. Henry made it.'

Captain Gordon bent to give it his appraisal. 'Henry's very clever.'

Henry, having just come up to join them, laughed. 'Ye'd be alone in thinking that, but I will take the compliment.' He greeted Captain Gordon, who had noticed something else on Dolly.

With a smile, the captain said to Maggie, 'Dolly has a new admirer, I perceive. Who gave her this?' He touched the second wire brooch, shaped like a heart, meant to be hidden underneath the doll's blue cloak.

Conspiratorially, Henry leaned closer and told him, 'That is a great mystery, we're not meant to know.'

Maggie withered both men with a look, rearranging the doll's cloak to cover the pin.

Gordon asked Henry, 'You didn't make that one?'

'No. Matthew did.'

Maggie said, 'It's like the one he gave to Lily.' Then, when she saw how that statement changed the faces on the adults standing round her, she looked up at Lily in dismay. 'Did I do wrong? He said to not tell Archie, but . . . oh, Lily!' And her hand flew up to hide her mouth as if she wished to force the words back.

Lily's own heart had just fallen sickly to her feet, but she told Maggie not to worry. 'Captain Gordon is a friend, and Henry's Matthew's brother. They will keep the secret.' She looked at both the men and with her eyes alone implored them to be honourable.

'Aye,' the captain rushed to reassure the little girl, and crouched to Maggie's level, his eyes kind. 'There's no harm done. But I would take care who I told that to in future. Small leaks,' he advised her, 'sink great ships.' She nodded solemnly, and Gordon reached into his pocket. 'I nearly forgot, I have a gift for you, and one I'll wager even Mistress Aitcheson will not find fault with, for it cost me nothing.' Taking out a paper packet, he unwrapped two small baked tarts. 'My wife did bake too many of these,' he told Maggie, 'so I said to her, I know a little lass who'll gladly take these off our hands. The one is apple, and the other raisin.'

Maggie looked at him, round-eyed, and thanked him. 'Could I save the raisin one for Matthew? He likes raisins.'

'Eat them both,' the captain told her. 'I have plenty more that I can give to Matthew.'

Henry sent him a good-humoured look. 'Ye see which brother is her favourite, and it's clearly not myself.'

Maggie didn't seem to know if she should take him seriously, but she saw a way to turn his pouting to her own advantage. 'Matthew does not let me ride upon his back like ye do,' she said hopefully.

The grin that Henry gave her was infectious. 'Does he not?' He turned and bent and let her clamber on, and as she wrapped her arms around his neck, with Dolly safely tucked between them, he said, 'Come then, my wee cadger's creel, we'll go and see what's new along the pier the day.'

'He'll make a wondrous father,' Captain Gordon said, as he and Lily stood and watched them go.

She had been thinking much the same thing, hoping Henry would be granted his own family one day, for it would be such a waste for someone of his patience and capacity for love to be unable to see it continued.

Captain Gordon said, 'It's rare to see a man of his age ready for the hearth and home. I can assure you I was not.'

'Ye seem well fond of children.' Lily knew her lack of trust in Captain Gordon's motives when it came to Maggie put a faint edge to her tone, but it could not be helped.

He glanced at her. 'Aye, but I did not begin my family until I was thirty. I was ready for it then.'

Lily realized, though his words might sound offhand, he was selecting them with purpose. It dawned on her that he was thinking of the heart-shaped brooch he had just learned about by accident, the one Matthew had given her, for

Gordon would know what it meant. She looked at him more closely. 'And ye think Matthew's not ready?'

'I think Matthew is yet young.' He had the air of someone at a crossroads, trying to decide which turning he should choose. At length he said, 'He does remind me of my brother. My half-brother, if you'd know his true relation to me, for my father did beget him on a servant two years after my own mother's death, so he was born into this life already at a disadvantage, as a bastard.'

Just like Matthew. Though he did not speak the words aloud, the implication could not be ignored, and Lily bristled. 'Children cannot choose the circumstances of their birth.'

'You're right. But our society is structured to constrain them by it, nonetheless. And if a man is driven by ambition, like my brother, those constraints are keenly felt. They turn to restlessness.' His hands were in his pockets now. 'My brother is a man of fine intelligence, like Matthew. He is forever chasing some new challenge. When the Revolution came here, I did send him into Russia to the care of General Gordon, who's a favourite of the Tsar. It's my hope he finds his fortune there. If nothing else, he'll find adventure.'

Lily did not need to hear him say the words. 'Ye think that Matthew should not marry me.'

'I think he's young,' the captain said again. 'I fear that if he settles here too soon, he'll never know how high he could have climbed. How far his own ambition could have carried him. I fear he will regret his choice in time, and grow resentful, and you both will be unhappy.' Captain Gordon held her gaze with level eyes. 'And I believe that, if you're honest with yourself, you fear it, too.'

The wind felt cold when he had walked away.

She wrapped her arms around herself, yet she did not feel any warmer. What he'd said had stirred the tiny whisperings of doubt that she'd been fighting to ignore. Sometimes at night, when she lay troubled in the darkness, she had tried to argue with those whispers, telling them that Matthew was as ready as he claimed to cease his wanderings and have a settled life. And then she'd see him at his work, and she would try to picture Matthew growing old here with his cart and horse in Leith, and even Lily knew that he was meant for greater things.

If it were simply something he could cure by moving elsewhere, that would be an easy thing to solve, for there were many places they could live after they married where they'd not be known to anyone, where they could start their lives anew. Sometimes she imagined that – the two of them together in a distant place, perhaps with a small garden, and a room with books to call her own. She dreamed of it.

But in her darker moments Lily feared that dream would never be within her reach, for whatever drove Matthew on his wanderings, whatever he was searching for, was something he would need to find alone.

She was looking out across the water, heedless of the people walking all around her, when she gradually became aware of someone at her side.

At first, he was the vague impression of a man, and she could not have said how long he had been standing there. Then, much like a half-remembered landmark taking shape out of a misty landscape, there he was – a strongly-built young man with fair hair caught back at his collar underneath a broad, black hat, and eyes that looked at hers as if they, too, were sifting through the memories. Struggling to believe.

He asked her, 'Lily?'

Lily tried to answer but the words refused to form and she could only nod, and then it scarcely mattered because Jamie swept her up into a crushing hug that lifted her clear off the ground.

Joyously, he whirled her round and Lily only learned that she was crying when she felt the chill air fan the tears that had begun to trickle down her cheeks.

'Ye are not dead!' He set her down but did not let her go. He only drew back so that he could better look at her, as though he needed to be certain. 'How are ye not dead?'

It was too long a story to explain and Lily did not try to. With one hand she brushed her tears away, and with the other she held tightly to his sleeve, remembering the last time she had heard him with his father passing by, and lost him. 'Don't leave,' was the first thing she managed to say.

Jamie dug in his pocket and pulled out a handkerchief for her. 'It's all right,' he said. 'Ye'll have the devil's own time getting free of me now, so ye will.'

Somebody whistled, sharply, and he raised his head and called across the crowd that he'd just be a minute. Looking down again at Lily, Jamie told her, 'I can't stop long, not the now, I'm meant to join the others on the ship afore the celebration.'

Lily sought to focus, still amazed that she was standing now with Jamie after all these years. 'What ship?'

'The *Instauration*. Shortly to be the *St Andrew*.' His grin was the same. 'What? Ye said that I could be a sailor.'

Lily's face had fallen, she could feel it. 'Ye are going to the colony?'

'I'll tell ye all about it,' Jamie promised. 'Later. Are ye living here in Leith? Where can I find ye?'

'Riddell's Close.' She told him where. And then remembered Archie. 'But don't come to the house,' she said, 'the people where I'm living wouldn't like it. Meet me here, instead.'

'Here on the Shore?'

She nodded. 'Over by the windmill.'

'Fine. Tomorrow morning, then,' he promised. 'Say, at ten o'clock?' The easy smile of the boy that she remembered flashed behind the features of the man as he bent down to draw her close to him again. 'I kent that ye could not be gone. I kent it here.' As Jamie straightened, he tapped his closed fist against his heart. 'I'm glad that I was right.'

He still had the same swagger to his walk. The crowd closed in around him until even his fair hair was difficult to follow in the shifting sea of people on the Shore, and Lily stood and craned her neck to see where he had gone.

At last she saw someone she recognized, but it was not Jamie.

It was Matthew. And his gaze was fixed on hers.

When he came across to join her, she could tell that he was jealous. Matthew was not one to hide his feelings, not with her. He nodded at the handkerchief she still held in her hand. 'Who was he?'

'That was Jamie. He's an old friend.'

Matthew scoffed. 'A friend.'

'Aye. We've not seen each other since afore I came here.'

She could tell from his expression there'd be little point in trying to share details of her history with the Graeme family. Matthew, in this mood, would not be listening, and she was working still to process her emotions after her reunion with her childhood friend. She'd bring Matthew with her when she met with Jamie here tomorrow, at the windmill, and she'd introduce them then, and Matthew would be able to see for himself that Jamie was no rival.

Thinking to reassure him on that point, she said, 'He's going to sail to the colony.'

'Is he?'

Lily said, 'And thanks to your Captain Gordon, I fear we may now have to hold Maggie back so she'll not volunteer for the voyage.'

'Why's that?'

Taking Matthew's cold hand in her own, Lily explained how the captain had shown Maggie the two great ships of the African Company, and told the child about colonies. But Lily was thinking more of what Gordon had said about how Matthew was too young yet to confine himself to married life.

Because when Matthew looked over the firth towards Burntisland, where the two ships of the company lay at their anchors, Lily was watching his face, and she saw it – the play of emotions that swiftly ran over his features, from envy to deeper frustration to yearning, then died like a wave come to naught on the sand.

And though her mind tried to reason against it, she knew in her heart then the captain was right.

Breathing deeply to soothe the sharp pain in her chest, Lily said, 'Matthew . . . I have been thinking.'

'Aye?'

'What if we waited? To marry, I mean. There's no hurry, and I would not have ye regretting your choice.'

His head turned. 'And do you regret yours?' He spoke sharply, his brown eyes demanding an answer. His jaw had set into the hard lines that meant he was holding in darker emotions.

'Of course not.'

'And I'm meant to believe that? So it's just a coincidence, is it, that you meet this . . . friend . . . and suddenly, you think we ought to wait to marry? What do you think I've been doing all these years? And now it's, maybe we should wait? Because you see a better prize on the horizon?'

Even as Lily recoiled from the anger in Matthew's voice, she heard the pain at the back of his words and knew where it was rising from – that hollow well of doubt he carried deep within him that, in spite of Barbara's reassurance to the contrary, he was a foundling for a reason. That he somehow failed to measure up to expectations, and would always be inadequate.

She doubted there was any cure for such a wound, unless it might be constancy, or love, and love was always worth an effort. She'd misjudged how deeply he was feeling what he thought was her betrayal, and he was misunderstanding everything that she was trying to say. As devastating as it was how quickly things had come undone, she knew their love was strong enough to put it back together in the morning, when his temper calmed.

'I ought to be enough for you,' he said. His voice was low, and there was fierceness in the way he said the words, yet there was also vulnerability.

Though Lily's view was misting over rapidly with unshed tears, she tried to keep her own defences fully down so he would see the truth that lay within her heart.

She told him quietly, 'Ye are the first man I have loved in this way, and ye'll be the last. Ye'll always be enough for me.'

His eyes searched hers, as though he truly needed to believe that.

But he turned from her, and without looking back, he walked away.

CHAPTER THIRTY

FRIDAY, 3 OCTOBER, 1707

TEN YEARS HAD PASSED, but I could see that Captain Gordon had not forgiven himself. Facing me now across the remains of our supper in the private chamber upstairs at Steell's tavern, he looked deliberately away and focused on the fire.

'I had no business saying anything,' he told me. 'I was younger then, and arrogant, and did not spare enough thought for the consequences of my speech. And so I cost a young couple their happiness, and lost a friend.'

'There was no way you could have known.'

'She never liked me much.' He said it in an offhand way. 'I never understood it. After that day, though, she had good reason. She could barely bring herself to look at me.'

I held my silence for a moment. 'It was not your fault, the first part.' I knew I was breaking faith with Lily in a sense, but Gordon carried enough guilt. 'She was in service as a child to a man who broke her trust as no child's trust should ever be betrayed. He gave her gifts. I think that seeing you give gifts to Maggie raised those memories for her, and those fears.'

'I see.' He looked troubled. 'Poor lass. Had I known, there are things I'd do differently.'

I settled back in my chair and reminded him, 'Clocks don't wind backwards.'

'No.' He granted this was likely a good thing. 'Still, it's a shame that we cannot reclaim those vanished days, and try to live them better.'

'Who's to say we would not live them worse?'

That made him smile. The rousing cheer that drifted upwards from the main room of the tavern underneath us brought him upright in his seat. He stretched his shoulders. 'Shall we put in an appearance belowstairs? I'm sure there is much gossip to be had, and we are out of wine.'

I warned him, 'I am told the walls here do have ears.'

'Oh, very certainly. His Grace the Duke of Hamilton likes to be kept informed. But he's on our side, for the most part,' Gordon said.

He meant the Jacobite side, of course, and his confidence that I'd agree with his politics called up a reflexive answer of loyalty that showed me why men would so freely follow him. 'Why "for the most part"?'

'If you would ask our enemies, they'd say the Duke of Hamilton is on our side. Most of our friends would say the same. But there are some who will remind you he is an ambitious man, and popular, and Protestant. And that his family lineage does also give him a strong claim upon the Scottish throne, so that perhaps the duke is not so keen to see our young King James restored as he might wish us to believe.'

'The duke intends to have the throne himself, you mean?'

He said, ''Tis only what some people say. But friend or foe, there's little that escapes his notice.'

'Does he have a hand in the invasion?'

'What invasion?' Gordon's face was total innocence.

I let it pass, and told him, 'Fair enough. You needn't tell me.' I could understand why he'd not wish to share the details of a game with stakes so high.

But Gordon took my measure. 'Let us say, if there were an invasion, and if the duke were involved, he'd not be trusted by all of our friends, and he would not know all of the plans. Which would make him more determined to discover them,' he said. 'He keeps his men among the patrons here. They are not difficult to spot. Let's see if you can manage it.'

I took his challenge when we went downstairs.

I did find two of them, from how they moved to sit at closer tables, seeming not to listen while in truth they hung on Gordon's every word. But it was left to Gordon to point out the third, discreetly – a large, jovial man who seemed for all the world to be so far gone in his cups that he'd not have remembered anything he overheard. I marked their faces, so I would remember them.

And then, quite unexpectedly, I saw another face I knew, half-hidden by a grey cocked hat. He had been sitting at a table near the door, but when he saw me notice him, he stood and pulled the collar of his grey coat close, and slipped out of the tavern like a shadow.

I excused myself from Gordon's group, explaining that I meant to take some air. It was no lie. The pipe smoke hung like layered webs within the room, and while the company and warmth were welcome, I felt the beginnings of a head-ache from the wine and noise and staleness of the space.

Outside, the night was clear and cold, a perfect half-moon hanging in the sky, with all the watching stars to serve as sentinels. I could see no one in Steell's Close nor in the High Street, though I looked in both directions, but I knew he could not have gone far. I also knew it would be best to face him now and get our meeting over with, instead of always wondering when it was going to happen.

There was silence tonight at the front of St Giles', and the dark, shuttered Luckenbooths held their own secrets. My footsteps rang hard on the stones of the street as I passed them all by.

Though the shadows lay thickly as always at the head of Forrester's Wynd, there was nobody there, either. And there was no candle shining tonight from Lily's window.

My mind had barely registered that fact before I'd started up the turnpike stair towards her door.

It was not, in looking back, the wisest thing to do. The hour was late, and I was not the only person looking for that light who knew its meaning. But I acted on pure impulse when I saw that darkened window, thinking only that the candle's absence meant something was wrong.

A troubling play of possibilities ran through my mind as I went up those stairs, and when I reached her door and found it had been left unbolted and ajar, I feared the worst. I drew the whinger from its scabbard as I stepped inside her lodgings.

All was silent. There was little light to see by, save the moonlight coming through the windows, for the fire in the hearth had burned too low to be of any use.

Lily spoke up quietly. 'I'm here.'

The oath I swore could not be helped. I closed the door securely. Slid the bolt home. Sheathed my blade. 'Why would you be so careless as to sit with your door open?'

Lily could have answered that I had no right to chastise her, but she did not. She only said, 'I knew that it was you upon the stair. I saw you.' She had dragged the cushioned chair close by the window with the candle, and was sitting curled up on its seat just far enough out of the light that she would not be seen, while she yet had a view of where the High Street met the wynd below. She would, indeed, have witnessed my approach. 'You often take your walks this time of night,' she added, and I lost my irritation then, because it caught me strangely in my heart to think she might have sat here watching for me.

Waiting for me.

And now that my senses were no longer on alert and had begun to function normally − at least, as normally as they could function in her presence − I could tell that something *was* wrong. All the vibrancy had drained from her and left her looking weary and dejected.

Making a decision, I crossed to the fireplace and stirred the small fire to life.

'Come, sit where it is warmer,' I said. 'You'll catch cold if you stay there.'

I moved the cushioned chair for her, and while she settled into it, I took a twisted paper spill from the container on the mantel and used it to transfer a single, tiny piece of flame from the now-glowing fire across the room to light the candle in the window.

I did not want any interruptions from the other man who I knew might be out there right now watching Lily's lodgings for a signal of distress. I stayed well to the side, so I would not be seen, then rejoined Lily at the hearth and took the cane-backed chair across from hers.

She knew a reckoning was coming. 'It is no use,' she told me. 'I'm beyond your help.'

'You said you trusted me.'

'I did. I do.'

'Then trust me now.' I held her gaze. 'I don't believe you ever married onto Jamie Graeme. Did you?'

In the pause that followed, I could feel the strong pulse in my own veins counting off the moments like a clock.

And then she slowly shook her head.

I asked her, 'Why? Why take the risk of coming forward with a false claim?'

Lily raised her chin, and her attempt to smile was heart-breaking. 'Because,' she told me, 'with Archie, there's always a price.'

CHAPTER THIRTY-ONE

WEDNESDAY, 29 JUNE, 1698

S HE'D BEEN UNWILLING TO believe, at first, that he had
truly left her. On the morning after Lily had watched
Matthew walk away – the same morning she'd first arranged
to meet with Jamie at the windmill – she had gone to
Matthew's lodgings to convince him to come with her to
that meeting, so that he could speak to Jamie for himself and
know the truth.

There'd been no answer at his door, and he had not been at
the stables in the Kirkgate where the carters kept their horses,
nor at work upon the Shore.

Day followed day, and by the end of that first long week
of December when she knocked on Matthew's door it had
been opened by a stranger, a new tenant, and another carter
had begun to hitch the mare named Lennet to their cart, and
Lily knew then Matthew had done more than leave to calm
his temper.

'He'll be back,' Henry had promised her with certainty, but
after nearly seven months now even Henry was beginning to
accept that Matthew, once again, was gone.

Neither Henry nor anyone else in his family had made Lily feel for a moment that she was to blame.

Jamie felt this was only right. 'It's not your fault,' he'd said. 'He was the one who decided to leave.'

'I'm not sure "decided" would be the right word,' had been Lily's reply. 'I'm not sure he was thinking so clearly. I injured him.'

'He made that cut himself, when he chose not to have faith in ye.' Jamie held firm. 'And if that's his nature, then it's best that ye did learn it now, and not when ye were facing times of trouble, for it's then ye need a man to stand beside ye and not leave ye.' Stubbornly, his head set at an angle she remembered from their childhood, he had glanced at her and added, '*I* would never leave ye.'

'Jamie.'

They'd been walking, for although they met each week at the windmill on the Shore, it was no private place to talk and Jamie never could stand still long anyway, so commonly they walked from there along the sea wall, down across Leith sands, across the broad expanse of windswept beach where every spring the horse races were held.

On that one day in particular, it had been late in March and there'd still been snow. The air had smelt of salt and coal smoke, and the chill wind blowing over the white waves stung Lily's eyes.

Jamie had said, 'All right, I'll let it lie.'

But she had known that he would not. He'd raised the subject once again in early May, and she had answered him the same as she'd done since he'd first made the suggestion in December.

And now here they were on this final warm Wednesday of June, with the gulls in high flight overhead, and she knew he was going to ask her again because finally the glass had turned and the sand had started measuring their last hours with one another. This morning the drummers had gone through the town calling all of the Company's men to be on board the ships by the following Monday and ready to sail for the colony.

Jamie had been making use of these past months. He'd had new suits tailored, and bought a new hat, and had taken his swords to be furbished. And after much waiting, he'd finally received his official birth brief – the single-page summary of pedigree and descent that men carried with them when they wished to settle in a foreign land.

He'd been concerned that, even though he had petitioned for his birth brief in the proper way and had provided a certificate outlining his descent as proof, he'd not be granted one because his father was an outlaw still in service to King James.

Lily hadn't shared his worry. 'See?' she told him now. 'It's as I told you. No one could deny a birth brief to the grandson of the Black Pate.'

Jamie, grinning at the mention of his grandfather, said, 'Aye, well, 'tis a good thing that he did not live to see these times. I don't doubt he'd have taken up his sword again.'

She knew that it was true. 'I miss your grandfather.' As distant as those happy days of childhood sometimes seemed, they had felt closer to her these past months with Jamie here, and it had saddened her to learn that both her grandmother and the old laird had been dead for some time.

Jamie nodded. 'Inchbrakie's not the same without him.

Uncle George prefers the town life, so ye'll almost never find him there. And with my cousin forced to flee to save his neck, the old yew will be waiting yet awhile afore new children come to climb it.'

Lily knew when he faintly frowned afterwards that he was thinking of Maggie. It was an easy association to make, not only because he'd been talking of children, but because the cousin he spoke of – the one forced to flee to the Continent last winter – was Maggie's father.

As everyone had feared, the family of the man Maggie's father had fought and killed six years ago had finally brought a charge of murder, and because that family was so firmly attached to King William while the Graemes were known Jacobites, Maggie's father had felt he'd have no chance persuading the lords it had been a fair fight. So he was now a fugitive.

In the beginning, when she'd started having these meetings with Jamie here on the wide sands of Leith, and they began filling in the blanks of their lost years with each other, Lily hadn't been sure whether she should say anything to him of Maggie.

Yes, they were kin, but what good would it do in the end if he knew that? As Barbara often said, *All the truth shouldn't be told.*

But then one day she'd turned up and Jamie had looked at her strangely and asked, 'Who was that wee lass with the fair hair ye were walking with, day afore yesterday, down by the pier?'

And she'd never told Jamie a lie. So that day he'd learned about Maggie and the way they were related. At first, he'd wished to meet her, but he had agreed with Lily it would be unwise. Not only would it not be fair to ask the little girl to keep the secret of his being there, but having Maggie meet a kinsman and then have him leave again so soon would only cause the child unnecessary heartbreak.

'She has lost so much already,' Lily said, thinking in silence that Maggie's deep grief over Matthew was daily the one thing that helped Lily manage her own, for it bound her to someone who not only mirrored her sadness, but desperately needed her not to give in to it. Needed her to remain strong.

Jamie watched Maggie through the spring, into the summer, unnoticed but with growing pride. 'She's a Graeme,' he told Lily one morning early in June. 'Ye can tell that she's a Graeme. Did ye see the way she runs?' And while he'd started off calling her 'my cousin's lass', he'd since claimed her as 'my own wee cousin, Maggie'.

He called her that now, underneath the clear sky of a late June morning, with the waves carried in on a quickening wind, curling white at their edges as they came to rest on the sun-warmed sand.

'Ye'll see that my wee cousin Maggie learns all the tales of Inchbrakie?' he asked Lily. 'Tell her the tale of Montrose and the yew. And of Grandfather. And you and me,' he said, 'when we were young. I ken her daddie would do the same, if he were here and were able to. She has a right to ken where she belongs.'

Lily promised.

'And ye have the money that I gave ye hidden in a safe place?'

'Aye. I'll see that Maggie gets it.'

Jamie said, 'It isn't just for Maggie. It's yours as well, if ye have need of it.' He looked at her with brief regret. 'I wish it hadn't happened to ye.'

'What?' she asked him.

'Any of it. I wish I'd been here to keep ye safe.' He stopped walking then, and glanced back at the masts and furled sails of the ships within the harbour.

Lily waited, knowing what was coming next.

''Tis not a life I like to see ye living, Lily,' Jamie said. 'Will not ye come away and marry me?'

She smiled. 'Ye cannot always be my rescuer.'

'I can,' he said, as stubbornly as if he held a homemade sword of branches tied together, and it only made her love him more.

She told him so. 'But not the way a woman loves a man she's meant to marry. Nor do ye love me that way. Ye ken ye don't, ye can't deny it.'

'People build their lives with less,' was Jamie's argument.

From habit, Lily touched the place above her heart where she still wore the little silver brooch pinned out of sight beneath her bodice, and she thought of Matthew, and tried not to, and replied, 'I don't want less.' And then to mask her sadness she tried lightening the mood by adding, 'Anyway, your mother would be less than pleased to see ye married onto me.'

'My mother would be pleased to see me married onto anyone,' he promised her. 'She fears I may follow the path of my brothers.'

'Then she does not ken ye well.'

'And who among us would have thought that Pat would end up as a monk?'

He had her there. His brother Pat, who'd yearned to be a soldier, had at last been given a commission in the army of King James, but having fought a duel and killed a friend he could not bear the guilt of that one lapse of judgement, so he'd left the field of battle for the monastery and become a Capuchin, known now as Father Archangel.

'And Bobby seems to have a mind to do the same,' said Jamie. 'He's been in and out of monasteries since he went to France. There's hope yet for William, he's young yet, and clever, and good with his studies, but I can assure ye my mother would have all the bells rung if I were to marry.' He grinned. 'I'll wear ye down.'

'Ye'll not. I will not spoil your future, Jamie. I'll not do it. Ye deserve a proper wife, and bairns. I will be fine and well here, ye've no cause to worry.' Lily turned her gaze towards the waves and blinked against the sunlight. 'Ye will write, when ye are settled in the colony?'

'Of course.' His arm came round her shoulder, strong and reassuring. 'What was it that Jean called us? Faithful friends? And so we are. And so ye said we would be unto death, no matter where we bide.' He looked where she was looking, to the restless water of the firth, and told her, 'Nothing's changed.'

She might have questioned that, but Lily held her tongue. They stood in peace a moment longer before starting back, and Jamie, because he was lost in thought, did something out of habit that he had not done with her of late.

He walked a step ahead.

It made her smile, faintly. Lily followed after, fitting her footsteps to his ones in the sand, as though she were a little girl once more upon the sunlight-dappled green paths of Inchbrakie woods, following Jamie on a new adventure. Only this time, she knew she could not go quite as far as he was going.

In the shadow of the windmill, Jamie stopped.

Lily liked the windmill, with its sturdy round stone walls that soared high like a castle turret, and its creaking sails that turned incessantly at work. But from here she saw the bustle of activity along the Shore and pier – the ships and small boats in the harbour, and the larger ships that lay at anchor in the Road of Leith beyond.

Jamie said, 'I have to be on board my ship by Monday.'

Lily felt a deep misgiving, standing there within that shadow. 'Ye are certain ye do wish to go? They have not even told ye where you're sailing to. It may be somewhere terrible.'

'It may be somewhere wonderful. What happened to the lass who wished to sail to Norway?'

'Norway's not so far.'

He smiled, and took a folded paper from his pocket. 'If ye change your mind afore I leave, ye ken where ye can find me. But if ye change it after I have sailed, I leave ye this – 'tis a letter stating my intent to marry ye, and signed by my own hand. If ye do take that to the Company's directors up in Edinburgh, they'll pay your passage to me in the colony.' He put the paper in her hands and folded his own larger ones around hers, holding firmly as he fixed her gaze with his. 'And hear me, now. If ye have need of me, whatever ye decide, ye use this letter and ye come to me, ye ken? Marriage or no, if there is trouble here, ye come to me. And bring my own wee cousin with ye. I'll keep the both of ye safe,' Jamie promised. 'We Graemes take care of our own.'

She knew he truly meant it, but she also knew that this was where their paths were meant to separate, so Lily tried to tease him. 'And if ye have a wife already? What then?'

'Then we will have a full house.' He grinned, and in that moment he was the boy on the barrels again at Jean's wedding, who'd wished he could marry her then, too, and take her to Perth with him so they would not be divided. 'Anyway,' Jamie said, and his eyes told her that he was remembering that moment also, 'who else would ye have?'

He bent, and gently kissed her cheek, and letting go her hands he turned and walked away. He turned back twice along the Shore to look behind and wave farewell, and Lily waved, too, but her smile was hard to hold in place, and without his hands over hers, her own felt cold.

Chapter Thirty-Two

STILL WEDNESDAY, 29 JUNE, 1698

RETURNING TO RIDDELL'S CLOSE, Lily was met at the door by Maggie who, taking her by the hand, half-danced and half-dragged her past the front rooms to where warm talk and laughter spilled into the back passage from Barbara's chamber, which meant Walter and his wife had brought the bairn.

Archie was not over-tolerant of bairns within his work room anymore, so since the birth of Walter's son in February, Barbara's chamber, normally off-limits to the family, had become the place to gather when the bairn was brought to visit. It was a comfortable room, with soft furnishings, and if it had not been designed for that function, well, 'What's more important than family?' asked Barbara of Archie, one morning.

Dryly he'd answered her, 'Earning your keep.'

'I've earned it twice over.' Barbara had matched his tone, ending the argument, likely because Archie knew she was right.

Barbara had fewer gentlemen visitors now, and she went

out less frequently. She seemed more tired these days. She often did not wake in time to take her morning draught, and was asleep again when Lily had just started to prepare for bed. She'd said to Lily several times there was no need to worry, she was only wanting rest.

Archie, on hearing her say that, had rolled his eyes. 'Ye're wanting feeding. Ye'll be naught but bones if ye keep going on as ye are.'

All of them were thinner, it could not be helped. Meat was scarce, as were barley and wheat, and although Captain Gordon still carried in cargoes of food when he could – no doubt some of it stored out of sight below decks with his ballast – their meals had grown plainer and smaller to make their provisions last until the harvest.

Barbara, in her selfless way, served up more for the rest of them than for herself, but Archie last week had set down a jar of honey-coloured paste beside her plate at dinner, saying, 'That's from the apothecary. He said if ye take a spoonful daily, it will help to make ye strong again.'

At first, Lily had been suspicious. But then she'd seen Archie's eyes, and realized he was genuinely worried.

'He does care for me, in his way,' Barbara had told Lily years before, and Lily's observations bore this out. It was a tragedy that Archie could not care for Barbara in the way that she deserved, but if he had a heart at all, then Barbara was the only person who had ever been allowed to come within its reach.

Even today, when Lily stepped into Barbara's chamber and joined the others, she noticed that Archie, who stood by the wall, wasn't watching the bairn. He was looking at Barbara with quiet concern.

But his head turned when Maggie brought Lily in. 'Home from your wanderings, are ye?'

'Aye.' She kissed Walter and his wife warmly. 'I'm sorry I'm late.' Lily hadn't been ready to come straight home after she'd watched Jamie leaving. She'd feared that her face would reveal her emotions, so she'd walked a while longer, taking the roundabout way from the Tolbooth Wynd into the Kirkgate and down past the churchyard and back up the curve of St Giles' Street into the close.

Walter said, 'Ye can hardly be late when ye don't ken we're coming.'

A tug at her hand. Maggie told her, 'Ye've missed the best part – he rolled over!'

It was a new trick that the bairn had apparently mastered just yesterday, and he repeated it now when Walter laid him on the blanket spread upon the floor.

Amid the cheering, Henry swept the infant up, blanket and all, pronouncing him a genius.

'He *is* clever,' Walter said with pride. 'The other day I think he called me "daddie".'

'Och, he's still too small for that,' his wife declared. 'Though it would be the way, now, would it not, for him to start with "daddie" and not "minnie"? Never mind that I'm the one who wakes to feed him in the night and walk the floors with him.'

Barbara reassured her all bairns did the same. 'And yet a lad is aye his mother's son. Ye'll never lose him.'

Lily looked at Barbara's face in her turn, thinking to see sadness, but instead she only saw a patient certainty. As though aware of her appraisal, Barbara looked at Lily, smiled, and settled in her favourite chair. 'Well then. What did ye see on your walk the day?'

Lily told her nothing of Jamie of course, but she did tell her of the new ship that had just arrived from Holland, and of the little dog she'd seen that had snatched up a seaman's hat and made a game of it, and led a merry chase all up and down the pier until both dog and hat were swimming in the harbour. 'But it ended well,' said Lily, 'for the seaman dived in after them, and saved his hat, and kept the dog.'

Maggie agreed that was a perfect ending to the story. 'Was it a sailor from one of the ships of the African Company? Will he be taking the dog to the colony?' And without waiting for Lily to answer, she asked Walter, 'Did ye hear the drummers, Walter? Weren't they grand? That means the ships are sailing soon. Would not ye wish to sail beyond seas to some foreign land? *I* would. I think it would be an adventure.'

Lily held her breath while watching Walter, knowing how much he'd once longed to do exactly that, but Walter looked at his wee son in Henry's arms, and reached a hand to stroke the bairn's soft head, and shared a smile with his wife.

'No,' Walter said to Maggie, 'I've no desire for foreign lands. Everything I need is here in Leith.'

Archie cleared his throat and, coming forward, motioned Lily to the door. 'That minds me. I've a bit of work to show ye.'

Barbara asked him, 'Now? Cannot it wait?'

'We'll be done afore dinner.'

Lily would have much preferred to stay and play with Walter's bairn, but every piece of work she did for Archie brought more money to the household so she followed him into the passage, uncomplaining. But she did have one thing she would do, first. 'I'll just fetch my apron, Archie.' For she still had Jamie's letter in her pocket, and it needed to be safely stowed upstairs within its hiding place.

'No need,' said Archie. With a hand he guided her along towards to the work room. 'I but mean to show ye what needs doing, I'll not keep ye long.'

On the table in the work room, Archie had set out the necessary papers and the pens. 'It is a birth brief that we're needing, for a young man going to the colony. The council did not grant him one because he could not prove to them his origins. His birth is, shall we say, disputed by the family. But he does have a testificate to show his genealogy.'

Sometimes when Lily looked at papers such as this one they were clearly falsified, drawn up all in one hand and badly done, but this one did look to be genuine. So it would seem the only thing that barred the young man from his future was that he'd been born as the result of fornication, illegitimate, and had thus grown from childhood in a world made smaller and less kind by other people's prejudice. It would not trouble Lily's conscience to write this young man his birth brief so that he might start his life in a new world, away from such constraints.

Archie informed her, 'He needs it by Saturday. I said that would be no problem.'

'No trouble at all,' Lily said.

'He must be on his ship by Monday,' Archie said. 'I do expect your friend got the same order.'

Lily's heart dropped, but she knew that sometimes Archie knew things, and sometimes he was just searching, so she strove for lightness as she asked, 'What friend?'

'The one ye walk with every Wednesday on the sands.' He said it casually. 'I must admit that at the first I did believe ye, for I thought our Lily would not tell a lie. If she says she has only gone to take the air, then that's what she is doing. And I kent that Matthew's leaving left ye melancholy.' *That*, she knew, was said to twist the knife, and it succeeded. 'Then a few weeks back, one of my lads says, Archie, did ye ken your lass has found a new man? So then I took notice.'

Lily sought to hide her inner panic with a mask of bravery. 'Am I not allowed a friend?'

'Of course.' The chilling thing with Archie was that, unlike most men who could do you harm, he did not raise his voice. He rarely changed his tone. Only his eyes changed, their humanity replaced by hardness. 'What was in the letter that he gave to ye this morning? May I see it?'

'It is private.'

'Nonetheless.' He held his hand out, waiting.

Lily knew she had no choice. Physically, she was no match for Archie. He would take the letter from her if he wished. She might have called for help, but who was there to help her? Matthew was long gone, and Simon – the only other of the brothers able to stand up to Archie – wasn't in the house today. However much Walter and Henry might love her, neither had the strength to defend her, and to ask it of them would be most unfair.

And as for Barbara, her body and heart had been broken enough.

Lily clenched her jaw, reached in her pocket, and handed the letter to Archie.

He read it in silence. On reading the signature, he said, 'Is he a relation then of your old friend Colonel Graeme, who formerly led the town guard?'

'Aye. His son.'

'Very nice. 'Tis a well-written letter with honourable sentiments.' Handing it back to her, Archie said, 'Burn it.'

She stared at him, feeling her cheeks flame in sudden defiance.

Archie lifted his eyebrows a fraction. 'That letter does give ye the power to leave us. Ye ken that I'll not let that happen. Think how it would devastate Barbara.'

Unmoved, Lily told him, 'The letter is mine. I'll not burn it.'

He shrugged. 'Ye must do as ye think best.' She knew that tone. Knew it, and feared it. He said, 'Did ye ken Walter's wife came to see me last year? No, 'twould be a bit more than a year ago, now. They'd been having some trouble with money, she said. Walter never could manage it well. She asked for my help.'

Lily guessed what was coming, but still she denied it. 'No.'

'Oh, aye. She's worked for me since then. In private, like. We have to keep it from Walter, he'd never approve, but he works such long hours he's not bound to notice. And ye've played a part in deceiving him, too, all those times ye looked after the bairn for her, when she said she was just off to the market or wanted a rest.'

Lily told him, 'You're lying. If she were back again and working for ye, Simon would have said something to Walter. Nothing goes on in the Paunchmarket that Simon doesn't see.'

'My dear,' said Archie, 'I'd never be such a fool as to put the lass back in the house on the Paunchmarket. No, there are always arrangements that can be made with the right gentlemen. Quiet. Discreet. It keeps everyone happy. Even the lass, I would wager.' His smile was thin. 'Once a whore, always a whore.'

Lily felt her hand clench round her letter more tightly. 'Barbara believes that ye have a soul.'

That small arrow appeared to strike home, but just as grazing an animal with a missed shot only made it more fierce, Lily's comment seemed only to make Archie more cruel.

'The bairn,' he said, 'might not be Walter's. It probably isn't. It would be a shame if he learned that. He's so much in love with the lad that I doubt he'd recover from such a hard blow.' Archie's voice was as smooth as a monument stone, and as cold, and she hated herself then for ever thinking he could have a heart. With the eyes of a man who knew well he held all the cards, Archie looked down once again at the letter she held in her hand and said, 'If ye would have me keep silent, if ye would spare Walter the pain of that secret, then burn that.'

Defeat did not mean Lily lowered her head, nor that she gave up thinking. Without saying anything, she moved past Archie to stand by the hearth.

'Tear it, first,' he instructed.

She did as he said. But while tossing the fluttering, pale strips of paper upon the coals, she folded one fragment carefully into her palm and concealed it there, counting on Archie not noticing, since both her hands were curled into tight fists. He'd think nothing of that minor gesture, for it was the way she had always reacted when she sought to hold back her temper.

'There, now. Ye've done wisely,' Archie said. 'Good lass.'

She turned and, still not answering, walked by him to the door, and Archie moved aside to let her pass, but not before he commented, 'I think it would be best if ye did not fare-well your friend afore he sails. Ye might forget the terms that we've agreed to.'

Lily paused within the doorway. Turning back with head held high she told him, 'I do keep my word, when I have given it.' And bravely added, 'See ye do the same.'

She did not flee along the passage, although every instinct deep within her urged her to escape. Instead she kept her pace as slow and measured as she could, to show he had no power over her, and that she was not frightened.

But she was.

Upstairs, within the safety of her chamber, that fear rose and broke its chains and made her hands shake as she knelt to ease the wooden chest below the window forward from its place so she could gently prise up the loose floorboard. Underneath, within the shallow, hollow space, she kept the leather purse of silver coins Jamie had given her to use if she had need. To this she added now the ragged slip of paper she'd been holding in her closed hand. She'd torn it carefully when she had torn the letter, so the writing would be well preserved, that she might later make a copy of those two words that made Jamie's signature.

She had not yet lost all of him. Not yet.

❧

Two more full weeks passed before the five ships of the Africa Company sailed with the morning tide in mid-July. Jamie's ship, the *St Andrew*, was flying the commodore's pennant and sailed at the head of the small fleet that carried the hopes of a nation within their sealed orders that yet held the secret of their destination. It was said there was no space on the hillsides for miles around for all the people who crowded from Edinburgh's castle hill right down to Leith's pier to watch those ships slip their moorings, sails filling with wind as they headed out into the firth.

Lily was not among them.

Barbara, who had passed a restless night with indigestion and was lying late in bed, said, 'I should think ye'd rather be out on the Shore and in the midst of the excitement, than in here with me.'

'I'm happy where I am.' Lily kept her focus on the stocking she was mending. 'Anyway, I'll hear the whole report from Maggie, when she does return.'

Lily had not said anything to Barbara of the devil's bargain she had struck with Archie – that weight was her own to carry – but it scarcely mattered. Barbara always sensed when something in the household was awry.

The chair where Lily sat was drawn up close beside the bed and Barbara had to roll her head against the bolster for a closer view of Lily's features. Lily tried pretending that she did not feel the scrutiny.

The older woman gently told her, 'I ken ye're not happy. I would warrant he's not, either. Hold your faith, and he'll come back to ye.'

She spoke of Matthew, plainly. Savagely the needle stabbed at Lily's finger and she missed a stitch. 'Who is it says I wish him to?'

But Barbara wasn't fooled. 'It was real, the love ye had for one another. It was real, and it was true.' A pause, and then a tiny flash of silver as she reached across to set her simple wedding ring atop the stocking Lily had been mending. 'Keep that with ye, so ye'll not forget.'

Stunned, Lily looked up from her work. 'I cannot take your ring.'

'Ye can. 'Tis mine to give, and I will have no argument. For years it has reminded me I was well loved, and it can mind ye of the same till Matthew comes again to give ye proof.' She smiled. 'I hope I will be here to see that day. But if I'm not, will ye do me one favour?'

Lily answered without hesitation. 'Anything.'

'Take Maggie with ye, when ye leave here. She would have a better life with ye and Matthew than she would left here in Riddell's Close.'

Of that much, Lily was completely certain, so it was an easy promise. But it still felt hollow. 'And if Matthew never does come home?'

'He will.' Barbara, while remaining firm on that point, did allow for a contingency. 'Could ye please fetch my strongbox?'

Barbara kept her strongbox underneath the bedstead. It was Spanish-made, of lovely dark wood and the size of a large, heavy book, ornately bound with strips of iron.

Lily slipped the silver ring onto her finger, set her mending to the side, and bent low to retrieve the strongbox. When she straightened with it, Barbara had the key.

'I keep the letters Maggie's father sent in here,' she said, and opening the box she showed to Lily a tight bundle of those letters, tied with string. 'He wrote more often in the year afore he married, but he still wrote after that, each time he sent the payment for her keep, to see that she was well. That she was happy.' Barbara touched the letters lightly. 'I have saved them for her, because it is very plain from how he writes that he is proud to claim her as his daughter, and 'tis plainer still that she'd be welcomed if she turned up at his door. If Matthew does not come, and I am gone, ye can take Maggie to her people up in Perthshire. They were once your people also, were they not? Well then.' She closed the box again and locked it. Slid the key beneath the bolster. 'This is where I always keep the key, and ye ken where I keep the strongbox. If that time comes, take those letters with ye, for they'll prove to young Patrick Graeme Maggie is his daughter.'

Lily wondered whether she ought to tell Barbara Maggie's father was a fugitive and no longer in Scotland, but in the end she did not bother giving her that news, for fear it might cause Barbara added worry. Nor was Archie ever likely to let Lily leave this house with Maggie, when he would not let her leave alone. *Ye ken that I'll not let that happen*, she could hear him saying in his calm and even way, and Lily felt the walls close in more tightly still around her.

Barbara saw her face and smiled in sympathy and reassurance as she handed Lily back the strongbox to return to its place underneath the bed. 'But Matthew will come home,' she said again. 'I ken my sons. I ken their hearts. And he has given his into your keeping.'

Maybe so, but it appeared to Lily he had found a way to live without it then, for summer reached its end and Matthew did not come.

The autumn followed, endless rains that brought a harvest yet more devastating than the last, the crops so poor that people faced the falling darkness of the season with a rising sense of desperation. And still Matthew did not come.

In late October, with food scarce already, they awakened to a frost and snow as hard and cold as if it were the dead of winter.

Barbara had no gentlemen to visit her beyond that day. She grew thinner while her stomach swelled, and then her legs began to bloat as well, and Archie called the doctor in to bleed her. 'I am sorry to be troublesome,' she told them.

Archie brushed the hair from her hot cheek, his mouth in a grim line. The next day he told Lily, 'Away ye go to Walter's house and watch the bairn awhile. His wife has work to do.'

Each time that she was sent to mind the bairn at Walter's lodgings, Lily died a little more inside. The shame on Walter's wife's face as she slipped home from wherever Archie had arranged to send her was a sight that Lily could not bear to see, and in the evenings, back within the bedchamber upstairs at Riddell's Close, Lily tucked Maggie more securely in the blankets than she used to do when settling her to bed, as though by doing that she'd somehow keep her safe.

And Lily lit the candle every night and set it in the window. Simon often looked for it, she knew. He'd told her this, although they so rarely saw Simon anymore that she could not be certain whether all her effort was for naught.

Still, it was something. One small light against the darkness. A little piece of hope that had no right to be so hopeful.

Were it not for hope, as Barbara said, *the heart would break.*

But Matthew did not come.

CHAPTER THIRTY-THREE

TUESDAY, 7 FEBRUARY, 1699

THE BAIRN DIED FIRST.

Still a month shy of his first birthday, he had caught a chill that soon turned to a fever and within the space of a few days he'd gone. And then Walter's wife, weakened from grief and starvation, took ill with that same fever, and by the week's end had followed her son to the grave.

Walter was inconsolable.

Barbara insisted on rising from bed for the burial, even though Archie did all that he could to forbid it. He cursed her red hair and her stubbornness, but she went anyway, leaning on Simon's arm.

It was the last time she left the house living.

Now, the evening after Lily's birthday in the second week of February, Lily was returning after taking Walter's dinner to him. It had not been much but he'd been eating far too little, so she'd sat with him for company and made sure that he'd eaten it, and tried to keep him from resorting too much to his drink, and she had listened while he talked.

And walking home along the Shore as twilight fell, she'd

seen a small boat drawing closer; heard the splashing of its oars and seen the warm light of its lantern. It had minded her exactly of the boat she'd seen that first time as a child, when she'd collapsed upon the ground in her despair and utter weariness and watched that light grow brighter, and heard Barbara's voice say, 'It's a lass!'

Watching this boat coming nearer now, she saw two figures seated in it – one the boatman, rowing, and the other a cloaked woman. Then the woman turned her head and looked at Lily. It was Barbara, with her bright hair and her lovely face. She smiled.

And faded in the air as though she'd been imagined, leaving no one but the boatman, rowing steadily towards the harbour wall.

A chill gripped Lily's heart, because she knew then what she'd seen. She spun around and ran for Riddell's Close.

But she arrived too late.

In Barbara's chamber, Archie had already closed her eyes. He sat beside her, with his hand on hers. His head was bent.

When he heard Lily's footsteps, he half-turned his head and she could see his own eyes were red-rimmed.

'Get out,' he said. And when she did not move, he stood and crossed to slam the door himself, to shut her out, to shut himself in with his private grief.

He was a hateful man and Lily could not pity him, but Barbara had been right. He'd truly cared for her, in his way, and it appeared she might have been the only person he'd allowed to reach that place inside him that had not completely frozen – that was still remotely human. And God help them all, now that Barbara was gone.

❧

By Easter everyone had heard the news that the African Company had received word from its colony, being the five ships that sailed out of Leith had all landed in safety at Darien in the Americas, founding a town that was now called New Edinburgh, in the new colony named Caledonia.

Lily took the atlas of the world down from its shelf and used it to teach Maggie part of that day's lesson. Archie's atlas was not near as grand nor brightly coloured as the one she'd loved to look at in the Graemes' house, but it did show the countries and the seas, and Lily could show Maggie where the colony at Darien lay, not far above the curving coast that sheltered Cartagena. 'Do ye see here, how this piece of land is narrow, in between the seas? Well, as it is, all ships that wish to sail to trade with India must either pass around the Cape of Good Hope, at the southern tip of Africa, or else go all the way down *here*, around Cape Horn, the southern tip of the Americas. But now, with Caledonia – that's our colony at Darien – our Company can bring ships in from this side, the Atlantic, and then carry all the cargo overland, because it's not so far, and load it onto other ships that they have waiting at the other side, on the Pacific. D'ye see? 'Tis a much shorter way that will save time and make us the master of both seas, and of the route to India.'

Maggie became briefly enamoured of maps, but not even that could take the place in her heart of the chivalrous knight Don Quixote. Although she could read his adventures herself, she still liked being read to, and when she was finished her lessons in writing, she claimed her reward of a chapter or two from her favourite book.

Lily was not bothered by the ritual. She was inclined, like Don Quixote, to escape reality awhile, because the world both outside and within doors was increasingly unpleasant.

Walter was descending into drink, and Henry was depressed, and Simon had been sent off to recover payment of a bond four days ago and had not yet returned. The famine was continuing unaltered and it seemed to Lily every day that she was walking in a bitter wasteland. So many horses were dying all over the countryside and at the side of the road from starvation that there'd had to be a proclamation made to have them buried.

In view of this, Lily enjoyed the hour when she and Maggie curled into the armchair and followed the tales of the would-be knight and his most loyal squire, Sancho.

Today Maggie frowned when they finished their chapter. 'I think it was very cruel of Don Quixote's friends to burn the books he loved to read, or keep them hidden from him. They were not good friends. I should not like to lose the books I love.' Which made her think of something. 'We can bring this book to London with us, can we not?'

'When d'ye think we'll be in London?' Lily asked that teasingly, but Maggie's answer was matter-of-fact.

'I don't ken how long the journey takes, but if we're leaving Saturday, as Archie says, then surely we'll be there afore the first of May. I worried that the gentleman might not find a good coach to hire, but Archie says he did, and then I worried also because when the gentleman first met me he said I would have to wait till I was ten afore I travelled, but then Archie said that was no bother, he could make me papers that would let me travel any time I needed to, and ... oh!' She clapped her hand over her mouth. 'Oh, Lily! Now I've spoilt it. We were going to surprise ye. Archie said ye'd like to be surprised, he said ye'd been so sad and that a journey would be good for ye.'

She looked so downcast, Lily hugged her tightly, trying hard to slow the panicked beating of her own heart. Striving for a normal voice, she said, 'No, I will act surprised. But we had better not tell Archie that I've learned of it, in case it disappoints him.' Very cautiously, she added, 'Who's the gentleman?'

'A friend of Archie's. He has a great house in London, and he says that we can stay there for as long as we do wish.'

There are always arrangements that can be made with the right gentlemen. Quiet. Discreet.

Lily kissed Maggie's fair head, and said a quick, silent prayer of gratitude that the child could not keep secrets. 'And ye say we're leaving on Saturday?'

'Aye. Saturday morning.'

Two days from now. Lily's mind raced. 'Well then. We'd best be packing our things. What, within this room, would ye take with ye to London?'

'This.' Maggie closed Lily's fingers around the book they had been reading, then slipped from the chair and retrieved her own copy book, pen, and ink. 'These.' Last of all, she unearthed from a cabinet the old, rolled certificate Lily had made for her when she was smaller, to make her a princess. 'And this.'

Lily took them all into her hands. 'I'll make certain to bring them. Now away off to the kitchen, my darling, and see that our broth doesn't burn, if ye please.'

Maggie, obedient, skipped to the door, and turned. 'Are ye sure that I've not spoilt the surprise?'

With a smile that held steady somehow, Lily said, 'Ye could never spoil anything.'

Alone, she tried to breathe, to think. She unrolled the certificate, remembering the time when they had made it all together as a family – Henry's wax seal, Simon's perfectly aged edges, Walter's signature with Barbara's bearing witness to the status of young Princess Maggie of her far-off and fictitious country. Lily thought of how, on that day, Matthew promised Maggie, 'In life, nothing is impossible.'

She drew strength from that promise now and, crossing to the work table, began to search among the inks, for she had much to do.

⤬

Henry, frowning, asked her for the third time, 'Are ye certain?'

'Think,' she told him. 'He just happens to send Simon off four days ago, upon a simple errand that he could have carried out himself, and where is Simon now? Not here,' she answered her own question, 'where he could be some protection for us. I don't doubt he's met with some misfortune. Even if he hasn't, by the time he does return it will be too late. Maggie's "gentleman" will have her held in London and we'll never see her afterwards, unless we act to save her. No, it must be now. Tonight,' she said, 'while Archie's in the Paunchmarket.'

He had been staying there these past few nights, while Simon was away, to keep watch on the women who did live and work within that house, but Lily knew he might return at any moment to look in and see how they were getting on.

He might even decide to remove Maggie to a different place, in preparation for her travels.

'He never intended I should go with her,' she said to Henry. 'He has only told her that to keep her calm and unsuspecting, but I can assure ye that his plan has been to hand her to this "gentleman" on Saturday, and take whatever payment he has coming in exchange.'

'Not even Archie, surely—'

'Maggie said that Archie told the "gentleman" he'd make her special documents to say that she was ten.'

Henry was puzzled. 'What does that prove?'

This was personal, for Lily. 'I'll not claim a knowledge of Scots law, but Maggie's being sent to London, and if ye do read that book of English trials just there, ye'll find that ten's a magic age, for girls. Below that, if a man does have relations with ye, it is counted rape. But once ye pass the age of ten, the man can say ye did consent.' She felt a sickness in her belly even saying it – the same sickness she'd felt when she'd first read those words within that book, and thought back to the day that Mr Bell had told her that her own tenth birthday was important because when she'd passed it, she would no more be a child but a young lady. 'Therefore,' he'd said, smiling, 'we must celebrate it in a special way.'

Lily saw, from Henry's eyes, that he was finally seeing and accepting the full horror of their situation. Looking at her helplessly, he asked, 'Where will ye go?'

'The less I tell ye,' Lily said, 'the less ye'll have to lie.'

He smiled, and smiles from Henry were a rare thing these days. 'Do ye not think I can tell a lie?'

'I think ye've told too many, living here,' she said. 'It's

not your nature.' He had always been the kindest and most uncorrupted of the brothers, and she told him so. 'I'll not contribute to your downfall.'

'Most would tell ye it's too late for that.' He was still smiling, but his eyes had altered and she knew that he was deeply moved. 'Ye have the papers that ye need?'

She nodded.

She did not have all the papers that she would have liked to have. That evening she had forced herself to enter Barbara's chamber – something difficult to do, because instead of giving solace to her, seeing all those tangible reminders of the woman she had loved so fiercely only brought the loss of her more sharply into focus, as when looking at a garment with a hole in it, no matter how you tried to keep your eyes from it, you only saw the hole.

The strongbox had been still in place beneath the bed, the key beneath the bolster, and it had not taken Lily very long to spring the lock. There had been papers yet inside the box. But Maggie's letters from her father, in their bundle tied with string, were gone.

Whatever purpose Archie had in taking them was yet unclear. That there *would* be a purpose, Lily knew beyond all doubt, and that knowledge spurred her on to finish her own work.

She'd made a birth certificate for Maggie, and although she could not recreate the letter Jamie wrote her, she had gone one better, making a certificate of marriage.

After all, unmarried women could not travel freely, and at any place they could be pressed into domestic service. Lily could not take the chance, with Maggie in her care, that such a thing might happen. She'd allowed herself the one small lie which sat upon her conscience the more easily because she knew that Jamie would forgive her for it, given all the times he truly had asked her to marry him.

His signature upon the false certificate was such a perfect copy of the one she'd saved from his burnt letter that she doubted whether he'd have known himself he did not sign it. If the directors of the African Company wished to compare it to any document he might have signed in their offices, they'd find that it matched.

Watching while Henry now took all the papers and fastened them into a file, Lily told him, 'Archie will be furious when he learns we are gone. Come with us. It would not take more than a couple of hours to draw documents for ye, or else if ye like we can just bring the paper and ink and I'll write them tomorrow, when we've found a safe place to lodge.'

Henry shook his head. 'I will be fine. And besides, ye will need me to aim Archie elsewhere, to buy ye the time to get free of him. Where are ye *not* headed?'

Lily considered this. 'North. We are not going north.'

'Then I'll tell Archie ye told Maggie tales of Inchbrakie this week,' Henry said. 'That will not be a lie, but it may keep him looking in the wrong direction.'

Things moved swiftly, after that.

Henry helped to waken Maggie and he carried her downstairs because they did not dare leave any lights but one half-shuttered lamp to burn within the downstairs rooms, lest Archie see they were awake so late and wonder why. That was the thing with Archie – although he was in the Paunchmarket, his eyes and spies were everywhere, as Lily had well learned. It made her nervous. Outside in the close, a door slammed closed, and Lily held her breath until the briskly clipping footsteps had receded out of hearing.

Maggie grumbled only slightly while she dressed. 'Why must I wear both of my petticoats at once?' she asked.

Lily hushed her. 'It is simpler than carrying them.' She, too, wore two petticoats, and two shifts beneath that, and Barbara's old straw hat with the brown ribbon tied securely on her head. Besides the file of papers, she carried a bundle of their clothing, neatly wrapped around their few books and belongings. When they reached a safer place, she'd buy a proper chest to store them in for travelling, but for tonight she'd have to take no more than she could carry in her arms.

Maggie had Dolly, who was also dressed for travel in her yellow gown and blue cloak, with the heart-shaped wire brooch hidden beneath it. 'Is it Saturday already?' she asked, sleepily.

A floorboard creaked behind them in the passage. Lily jumped, and turned, expecting to see Archie standing there, but it was nothing. Just the old house settling.

'Almost,' she told Maggie in a low voice. 'And we'll have to walk a ways to meet the coach.' There would be time for her to share the truth with Maggie – all the truth – when they were somewhere safe. For now, a few more hours of ignorance could surely do no harm. She heard her grandmother's approving voice say, 'Let her keep her childhood.'

Henry cautiously stepped into the close before them, walking its length up and down to look into the shadowy places and see for himself that their way would be clear. When he came back inside he knelt in front of Maggie and quietly told her, 'Now, give me a kiss.' She did. 'And keep ye warm. And mind whatever Lily says. And be a good lass always.'

'Are ye coming up to London, too?'

'Someday,' he said. 'Someday I will.' He held her very tightly. Then he kissed her hair, and let her go, and stood.

Lily had no words that could tell him how her heart felt, but she knew he knew.

She reached for him in silence and he held her for a moment, hard, then set her from him with reluctance. 'Go,' he said. 'And don't write letters, he's too clever. Don't leave any trail that he can follow.'

'Henry . . .'

'Don't look back,' he said, 'no good will come of it. I'm going to close the door.'

She knew how much it would have broken Henry's heart – Henry, who for all his life had wanted nothing more than a real family – to push them so gently from the passage out of the door into the waiting night, but still he did it, and she saw his eyes and watched him try to give her one last smile.

Lily did not obey his last words. She looked back. He'd closed the door, as he had said he would. The little house in Riddell's Close looked lonely and forlorn.

Maggie, too, had looked behind. Her small hand holding onto Lily's tightly, she said in a sad whisper, 'But we did not light the candle.'

'No,' said Lily, looking from the empty window that had been her own for all those years, and was no longer, to the other windows that were watching them in silence. 'Not tonight.'

Shivering, but not from cold, she took a firmer hold of Maggie's hand and turned towards the road to Edinburgh, her steps as soft and swift as though the devil were behind.

Some things were better done in darkness.

CHAPTER THIRTY-FOUR

FRIDAY, 3 OCTOBER, 1707

IN THE FLICKER OF the firelight, Lily's face looked sad as she remembered. Sitting curled into her cushioned chair, she said, 'I did not know what else to do. There was nobody left to ask for help, not really. They'd all gone.'

I leaned towards her in my chair and took her hand in both of mine. '*I've* not left you,' I said. 'And I am not going anywhere.'

She gave my hand a grateful squeeze and let me keep possession of it, so I counted that a victory.

'But,' I said, 'you've not yet made it clear how Archie came to be involved in this affair. How did he find you here in Edinburgh?'

'How does he ever find a person? He has ways, and I'd grown careless. Maggie had this offer of a teaching job, and oh, you should have seen her. I could not have told her no. I told myself, since we were living very modestly and under different names, perhaps it would not be a problem. And then one day I came out of the Luckenbooths and there he was.' She said it very evenly, although it must have been a terrifying moment for her.

'Maggie was not with you then?'

She shook her head. 'She does not know that Archie knows where we are living. I have kept that from her.'

'Well, you'll have to tell her something, to prepare her, for I cannot guarantee that Gilroy will not want her testimony.'

Lily nodded, but she looked towards the fire, her eyes filled bright with unshed tears. 'It's very hard, you see, because I've tried to shield her from it all. It's Maggie who will suffer if I fail.'

I was not following. 'What is it Archie wants from you, exactly?'

'He was very plain. He said he'd learned that I was living here under the name of Mrs Graeme, and that he remembered well the letter Jamie gave to me – the one he made me throw upon the fire. He asked me whether I had married Jamie, and when I gave him no answer, he replied it did not matter, all that truly was of consequence was if the marriage could be proved. For if it could not . . .' Lily took a moment to collect herself, continuing more calmly, 'Archie still has Maggie's letters from her father. If I fail to prove to the commission I was Jamie's wife, those letters will come out and Maggie's future will be ruined. Her birth will be exposed as illegitimate, and her employers at the school are careful who they hire, because their parents demand teachers of a certain moral quality.'

I thought, I could not help it, of how Helen Turnbull had been quick to judge the poor wife of Lord Grange for having been the daughter of a criminal, and I knew well how any whisper that a person's birth was illegitimate could close a door to them that might have otherwise stood open.

Her hand rested lightly in mine while I thoughtfully

rubbed my thumb over the back of her knuckles. 'Did he know you had the certificate?'

'No. He expected that I'd have to make one. It pleased him to learn I would not, for it saved him time and the cost of supplies.'

'This may seem an odd question,' I told her, 'but I have my reasons for asking. Do you have the sense Archie's aim is to simply collect any claim that he can? Or does he seem to have a particular interest in James Graeme?'

Lily frowned faintly. 'He showed me an edict the Commissioners of the Equivalent put out, inviting Jamie's spouse – and bairns, if any be – to come before them with a claim. I simply did assume he'd seen the edict posted, and on learning I was here had made a move of opportunity.'

I said, 'You're very likely right.'

'Why? What else could it be?'

'I don't know.' Truth was always best, but there was no need to tell all of it. 'It's only that the claim does seem a small amount of money, for a man like Archie Browne to go to so much trouble over.'

Lily's face cleared. 'He's not doing it for money. It is not his own idea. He does take his orders from a man above him. That was evident,' she said, 'at our next meeting, when I gave him the certificate.'

'And where was this?'

'At Pat Steell's tavern, in a private room upstairs.' She'd feared the worst, when Archie had escorted her upstairs to meet a stranger in that room, particularly when they'd found the stranger waiting for them, sitting up in bed with the bedcurtains partly drawn. But nothing more had happened than the other man had read the document, asked Lily some brief questions, and then given his approval. 'Very good,' he'd said to Archie. 'I shall tell His Grace, and we'll proceed from there. With luck, it won't take long.'

I stopped her there. 'You're sure he said "His Grace"?'

'I'm certain of it.'

I was not an expert on the forms of social address, but I did know that few people were raised high enough to merit being called 'Your Grace', a form most commonly reserved for dukes. And while I'd not accuse a man on nothing more than my suspicions, I knew of but one duke who had close ties to Steell's tavern.

'This man you met at the Cross Keys,' I asked Lily, 'what did he look like?'

'He stayed behind the bedcurtains. I never did see him directly. Except he was fat, and his manner was pleasant.'

He might be the same jovial man I had seen there myself tonight, who had been trying too hard to appear drunk, and sitting behind Captain Gordon. 'And what happened after that?'

'He kept the marriage certificate, and we left. I was told he would see it was presented on my behalf to the Commissioners for the Equivalent. I did not see it again till the day I was summoned to meet your friend Gilroy. And you.'

That was a day I would always remember. 'And have you been back to the Cross Keys since?'

'No. If Archie wishes to see me, he sends word that I am to meet him at St Giles'.'

'You find him with the Regent Murray?' I guessed, thinking back to last Sabbath, when I'd found her waiting beside the great tomb of the venerable regent where so many people met to strike their deals and pay their debts, and on whose plaque dejected Justice drooped while Faith kept writing in her book as though determined not to give up hope.

'Aye.'

'And if you wish to meet with *him*?' I asked.

The light was dim within the room, but I could see her fear. 'You are not thinking to confront him?'

'Do you know where he does lodge? Henry says he is rarely to be found at Riddell's Close these days.'

'I'm not surprised,' said Lily. 'Archie is a wanted man, he told me so himself. In fact—' She caught herself, and looked away as though she could not meet my eyes.

'What is it?' When she stayed silent, I said, 'I know there's a warrant for Archie's arrest. Gilroy told me. He said Archie forged a will to help some people claim funds falsely from the Equivalent. So, you see? It is no secret.'

She withdrew her hand from mine and made a fist of it in her lap. 'What you do *not* know,' she said, 'is that it was no small amount that they were trying to claim. And because of the number of schemes such as this that are currently being attempted, the word is, should Archie be caught, he'll be hanged.'

'They don't hang people for forgery.'

Her soft eyes almost pitied me my ignorance. 'He's been told they'll make an exception in his case,' she said, 'so he'll be an example, and stand as a warning to others.'

I could find no space in my heart to feel sympathy for him, and said so. 'He has earned his ending. And if he is hanged, you'll be free.'

Lily looked down, but not before I saw what looked like a tear glisten briefly in light from the fire on her cheek.

'Lily,' I began, and then I looked away as well, and searched for words. The ones I finally found were, 'You must tell me all of it, if I'm to be of help.'

'You cannot help.' She sounded very sure. 'Whichever way I try to move upon the board, he has me trapped. If I warn Maggie or try moving her to safety, he'll reveal the letters. If I fail to see the marriage proved, then he'll reveal the letters. And if I reveal *him*, or seek help ...' Another tear trailed where the first had gone. This time I saw it clearly.

'Then what?' I asked, gently. 'Lily, what?'

She drew a shaking breath. 'Then he will say that it was me that forged the will, and turn me in. The others in the scheme have sworn in writing he was innocent, I've seen the papers they did sign. So he will stay in hiding, I will take the blame, and he will see me hang.'

She looked at me, and although I felt rising anger at the man who caused her such distress, I wanted at that moment no more than to take her fear away from her, and so I said the first thing that occurred to me. 'You are not trapped. It's but a stalemate.'

My reward was her small smile at hearing her own words returned. Her hand unclenched and, raising it, she wiped her cheek and asked me, 'How is it a stalemate?'

'Did not Colonel Graeme teach you that, when all the moves that you had left upon the board would lead you to disaster, you could still make a retreat?'

'To where?'

'I'll find a path,' I promised her.

She did not look persuaded. But at least I'd made her smile.

And then, because I knew that it would make her pleased to think of Colonel Graeme, I told her what I knew of the invasion that was rumoured.

'There is always an invasion,' Lily said.

'Aye, that's what Henry says.' And then we talked of Henry, but it soon became clear Lily did not know of Henry's injury, and I did not wish to be the one to tell her, so instead our talk turned further back in time and touched on other questions, other blank spots in the stories I'd been told. She spoke freely. When we came to Mr Bell she was more halting, yet we talked of those days too, and I confessed that I had visited the swordslipper, and that I'd spoken to his daughter, Marion.

'Poor Marion,' said Lily. 'I did like her. She was good to me.' And then, 'Perhaps I'll write to her.'

I said I thought that was a fine idea.

'Though I am glad you went to see her first,' said Lily, 'for at least she does know now that I'm alive. It would be a great shock, I think, to get a letter from a person you believed was dead.'

There were shadows in the corners of the chamber and I felt, while we were talking, that the dead were somehow with us, settling in to listen, too. I felt the living ghosts as well, of what had been and might have been – the more so when the candle in the window guttered and went out on a slight, wispy puff of smoke that hung a moment in the air.

That startled Lily, who'd been sure she'd had three hours left yet of that candle. Then she realized we'd been talking for that long. 'I am so sorry.'

'Why? I have enjoyed our talk. Besides, I'm not expected

back at Caldow's Land till morning. When I left with Captain Gordon, he implied our night would be . . . debauched.'

'I'm sorry to have spoilt it.'

Once again I turned her own words back upon her. 'You could never spoil anything.'

The warmth I felt between us did owe nothing to the fire. Her instinct, unlike mine, was to escape it, and I could not blame her. Burns were dangerous.

I kept my seat while Lily rose and took the cups we'd used for wine while we were talking. As she passed me, I could see the weariness upon her face that came not from the lateness of the hour, but from the loneliness of how she lived.

Again I thought of Helen Turnbull, in the comfort of her rooms at Caldow's Land, who in the absence of her husband – even with him – had the housekeeping assistance of MacDougall and the maid, while Lily kept these lodgings on her own. No matter this was but a single room, it still took effort, and with no one else to share the burden or to keep her company most days, the work must have seemed unrelenting.

I looked around. The coals within the fireplace needed to be banked up properly so that they'd not burn perilously through the night, but would still hold enough heat in the morning to come once again to life and let a new fire be rekindled. That, at least, was one small thing that I could do for Lily while she cleared our cups away. I was finishing the final task of covering the embers with a thin layer of ashes when I felt the weight of silence at my back, and knew that I was being watched.

Still bending at the hearth, I glanced behind, over my shoulder.

In a quiet voice, she said, 'You're a good man.'

Having heard her tales, I understood the weight of those words now in a way few men could. 'I'm not,' I told her, 'actually. I'm truly not.' I stood, and closed the space between us, and she did not move but waited for me, her face tilting up as I came nearer. 'You've had wine,' I said, reminding myself of that fact as much as her.

'Aye, half a cup. 'Tis not enough to meddle with my reason. Most men would attempt to give me more.'

'I'm not most men,' I said.

'I ken that.' As though she could feel the conflict in me and desired to calm it, she reached up and lightly touched my face and told me, 'Stay.'

My life had left me hardened. I had seen and done things in it that were better left unsaid, and I had travelled far beyond the comforts most men knew, and learned to live with none. I'd grown resilient. I had fought men, and I'd killed them. And yet standing now before this woman – and before her only – I felt vulnerable.

I said, 'I'd like to hear you call me Adam. Could you do that?'

Lily nodded. 'It's a fine, strong name,' she told me. 'Adam.'

'Say it over.' I was asking her, not ordering, my head already lowered so we breathed together.

'Adam.'

In my life I'd kissed more expertly, but never with more passion, nor more tenderness. Time stopped for me, and then I stopped as well, because my hand, which had been travelling its own path, had slipped underneath the neckline of her bodice, where the thin, smooth linen of her shift edged over her firm stays. And there my fingers touched a tiny object that dislodged itself into my palm.

I drew my head back and looked down. It was the little silver brooch, the heart-shaped brooch topped with a crown, that was itself made up of smaller hearts and roses.

Lily's hand came briefly into mine as she took back the brooch from me and pinned it where it had been on her stays, above her own heart, saying, 'It does hold the memory of a time when I was loved.'

With the fingertips of both my hands I gently brushed the darkly curling hair back from her face to either side of those blue eyes.

'Love,' I said, 'should be more than a memory.'

Lily reached for me, and told me, 'So then stay.'

And then I knew that I was right and she had been mistaken, for a good man would have told her no, and kissed her one last time, and made her lock her door against him as he left her there alone.

A good man would never have lifted her, the way I did, and carried her across to where the bed lay in the corner of the chamber. He would not have stood without a protest while she pushed his coat impatiently down from his shoulders, tugged his shirt over his head, and brought his mouth back down to hers.

I was not a good man, as I'd warned her.

So I stayed.

CHAPTER THIRTY-FIVE

SATURDAY, 4 OCTOBER, 1707

THE GUARD WAS NOT inclined to let me in. I did as I had done with the first guard at the portcullis gate, and showed again the pass the Earl of Seafield had provided me, that I had kept against such an occasion in my pocket. 'It does plainly say that I'm to be admitted on demand at any hour,' I pointed out, and stood my ground before the guard.

He did not win the argument, but made me leave my weapons.

Robert Moray was awake. The stubble of his beard had filled in slightly since I'd seen him last on Monday, and again he wore no coat nor wig. This time he did not bother donning either, only faced me in his shirt sleeves with the weary air of someone plagued by tiresome formalities. 'What now?'

We'd moved beyond polite good mornings, then. I said, 'You have been less than truthful with me.'

It was so early in the morning still that no light penetrated through the small, barred window of his prison chamber. The high, vaulted ceiling and stone walls were cast in stark relief of light and shadow by two standing rushlights that allowed me to see his expression. 'Tell me when I've lied.'

I found that an irritating challenge, because he had been so clever with his words I could not find a single instance to reply with, so instead I took a new approach. 'You did not tell me everything the last time I was here, nor yet the time before that.'

'Ah.' He sat, and indicated I should do the same. 'Well, that's a different thing from lying, surely? All men do leave pieces out when they tell tales, it is no crime.'

I could not argue that. But, 'You knew Lily was alive.'

That realization had struck me with certainty when I'd woken an hour ago, with Lily's head upon my shoulder. I'd been dreaming of the Shore at Leith, and of James Graeme swinging Lily round, amazed and joyful that he'd found his friend again, and in my dream, Lily had looked towards me and explained, 'It would be a great shock, I think, to meet a person you believed was dead.'

I said to Robert Moray now, 'When Lily was a lass of ten, they found her lantern by the loch at Duddingston. They found her hood beside the broken ice. The story was that she'd been pining for her father, and had taken her own life. I know this. I was told this. Everyone was told this. Colonel Graeme stopped his custom with the swordslipper because of it.' I watched his face while I was talking. He was very good at not revealing his emotions, but I saw the subtle change that told me I was right. I carried on, 'But when I came here that first day with Lily, while I'll grant that you did not expect to see her, you were not surprised to see that she was living. Which does tell me you already knew that Lily was not dead.'

Once in battle I'd disarmed a more accomplished swords-man when he had not been expecting it, and now I saw an echo of the look that man had given me play over Moray's features. His mouth curved. 'Ye've missed your calling, Sergeant Williamson. Ye should have made a study of the law.'

'I am no educated man. I've neither wit nor patience,' I confessed, 'to duel with words when there is action to be taken. Lily needs my help, and I would ask you to be honest with me.' I asked the question, straight. 'How did you know she was alive?'

He studied me a moment longer, then he came to a decision. 'In December, of the year before my cousin Jamie sailed to Darien, I did return to Scotland on the business of King James. In Leith, I saw my cousin, and he told me he'd seen Lily. He was troubled,' Moray said, 'for although grateful to have found her, he did fear she was unhappy.' A pause. 'He told me he had asked her would she marry him.'

I waited. 'Did he tell you what she answered?'

'Evidently it was yes.'

He did not know the truth, then – that the marriage had not taken place; that Lily had refused his cousin, and had only forged that false certificate so she could take young Maggie Graeme to safety.

But Moray's lack of knowledge might be useful. The most direct way out of Lily's problem was to prove the marriage, and for that there would be few things better than a witness.

'Since you care for Lily and you wish to be of help to her,' I said, 'I take it you'll sign a testificate to state exactly that? Your cousin James asked her to marry him?'

'It is because I care for her,' he said, 'that I cannot.'

I felt a rush of pure frustration. 'Why not? Speak plainly, if you can.'

'I'm sure ye'll work it through.'

I did not lose my temper, to my credit, but I lost my patience. 'I am done with wasting time,' I told him. 'Lily's not your playing piece, and this is not a game.'

His voice turned cool. 'I would remind ye which of us is free to leave this chamber and go home, and which of us must daily wonder if he is to keep his head. Believe me when I tell ye I am well aware 'tis not a game.'

It was the closest I had seen him come to showing worry for his safety, but he tamped it down again and carried on in a more even tone, as though he were my schoolmaster.

'It isn't me they want, it's John. Ye heard them say so for yourself.'

'Yes. At the Earl of Seafield's. They believed he'd been here planning the invasion.'

Moray said, 'My brother John does have the confidence and trust of young King James and of the queen his mother, who counts John among her favourites at the court of Saint-Germain. The English – and their allies here in Scotland – know that, if there's an invasion coming, John will ken its secrets.'

I suspected he did not speak half so freely with most men, and that it likely went against his better judgement and his nature to do so with me. In recognition of that, I chose not to ask him if there would be an invasion in the spring. It did not matter.

'But,' he said, 'they don't have any way to draw John out where they can capture him. I don't doubt when they put me in here, they were hoping he might try to rescue me, but John's not such a fool – nor would I ever thank him for risking our cause and his life in exchange for mine. But if John had a wife? And if *she* were in this prison? He'd tear the town apart to set her free, and well they ken it.' Moray told me, in the even tone men use when they do swear an oath, 'Our women are the heart of us, and no man of my family would do any less.' He paused a moment. Asked me, 'Are ye following?'

I was beginning to, and yet I was uncertain, so he spelled it out.

'There is another man who kens the secrets that my brother holds. My uncle, Colonel Patrick Graeme. Do ye follow now?' He saw the confirmation in my face, and carried on, 'My uncle is a man of honour. He would come for Lily any time she were in trouble whether she were Jamie's wife or no. 'Tis fortunate the duke is unaware of that.' On seeing my reaction he remarked, 'It is the Duke of Hamilton behind this then?'

'I think so, aye.'

'That's not surprising. Seafield might be clever, but he lacks the motivation to put all these wheels in motion, and he never could charm Lord Grange into doing him a favour. No, it had to be the duke, there like a spider at the centre of his web, controlling everything. I should imagine it was just too great an opportunity to miss – these payments being made, from the Equivalent.'

The plan was simple and straightforward. As it stood, with James Graeme officially unmarried, his sole heir would be his father, Colonel Graeme, who would then be sent the payment owed to Jamie. No competing claim had yet been filed with the commissioners, since Lily's claim had not been put in front of them. The duke, when he had first seen her certificate, had likely noticed the same problem Robert Moray pointed out at our first meeting – the same problem Moray told me would have prompted the commissioners to disallow the claim: there was no way to prove it with so little evidence.

Which would explain why the duke had then resorted to a secret inquiry, and passed the certificate on to Lord Grange.

'Lord Grange has Gilroy,' Moray said, 'who, as you've seen, is very good at what he does. He's like a bulldog with investigations.'

Frowning, I asked, 'Do you think Lord Grange is in the scheme?'

'I shouldn't think so. Not his style. He'd take the duke's word at face value, that it was a task that needed to be done, that's all.'

I thought on this. 'So, Gilroy and I get the proof that James and Lily married, and we send this back to the commission . . .'

'And then the commissioners declare the marriage valid.' Moray nodded. 'And my uncle, being now informed he is no longer heir, learns Jamie had a wife. I'd think about this time the duke will also move behind the scenes to see that Lily's taken up and put in prison. Not in here,' he said, 'but in the Tolbooth. Have ye ever seen the Tolbooth, Sergeant Williamson?'

I had. I did not wish to ever see the inside of that place again.

He said, 'Would ye wish to see Lily there? And under torture? Because I can promise ye, that's what they do intend.

They will use any means to draw my uncle out into the open, and God help both him and Lily if they're able to succeed.' His mouth made a grim line. 'So no, I will not sign your document. And if ye care for Lily as I think ye care for Lily, ye will let the matter drop, for then she'll be no further use to them.'

I did not waste breath explaining that it would not be so simple. He had told me much, and there was nothing more that he could do that would help Lily. Telling him the full breadth of the dangers she was facing would but add to his own burdens.

I could manage things alone.

I stood, and thanked him. Briefly I considered reassuring him that I'd tell no one what he'd said about his family, but I reasoned he would not have told me in the first place if he'd thought that I'd repeat it, so I only said, above our handshake, 'I will keep her safe.'

'I'm counting on it,' he replied.

I had a strange, uneasy feeling when our eyes met that I'd not see him again, and I sensed Robert Moray knew it, too. But all he said, when I had nearly reached the barred door of his prison chamber, was, 'And, Sergeant Williamson? Take care to watch your back.'

❧

As warnings went, it was well timed.

I heard the footsteps falling in behind me as I started down the castle hill. I stopped, and turned. The morning light had raised a mist that lightly hung between the houses, and a man in a grey coat might shelter in a dozen places and remain unseen.

I could see no one, yet I knew full well that I was not alone. Firmly, I said, 'She is with me, now. I am taking care of her.'

No answer came.

But when I turned again and went on walking, no one followed.

I was busy with my thoughts.

Brave though it might be to claim that I was taking care of Lily, it was something else again to do it with the right effect.

If she succeeded in her claim to prove the marriage – if we could find sufficient evidence that would convince the men of the commission she had been James Graeme's wife – her life would be in danger from the Duke of Hamilton, who sought to hold her hostage as a means to draw out Colonel Graeme.

On the other hand, if Lily failed to prove the marriage, then as punishment the letters Archie held from Maggie's father would all come to light, and Maggie's future would be ruined.

There was yet a third threat Lily might not have considered, but that I was only too aware of – even if she did as Archie asked, and saw the marriage proved, he might betray her anyway. She had escaped him once, and to a man like Archie, that was unforgivable.

If he indeed had gathered documents that threw suspicion for his own crimes upon Lily, he'd not hesitate to use them once she'd served her purpose, and he'd gladly stand and watch her hang.

She might hang, too, or be imprisoned at the least, if Gilroy came to the conclusion the certificate was forged, beyond all doubt, and took the matter to the courts.

She'd be beyond my help, then.

But for now, I had control of the inquiry. Gilroy had not yet returned from Dundee. And with a few days more to plan, I could find Lily that safe passage from the chess board that would let her make a safe retreat.

These thoughts and more were in my head as I came up the curved forestair of Caldow's Land. I nodded a vague greeting at MacDougall as he let me in.

'What hour d'ye call this, then?' he demanded.

Helen, sitting at the breakfast table near the windows, told him in a cheerful voice, 'He's been with Captain Gordon, do not scold him so.' And then she added, 'Come and join us, Adam. Gilroy was just telling me about his niece's wedding.'

There he sat, inscrutable as ever, eyebrow raised a fraction as he judged my slightly rumpled clothing. As I took my seat, he said, 'I'm far more interested in hearing how you've spent your week. I'm told by Mrs Turnbull that you have found Maggie Graeme. Well done. When shall we arrange to speak to her?'

MacDougall poured my ale. It was the one time I'd been grateful for him.

Helen put in, 'Did not Mrs Graeme tell us that her husband's cousin had her day off work on Mondays?'

'Yes.' It satisfied me to hear my voice sounding wholly natural. 'I think that Monday would do well.'

Agreeing, Helen said, 'Then you would have her testimony written up in time.'

I asked, 'In time for what?'

Gilroy passed me the bread, explaining, 'Mrs Turnbull's had a letter from her husband.'

'Yes,' she told me. 'He expects that he'll be here on Tuesday afternoon, or Wednesday morning at the latest. So you'll soon be free to pass your duties on to him.' She smiled. 'Will that not be a great relief?'

Relief was not the word I would have used. Within the space of a few minutes, my control upon the situation and the time in which I had to act had both become restricted.

But I only drank deep of my ale, avoiding Gilroy's eyes, and said to Helen, 'I do look forward to seeing him.'

Because, as Robert Moray had explained, not saying everything was not the same as lying.

CHAPTER THIRTY-SIX

MONDAY, 6 OCTOBER, 1707

Lately i'd been listening to Lily's reminiscences, and Henry Browne's, and those of Captain Gordon. I could picture Maggie Graeme only as a child.

This self-assured young lady who faced Gilroy and me now in Lily's lodgings seemed to bear such small resemblance to the picture I'd imagined that I knew I had been staring. But I caught, from time to time, a trace of childish vulnerability in how she moved her head, or pleated folds into the fabric of her skirt while she was talking, or tried not to meet my eyes.

She'd grown to be a lovely woman, both by all the standards of society – her golden hair and charming features and melodic speaking voice – and by the smaller measures that revealed how she was raised, at first by Barbara Malcolm, then by Lily. Maggie's manners were not in the least affected, they were natural. She did all things by reflex and because it was the proper thing to do, not because she wanted praise or any action in return. She thought before she spoke, and when she did speak it was with the expectation that what she said would be valued. And she always treated Lily with respect.

Even if I'd not known their history and how much they'd had to overcome together, I'd have guessed that they were family from the way they interacted. Family, so I'd come to learn in life, was not merely the people you were bound to by your blood, but those you bound yourself to by your choosing. It was very clear that Maggie Graeme had chosen Lily.

'Come and sit,' said Maggie now. 'We have all that we need.'

As Lily took the chair beside her, Maggie looked across at Gilroy, who was seated next to me. We'd brought the table once again before the hearth, to make it easy to take notes. Gilroy, when confronted with the fact there were but three chairs in the room, and one of those half-broken, had excused himself for a few moments, gone downstairs, and then returned with two plain wooden chairs he'd borrowed from the shopkeeper below.

With Gilroy, I was never sure if he obtained things because people were disarmed by him or threatened, but whatever his approach it was successful. So the women had the better chairs, and he and I the plainer ones, and with wine to drink, our papers set upon the table, and our pens inked, we began.

Maggie surprised us all, at the beginning, when I asked her if she'd ever seen Lily together with James Graeme.

'Only once,' she said. 'The day after St Andrew's Day. The day that . . .' She glanced up at me, as though unsure how much I knew. 'The day my brother went away.'

I hadn't been expecting this. I looked across at Lily, who seemed stunned, and said to Maggie, 'You have never told me this.'

'It never seemed like something I should mention,' Maggie said. 'And I did fear I'd get in trouble, for I was not meant to be out on the pier. I used to do that sometimes – slip out on my own, when everybody else was busy with their work. I liked to see the ships. I didn't stay out long, so I was never missed. And that day, you'll remember, there was *so* much going on, and I just wanted one more look at it before I did begin my lessons. But when I came near the windmill, you were there already with a man, and you were talking. You did call him Jamie, and I did not hear what else you told him, but I did hear him reply, "A Graeme would not leave you." And then you began to weep. He tried to comfort you. So I turned back. And that's when I saw Matthew.'

Gilroy said, 'Your brother Matthew?'

'Yes. He'd come down from his lodging, and was standing on the pier as well. I don't believe he noticed me, I was well back between the houses. He was watching Lily and James Graeme. And then he turned back, too. Like I did. And he went away.'

I made a note upon the paper, feeling Lily's eyes upon me, wondering if we were thinking the same thing, or if her thoughts were turning backwards to that day upon the pier and what might have gone differently had Matthew not ignored her knocking at his door that morning, while my own thoughts were more fixed upon the fact that Maggie having seen James Graeme there with Lily might now be a problem.

If we proved the marriage, Lily was in danger.

If we did not prove it, Maggie's reputation was in danger.

My job was to buy us time, and see the scales did not tip steeply either way until I found the best path out of our dilemma.

Taking hold now of the conversation, I steered straight past all the intervening turmoil, over any hint of scandal, and came firmly back to shore with, 'And when did you first learn that James Graeme was your cousin?'

'Lily told me on our journey west from Edinburgh,' said Maggie.

I knew Lily had said other things to Maggie then, as well. Among them, she had told the child that Archie was a bad man, and he meant to do them harm. But Maggie mentioned none of this. She only said, 'I was fair pleased to learn that I had cousins, and to learn that I had cousins who did live in the same place where Lily once had been a child herself was wonderful. And better still to learn that we'd be going soon to live in the new colony with James, at Caledonia.'

'And that,' I said, 'was when you first saw the certificate of marriage?'

'Yes.'

Lily was yet unaware of the great trap the Duke of Hamilton had set for her. I had not wished to burden her with any added worry. She still would think her greatest hope of getting clear of Archie would be to see the marriage proved, and since Maggie believed Lily had actually been married onto James Graeme, Lily would have advised Maggie to answer our questions with truth.

I tried now to gently counter the effects of that approach, so that the scales stayed balanced, for I did not want Gilroy to come to any firm decision yet.

I said to Maggie, 'But you don't recall a wedding ceremony.'

'No. But then I was child, and Lily said they married all in private.'

Gilroy asked, 'And when you got to the colony, what happened then?'

Maggie looked briefly from Gilroy to me. 'Then you do not know?'

And so she told us.

Chapter Thirty-Seven

Monday, 14 August, 1699

Maggie had made a new friend over breakfast that morning.

The girl, Sophia, was her own age, her own height, and shared her own dislike of wearing hats. Her hair gleamed copper in the sunshine and made Maggie think of Barbara.

She and Lily had been waiting here now since the end of May, among the swelling groups of people thronging into Greenock for the preparation of the next ships that would sail to Caledonia. The people came and went. A lot of men, many in uniform, all milling round importantly. A steadily increasing flow of women – mostly young, like Lily, although some were middle-aged. But there had been few children.

Maggie had been very glad to find Sophia at the breakfast table.

She'd been gladder still to have her company outdoors.

The house they boarded in was not within the town of Greenock, but adjoining it along the south bank of the river Clyde in the small townlet known as Crawfurdsdyke.

It was not Leith, but Maggie had grown used to it.

The Clyde was not the Firth of Forth. The water would not be so wide to cross, and it looked calmer, and when the west wind blew the clouds, the hills that rose so gently on the river's further side were chased by sun and shadow in a different way from those at home.

There was only one true street to speak of in Crawfurdsdyke, running along parallel to the river and on into Greenock. Some houses, including the one they were boarding in, lay between that and the water's edge. Some others had been built south of that road, fronting onto it. And beyond those lay the farms and the woods and behind all of *that* rose more hills, holding everything snugly enclosed.

But there was still a harbour, with a sea wall and a pier of rough-hewn, reddish stones, laid tightly without mortar. It was twice as tall as Maggie, twice her height across in breadth, and curved out into the bright water of the Clyde like a stone scythe.

She and Sophia walked along it, each of them holding one of Dolly's hands, the way Lily and Henry once held Maggie's hands when they walked her along the Shore at Leith when she was small.

Maggie was finishing her story. 'But it was all right because Don Quixote and Sancho Panza rode out together at night all in secret on their first adventure, too. They gathered their money and left without saying goodbye, only we said good-bye first to Henry.'

They'd come to the curve of the pier, from where they had the best view – not only of the smaller fishing boats sheltered within the close curve of the pier, but of the larger ships lying at anchor now out in the Greenock Road, and the activity going on all round them.

There were four ships now, though Maggie had eyes for but one of them – the *Rising Sun*, which had been there to greet them in May when they'd first arrived, richly resplend-ent in all her red paint with her carved, gilded ornaments painting the Clyde's current glittering gold with their scat-tered reflections. Most beautiful, in Maggie's eyes, were the two rising suns, with their rays spreading out, fore and aft, so whichever direction one viewed the ship from, a new day was about to begin.

'Thirty-eight guns,' Maggie said, even though Captain Gordon was not there to hear, nor admire her for making the count. Then, to cover the fact that she missed Captain Gordon, she turned to Sophia and said, 'That's the ship we'll be sailing on.'

Sophia sighed. 'I do wish that I was sailing, too. But Mother says she'll send for us when she is certain that my daddie has our house built properly. He went ahead last year.'

'My cousin did, as well,' said Maggie. 'He did marry onto Lily, all in secret, like, afore he went. I'd hoped she'd marry onto Matthew, but ...' Her voice trailed off. She raised her free hand in a gesture she'd seen Lily often do, to shield her eyes against the sunlight on the water. 'Lily says my cousin's very nice, and that he'll keep us safe.' Which made her think. She asked Sophia, 'Who will keep you and your sister safe, with both your parents gone to Caledonia?'

'My aunt and uncle.'

That was good then. Just so long as she was not alone.

Kicking at a stone, Sophia added, 'They are to meet us here this morning. They are staying at an inn nearby.'

'They do not live here?'

'No. They live far south of here,' she said, 'near to Kirkcudbright.'

Maggie, having never heard of that town, heard its name the way Sophia voiced it now – Kir-*coo*-bree – and she stored it in her memory so that she could find it later on a map.

When they were finished walking on the pier and looking for a new adventure, Maggie said, 'I ken what we should do,' and led the way along the shore to the two-storey house where she and Lily shared an upstairs room and where Sophia and her mother and her older sister had arrived last night.

It was among the larger of the houses here, with crow-stepped gables and a slated roof instead of thatch. It had been built for Captain Reid, who'd been the skipper of a merchant ship, but he'd been lost at sea and now his widow took in boarders and did dressmaking and knew how to make sugar candy.

Maggie liked her very much.

As Maggie and Sophia came into the kitchen, Mrs Reid looked round and asked them, 'Well? What is it that you're after?' But she asked it cheerfully, as though she, too, were pleased that Maggie had at long last found a friend.

'Can we look at the book of maps?' asked Maggie.

'"May we". And say "please".'

'May we look at the book of maps, please?' It had not been published as a book of maps – it was a book of Scotland's history, but within its illustrations it contained a series of impressive maps that Maggie much admired.

The book belonged in Captain Reid's small library, and Mrs Reid was careful who had access to that room, but after having watched for many nights while Lily read to Maggie from the tales of Don Quixote, Mrs Reid had one night opened up that room to them and said, 'You may find more to read the child in here.'

There was a writing table in that room as well, so Maggie once again began to have her lessons every day with pen and copy book, which made her very happy.

Mrs Reid remarked to Lily, 'She does have a lovely hand. You've taught her well.' She'd gone to school herself, in Glasgow, and had been apprenticed there to a dressmaker of good reputation who had served fine ladies. 'If you wish the child to do the same,' she said to Lily once, 'you will correct her way of speaking, and your own, so none will judge your status by it.'

Lily had apparently been taking this advice, and she had altered her own way of speaking as a model and reminder so that Maggie had begun to also say 'you' now instead of 'ye', and 'know' instead of 'ken', and speak more like the English.

Wishing to impress her friend, she tried hard to remember this when Mrs Reid retrieved the book of maps. 'Come,' Maggie told Sophia, 'you can show me where you live.'

But when she started to sit at the kitchen table, Mrs Reid advised her, 'Not there, I've been mixing things. Go through into the parlour. I believe your cousin's still playing at cards with Mrs Paterson.'

It still felt odd to think of Lily as her cousin, but James Graeme was her cousin, and now Lily was his wife, so that made Lily Maggie's cousin also. It did take some getting used to.

In the parlour, they indeed found Lily with Sophia's mother and Sophia's older sister, Anna, who was too sophisticated to come join them as they spread the map book open on the floor and searched to find Kirkcudbright.

'That,' said Maggie, when Sophia found the place and pointed to it, 'is the strangest way to spell it.'

And they searched then for odd-looking names, and tried to think of ways that they might be pronounced.

They were enjoying this so much that Maggie nearly didn't notice when the man in the green coat arrived.

He'd been sent from the African Company, and asked for Mrs Graeme.

He took his hat off, an action that knocked his wig slightly askew. Maggie wanted to fix it, but she knew that doing so would be unspeakably rude, so she stayed where she was, but it bothered her having to look at that one detail out of alignment.

The man's smile was thin. 'It was difficult finding you,' he said to Lily. 'The Company kept a most improper record when you passed through Edinburgh. I'd not have known that you even existed if not for the clerk you did speak to, and even he barely recalled you. I say this,' he said, 'not to chastise you, but to explain and, I hope, to excuse my delay.'

Lily answered with a tight smile of her own, and then they talked briefly of how he had managed to find her in Greenock, which seemingly hadn't been easy, and Maggie lost interest, drifting back into the game with the maps, until she heard the man saying, 'I'm sorry', and Sophia's mother exclaimed, 'Oh, my dear!'

Maggie looked up, and Lily was standing, her hands slowly closing to fists.

The man said, 'It has been confirmed, I'm afraid, by two colonists who have but lately returned. It did happen last year, on the twenty-fifth day of October, on the journey down to the colony.'

Lily said quietly, 'So Jamie never did reach Caledonia.'

'No, it is very unfortunate. We do mourn every man lost in this venture. There were a good number who died of the flux or of fever at sea, like your husband. I'm so very sorry.'

It couldn't be true, Maggie knew. The man must be mistaken. Her cousin James couldn't be dead. She had heard him promise Lily that, 'A Graeme would not leave ye.' And a Graeme never lied. Lily had told her so. Which meant her cousin James could not be dead.

She wanted to explain that to the man, to say, *He is not dead. We're going on the* Rising Sun *to join him, and he's going to keep us safe.* But no words came.

Lily had turned her back to all of them, and crossed to stand before the window.

'The body . . .' she began. 'What did they . . . ?'

With a cough, the man said, 'When they are at sea, they have the ceremony there.'

She gave a single nod, and for a stretching moment she said nothing, looking out towards the shining water of the river Clyde, with all its anchored ships and windless sails.

'I'm glad he is not buried,' she said finally. 'I am very glad to know he's in the sea, because the sea is always moving, and I cannot think of Jamie keeping still.'

'Of course you'll stay with me,' said Mrs Reid, and there was no more argument.

It had been very hard the day the drummers had gone all along the shore, beating the call for everyone to board the ships because they were about to sail. And it was even harder two days after that when Maggie stood with Lily, hand in hand upon the pier, and watched the lovely *Rising Sun* glide off upon the ebb tide down the Clyde towards the open sea.

She said, 'We were supposed to go to Caledonia.'

'I know,' said Lily, squeezing Maggie's hand. 'I know we were.'

'That was *our* ship.' Then, because she could not bear to watch that hopeful golden sunrise on the ship's stern sailing ever further from her, Maggie pressed her face hard against Lily's heart and sobbed, and Lily stroked her hair and held her.

'There will be a ship for us one day,' said Lily, in a soothing voice, 'I promise ye.'

'"You",' Maggie told her, muffled, and they both smiled.

'All right, then. I promise *you*, you'll have another ship.'

'It will not be the *Rising Sun*.'

'It might be better. Nothing is impossible.'

It was the truth, while they still had each other. And while they had Mrs Reid, who grew to be like family.

Mrs Reid taught Maggie how to stitch a perfect seam, and how to set a sleeve, and how to make the smallest, finest tucks to give a garment its desired shape. After a year of learning, she was able to assist in small ways when there was a larger project Mrs Reid was working on.

But best of all, whenever Mrs Reid was called up to the Mansion House at Cartsburn, Maggie got to go along to help.

The Mansion House was where the Crawfurds lived – the Baron of Cartsburn and his family – who did own the whole of Crawfurdsdyke. Their house was grand, and set within a garden by the running water of the burn, with trees all round, and the green hills behind.

There were children in the house, which Maggie found exciting. Not that there weren't children in the houses closer to their own, but Maggie had not found a friend among them. And although sometimes a boarder brought a child along who wished to play, the boarders did not stay beyond a short handful of nights and days and those playmates were soon departed.

But at Cartsburn House, within the Crawfurd family, there were two girls close to Maggie's age. She had met them when she'd gone the first time to help Mrs Reid do fittings for them, and she'd found them very friendly.

Mrs Reid had said to Lily later, 'If you would imagine fitting sparrows in a field, all hopping round and chirping at the same time, that's what it was like.'

But she took Maggie with her the next time she went to Cartsburn, and the next time after that, and Maggie and the Crawfurd girls grew still more comfortable with one another.

One day, on arriving, there was music playing in the house, and Maggie had been mesmerized. Peering round the open doorway to the grand front parlour, she saw one of the girls sitting next to her mother in front of a long, box-shaped instrument set upon legs, with a raised lid on which there was painted a landscape with fields and white clouds.

Lady Cartsburn's hands were on the white and black keys

of the instrument, making the music, and something within Maggie rose in response like a bird seeking somehow to soar in those painted clouds.

Holding her breath, she stood, transfixed and listening.

Afterwards, she asked the Crawfurd girls what they called the incredible instrument, and she learned it was the virginals, and that it had come from Italy, and that they hated to play it, but their mother wished them to be proper ladies and so they were bound to take lessons. They showed Maggie how the keys plucked at small strings, and allowed her to touch one, to make a note sound.

'Maggie.' Mrs Reid, standing behind in the doorway, was watching them closely. 'It's time to go.'

So Maggie played one last note on the wonderful virginals and thanked the Crawfurd girls and, with reluctance, trailed Mrs Reid home.

Some days after that, Lily asked Mrs Reid, 'Did you wish me to enter the week's accounts for your work up at the Mansion House?'

Mrs Reid shrugged and replied, 'There is no payment to add this week, nor will there be one for some weeks to come. Lady Cartsburn and I have agreed upon new terms.'

And so Maggie started to have music lessons each week at the Mansion House.

Lily would take her, because Mrs Reid said she thought Lily might like to walk in the gardens awhile and enjoy the peace while she was waiting for Maggie. It would make a change from the hours she spent cooking and keeping house. For some reason, that had made Lily cry quietly, but she had hidden her tears and thanked Mrs Reid, and every

Wednesday, while Maggie was spending her happy hour with Lady Cartsburn and learning to play on the virginals, Lily was walking in all weathers out in the Mansion House gardens, along the burn and through the towering trees of the deep woods behind.

Lady Cartsburn walked Maggie out one afternoon at the end of the lesson and met Lily underneath the lime trees by the gate.

She laid her hand on Maggie's shoulder. 'She is very, very good. I fear she's passed beyond the limits of my own ability. There is a lady who retired locally who once performed at London, and at Paris. I should like to bring her in, if you are willing, to continue Margaret's lessons.'

Maggie's flush of pride was drowned beneath a cold wave of reality. She knew a private music teacher would be something they could not afford.

As though she understood that, Lady Cartsburn carried on, to Lily, 'I am told by Mrs Reid that you've a lovely writing hand. I wish my girls to learn their letters well. I wonder, do you think we could arrive at some sort of arrangement? An exchange?'

Lily nodded, as though words were not available.

Against the gate, a spider's web was blowing loose, and in its strands a small white moth had caught its feet and could not flutter free. Maggie did not think she'd have noticed it at all if Lady Cartsburn had not gently reached to break the web and loose the moth and set it high up on the facing wall where the returning spider would not be a threat.

'Sometimes,' said Lady Cartsburn, 'I believe God gives us

gifts that carry us to places where we might not otherwise have gone, if we are able but to use them.'

Even young as she was then, Maggie believed she understood what Lady Cartsburn meant – she meant that Maggie's love of music and her skill at playing it might one day lift her higher than a common life. Beyond the confines of the world of Riddell's Close and Crawfurdsdyke, to worlds she might not otherwise have known.

'Perhaps,' said Maggie later on that night, as Lily tucked her into bed, 'my music's meant to be my ship, and not the *Rising Sun*. Perhaps it is my music that will carry me to new worlds of adventure.'

Lily's kiss, soft on her brow in the same way it had been each night Maggie could recall, came with the same promise. 'There, that's to sweeten your dreams.'

Maggie's dreams were sweet.

She went on dreaming, and learning, and working hard.

Until the day Mrs Reid was struck down by a sudden fit, and in an instant, their world changed.

Outside the church, Lady Cartsburn approached Lily.

'I understand that Mrs Reid did leave you money.' Lady Cartsburn's voice was kind. 'The house, of course, was not her own to leave, but we'd be pleased to have you stay on as our tenant. Though there is another course you might consider.' With a glance and smile at Maggie, she went on, 'I have a friend who has a school for girls at Edinburgh, and she's in need of a young lady of good temperament, she tells me, to teach music. I'd be glad to write a letter to her, recommending Margaret.'

And so then, as Lily promised, there at last had been a

ship for them, of sorts, if not the one they'd planned to sail upon, and not exactly shaped with prow and masts and sails. But even so, a ship, if one looked hard enough to notice, and they'd had the sense this time to leave the pier and climb aboard.

Chapter Thirty-Eight

MONDAY, 6 OCTOBER, 1707

Gilroy could be difficult to fathom. I was privately inclined to side with Moray and agree that Lord Grange was not part of any plot the Duke of Hamilton had put in motion, and thus Gilroy had been given no direction when it came to our inquiry beyond searching for the truth.

Gilroy would otherwise have been impatient to see Lily's marriage proved, regardless of how thin our evidence might be. Instead, from the beginning and through our investigation, he'd maintained his staunch belief the marriage was a fraud, which would imply he was impartial.

Then again, he had asked both Moray and Lily about Moray's brother John, and if they knew where John was now – which, while it might be innocent, might also have to do with the duke's efforts to learn more about the Jacobite invasion.

As Seafield had said outright, other members of the family may be fine to capture, but the fact was, everybody truly wanted John.

That Gilroy had shown interest in him meant there was

an outside chance that Gilroy might himself be in the duke's employ, and I could not entirely let down my guard, nor trust him.

When I looked at his impassive face, I could not help but think of Robert Moray telling me he looked on Gilroy as a man who followed orders and was loyal. And again, I did agree. I simply wasn't sure to whom Gilroy was loyal, nor whose orders he was following.

By contrast, it was obvious to me the fat and jovial man past Gilroy's shoulder, who for the past quarter of an hour had been persistently attempting to move closer to our table here within Steell's tavern, was an agent of the Duke of Hamilton.

He was the same man I had seen on Friday night when I'd been here with Captain Gordon, and he'd very likely been the same man who'd stayed half-hidden behind the bedcurtains upstairs when Archie had brought Lily here to hand off the certificate of marriage. It could not be a coincidence that, from the moment we'd walked in, he'd taken a great interest in us and our conversation, changing tables three times now so he was nearly close enough to overhear what we were saying.

Gilroy, unaware of what was going on behind him, raised his cup of wine and told me, 'I see you did not take my advice.'

'And what advice would that be?'

'Did I not distinctly warn you it would be unwise to get involved?'

'With whom?'

His sidelong glance knew better, but as though agreeing to switch topics he sat back and looked me over. 'You've a button missing from your waistcoat.'

'I expect I'll find another.'

'You'll find one exactly like it,' he informed me in an idle tone, 'upon the floorboards next to Mrs Graeme's bed.'

I tried not to react, but I suspect I held my own cup to my mouth a fraction longer than I needed to before I set it down.

'The thing is,' Gilroy said, 'a man should be a realist. When a woman seeks to charm you in the middle of an inquiry, it's likely she's less interested in you than in the ways you might be influenced.'

I bit back what I might have said, and only answered, 'You assume I'd let myself be influenced.'

'You may believe you wouldn't, but—'

The jovial man had moved again, to take a seat directly behind Gilroy. I'd been waiting for this moment.

Knowing everything I uttered would be overheard, I interrupted Gilroy. 'You'd be wrong, because I don't think we will ever have the evidence to prove the marriage. I don't think it's possible.'

He stared at me. Drank slowly. Then asked, 'What changed your mind?'

'You did. With your persuasive arguments.'

'What arguments?'

'Your stubbornness then.'

Gilroy still looked wary. 'So we're in agreement?'

'Aye. The witnesses are dead. We've found no one who knew them as a married couple. I agree the inquiry is but a waste of time, and we should write to the commissioners and recommend that they dismiss the claim.'

'I see.' His mouth curved faintly, registering victory. 'Then I suggest a toast to the occasion, Sergeant Williamson, for most of the commissioners will soon be in their beds. Our letter can wait till the morning.'

No doubt his true reason for wishing to celebrate was that he would soon be rid of me, but I still lifted my glass. Behind Gilroy, the jovial man rose and quietly headed towards the door, and at the edge of my vision I saw him step out of the tavern and into the night.

Gilroy said, 'Here's an end to our labours.'

A toast I could drink to, with hope.

❧

I didn't stay long at the Cross Keys after that.

As I walked back up the darkened High Street, it struck me that I had neither seen nor heard the man in grey since I'd come down the castle hill the morning before yesterday. Some people might have felt relieved. It made me feel on edge.

I tried to keep my footsteps quiet as I climbed the stairs to Lily's lodgings, but she met me at the door.

'What is it?' she asked, when she saw my face. 'What's happened?'

'Nothing's wrong.' I stepped inside, and when she closed the door behind me, I said, 'I've called off the inquiry. The wheels are set in motion now.'

Her own face fell. 'You might have warned me this would be your plan.'

'Until an hour ago I didn't have a plan. I am developing it as I go, that's why it is in motion. It does still have moving parts. It may yet change.'

Lily did not find that very reassuring.

I said, 'Trust me.' Then, because there was still one thing that she did not know, I briefly told her of the Duke of Hamilton's involvement, and of Robert Moray's strong belief the duke was trying to draw Colonel Graeme out to capture him.

'The duke's spies know we've called off the inquiry,' I said, 'and they'll go straight to him with that information, so in his view you'll be of no further use. You will be safe from him.'

'But not from Archie,' Lily argued. 'He'll be angry when he hears. He'll want to meet me.'

'Which is why we need to get you now to safety.'

'Where?'

The nearest place that came to mind was Caldow's Land, with Helen Turnbull. 'We can tell her there were noises in the shop below, and they did make you nervous. She'll not mind if you do sit with her awhile.'

'And where will you be?' Lily asked me.

'With the Regent Murray, meeting Archie in your place.'

She grabbed my sleeve and told me, 'That is *not* a good plan.'

'Perhaps not, but I do warrant it will work.'

She shook her head a little helplessly, as though aware that nothing she could say would change my mind. 'Why did you stay?'

I grinned and said, 'Because you asked me to.'

Lily blushed. 'That is not what I meant. I meant why did you stay in Edinburgh when you could have been clear of this? It never was your fight.'

'Of course it was.' I felt my grin fade as I told her, 'I could not have left you.'

She was too close but she came closer still. 'Why not?'

Showing her was easier than telling her. The kiss was light this time, but it did not last long.

Lily pushed me back sharply and said in surprise, 'Matthew!'

I wheeled and followed her gaze to the man who had stepped through the door she'd forgotten to bolt. He'd entered by the turnpike stair so silently he was but a grey shadow in the doorway, standing watching us together.

'Ye're looking after her, are ye?' he said to me. 'Anyone could have come in, and the both of ye would now be dead.'

Lily stared at him, and then with her heart in her eyes, she rushed past me and into his arms. 'I was so worried! When I did not see you in the street, I feared the worst.'

I looked at them and saw how he was holding her and in that moment my plan changed, and I knew what I had to do.

Emotions were an easy thing for me to hide. They always had been. It was not so difficult for me to hide my feelings then and tell him, 'Go, then. See you take her somewhere safe.'

Waiting, too, was something I was used to. While I walked the floor of Lily's lodging, waiting for the paper to be slipped beneath her door by Archie's messenger to call the meeting – which I guessed would be tonight – I held my racing thoughts in check.

I idly turned the pages of the book that she'd left lying on the table – the book that I had loaned to her of plants of the Americas, still with my note that marked the page that held the illustrations of the ferns. She'd finished with this now, she would not need it any longer. When I'd done what I must do, I would come back here and reclaim it.

I bent once to retrieve the telltale button that had fallen

from my waistcoat and was lying on the floorboards by the bed. It was a small thing, but I held it for a moment before tucking it securely in my pocket. There could surely be no harm in keeping something that, as Lily put it, held the memory of a time when I was loved.

And yet.

A man should be a realist . . . Gilroy's words became my point of focus. Lily Aitcheson was Matthew's lass, for now and always. Everybody knew that. Archie Browne would know that, too. And he would never give them peace.

He'd never stop, so someone had to stop him.

⁂

He seemed smaller than the image I'd been holding of him in my mind.

It might have been because we stood within the shadow of the monument built to the Regent Murray – that hard man of little mercy who had turned upon his flesh and blood and found betrayal had a price.

It might have been because this section of the southern transept of St Giles' was lit by only moonlight at this hour, and all things had been cast into uncertain shades of blues and greys and pale, dead ivory, and were thus distorted.

But more probably it was because age had left Archie Browne reduced in every way. Age did not do so with all men. I had known several men of twice my years who sat as upright in the saddle as their younger peers and walked as sturdily behind the plough, and who remained as vital in their minds as they had ever been until the day we laid them in the ground. The years instead had withered Archie in the way a leaf will blacken from an unseen rot.

At first, when he approached me, there was part of me that almost felt the slightest twist of pity.

But then he began to speak, and all the vitriol spilled out, and there was no way not to see the danger he still posed to those unfortunate enough to fall under his power.

'She has made a grave mistake,' he told me. Patting the large pocket of his coat that I assumed held Maggie's father's letters, he said, 'These will now be published, to the shame of Lily's precious Graemes and the lass she holds so dear.'

'The lass you helped to raise,' I pointed out, 'as you did help raise Lily. Do you not feel any bond of family?'

'Family' – Archie spat the word – 'does not abandon ye.' His grim expression, in that moonlit corner of the church's transept, was a thing unholy. 'She will pay for that, as well.'

It was not lost upon me that we were now standing at the place where people long had paid their debts, and Archie's ledger bore the names of countless souls he'd damaged. All the women who had suffered in that sad house in the Paunchmarket, and given up their dreams there. Simon, who could not come freely home but had to wander now in exile. Walter, whose own dreams of travel and of learning had all come to naught, and now lay buried in the South Leith churchyard with the bodies of his wife and bairn. Henry, with his broken body and his bitter memories, left alone in Riddell's Close. Matthew, who, while he might have Lily, had to live with knowing he had not been there to help his brothers at the time when they'd most needed him. And Barbara, patient Barbara, who'd once bound them all together.

Those names, already written down in Archie's ledger, were the product of his sins, and I could feel the ghosts of some of them around me now within this shadowed space.

But I was thinking more of Maggie, yet untouched by him. Unbroken. And of Lily. Mostly Lily.

I told Archie, 'She will be beyond your reach.'

'And who will keep her safe?' he taunted. 'You?' He looked me up and down, and with a snort dismissed the notion. 'Henry? Henry could not keep himself safe, when it counted.'

I had learned to let an insult pass when it was aimed at me, but I did rise to that one, being it was aimed at one not there to make his own defence. 'I would not mock his accident.' I gave the warning evenly, but Archie did not pay it heed.

'His accident?' His thin face crinkled in a smile. 'Is that what he did call it? I gave the lad a leathering, that's what. He let them go. He was supposed to be their keeper, and he let them go.'

Ever since I'd come into the transept, I'd been second-guessing my decision, re-evaluating every angle of my plan. There'd been a moment, while I'd stood and waited here for Archie, when I'd studied that brass plaque upon the tomb and looked at Justice with her broken sword, and thought perhaps she did not need my intervention after all. Perhaps she would pick up her sword and see the matter to its end.

But each man has his breaking point, I'm told.

Henry was mine.

Henry, who everyone agreed had been the easiest to love of all the foundling boys within that house in Riddell's Close. Who'd been quick to laugh and quick to love and so good-natured everyone remarked upon it. Who had wanted nothing more from life than a real family.

Who had lied to me, and said, 'I was a carter, Sergeant Williamson,' to hide the truth that he had never worked outside the front room of that house, as Archie's clerk. That it was Archie's beating, not a horse and cart, that broke his bones so badly that the doctor had once thought he'd never walk again.

'He needed to be taught a lesson,' Archie told me, although as he spoke the words I think he caught his error. He was looking at my face.

I felt the rising rush of blood, and then the heightened sense of calm, and welcomed both. I was prepared when Archie took the pistol from his belt.

Coldly I struck it from his hand, and heard it clatter on the stone floor.

My voice was cold, too, without violence. 'You should not have told me. Or at least you should have lied, as Henry did, and let me think it was an accident.' The time had come to finish things. He tried to back away from me. I took a step towards him. 'Because then I might have found it in my heart to let you live.'

CHAPTER THIRTY-NINE

FRIDAY, 17 OCTOBER, 1707

WITH MY FRIEND LIEUTENANT Turnbull back, a change
had come to Caldow's Land. More than a week had
passed since he'd come home. Our lives had settled into a
predictable and regimented order, and although it would
have killed my soul to live confined by rules for ever, I'll
admit I found it soothing, in the short term, after what had
come before.

Turnbull had been grateful for the service I had done by
taking his part in the inquiry. 'I'd not have had the patience
for it,' he confessed, but he'd gained the reward. Not only had
Lord Grange sent formal thanks, but yesterday had brought
an invitation to attend a private dinner with Lord Grange and
several friends, a prospect that had Helen so excited she could
barely eat her breakfast.

'And of course it *would* be when I am too large to fit into
my best gown,' she complained.

'You will look lovely in your blue one,' Turnbull told her.

'I do thank you for your confidence. Except my blue one
always makes me look too pale, I think. A little like a corpse.

Which does remind me' – Helen danced with lightness from one topic to another – 'you recall that man they found dead at the Regent Murray's tomb on Tuesday morning last past?'

Turnbull said he was not likely to forget. 'You've talked about him daily since I have come home.'

Ignoring his remark, she said, 'A friend of mine has overheard there was a warrant out for his arrest, and that he sought to take his life by his own hand as an escape from a more painful execution.'

'For what crime?' asked Turnbull.

'I believe he was a forger,' Helen said.

'Well then, your friend is wrong,' was Turnbull's answer, 'for I've never known the courts to hang a man for forgery.'

'Perhaps he had intended to escape his guilty conscience, then,' said Helen, 'for they found a pistol near him, but the final judgement seems to be that he did lose his footing and fall back and strike his head against the monument.'

I drank my ale and offered nothing, mainly because Helen was not altogether wrong. That was essentially what happened, except Archie wasn't trying to escape his execution or his conscience – when he'd tripped and fallen back and struck his head its fatal blow against the Regent Murray's tomb, his frightened eyes had been on me.

And I was fine with that. I'd stood a moment in the moonlit silence, looking at the brass plaque on the tomb, and I'd decided Justice after all had played her part. The debt was paid.

Helen seemed to hesitate. 'My friend does also tell me Dr Young will soon be travelling to London with his daughter, Violet, there to spend the winter.' With a glance at me, she added, 'I am sorry, Adam.'

I assured her it was of no matter. 'I would do the same, if I were Violet's father. He will find a better match for her in London, I should think.'

Turnbull was looking from his wife to me. 'What's this?'

Helen explained, 'Adam was hoping he might find himself a wife while he was here. I thought that Violet Young would suit him very well. I was apparently mistaken.'

'She was not my matching half,' was how I summed it up, which earned a smile from Helen.

'She was perfect. You were simply too particular.'

Someday, perhaps, I'd freely speak of how I'd met the woman who was made to be my matching half, and how I'd given her my heart, and how I'd let her go. But not today.

'If you're not careful,' Helen carried on, 'you will end up a lonely bachelor like your friend upstairs.'

I had enjoyed my visits with the Latin master these past several days, and rose to his defence. 'He is not lonely. He has books.'

With understanding, Turnbull asked, 'How many have you bought?'

'A few.'

To Helen, Turnbull said, 'You should have seen the books that Adam brought to Caledonia. I thought the ship would sink, he had so many.'

'You did meet each other in New York, I understand.' I knew she had been waiting for the tale of how we'd met, and I could see her sitting forward in her chair as Turnbull nodded.

'That's right. Adam helped us find another ship, when ours was not allowed to leave the harbour.'

She asked, 'So then you had abandoned the first colony?'

He winced a little at her choice of words, but did not argue, and I did not blame him. There had been so much dispute among the colonists of that first voyage as to why they had not stayed to see it through, so many accusations thrown, so many differing accounts, and so much hatred heaped upon those men who had returned to Scotland only to be branded traitors, that he likely thought it best to let it lie.

He told her, 'Yes. We'd parted ways when we left Caledonia, to start our voyage home. Our ship and one other wound up at New York. This was in August, ninety-nine. We did not know the Company was fitting out a second fleet of ships to sail from Scotland.'

And that second fleet of ships, the *Rising Sun* among them, would have been the expedition that sailed from the Clyde that month – the same one Lily nearly joined with Maggie, before they'd learned of James Graeme's death.

'We were unaware of this,' said Turnbull, as though he wished Helen to be very sure on that point. 'But Captain Drummond – you'll have heard me speak of him, he was one of the councillors of the colony – he was already keen to return. He disagreed with the reasons the others had given for leaving, and if he'd had his way, we'd have stopped in for provisions at New York, set down our sick men, taken on new ones, and gone straight back to Caledonia. But the governor of New York did not wish to help us.'

I chose not to correct his choice of words, because I knew my friend's heart had remained so loyal to King William that he likely found it easier ignoring the plain truth that New York's governor had been forbidden, by a royal proclamation, from giving us aid.

Turnbull said, 'We luckily had many Scots at New York who did take our part and try to help us, and the local merchants did arrange a new ship for us, underneath the nose of their government.'

And that's where I had come in, as a warehouse clerk, helping them find their provisions. 'Your husband recruited me,' I said to Helen. 'He showed me over the ship. Then, since any adventure had seemed to me better than being a clerk, I resigned my employment and sailed on her.'

'*I* nearly didn't,' said Turnbull, and smiled. 'They got under sail in New York harbour so suddenly, trying to slip out before they were stopped, that I didn't get word until they were well under way, and I was forced to chase after them in a boat or be left behind.'

'Is that when you left your parrot?' Helen asked him.

He nodded. 'I'll warrant now in New York there's a parrot from the Darien coast that wonders what it's doing there, but I could find no one to send it on to my cousin in Scotland, and I was too rushed to return it with me to the colony, so it remained with my friends,' he said, 'on Staten Island.'

We talked less of the time we'd spent in Caledonia. Most of it had been unpleasant. We'd arrived to find our fort burnt by the Spanish, and a very short while later our ship had been joined by the fleet of the second expedition, and turmoil began. The arguing among the councillors. The people who had wished to stay, and those who'd wished to leave. Those who had wished to build again, and those who'd wished to turn their backs on the attempt. And then, of course, there had been Captain Drummond.

I confess that when I'd heard his name first in New York,

I'd thought it could not be the same man I was thinking of, for surely the directors of the Company would never make a councillor of the man who'd been a leader of the massacre at Glencoe – who in the dark times following our Revolution had not only repaid the MacDonalds' hospitality by slaughtering their women, men, and children, but who, so it was said, had personally killed two lads who'd begged for mercy, when another captain hesitated.

Drummond was an able soldier, but he was not liked nor trusted by the men of the new council. He urged them to take action. They did, having him imprisoned under guard.

Turnbull, as his lieutenant, was imprisoned, too. A man who protested was hanged, and through it all I'd thought of nothing so much as that evening at Wood Creek those years ago when I had sat with Jacob Wilde beneath the pines and watched the war council, when other men were in such disagreement.

Wilde had told me then, 'You cannot take the measure of a man when things are working well. It's only when the plan goes badly wrong and everything is broken that you'll see what he is made of – if he breaks, too, or builds something from the pieces that remain.'

Turnbull had not broken.

And in time another ship had brought to us another leader who had built what he could from the wreckage, taken charge, released the men who were imprisoned, and led a defending force against the fort the Spanish had just built nearby at Toubacanti.

Turnbull talked of *that*. He did allow that Toubacanti had been a brave fight. Even though the shot he'd taken to his shoulder had come from an ambush, Turnbull argued that no men on either side could be called cowards. 'The Spaniards stood firing until our own men could reach out and grip the muzzles of their guns, but at last we had the better of them and we gained possession of their fort. *That* was a good day,' he told Helen.

It had not lasted. Only a month later, we'd been once again preparing to withdraw from Caledonia, and this time there would be no return.

Turnbull still believed it could have been successful. 'Caledonia was a place that would have well provided for us, if we'd been supplied with bread, for there was always new fruit growing ripe each month. And all around, the woods were stocked with deer, and goats, and rabbits, and so many different types of fowl that I could not begin to list them. We were taking turtle with our own boats from the bay. And fish. The bread was all we wanted.'

Helen said, in her opinion, we had been in want of better councillors.

He smiled. 'True. If I had to do it over, I'd choose only people who were loyal to the king, but as it was we had the Highlanders and Jacobites and everyone all mixed among us, and so we were bound to fail.'

See, this is the problem with our colonies. We brought these disagreements from our old land to our new one. Jacob Wilde had told me that as well, and he was right.

I felt sure that the Highlanders, so many of whom had sought to escape the overbearing Kirk by going to the colony to make a new start there, would have been happier without the disapproval of the ministers the Company had sent – all

Presbyterians – and without a murderer of Glencoe being sent into their midst.

That we carried our divisions where we went and let them weaken us was certainly a failing, but it was not the only thing that made us fail.

Some blame the toll of sickness and starvation and the unrelenting rains. It's true I caught my tertian fever there, and many died, but I was only there a short while, and I've heard accounts from others, who were there at other seasons, of the fineness of the weather, so I cannot judge.

There was sickness here in Scotland in that same year, bitter weather, and starvation, and our people did survive.

Some blame the Spanish, and it was indeed their forces who in those last hours compelled our leaving, watching us depart.

But the land we chose for Caledonia was not owned by Spain. When we arrived, it did belong to no one but the Tule – the natives who did live there – and they'd given us permission to create our fort and town upon the bay.

And the Spanish, while they fought us, weren't entirely to blame.

Whenever Spanish ships attacked King William's other colonies, his navy hurried to their aid. With us, no help came. That was not by accident.

King William, while he gave his charter to the Company when it was formed, had then done all he could behind the scenes to see it fail. The royal proclamations had been sent, not only to New York, but to all English colonies, forbidding them to trade with, correspond with, or give aid to our Scots colony upon the coast of Darien.

The goods we'd brought to trade were useless, then. We could not buy provisions.

All because the English could not bear to let us be successful – could not bear to have our merchants and our trade outpace their own. Their East India Company must have its sure monopoly, no matter if it meant our nation suffered.

That was why our venture failed – because we could not fight each other and the Spanish and the elements together, while our own king at every turn did stab us from behind.

I said none of this to Turnbull, for I knew well where his loyalties did lie.

He carried on, 'The late great King William was a good judge of men and their principles, as he did show us at the happy Revolution, and Queen Anne seems to be also, for this Union is our chance to move beyond our disappointment over losing Caledonia, and to build a brighter future without fear of any plots or schemes from Jacobites.'

Helen, seeming to have had enough of this talk, said, 'And I had better move beyond our breakfast table if I am to make myself presentable for dinner with Lord Grange.'

Her husband rolled his eyes. 'It's not for hours, yet.'

'It will take me hours.'

As I stood to help her from her chair, she looked up at me with a faintly sad expression. 'Can we not persuade you to come, too?'

I said, 'I'm not invited.'

'I am sure that was an oversight.' She looked to Turnbull. 'Would you not agree he would be welcome?'

Cutting in to spare my friend, I said, 'At any rate, my horse is hired. 'Tis all arranged.'

She sighed. 'You are determined then to leave us?'

I knew she'd grown genuinely fond of me. I gently said, 'You will be going down next week to Standhill, to begin your lying in. I should have had to leave you sometime.'

'But this is too soon.' She held my hand securely. 'Captain Gordon's very certain of this ship on which you're sailing?'

'Aye. The skipper is a friend of his. I shall be very safe.'

'I'd feel better if you sailed with Captain Gordon. Such a dashing man. A widower, I'm told.'

'He is.' The gossip mills ground quickly and efficiently.

'Perhaps I could find *him* a wife, if you won't have one.' With a smile she said, 'See that you write to us.'

I gave her back the smile, but kept my silence, for I could not promise that I would.

Sometimes friendships forged in war were of a different nature, so dependent on the forces and the pressures that created them that, once you did remove them from that time and place, they never could resume their former shape.

When we said our farewells, before they went downstairs to meet their coach, I realized it was probably the last time I'd see either of them.

Turnbull had been my commander. He was yet my friend. He had earned – and I hoped that he never would lose – my respect. But the truth was, we had very little in common, and I'd not be missed in his life any more than he would be in mine.

I had a few hours to fill before the time of my departure.

I'd arrived at Caldow's Land with little. Most of what I would be leaving with, I had already packed into my knapsack and the leather portmanteau that I had carried with me now for years. One thing I'd sent down yesterday ahead of me, that would be waiting in my cabin on the ship, was the box of books I'd managed to assemble, starting first with the new volumes I had purchased from the Latin master, and then choosing several from a bookseller and printer in the High Street, before adding in the law book and the illustrated French book of the plants of the Americas.

That last I'd held a little longer than the others, leafing through its pages and remembering when I'd loaned it to Lily, but at last I'd put it in the box and nailed the lid shut firmly.

This was not the moment to indulge in sentiment.

MacDougall found me now within the writing chamber, putting things to rights. I turned.

He faced me with the same distrust. I knew it did not matter to him that I had worked diligently in his master's place on the inquiry, given Turnbull all the credit, asked for none. Men like MacDougall went through life expecting to see nothing but the worst in men, and so became blind to the good.

He studied me with narrowed eyes. 'Ye're nearly finished, then?'

He wanted me to leave the room. To leave the house. To leave their lives.

I gave a nod and said, 'Time I was gone.'

MacDougall grunted. 'Ye've a visitor.'

I couldn't think who . . . ?

Gilroy thanked MacDougall. Stepped around him, and dismissed him. He was carrying his file of papers, neatly tied.

I thought I understood how Robert Moray must have felt when I'd surprised him in his prison chamber at the castle that last morning, and, like him, I felt a moment's urge to simply sigh and ask, 'What now?'

But I did not. I greeted Gilroy with a patience that I did not feel.

He said, 'I'll try not to detain you, for I hear you have a ship to meet, but this might be important.'

'Please.' I indicated he should take the seat before the scrutore.

He closed the door behind him, so that we could talk in private. 'It is about the man in grey who stood within the entrance to the close across the street, perhaps you noticed him? Well, Mrs Graeme noticed him, the one day we did walk her home, but she seemed keen that we did not, which made me wonder whether Matthew Browne might have returned. For, as you know, I've always felt she was not doing this alone.'

He set his papers on the writing surface of the scrutore and untied the file.

'I asked my stabler friend in Leith what he remembered about Matthew Browne,' he said, 'specifically. And then I did some research of my own.'

Gilroy, with everything prepared now, turned his head to me, and even having worked with him so short a time I knew from his expression he had made a new discovery.

He said, 'I believe you might be very interested in what I've found.'

ᐱᐁ

There was a candle in the window of the house in Riddell's Close. I hesitated for a moment, then I raised my fist and knocked a single time upon the door.

The night wind rose against my back and chased the ghosts along the dark curve of the narrow close, with all its waiting, blackly-watching windows.

And then the door swung open.

Framed within the warmly golden light stood Lily.

I forgot the cold.

She wore a petticoat and bodice in a print of orange flowers and green vines – not new, but kept with care – and I had never seen her look more beautiful. Her eyes searched my expression and she offered an uncertain smile.

Behind her in the passage I saw Henry, standing near the door to the front room. And coming down the staircase was a tall and well-built man I would have recognized even without the grey cocked hat and coat, who surged towards me now as Gilroy stepped out from the shadows just behind me.

Swiftly, I moved as a shield in front of Gilroy, and I told my brother Simon, 'It's all right. He knows.'

VII

I MUST GO BACK, I'VE missed a step, and you will be confused. When Gilroy came to see me earlier at Caldow's Land and faced me in the writing chamber, with his papers ready on the surface of the scrutore, I did have a fair idea what was coming next.

He's like a bulldog with investigations, Robert Moray warned me, and I'd several times seen wheels and gears at work behind his level gaze, and known that he was piecing things together.

There were wheels and gears at work as he set out his papers on the scrutore, but he kept his eyes down as he started.

'Let me tell you what I've learned of Matthew Browne. My friend the stabler nearly did not speak of him, because he says it's one of the most tragic tales he knows.'

I felt the old house settle round us, all the beams and floorboards creaking with the weight of years as if it were a burden to be borne.

Gilroy went on, 'The stabler holds it bad enough the foundling lads were brought to Riddell's Close by Archie Browne not from compassion, but to be raised there as criminals. But this' – he handed me a two-paged document – 'the stabler calls an even greater crime.'

It was the copy of a transcript from a trial, from autumn 1685, for house breaking and common theft.

'Matthew,' Gilroy told me, 'would have been but twelve years old when he was put on trial for that. The two men tried with him were known and hardened thieves. The stabler could not say why Archie Browne had trusted Matthew to them in the first place, but there was some talk that Barbara Malcolm had been giving thought to taking all the boys and leaving Archie, and that Archie might have wanted Matthew to be caught and punished to show Barbara there would be a price to pay if she tried to break free.'

I read the pages through in silence. It was a grim record of the testimony, and the evidence was plain.

'He must have been afraid,' said Gilroy. 'He was all alone. He'd been held in the Tolbooth, in the vilest of cells, with rogues and murderers. And at his trial, he saw the other men condemned to death before him. He must have been terrified.' He handed me a third page and said, 'But he was reprieved, because there had been private testimony given to his character. A soldier of the town guard, by the name of Corporal Morison, did swear by this testificate that Matthew Browne, on entering the kitchen of a house within the Canongate, climbed through the window and refused to then unbar the kitchen door for his confederates, because there were two maids there and he sought to keep them safe from harm.'

That paper, with the words and copied signature of Lily's Corporal Morison, did shake a little in my hand, I freely do admit it, but I gripped it tightly and regained control.

I said, 'I'm not sure that a lad of twelve would think it a reprieve to be condemned to transportation to the colonies.'

He granted that. 'No, likely not. Nor would his mother think much of the man who'd organized that transport. And I'd go so far as to suggest that, if his mother were a ... shall we say, a working woman, and the man were fool enough to try to come and use her services, he'd well deserve it if she threw a bottle at his head.'

I met his eyes. 'You speak of Mr Fearne.' The same man Simon nearly beat to death, that day at Riddell's Close.

Gilroy confirmed this. 'Mr Fearne was but the middleman. The one who found the ships. I found the skipper who transported Matthew. He took other prisoners as well on that same voyage. For the most part, they were Covenanters who'd risen that summer with the Duke of Argyll in his last rebellion. All of them were taken, on that voyage, to Barbados, to be sold as servants for ten years.'

Here Gilroy paused. The house had seemed to breathe and settle once again, but this time Gilroy stood, and crossing to the door he opened it.

MacDougall stood a little distance off, pretending not to have been trying to hear what we were discussing. It would not have been an easy thing to overhear us, for we'd kept our voices quiet, but still Gilroy called MacDougall over.

'I'm afraid,' said Gilroy, 'I forgot to post these letters. Do you think that you could do it for me?'

'What, now?'

'Yes.'

MacDougall went, but he was grumbling when he left us. Gilroy waited until we had heard the front door clicking shut, and closed the writing chamber's door before he carried on. 'The skipper who transported Matthew to Barbados did recall him vividly, because he was so careful who he sold him to. He had a lad himself about that age, and wanted to make very certain Matthew would be cared for, so he sold him to a family,' Gilroy said, 'whose name was Williamson.'

I handed back his papers and he took them and we looked at one another for a moment.

Then he asked me, as if it were the most natural of questions, 'How long were you in Barbados?'

'Four years.' There was not much that I could say about that time. About those people. I had been their servant. I was never family. I'd been shown no kindness.

Gilroy did not press for details. 'And from there, the family moved to Long Island, New York?'

'Yes.'

'How did they convince you,' he asked me, 'to take their son's place in the local militia?'

That part had been easy. 'They offered to give me my freedom.'

I'd won it, regardless, if not in the way they'd envisioned.

'And afterwards, you did work for a year or so in New York. Then you came back home to Leith?'

'For awhile.'

'But you later returned to New York?'

'Yes,' I said.

'When you left Lily Aitcheson.'

Questions about my own past I might answer, but I grew more guarded when it came to anything dealing with Lily. I felt my jaw set defensively. 'When did you know?'

'The day we went to Riddell's Close.' There was no hesitation. 'I have brothers. I could see what you and Henry were, no matter how you tried to keep it hidden.'

So all his talk when he'd begun, about the man in the grey coat and how the sight of him made Gilroy curious enough to ask his stabler about Matthew Browne – that was a lie. I called him on it, and received the calm look in return.

Instead of answering, he asked me, 'Do you have your birth brief close to hand?'

'My what?'

'Your birth brief. I should like to see it, if I may.'

There was no point telling him I didn't have one. I was going travelling, and Gilroy very likely knew to where. 'Wait here,' I said.

It did not take me long to fetch the single document from where I'd safely stowed it in my portmanteau. When I returned, Gilroy was standing at the scrutore, studying the square door of the small central compartment.

'The thing is,' he said, noticing the way that I was watching him, 'these scrutores tend to have a secret drawer somewhere around . . . here.' With an expert touch he slid aside the inset piece of wood that kept the drawer concealed, and from the hiding place removed three letters. They were all addressed to me, in Lily's handwriting. It had not been an easy thing for us to keep our correspondence hidden from the others – I'd relied upon the kindness of the Latin master upstairs to receive the letters for me – but we'd needed some way to make our arrangements.

Gilroy said, 'You'll want to take these with you, when you leave. And this.' He added to them one more paper from his file. I had to read it over twice before I could be sure I'd read it properly.

I told him, 'It's a pardon.'

'For your brother Simon, yes. Lord Grange did see to that, at my suggestion. It was very obvious, from testimony at the time, your brother did not know the bond he'd been sent to redeem was forged. Since Archie Browne gave him that bond, and Archie Browne has, since his death, been shown to be a forger and a liar of the first order, it hardly seems fair Simon should be made to pay the penalty.'

He held his hand out for the birth brief and, unrolling it, read through the neat, lined levels of its pedigree. 'It's very good. She made this for you, did she?'

Part of me did want to trust him. I tried focusing my mind upon the motto on the whinger that reminded me to take good care in whom I placed that trust, particularly when it came to someone else's freedom, and I did not answer.

Gilroy seemed unbothered. 'I would guess she used a page from your book with the plant pictures,' he told me. 'It was large enough. She's made a few mistakes, though. Here, and here. And then of course you did not have the right names for the generations beyond Adam's parents. Anyone who thought to look into the records would discover this was false.'

He turned and threw it on the small fire in the hearth before I guessed at his intent.

I swore, and took a step towards him, but he held his hand up and said, 'You'd do better with the real one.' And produced a second birth brief from within his files.

Had he conjured it from thin air I'd not have been more astonished. 'How did you . . . ?'

Taking the first set of papers he'd shown me – the ones from the trial – he began feeding them to the fire.

'The way I see it,' Gilroy said, 'there was a lad named Matthew Browne, once. Born a foundling, raised at Leith, who was ill used and sent to the Americas. But there his trail ends. It was never Matthew who marched up from Albany to fight the French, and it's for certain Adam Williamson came back.'

He said it in a sure tone, as if he understood the stigma of the Browne name and how badly I wished to be free of it and everything it represented.

'Some say Matthew Browne came back to Leith awhile,' said Gilroy, 'but I am not certain that he did. I think the man people saw then was Adam Williamson as well, he only needed to find out who he was meant to be.'

I did not know how to reply. 'He took his time.'

'We get there in the end.' He held his hand out. 'It's been good to know you, Sergeant Williamson.'

Above the handshake, I found myself searching for words that would not sound inadequate. None came, at first. And then suddenly, there they were.

I asked him, 'How would you like to come dance at my wedding?'

CHAPTER FORTY

FRIDAY, 17 OCTOBER, 1707

W E HAD TO WAIT for Gordon.

He arrived just after seven in the evening, very dashing in his blue coat with gold buttons and gold braid. 'I found this bit of baggage lying about,' he said, as he drew Maggie across the threshold with him, 'so I thought I'd bring her with us.'

She apologized. 'It's my fault we are late,' she said. 'My classes ran on longer than they ought to have.'

Behind her came a gentleman who looked to me as though he might be seventy or so, with steel-grey hair showing beneath his hat, and kindly eyes that met mine warmly.

'Mr Cant?' I shook his hand. 'I'm Adam Williamson.'

'A pleasure. May I ask' – he glanced around – 'where is my Lily?'

There may well have been more heart-warming reunions, but I can't say I have witnessed them.

There may, too, have been more memorable weddings, but I haven't taken part in them.

It did seem only fitting we should marry, not within a

church or great cathedral, but there in the front room of the little house in Riddell's Close, where we had passed so many hours together, with our friends, our joy, and Barbara's loving spirit crowding out the darker memories.

We used Barbara's ring as well – that bit of silver that did carry love as deeply and as surely as the little silver heart I'd given Lily all those years ago, that she had worn above her own heart where no one could see it, and that she wore now for all the world to see, pinned to the bodice of the orange-flowered gown.

I could not tell you now the words we echoed after Mr Cant, nor yet the promises we made, but I can still see Lily's eyes and feel the warm excitement of her kiss, and that was all the promise I did need.

Maggie and Gilroy were our witnesses.

As Gilroy took the pen in hand, Lily came up beside him and remarked, 'We have a problem.'

Gilroy turned. 'And what is that?'

Lily looked down at the certificate and sighed and said, 'This marriage was irregular.'

His mouth turned upwards at its corners. 'I'll sign a testificate to help you see it proved.' He signed his name, and Lily read it.

'I would not have thought you were a Richard. 'Tis a noble first name.'

'I am named for a nobleman,' Gilroy revealed. 'Richard de Mornay, who once was my father's employer and truest friend. He lost most of his fortune and family in Cromwell's wars, and lost yet more in the year of the plague that came afterwards – but it was then, when he could have easily guarded what little remained to him, that he risked all to give aid to my father and mother when they most had need of it. They were in love, you see. Had been for years. Yet my mother was then to be given in marriage to an aged man of cruel temperament, and there was nothing my father could do, so he thought. Until Richard de Mornay, he said to him, "Some days, the law does not step to the same drum as justice." And so on the day of the wedding, de Mornay attended and brought a fine horse as a gift for the bride, and distracted the bridegroom, allowing my mother to use that same horse to escape, with my father beside her. They married, and came north to Scotland, and I am the happy result.'

As with all of Gilroy's speeches, he delivered it so levelly he might have been discussing legal documents, but still it was like cracking a grey stone to find a glistening interior with unexpected colours.

Lily looked emotional. 'Is that why you're helping us? Because your parents were given help, once, and you felt it a debt that you had to repay?'

Gilroy angled a thoughtful look down at her. 'I felt my namesake's example was one I should follow. When law does not step to the same drum as justice, you do what you can for your friends.'

It was my turn, at that, to be gripped with emotion, and pride that he'd call me his friend, for I did not think Gilroy would give many people that honour.

He was, to the end, an inscrutable man, and it pleased me to think Robert Moray, astute in so many ways, had been mistaken when he had thought Gilroy predictable.

Moray had said, 'He'd not venture his neck for another man.'

Gilroy had proven him wrong.

'Never fear,' Gilroy assured me later on, when we were standing to the side and I warned him Lord Grange might not be best pleased to learn that his clerk had been at our wedding. 'Lord Grange doesn't know the half of what I do, and is the better for it. He has business of his own to keep him occupied.'

There was something I'd wanted to ask him. I asked him now. 'Did Lord Grange know?'

'Know what?'

'The details of the scheme the Duke of Hamilton had plotted, to draw Colonel Graeme out into the open, using Lily.'

His eyebrow lifted. 'I confess I cannot know Lord Grange's mind, no more than I can know the workings of the duke's,' he said. 'I can but tell you I only began to think that such a scheme might be in play after you'd been invited to your dinner at the Earl of Seafield's.'

I parried that with, 'I suspected *you* might be in on the plot. You kept asking where John Moray was.'

'I had been instructed to.'

'By Lord Grange?'

He raised one shoulder in a shrug. 'Lord Grange passed me my instructions. Who had written them, I cannot say. I did not think to question them until I realized that this inquiry was not what it appeared to be.'

'And then you knew why they were looking for John Moray.'

'Aye. And I stopped helping them.'

Our conversation ended then, for Maggie had begun to sing, and after two songs she grabbed Gilroy's hands and dragged him in to join her, and as if he'd not surprised us all enough for one night, he sang us three verses of 'I Love My Love In Secret' in a baritone that brought fair tears to Lily's eyes.

As I stood alone with Gilroy at the door that night and bade farewell to him, I said, 'You truly do have a romantic soul, and I am grateful for it, but you'll want to keep it hidden well from Helen Turnbull, or she'll make you the object of her matchmaking endeavours when she does return to town.'

He smiled faintly. 'She can try. But she'd do well to read her Plato, and refresh her knowledge of his theory of the matching half.' To my blank look, he said, 'The theory runs that all of us are halves of beings that were once whole, yes? Well, Plato reasons that some of those beings were male and female intertwined, androgynous, so when they were divided, you would have a man and woman searching for each other to be reunited. But he also claims that some of those original, whole beings were of one sex to begin with – wholly female, for example,' he explained. 'Or wholly male.'

I took his meaning. 'So, you're saying . . .'

Gilroy fitted on his hat. 'I am saying, Sergeant Williamson, if Helen Turnbull tries to see me wed to Violet Young, I wish her luck with that,' he said, 'because my matching half is not a woman.'

I wasn't shocked – I'd seen too much for such a thing to shock me – but his revelation did surprise me, for if he had made it to a different person, he'd have risked exposure and arrest. Perhaps he felt secure, because he knew *my* secrets, that

I would not reveal his. But I preferred to think it was because I'd earned his trust, as he'd earned mine.

He shook my hand, and wished me well, and headed out into the night. I watched him striding down the close.

In the front room, I found Gordon, holding court. He clapped me on the shoulder and congratulated me again. 'I've left a few bottles of brandy in the kitchen.'

Gifts, again. I said, 'You'd best tell Simon. He will be the only one left living here after we sail tomorrow.'

'Are you taking Henry with you?'

'Aye.' I would not leave him lonely. Not again. 'Simon said he would rather stay and keep watch over Maggie.'

Gordon thought that choice very responsible. 'I sail tomorrow, too,' he said, 'now that I have my men on board again, or nearly all of them. I will be headed north, and I'll warrant Colonel Graeme will be soon there with our friends. I'll see he gets word that he's heir to Jamie's wages.'

I said, 'Make sure he sends a factor down here to collect them – that he does not come himself.'

'I have your warning,' Gordon reassured me, 'and I will deliver it.' He looked at me with something of the air of a proud father, though we were divided by no more than ten years in our ages. 'I did think you once too young to settle down and marry. I am happy to see I was wrong.'

'No, you were right when you did say it. You were right. I was not ready.' Looking back along the passage to where Lily stood with Maggie, talking now to Mr Cant, I said to Gordon, very certain, 'I am ready now.'

I was.

I'd been the greatest fool a man can be when I was young.

I'd walked away from someone who had given her whole heart to me, and there'd not been a day since then that I'd not missed her touch and felt regret, and I knew well that I did not deserve to have her offer me her heart again.

And yet . . .

Sometimes life gave you back the things you'd lost.

Upstairs that night, in the small chamber where we had shared our first kiss, I stood with Lily, arms wrapped tightly around one another, saying nothing, doing nothing, feeling that we'd come full circle.

This, I thought, was my beginning.

I was Adam.

'You're the first man I have loved,' she said, her voice not much above a whisper, and it was as though she knew I needed those words then. 'The first man and the last man. You will always be enough for me.'

Then she kissed me. Then my wife reached up to me and kissed me.

'Come to bed,' she said.

I did. But first, I leaned to blow the candle out. It was not needed anymore.

I knew that all was well.

VIII

I WAS A YOUNGER MAN when I first met her in our house in Riddell's Close – though I should tell you in all fairness that was not the first time I had ever seen her, for her face had lived within my mind and memory from the moment I dropped through that window into the Bells' kitchen, turned, and found her looking at me through her tears.

I was a younger man . . .

I promised I would tell the story as I felt it should be told, and if you've read this closely you will find I've sought to tell the truth.

My study is a quiet room, but these past days it has seemed lively with the ghosts of those long gone, who've wished to come and visit me – Captain Gordon, always with a gift tucked in his pocket and his coat well-brushed, and Walter, with his dreams and hopes and arguments, and when the evening's drawing in, my mother, Barbara, with her lovely face and eyes that find mine in the firelight.

These shades, and others, have been welcome visitors of late, and yet no human guests could have been more demanding.

'Tell them this,' they've seemed to say, or 'you can surely not forget that part.' And so I've laboured on, to write the whole of Lily's tale, and mine, that you may judge the truth of it against the rumours that still rise.

Two of these phantoms in my study have been strangers – Colonel Graeme and his son – although I met the colonel long ago, when as a lad I was imprisoned in the Tolbooth. He showed kindness to me then. He gave a blanket to me, and advised me I would walk a better road if I kept better company. I have imagined that his son would have the same kind eyes.

In my life, the thing I most regret is leaving Lily on the pier that day in Leith. I should have stayed. I should have listened to her, trusted her, and not let my own feelings of inadequacy blind me to the truth that she would never have betrayed me with another man – but when I saw her standing with James Graeme by the windmill, after what I'd seen the day before, and Lily saying she no longer wished for us to marry right away, I thought the worst, and ... well, that is not true. I did not think at all. I acted purely out of pain, and impulse.

Though she has forgiven me, I know that my apology could not erase the moment, nor the harm it caused, and I have had to live with that.

But I regret, too, that by leaving then, I lost the chance to meet James Graeme, who'd been so important in her life – a man I would have liked. A man I would have counted myself fortunate to know.

So it has been a pleasure, and a kind of benediction, to have had the chance to meet him in the writing of this tale. And in the evenings when I sit beside my fire, my whisky in my hand, my thoughts drifting, I have found it easy, if I change the angle of my head and let my eyes half-close, to picture Jamie sitting in the chair that faces mine, an old companion – as he might indeed have been, had he but lived.

But those are shades.

Beside that chair right now, the cat is lying with her kittens in her basket. It seems only yesterday they were too small and helpless to do anything without her, but today they're tumbling out onto the carpet. Henry's granddaughter will be beside herself when she does come to visit us with all the family at the weekend, from Cross Harbor.

Henry takes great pride in all his grandchildren. They mind him not only of his own bairns, but of the children he did teach for so long at our school here in the town – so many he can barely cross the street these days but someone stops him for a conversation. Still, although he holds no favourites, he does play a little softer with his granddaughter, the only lass among so many lads. And I'd be lying if I said it did not soften my heart, too, the day I watched her climb into his lap, so he could sit awhile and read to her, and Henry laughed and asked, 'What book this time?'

But there is only one book that she loves: *The History of the Most Renowned Don Quixote of La Mancha: And His Trusty Squire Sancho Panza.*

It is a family weakness.

Maggie read it to her, also, when she and Simon came to see us this past spring. It was their second visit to America. I hope it will not be their last.

She writes with regularity, as do Marion Bell and her husband, and if Maggie's letters do not come as often as we'd like them to, we can rely upon those sent by Richard Gilroy, who has been a steadfast friend and from his rising vantage point has kept watch over both Maggie and Simon.

Maggie's music, which she now performs as well as teaches, has indeed become her ship, as she predicted, and it carries her to great adventures. She was built to have adventures, I believe. It's in her blood, says Lily, being she's a Graeme.

But I've known that from the time she was a bairn.

When I first handed her the letters from her father that I'd taken out of Archie's pocket on the night he died, Maggie took them with both hands and thanked me, and said, 'Someday, I will go to France and look for him.'

She did. Although to tell the story truly, it was Colonel Graeme who did come to fetch her into France, but that's a tale best told by Maggie, for she tells it well.

But wait ... my critic wants to have a word.

She has come to read this over and correct what I have written. This is properly her room, not mine, lined with its shelves of all the books that she so loves, and the warm lamplight in the evenings, and the windows looking to the changing sea.

'You could have been more clear,' she says, 'at the beginning.'

'I was clear enough.'

'You did not tell them all the truth.'

I've always liked the answer Robert Moray gave to me, and so I use it now: 'All men leave pieces out when they tell tales,' I say. 'It is no crime.'

She sighs, and picks a kitten up and puts it in the basket.

'They will get there in the end,' I promise. Readers always do.

'You've been too long indoors,' she tells me, 'and the day is fine.'

She stands beside me. Holds her hand out. 'Let's go see the ships.'

It is her favourite thing to do, still.

Years ago, I cleared some of the trees along the forest's edge to let the sunlight through enough so she could have her garden, and it drives its roots more deeply every year, spreading scent and colour in the most unlikely places.

Jacob Wilde's old house yet stands like a white beacon on the hill across the bay, and now his son has brought his own young family there to live. Their boats pass briskly back and forth between their own cove and our town.

Lily likes to look, not to the bay, but to the larger ships that travel through the Sound between New York's great harbour and the open sea.

When I was but a lad I used to stand upon this hill and feel a pain at every passing sail, because I wished the ships would carry me to somewhere else – to somewhere I'd belong.

I do not feel that, anymore.

Now, when I see a sail pass by, I no longer feel envy for those sailors who are looking back to shore, where I am standing close by my own home and hearth in comfort.

I think often of the vanished days that Captain Gordon spoke about – the ones that are behind us that we cannot live again – and how he wished it might be possible to make the clock run backwards so that we could live those days a second time, and live them better. But he had it wrong, I think, because I would not wish to change the way I lived them. I'd not be the man I am if I had not lived every hour of them, for all the pain they brought me and for all the pain I caused. Those vanished days that seemed at times so dark and so devoid of purpose had their moments still of light and happiness, which I have come to realize through the writing of this narrative. And in the end, they led me back to Lily, to the woman who has always made me whole. Who grows more beautiful, to my eyes, with each day that we are given.

I have come a further distance than I ever had in mind when I began that walk in darkness up the street to Turnbull's lodgings; further still from where I started, in that narrow close in Leith. But I have finished with my wanderings.

And so the time has come for me to lay my pen down, and to leave you here amid the others who have joined me in this chamber these past days, and who have kept me such good company.

Let other men write braver tales.

I am no longer weary in this home that we have built on the foundations that were left to me, where my wife waits with hand outstretched to hold my own. Where she yet holds my heart.

Where she remains – as she has been from our first meeting – my own lass.

For now and always.

ABOUT THE CHARACTERS

ONE OF THE MOST beloved of Scottish writers, Robert Louis Stevenson, says in his *Essays in the Art of Writing* that a novel 'is first cloudily conceived in the mind ... On the approach to execution all is changed.'

That was certainly true with this novel.

It was conceived, and cloudily, when I sat down with *Darien: The Scottish Dream of Empire* by John Prebble, and read this: 'A hundred women were sailing with the expedition at the Company's expense ... Most of them were loyal wives, and all but a few of them are now nameless.'

Nothing sets a brighter match to my imagination than learning about those whose lives have been largely forgotten, and when I discovered that my old friend Colonel Patrick Graeme – whose footprints I'd traced through two of my own novels – had a son who'd sailed on the first voyage to the ill-fated Scots colony, I knew I had a book to write.

I thought, at the beginning, it would be a grand tale of adventure, telling what had happened to the colonists at Darien – but in the execution, all was changed.

Other characters rose up to take the lead.

I was already prepared for Colonel Graeme to demand more space. He'd done this to me in my book *The Winter Sea*, where I'd first met him, and had stubbornly remained in my subconscious until I picked up the dropped thread of his family's story in a later book, *The Firebird*.

Like most of the real-life characters I write about, the colonel has escaped the notice of many historians and so moves like a shadow through the history books. Thankfully the Privy Councillors at Edinburgh kept minutes that record when they sent Colonel Graeme, as the captain of their town guard, to collect a prisoner, or when he asked for leave to go to London, or when he was given shoes and plaiding for his soldiers – and so, bit by bit, with help from correspondence left behind by others, I can try to reconstruct his life.

I always hope to find his own voice when I do my research. I find echoes of it. Documents that bear his name, or even bear his signature.

I enter every archive in the hope I'll find a letter that he's written to a member of his family, or, best of all, a portrait, so that I could finally 'meet' him face-to-face.

And yet, after these years of having him here in my writing room, he seems an old companion, and even though for now I must rely almost entirely upon what others say of him, I feel I've come to know him well.

One anecdote, from an unlikely source, gives us a window on his character.

In the autumn of 1707 – at the same time this novel is set – Queen Anne's spymaster, Robert Harley, being keen to learn whatever he could about the invasion plot, sent spies into the north of Scotland. One of these was a former friend of Colonel Graeme's, who had offered now, for money, to betray him.

In a report to Harley dated Christmas Day 1707, this spy wrote that an order had been given to a local officer to apprehend Colonel Graeme, but 'this officer kept the order above four months and never did it, at last it was given to another officer and he had it three months, at last the Colonel came to a house by chance where this officer was, but alone, the master of the house did know of the thing and advertised the Colonel not to come in, but the Colonel being a ... bold brave man said since he is alone he shall catch a Tartar if he offers anything to me; and the Colonel actually went up and drank all the night with this officer ...'

Which doesn't only tell us of the colonel's courage, but of the respect that he commanded from the Highlanders – even from those who were not on his side.

There's no denying he earned that respect through his own actions, but I don't doubt some of it was given to him also for the simple fact he was the son of the Black Pate, who'd ridden with the great Montrose (who in Scotland is more commonly referred to by the French form of his title, marquis, instead of the English marquess, so in this book he's the Marquis of Montrose).

I'd first 'met' the Black Pate in *Or and Sable: A Book of the Graemes and Grahams*, Louisa Grace Graham's history of her family and its origins, published in Edinburgh by William Brown in 1903.

But it was another man I encountered in *Or and Sable* who ended up taking my story off course in a way Robert Louis Stevenson would, I'm sure, have recognized and understood.

In her section on Colonel Graeme, the author of *Or and Sable* did what I've just done – she used an anecdote to try to show his character. She told how he'd attempted, unsuccessfully, to save the life of one of the town guardsmen under his command, a man named Acheson (her spelling), who'd killed a violer playing in the dead of night.

The unfortunate 'Acheson' stayed with me. Characters do that sometimes.

And when I next went to Edinburgh, I asked my friend Alison Lindsay, Head of the Historical Search Rooms at the National Records of Scotland, if she could help me learn anything more about him.

Between the pair of us, we filled the gaps. I changed the spelling of his surname to Aitcheson – a composite of the ones I came across while searching through the records. By the end, I knew his first name: Edward. I knew when he'd married his wife, Jean, and where. I knew the dates when they'd baptized their little girl, Elizabeth, and their son, James. That made it harder, somehow, because then I knew that baby James was barely two months old, if that, when . . .

Well, it made it harder. But I wrote the scene.

I kept firmly to the historical record, which states that Edward Aitcheson was executed on 17 June 1685, in the churchyard of what most people in Edinburgh at that time would have called the College church, but which I've chosen to call by its alternate name, Trinity Church, for clarity. This was not the public place of execution, and he was not hanged but shot.

Those are the facts; but common people disappear so easily into the written record, and I haven't yet been able to establish beyond all doubt what became of Jean and their two children, so I strayed from straight facts when it came to their life afterwards. I was content to let Jean be the same Jean Atchison who, in the real-life registers of Edinburgh, was married to John Morison, a soldier, on 29 October 1685 (ignoring that Jean would more likely have retained her maiden name of Durhame). I liked that ending for her better than thinking of her all alone.

I did give Edward one more daughter, though.

I gave him Lily.

She is my creation, as are her fictional mother and grandmother.

I strayed from straight facts also when I placed the house of Mr Bell, the swordslipper, in Bell's Close, for I know I will get letters from historians reminding me that Bell's Close was not known by that name at that time. They are right. The close took the name Bell's Close from a much later Mr Bell, a stabler and carrier, who lived there in the 1770s, and for a while before that it was known as Hope's Close, but since I could find no definitive record of what it was called at the time when my characters lived there, I let it be Bell's Close again.

The swordslipper, like everyone who lives within his house, is my creation, but because his treatment of Lily was drawn from my own experience and, in case anyone reading this has met their own Mr Bell, I'd like to emphasize, as Barbara does to Lily, that what happened never was your fault and there are helplines you can call, if you have not already done so.

In my story, Adam visits Bell's Close in the last week of September 1707. In real life, two months after that, on 28

November, a great fire broke out in that part of the Canongate head. It began around two in the morning, according to one eyewitness quoted in Chambers' *Notices of the Most Remarkable Fires in Edinburgh*, who said, 'when I came to the window, I saw the terrible light; both sides of the Canongate were on fire.'

That witness saw the fire as a sign of God's judgement on the place. I saw it as a chance to free my fictional character Marion from her oppressive circumstances, and give her the happier life hinted at in Adam's epilogue.

Fires were a continual hazard in Edinburgh. The following August, another one began in Steell's Close, burning backwards from 'the great lodging possest by him' into Borthwick's Close and up to the High Street. Those flames, so close to St Giles', would have been cause for concern, as would the damage to the Cross Keys tavern, which had, as I've portrayed it, been a landmark on the High Street for some years, known for its musical landlord, Patrick Steell.

You'll find his name spelled variably in the records of the time, as Steele or Steil or Steill, but for the documents he or his family signed – his marriage, the baptism of his daughter Christian, his death record, and his will – it was spelled uniformly 'Steell', so that's the way I've spelt it here.

The fame of Pat Steell's tavern was its 'parliament' of patrons – among whom was the powerful 4th Duke of Hamilton.

I have a code I keep to when I deal with real-life characters: I don't make anyone a villain unless I can do it with a clear conscience. That person is no longer here to defend themselves, and I must be convinced, from my research, that I'm portraying them correctly.

In the case of the Duke of Hamilton, apart from his own actions, it was the words of those who knew him best that, in the end, convinced me – particularly those of his long-time friend Nathaniel Hooke who, being sent to Scotland from the court of Saint-Germain in the spring of 1707 to prepare for the coming invasion attempt, came to the dismayed conclusion that the duke could no longer be trusted. 'I was quickly convinced that he did not act sincerely,' Hooke wrote in his memoirs, adding, 'it came into my mind that he had still an intention of seizing the throne himself.'

The Earl of Seafield is a more ambiguous figure and therefore trickier to bring to life on the page but, where I could, I've used his own words in his dialogue, so that he may speak for himself as much as possible. The part he played in questioning Robin Moray is factual, and the house Seafield lived in then – called, by coincidence, Moray House – still stands today in the Canongate.

I confess I gave Adam, who became one of my favourite fictional characters, my own love of walking Edinburgh's Royal Mile, but Adam would find his nightly walk greatly changed were he to do it today.

The Netherbow was taken down in the mid-eighteenth century to widen the street, although its bell, after some adventures, can now be found overlooking the Canongate once again, above the Scottish Storytelling Centre, beside the John Knox House.

And Forrester's Wynd – sometimes shown on old maps as Foster's Wynd – was swept away in the 'improvement schemes' of the nineteenth century, leaving no trace of the rooms where I lodged Lily in the house owned by the real Sir

John Foulis, whose published account book provides a useful window on the daily life of people of the period.

But Hamilton's Close, where Simon lounged in the shadows, survives today as Fisher's Close. From its entrance you have a clear view across what once was called the Landmarket – what we now call the Lawnmarket – to Gladstone's Land, the very real seventeenth-century building that became the model, both inside and out, for my fictional Caldow's Land.

Lieutenant Turnbull was never a tenant at Gladstone's Land, but he existed in actual fact, as did Helen, his wife. It's my hope they had more cheerful servants in real life than those I created and gave to them. All their family connections as mentioned are real, as are Turnbull's endeavours to seek a promotion, while others with better connections advanced before him.

He was still a lieutenant on 12 December 1707 when he and Helen baptized their firstborn child at Standhill – a daughter they called Anna. But by the time their daughter Helen was born in 1711, Turnbull had finally advanced to the rank of captain. Several years later (one source says around the year 1717), he became deputy governor of Dumbarton Castle, a post he held until his death. His obituary, from the *Derby Mercury* of 2 July 1756, reads: 'At Dumbarton-Castle, on the fifth of May last, died Robert Turnbull, Esq.; of Stand-Hill, Lieutenant-Governor of that Garrison, in the eighty-sixth year of his Age. He served sixty-eight Years in the Army with Approbation, and was the only remaining Officer of those who went upon the Darien Expedition.'

If Mr Gilroy – a fictional character who turned up entirely

unexpectedly in this novel, and whose parents' story began over a quarter of a century ago in my novel *Mariana* – were to venture down to Leith today in search of information, he'd find things greatly changed, although the Links are still there to be walked upon, the Shore can still be found, and the stone tower of the windmill stands as sturdily as ever at the end of it. South Leith Church, much reconstructed and restored, occupies the same site that it did when Mr Andrew Cant first came to preach there in real life in 1671, before he was transferred to Edinburgh's Trinity parish in 1679, where he was still the minister that June day six years later when a soldier of the town guard, Edward Aitcheson, was executed in his churchyard.

At the Revolution, he was deprived of his position for refusing to read the proclamation 'disowning James VII, and acknowledging William and Mary' but he continued to serve those of his faith clandestinely. In July 1708 he was one of five Episcopal ministers imprisoned for doing so, and in 1716 he was told again to stop preaching illegally, and fined for refusing to pray for King George. Undaunted, Mr Cant carried on, and was appointed an Episcopal bishop by the exiled King James VIII in 1720. He died in Edinburgh ten years later. Depending which source you believe, he was either in his eighty-first or ninety-first year.

The Jacobite church where he preached in the last several years of his life, Old St Paul's in Edinburgh's Carrubber's Close, is still in use as a church and worth visiting.

The house in Riddell's Close in Leith does not exist and never did. The close has been lost to development, and so I built a house for Barbara Malcolm from the sketches and descriptions and old photographs of ones that had once stood nearby.

The character of Barbara is herself a compilation of a handful of the women I encountered in the registers of South Leith parish church, whose lives were anything but easy in those unforgiving times.

It's just as well my fictional notary, Archibald Browne, was not a real person – although there actually *was* a real-life notary named Mungo Strachan who attempted a very similar swindle of the Commissioners of the Equivalent in the autumn of 1707 with the help of several accomplices, aiming to collect the wages of a dead Darien sailor by having a woman from Leith pose as the man's sister. The trial was a sensation, and when Strachan and one of his fellow forgers were brought up for sentencing before the Lords that December, it was felt 'that their guilt was so fragrant and palpable, that there was a necessity for some example to discourage such impudent growing boldness, and such flagitious contrivances deserved death,' so despite the fact forgery usually rated a fine and some time in the pillory or perhaps banishment, both Strachan and his fellow forger were hanged, 'as an example to the terror of others.'

The punishments for criminals were swift, and often harsh by modern standards.

Transportation was a common one, and at that time in Leith it was a profitable business for such men as Alexander Fearne, the real-life merchant who was authorized by the Privy Council to receive 'all such vagrant persones and other criminalls as should be delivered' to him and arrange their transport 'to the plantations in Barbadoes or another of his

Majesties plantations in America' where they were to 'be disposed of in the usuall maner', meaning sold into servitude. I put my fictional young Matthew Browne aboard Fearne's ship the *John and Nicholas*, which sailed from Leith to Barbados in December 1685.

In charting Matthew's course, I admit to being guided by the younger years of one of my own ancestors, Anthony Lamb, who in his days working as an apprentice in London made the mistake of befriending the notorious burglar Jack Sheppard. Lamb foolishly agreed to leave the street door of his master's house open so Sheppard and another thief could enter one night and rob a fellow lodger there. Of course he was caught – as was Sheppard, eventually. Sheppard was hanged at Tyburn later that same year, but Anthony Lamb, fortunately for me, was instead transported to the Americas, where in time he made his way to New York City and established himself as a notable maker of mathematical instruments. Anthony Lamb's son, John, became a prominent figure of the American Revolution and was given the command of West Point by George Washington in 1779. John's sister, Elizabeth, married into the Halletts of Long Island, the family that inspired my fictional Wilde family, touched on in this book and in my novel *Bellewether*.

Not all transported felons were so fortunate. The Englishman William Eddis, writing in 1792 – more than a hundred years after I sent young Matthew on that ship out of Leith – describes the conditions of life for convicts sent from Britain to America, in terms that would have been recognizable to both my ancestor and Matthew: 'These unhappy beings are, generally, consigned to an agent, who classes them suitably to their real or supposed qualifications; advertises them for sale, and disposes of them, for seven years, to planters, to mechanics, and to such as choose to retain them for domestic service. Those who survive the term of servitude, seldom establish their residence in this country: the stamp of infamy is too strong upon them to be easily erased: they either return to Europe, and renew their former practices; or, if they have fortunately imbibed habits of honesty and industry, they remove to a distant situation, where they may hope to remain unknown . . .'

I would imagine many who returned to their old homes, as Matthew did to Leith, would have had difficulty settling in completely to their old lives, as he did. Since he was my own creation, as were all his foundling brothers, I was able to explore this on the page without constraint.

That said, I did place one real person in that house in Riddell's Close: young Maggie – little Margaret Graeme – the illegitimate daughter of Margaret Malcolm and Patrick Graeme, later 7th Laird of Inchbrakie. I stumbled on the record of her birth while doing research. What became of her, or of her mother, I have not yet learned. It would not have been unusual for Margaret Malcolm to have died in childbirth, as I describe. So many women did. As I know well from my own family history research, records left are often incomplete and do not tell us all. Those times were turbulent – and ordinary people, as I've noted, can be difficult to trace.

But while the life I gave to Maggie might have been my own invention, she began her own life every bit as real as all the other Graeme and Moray children running through these pages.

There were seven Moray children in this generation born at Abercairney (as a side note, the estate's name is now spelled as Abercairny, but when I began to write my books, I used an older spelling and have chosen to retain that now to be consistent).

To avoid confusion, I did not put all the children on the page. William, the eldest, grew to be the laird in his turn, commanded a troop of horse at Sherrifmuir, and passed the estate to his heirs, who still hold it and care for it. Anna married David Graham, 10th of Fintry, while her sister Emelia married James Graeme, 9th of Garvock, keeping their family well bound to their mother's kin, which sometimes earnt them the aid of the younger Marquis of Montrose.

James, their second-youngest brother, died young.

But Robert – called Robin by his family and close friends – came closer to the threescore years and ten the Bible felt a man should have, and he lived many of those on the edge, no stranger to adventure.

Although his time spent in what is now the Lower Argyll Tower of Edinburgh Castle cannot have been comfortable, he was home again by Christmas. His old friends did not let him down, for on 13 November 1707 the Earl of Mar – who was then at the Palace of Whitehall, in London – wrote to tell his brother, Lord Grange, 'I have got the Queen's hand to a warrand for seting Robt Moray at libertie'.

Robin was released from prison in December, but his time by his own hearth was brief.

The following spring, after the failure of the Jacobite invasion attempt, he was taken up again with other Scottish noblemen and members of the gentry suspected of being involved in the plot. They were marched as prisoners to London in three divisions, sent from Scotland a week apart from one another. Robin was in the first division, which left Edinburgh on 29 April 1708, and was along the way exposed to all the coarse humiliation heaped upon them by the English standing at the roadsides.

It was while he was on this march and separated from his family – unable to protect them and most likely worried for their welfare – that his second son, named John, was born.

He would not get to hold his son for many months. Despite the efforts of his noble friends, he was held prisoner in the Tower of London until he was finally able to arrange his release in January 1709 in exchange for posting £6000 bail.

None of this seemed to stop him from continuing his service to the exiled King James VIII, although he did it in clandestine style – at least until the Jacobite rebellion of 1715, when he came out into the open with his sympathies, serving, like his brothers Maurice and William, in a regiment of horse.

In late October he was captured in a surprise night raid on Dunfermline. Held under close guard at Stirling Castle for almost a year, he was then moved with other prisoners to await trial at Carlisle, in England, the British government having conveniently decided that the wording of one of their recently passed Coercion Acts gave them the right to breach the Acts of Union, which had promised Scottish subjects that they would be tried in Scotland, by their own laws.

Robin was condemned to die on 27 December 1716 – but the execution was not carried out, and he remained a prisoner at Carlisle until the general indemnity issued by King George in July 1717 set him free again. He had been imprisoned, unable to be with his wife and young children, for nearly two years. I cannot imagine the range of his feelings as he made his weary way home to his family.

The joy of his homecoming wasn't to last. His wife, Janet, fell ill shortly after his return, and by mid-October that year she had died, leaving him with three sons and two daughters.

He never remarried, that I've found a record of.

If he continued his service to King James, he did it discreetly. I've found only one mention of Robin travelling over to France afterwards, in 1721, on some business that took him to Paris, from where he returned home to Scotland with his brother Maurice, who'd lived in France from the time he had carried some money and messages there for King James in the wake of the '15 rebellion.

Robert Moray died at home in Perthshire on 27 January 1733, having managed, in spite of the dangers and intrigues he'd weathered, to live till his sixty-third year.

Most history books don't mention him, but I feel that a man who lived a life like his deserves to be remembered, so I hope you will indulge me for the space that I've allowed him here.

He might turn in his grave to know one of his grandsons, Robert Keith, grew to be a diplomat in service to the government of Britain – that same government that held Robin for so long in prison, and came close to killing him. He'd doubtless turn a little faster in his grave if he were told Sir Robert Murray Keith – his own great-grandson – not only continued to serve Britain as a diplomat, but earned some fame by rescuing the sister of King George III when she was held a prisoner in Copenhagen. Still, it might be some solace to him that one of his great-granddaughters – Anne Murray

Keith – was well known to the great novelist Sir Walter Scott, who used her as the inspiration for the character of Mrs Bethune Balliol in his novel *Chronicles of the Canongate*, and who, after her death, wore a memorial ring with her name inscribed upon it, to remember his 'excellent friend'.

Robin's brother John Moray isn't often mentioned in the history books either.

The story of John Moray's part in the true-life Franco-Jacobite invasion attempt that happened in the spring of 1708 became my book *The Winter Sea*, where Captain Thomas Gordon first stepped from the pages of the history books and took on life for me, as well.

I won't tell either of their stories in great detail here, except to mention that when Queen Anne died in 1714, Captain Gordon, who could stretch his Jacobite loyalties sufficiently to serve under a Stewart queen, could not stretch them far enough to swear allegiance to King George, whom Jacobites referred to as the German 'Prince of Hanover'. Resigning his commission, he left Britain and went into Russia where he rose to prominence as one of Peter the Great's most trusted admirals, while continuing to do what he could to advance the interests of King James VIII in exile.

His time in Russia at the heart of the Jacobite community in St Petersburg is partly told in my novel *The Firebird*, a story which also allowed me to trace the steps of Robin Moray's youngest brother, Maurice, and Colonel Graeme's soldier-turned-Capuchin-monk son, another Patrick, who appears in this book as young Pat in the children's game of Covenanters and Montrose, but is known more commonly to history as Father Archangel.

Father Archangel claimed in his own family tree that there were four of them – four brothers – born to Colonel Graeme and his wife (although again, to keep things less confusing, I have only put two on the pages of this novel).

William was the youngest. He became a doctor. Robert died at twenty-one, a monk, like Father Archangel, who lived past his threescore and ten years, dying in Boulogne, France, where he'd risen to be the *Guardien des Capucins* – the Superior of his house.

And there was James. I call him Jamie in this book – partly because he appears first as a child, when the name Jamie seemed more fitting for friends and family to use – and because in the letters I read from the period, few of the adults named James were referred to by their full name, either, but commonly nicknamed Jemmy or Jamie.

When I first read Louisa Graham's description of Jamie in *Or and Sable*, I was convinced I'd found a central part of the great story of adventure that I planned to write about the Scots in Darien.

She told a stirring tale of how, while sailing near the colony, he and his fellow crew members aboard the ship the *Dolphin* were captured by the Spanish, taken first to Cartagena, then to Spain, where they were held in prison and condemned as pirates, only narrowly escaping execution before finally returning home to Scotland.

It was quite a story, and as I researched the details, it became more fascinating – but there was one problem: that same research proved to me, beyond all doubt, that the James Graham taken by the Spanish was not 'my' Jamie.

The index book of the African Company shows there

was indeed a James Graham who sailed aboard the *Dolphin* on that expedition down to Darien in 1698. But there was also a 'James Graem' on that same voyage who sailed on the *Saint Andrew*.

And in all the documents I have before me – from the Company's registers, to their certification in August 1707 that James Graeme had wages owed to him that needed to be paid from the Equivalent; to the agreement Colonel Graeme, safely in the north of Scotland, signed to have a factor travel down to Edinburgh to do the dealing for him; to the last Testament Dative on 8 October, naming Colonel Graeme as Jamie's nearest kin and heir and granting him the wages owed – the name of Jamie's ship is clearly stated.

'The deceast James Graeme my son,' writes Colonel Graeme, 'who was midshipman and sailor on board the ship the *Saint Andrew* belonging to the Company of Scotland.'

It's my belief that the James Graham whose story Louisa Graham wrote about in *Or and Sable* was, in fact, a cousin – son of Harry Graham of Braekness. *That* James Graham, after his ordeal in Spain, finally returned to Scotland to give his report to the Company, marry, and live a long life.

'My' Jamie was not so fortunate. Sometime during that expedition, he died.

I'll admit that I was disappointed when I realized he was not the same James Graham who'd been on the *Dolphin*, but I still believed he might have made it to Jamaica with what remained of the crew of the *Saint Andrew*, so I turned my focus there, and the Darien half of the book altered shape in my mind again, adding a possible new section.

But I don't properly plan out my novels – they take their

shape from my subconscious, and on the day Lily and Maggie were meant to set sail from the Clyde, my subconscious was keenly aware of that paper that had been brought back from the colony, listing the names of the people who'd died on the voyage, among them one James Graham, volunteer.

And in my heart, I knew. Even before my own research persuaded me, I knew.

My mind didn't want to believe it, at first. It raised arguments.

'Graham' was not the right spelling, for one thing – the Graemes of Inchbrakie used the 'ae'. But coming, as I do, from a family of amateur genealogists, I knew that was no argument at all, since surnames are often misspelt in such documents. After all, the Testament Dative for Jamie's uncle John Graeme – Colonel Graeme's brother – who also died in the Darien expedition, misspells *his* name as 'Graham'.

All right, my mind argued. The James Graham on the list was called a 'volunteer', when Jamie had been a midshipman. But when I traced through the records of the others on that list, I found men like William Miller, who on the list was also called a volunteer, but who had no corresponding Testament Dative in the otherwise scrupulous records of the Company unless he was the William Mill, a 'sailor and midshipman aboard the ship *Unicorn*' whose Testament Dative records his surname as both Milne and Mill in the same line, and who, like Jamie, died on the Darien expedition.

The African Company might have kept poor records of the women who were part of its two expeditions, but they did keep records of the men whom they employed, and I've found only two James Grahams.

In the end, there's only one Testament Dative in that name among the records of the Company for wages owed to those who died at Darien. And in the end, I had to accept that the name on the Company's list of those who'd died before they'd reached the colony could probably belong to just one person.

'The deceast James Graeme,' I could hear Colonel Graeme saying, in a gentle voice. 'My son.'

And so, with Maggie and Lily, I stood on the pier and watched the *Rising Sun* sailing westward, without us.

It may be that someday I'll write that grand Darien novel – that sweeping tale of adventure. But this book decided it wanted to be something different.

Robert Louis Stevenson, had he been sitting drinking whisky with me on the day that I first (cloudily) conceived it, might have warned me it would change, but I doubt even he could have predicted how much more this version of the story would have taken hold of my heart than the one that I began.

My writing room has been as full of phantom visitors as Adam's study while I've worked on this novel, as the now-familiar shades of Abercairney Morays and Inchbrakie Graemes move around me, telling tales.

They have more left to tell, I think.

And when I go to Abercairney next, perhaps I'll stand awhile beneath the old Inchbrakie Yew, at evening when the shadows fall just right between the trees, and change the angle of my head and let my eyes half-close – to see if, for a moment, I might glimpse an old man, once a soldier, walking to the now long-vanished castle, with a child holding fast to either hand.

A WORD ABOUT ACCURACY

ANY STORY SET WITHIN another time presents a challenge – how to tell it well, and not distort the past, yet not confuse the reader.

There are compromises.

Several of the characters in this novel would properly be speaking Scots, but to write their speech phonetically would render it difficult for many modern readers to understand, so I've opted to rely more upon cadence where I can. In Scotland, the long undergarment women wore beneath their clothing was a smock – but since that name conjures the wrong image in the modern mind, I've replaced it with *shift*. And while Scottish people of the time used dollars as their currency and said 'gotten' in everyday speech, it's difficult to convince a modern reader these are not Americanisms, so my characters use neither.

As a historical novelist I sometimes find myself having to be inaccurate to *seem* accurate.

But for the rest, I've tried to paint a picture that's as true to life as possible, by drawing on the letters and the other varied writings that the people of those times have left behind.

All dates are noted in the Old Style of the Julian calendar, with the Scottish exception being that their new year began not on 25 March as in England, but on 1 January.

A Note of Thanks

I'M VERY GRATEFUL TO Bill Drummond Moray, twenty-second Laird of Abercairny, who knows his family's history better than I ever will, and who, with his wife Emma, has been generous and kind to me with all of my enquiries.

My thanks also to his brother, John Drummond Moray, for taking time to walk with me across the field to show me where the first great house his forebears built at Abercairny had once stood.

Anna and Daniel Moray Parker are owed more than simple thanks, and well they know it. This book would not be what it is were it not for the help they've given me – the warmth with which they've always welcomed me to Abercairny, and their willingness to answer any question I might ask. Their children – Noah, Francis, Jacob and Minerva – have been equally as helpful, each in their own way, and I am beyond grateful to them all.

Just as Anna and her children are direct descendants of the Laird of Abercairny mentioned in this novel (and by a happy twist of genealogy, of Captain Thomas Gordon), Alex

Graeme is descended from the Black Pate through his grandson Patrick (Maggie's father).

Alex, award-winning owner of Unique Devon Tours, thoughtfully provided me with his own family history notes, and throughout the writing of this novel has stood ready to supply me with any information I might need about the Graemes.

Alison Lindsay, Head of the Legal and Historical Search Rooms at the National Records of Scotland, has already been mentioned in my previous note About the Characters, but deserves to be mentioned twice for her continuing support and friendship, and for her ability to always and inevitably find *the* single reference I despaired of ever finding. I will owe her dinner till the end of time.

To all the staff and volunteers at Gladstone's Land, but most particularly to Anna Brereton, Visitor Services Manager there, my thanks for making all my stays within the upstairs flat seem more like homecomings, and for the time and effort taken to show me behind the scenes so I could craft *my* scenes.

I owe a debt of gratitude to Nigel Nairne and Allan Somerville – who, fortunately for me, were both working as Senior Castle Guides at Edinburgh Castle (although Allan, after more than thirty years of service, recently retired) on the day I wandered up to them and asked if they knew where, precisely, Robin Moray would have been held prisoner. They not only shared their valuable time and their knowledge of the castle's history, but let me stand in Robin's footsteps and see briefly through his eyes. A rare gift, for a writer.

To Lara Haggerty, thirty-first Keeper of Books at the incredible Library of Innerpeffray – established nearly three centuries ago as Scotland's first free public lending library – my thanks for sharing some of the books, including the atlas, that made their way into this story, and for letting me hold history in my hands in the shape of the little Bible that was carried by the great Marquis of Montrose, still with his jottings in the margins. It's a moment that I never will forget.

My thanks to Sandy Robb, for helping to set me on the path to Duddingston.

Appreciation and a drink are owed to Ian Rankin, who, among his many kindnesses, gave me the visual details I needed for my winter scenes at Duddingston, including the swan that was trapped in the ice.

Having been, for the best part of my life, one of those people found lining the walls on most social occasions, it has been both a quiet surprise and a pleasure to find myself part of a writing group in middle age, and my friends Elizabeth Boyle, Kathy Chung, Eileen Cook, Crystal Hunt, Mary Robinette Kowal, Liza Palmer and Nephele Tempest have been, and continue to be, a constant support.

To my agents, Felicity Blunt and Shawna McCarthy, thank you for always believing in me.

The editing of this book was very much a team effort.

Thanks to Clare Hey at Simon & Schuster UK, Laurie Grassi at Simon & Schuster Canada and Deb Werksman at Sourcebooks for their combined work in making this novel the best it could be.

Thanks to Judith Long at Simon & Schuster UK and Susan Opie for their meticulous copyediting, to Pip Watkins for designing the beautiful cover, to Jill Tytherleigh for designing the Graeme family tree, and to the sales team, publicists and all the other staff at Simon & Schuster who work so tirelessly behind the scenes to bring my books to life. Your work may not always be seen, but it is very much appreciated.

To the booksellers, a special thank you from the little girl in me who helped my mother in *her* bookstore and is always grateful for the work you do on my behalf.

And thank you so much to all the librarians, who with reviewers, bloggers and so many others help connect my stories to their readers.

To those who gave me help whose names I didn't think to ask, and those who helped but whom I have forgotten to acknowledge here, please know I'm in your debt.

Finally, to my own family – my mother, who always reads the stories first and helps to shape them, and my father, who with this one helped me find my voice for Adam, and my husband and my children, who endure my living in another age for two years at a time – I give my thanks, for all their love and patient understanding.

Turn the page for an extract from

The WINTER SEA

CHAPTER 1

I T WASN'T CHANCE. THERE wasn't any part of it that happened just by chance.

I learned this later; though the realization, when it came, was hard for me to grasp because I'd always had a firm belief in self-determination. My life so far had seemed to bear this out – I'd chosen certain paths and they had led to certain ends, all good, and any minor bumps that I had met along the way I could accept as not bad luck, but simply products of my own imperfect judgement. If I'd had to choose a creed, it would have been the poet William Henley's bravely ringing lines: *I am the master of my fate; I am the captain of my soul.*

So on that winter morning when it all began, when I first took my hire car and headed north from Aberdeen, it never once occurred to me that someone else's hand was at the helm.

I honestly believed it was my own decision, turning off the main road for the smaller one that ran along the coastline. Not the wisest of decisions, maybe, seeing as the roads were edged with what I'd been assured was Scotland's deepest snow in forty years, and I'd been warned I might run into drifting and delays. Caution and the knowledge I was running on a schedule should have kept me to the more well-travelled road, but the small sign that said 'Coastal Route' diverted me.

My father always told me that the sea was in my blood. I had been born and raised beside it on the shores of Nova Scotia, and I never could resist its siren pull. So when the main road out of Aberdeen turned inland I turned right instead, and took the way along the coast.

I couldn't say how far away I was when I first saw the ruined castle on the cliffs, a line of jagged darkness set against a cloud-filled sky, but from the moment I first saw it I was captivated, driving slightly faster in the hope I'd reach it sooner, paying no attention to the clustered houses I was driving past, and feeling disappointment when the road curved sharply off again, away from it. But then, beyond the tangle of a wood, the road curved back again, and there it was: a long dark ruin, sharp against the snowbound fields that stretched forbiddingly between the cliff's edge and the road.

I saw a car park up ahead, a little level place with logs to mark the spaces for the cars, and on an impulse I pulled in and stopped.

It was empty. Not surprising, since it wasn't even noon yet, and the day was cold and windy, and there wasn't any reason anyone would stop out here unless they wanted to walk out to see the ruin. And from looking at the only path that I could see that led to it – a frozen farm lane drifted deep with snow that would have risen past my knees – I guessed there wouldn't be too many people stopping here today.

I knew I shouldn't stop, myself. There wasn't time. I had to be in Peterhead by one o'clock. But something in me felt a sudden need to know exactly where I was, and so I reached to check my map.

I'd spent the past five months in France; I'd bought my map there, and it had its limitations, being more concerned with roads than with small towns and ruins. I was looking so hard at the squiggle of coastline and trying to make out the names in fine print that I didn't see the man till he'd gone past me, walking slowly, hands in pockets, with a muddy-footed spaniel at his heels.

It seemed a strange place for a man on foot to be, out here. The road was busy and the snow along the banks left little room to walk beside it, but I didn't question his appearance. Anytime I had a choice between a living, breathing person and a map, I chose the person. So I scrambled, map in hand, and got my car door open, but the salt wind blowing off the sea across the fields was stronger than I'd thought it would be. It stole my voice. I had to try again. 'Excuse me . . .'

I believe the spaniel heard me first. It turned, and then the man turned too, and seeing me, retraced his steps. He was a younger man than I'd expected, not much older than myself – mid-thirties, maybe, with dark hair whipped roughly by the wind and a close-trimmed dark beard that made him look a little like a pirate. His walk, too, had a swagger to it, confident. He asked me, 'Can I help you?'

'Can you show me where I am?' I held the map towards him.

Coming round to block the wind, he stood beside me, head bent to the printed coastline. 'Here,' he said, and pointed to a nameless headland. 'Cruden Bay. Where are ye meant to be?' His head turned very slightly as he asked that, and I saw his eyes were not a pirate's eyes. They were clear grey, and friendly, and his voice was friendly too, with all the pleasant, rolling cadence of the northern Scot.

I said, 'I'm going north, to Peterhead.'

'Well, that's not a problem.' He pointed it out on the map. 'It's not far. You just keep on this road, it'll take you right up into Peterhead.' Close by his knee the dog yawned a complaint, and he sighed and looked down. 'Half a minute. You see that I'm talking?'

I smiled. 'What's his name?'

'Angus.'

Bending, I scratched the dog's hanging ears, spattered with mud. 'Hello, Angus. You've been for a run.'

'Aye, he'd run all the day if I'd let him. He's not one for standing still.'

Neither, I thought, was his master. The man had an aura of energy, restlessness, and I'd delayed him enough. 'Then I'll let you get going,' I said as I straightened. 'Thank you for your help.'

'Nae bother,' he assured me, and he turned and started off again, the spaniel trotting happily ahead.

The frozen footpath stretched ahead of them, towards the sea, and at its end I saw the castle ruin standing stark and square and roofless to the swiftly running clouds, and as I looked at it I felt a sudden pulling urge to stay – to leave the car parked where it was and follow man and dog where they had gone, and hear the roaring of the sea around those crumbled walls.

But I had promises to keep.

So with reluctance, I got back into my hire car, turned the key and started off again towards the north.

～⁂～

'You're somewhere else.' Jane's voice, accusing me but gently, broke my thoughts.

We were sitting in the upstairs bedroom of her house in Peterhead, the bedroom with the little chains of rosebuds on the wallpaper, away from the commotion of the gathering downstairs. I gave myself a mental shake, and smiled. 'I'm not, I—'

'Carolyn McClelland,' she said, using my full first name in the way she always did when catching me about to tell a lie, 'I've been your agent for nearly seven years, I can't be fooled. Is it the book?' Her eyes were keen. 'I shouldn't have dragged you over here like this, should I? Not when you were writing.'

'Don't be silly. There are more important things,' I said, 'than writing.' And to show how much I meant that, I leaned forward for another close look at the sleeping baby wrapped in blankets on her lap. 'He's really beautiful.'

'He is, rather, isn't he?' Proudly, she followed my gaze. 'Alan's mum says he looks just like Alan did.'

I couldn't see it. 'He's got more of you in him, I think. Just look at that hair.'

'Oh, the hair, God, yes, poor little chap,' she said, touching the bright copper-gold softness of the small head. 'I did hope he'd be spared that. He'll freckle, you know.'

'But freckles look so cute on little boys.'

'Yes, well, be sure you come and tell him that, when he's sixteen and cursing me.'

'At least,' I said, 'he won't begrudge the name you gave him. Jack's a nice, good, manly name.'

'The choice of desperation. I was hoping for something that sounded more Scottish, but Alan was so bloody-minded. Every time I came up with a name he'd say, "No, we had a dog called that," and that would be the end of it. Honestly, Carrie, I thought for a while we'd be having him christened as "Baby boy Ramsay".'

But of course they hadn't. Jane and Alan always found a way around their differences, and little Jack Ramsay had made it to church today, with me arriving in time to stand up as his godmother. That I'd managed to do it only by breaking every speed limit between my stop in Cruden Bay and here had left the baby so supremely unimpressed that, when he'd first laid eyes on me, he'd yawned and fallen fast asleep, not even waking when the minister had doused his head with water.

'Is he always so calm?' I asked now, as I looked at him.

'What, didn't you think I could have a calm baby?' Jane's eyes teased me, because she knew her own nature. She wasn't what I would have called a calm person. She had a strong will; she was driven, and vibrant, so very alive that she made me feel colourless, somehow, beside her. And tired. I couldn't keep up.

It didn't help that I'd been struck by some virus last month that had kept me in bed over Christmas and taken the fun out of New Year and now, a week later, I still wasn't back to full speed. But even when I was in good health, Jane's energy level was miles above mine.

That was why we worked so well together; why I'd chosen her. I wasn't any good myself with publishers – I gave in far too easily. I couldn't stomach conflict, so I'd learned to leave it all to Jane, and she had fought my battles for me, which was why I found myself, at thirty-one, with four bestselling novels to my credit and the freedom to live anywhere, and anyhow, I chose.

'How is the house in France?' she asked me, coming back, as she inevitably would do, to my work. 'You're still at Saint-Germain-en-Laye?'

'It's fine, thanks. And I'm still there, yes. It helps me get my details right. The palace there is central to the plot, it's where the action mostly happens.' Saint-Germain had been the French king's gift of refuge to the Stewart kings of Scotland for the first years of their exile, where old King

James and young King James by turns had held court with their loyal supporters, who'd plotted and schemed with the nobles of Scotland through three luckless Jacobite uprisings. My story was intended to revolve around Nathaniel Hooke, an Irishman at Saint-Germain, who seemed to me to be the perfect hero for a novel.

He'd been born in 1664, a year before the Plague, and only four years after the restoration of King Charles II to the battered throne of England. When King Charles had died and his Catholic brother, James, came to the throne, Hooke had taken up arms in rebellion, but then had changed sides and abandoned his Protestant faith for the Catholic Church, becoming one of James's stout defenders. But it wasn't any use. England was a nation full of Protestants, and any king who called himself a Catholic couldn't hope to keep the throne. James's claim had been challenged by that of his own daughter, Mary, and William of Orange, her husband. And that had meant war.

Nathaniel Hooke had been right in the thick of it. He'd fought for James in Scotland and been captured as a spy, and held a prisoner in the fearsome Tower of London. After his release he'd promptly taken up his sword again and gone to fight for James, and when the battles all were over, and William and Mary ruled firm on their throne, and James fled into exile, Hooke had gone with him to France.

But he did not accept defeat. Instead, he'd turned his many talents to convincing those around him that a well-planned joint invasion by the French king and the Scots could set things right again, restore the exiled Stewarts to their rightful throne.

They nearly had succeeded.

History remembered the tragic romance of Culloden

and Bonnie Prince Charlie, years after Hooke's time. But it was not in that cold winter at Culloden that the Jacobites – quite literally, the 'followers of James', and of the Stewarts – came closest to a realization of their purpose. No, that happened in the spring of 1708, when an invasion fleet of French and Scottish soldiers, Hooke's idea, anchored off the coast of Scotland in the Firth of Forth. On board the flagship was the tall, twenty-year-old James Stewart – not the James who had fled England, but his son, whom many, not only in Scotland but in England, accepted as their true king. On shore, assembled armies of the highlanders and loyal Scottish nobles waited eagerly to welcome him and turn their might against the weakened armies to the south.

Long months of careful preparations and clandestine plans had come to their fruition, and the golden moment seemed at hand, when once again a Stewart king would claim the throne of England.

How this great adventure failed, and why, was one of the most fascinating stories of the period, a story of intrigue and treachery that all sides had tried hard to cover up and bury, seizing documents, destroying correspondence, spreading rumours and misinformation that had been believed as fact down to the present day.

Most of the details that survived had been recorded by Nathaniel Hooke.

I liked the man. I'd read his letters, and I'd walked the halls of Saint-Germain-en-Laye, where he had walked. I knew the details of his marriage and his children and his relatively long life and his death. So it was frustrating to me that, after five long months of writing, I still struggled with the pages of my novel, and Hooke's character refused to come alive.

I knew Jane sensed that I was having trouble – as she said,

she'd known me far too long and far too well to overlook my moods. But she knew, too, I didn't like to talk about my problems, so she took care not to come at me directly. 'Do you know, last weekend I read through those chapters that you sent me—'

'When on earth do you have time to read?'

'There's always time to read. I read those chapters, and I wondered if you'd ever thought of telling things from someone else's point of view ... a narrator, you know, the way Fitzgerald does with Nick in *The Great Gatsby*. It occurred to me that someone on the outside could perhaps move round more freely, and link all the scenes together for you. Just a thought.' She left it there, and no doubt knowing that my first response to anyone's advice was staunch resistance, changed the subject.

Nearly twenty minutes later, I was laughing at her dry descriptions of the joys of changing a newborn, when her husband, Alan, thrust his head around the doorway of the bedroom.

'You do know there's a party going on downstairs?' he asked us, with a scowl I would have taken much more seriously if I hadn't known it was all bluff. He was a softie, on the inside. 'I can't entertain this lot all on my own.'

'Darling,' Jane replied, 'they *are* your relatives.'

'All the more reason not to leave me alone with them.' But he winked at me. 'She's not got you talking shop, I hope? I told her she's to let you be. She's too concerned with contracts.'

Jane reminded him, 'Well, that's my job. And for your information, I am never in the least concerned that Carrie's going to break a contract. She has another seven months before the first draft's due.'

She'd meant for that to cheer me, but I think that Alan must have seen my shoulders sag, because he held his hand to me and said, 'Come on, then. Come downstairs and have a drink, and tell me how the trip was. I'm amazed you made it all that way in time.'

There were enough jokes floating round about my tendency to get distracted when I travelled, so I opted not to tell them anything about my detour up the coast. But it reminded me, 'Alan,' I asked, 'are you flying tomorrow?'

'I am. Why?'

Alan's little fleet of helicopters helped to serve the offshore oil rigs dotted through the North Sea off the rugged coast of Peterhead. He was a fearless pilot, as I'd learned the one and only time I'd let him take me up. I'd barely had the legs to stand when he'd returned me to the ground. But now I said, 'I wondered if you'd fly me up the coast a bit. Nathaniel Hooke came over twice from France, to intrigue with the Scottish nobles, and both times he landed at the Earl of Erroll's castle, Slains, which, from the map I've got, the old one, looks to be somewhere just north of here. I'd like to see the castle, or what's left of it, from out at sea, the way it would have looked to Hooke when he first saw it, coming over.'

'Slains? Aye, I can take you over that. But it's not up the coast, it's down. At Cruden Bay.'

I stared. 'Where?'

'Cruden Bay. You would have missed it, coming up the way you did.'

Jane, sharp as ever, noticed something in my face, in my expression. 'What?' she asked.

I never ceased to be surprised by serendipity – the way chance happenings collided with my life. Of all the places that I could have stopped, I thought. Aloud I only said, 'It's nothing. Could we go tomorrow, Alan?'

'Aye. Tell you what – I'll take you early so that you can have your look from out at sea, and if you want when we get back I'll watch wee Jack awhile and Jane can drive you down to have a wander round. It'll do you both good, get a breath of sea air.'

And so that's what we did.

What I saw from the air looked much larger than what I had seen from the ground – a roofless, sprawling ruin that seemed to sit right at the edge of the cliffs, with the sea boiling white far below. It sent one small cold thrill down my spine, and I knew that familiar sensation enough to be frankly impatient to get on the ground, so that Jane could take over and drive me back down.

There were two other cars in the car park this time, and the snow of the footpath showed deep, sliding prints. I ploughed ahead of Jane, and raised my face towards the salt blasts of the wind that left a taste upon my lips and set me shivering again within the warm folds of my jacket.

I confess I couldn't, afterwards, remember any other people being there, although I knew there had been. Nor could I recall too many details of the ruin itself – just images, of pointed walls and hard pink granite flecked with grey that glittered in the light ... the one high square-walled tower standing solid near the cliff's edge ... the silence of the inner chambers, where the wind stopped raging and began to moan and weep, and where the bare roof timbers overhead cast shadows on the drifted snow. In one large room a massive gaping window faced the sea, and when I stood and leaned my hands against the sun-warmed sill I noticed, looking down, the imprints of a small dog's paws, perhaps a spaniel's, and beside them deeper footprints showing where a man had stood and looked, as I was looking, out towards the limitless horizon.

I could almost feel him standing at my shoulder now, but in my mind he'd changed so that he wasn't any more the modern stranger I had talked to in the car park yesterday, but someone of an older time, a man with boots and cloak and sword. The thought of him became so real I turned . . . and found Jane watching me.

She smiled at the expression on my face. She knew it well, from all the times that she'd been present when my characters began to stir, and talk, and take on life. Her voice was casual. 'You know that you can always come and stay with us, and work. We have the room.'

I shook my head. 'You have a baby. You don't need a houseguest, too.'

She looked at me again, and what she saw made her decide. 'Then come on. Let's go down and find a place for you to let in Cruden Bay.'

CHAPTER 2

MAIN STREET IN CRUDEN Bay sloped gently down-hill and bent round to the right and then left again, curving away out of sight to the harbour. It was narrow, a line of joined cottages and a few shops on the one side, and on the other a swiftly running stream that surged between its frozen banks and passed a single shop, a newsagent's, before it ran to meet the wide and empty sweep of beach that stretched away beyond the high snow-covered dunes.

The post office was marked by its red sign against the grey stone walls, and by the varied notices displayed in its front window announcing items for sale and upcoming events, including an enticingly named 'Buttery Morning' to be held at the local hall. Inside the shop were postcards, books, some souvenirs and sweets, and a very helpful woman. Yes, she knew of one place in the village that might suit me. A little cottage, basic, nothing fancy on the inside. 'It was old Miss Keith's before she passed away,' she said. 'Her brother has it now, but since he has a house himself down by the harbour, he's no use for it. He lets it out to tourists in the summer. Winters, there'll be no one there except his sons from time to time, and they're not often home. The younger lad, he likes to travel, and his brother's at the university in Aberdeen, so Jimmy Keith would probably be glad to let you have the place these next few months. I can give him a phone, if you like.'

And so it came to pass that, with a newly purchased pack of postcards stuffed into the pocket of my coat, I walked with Jane along the path by the rushing stream and down to where the road bent round and changed its name to Harbour Street. The houses here were like the ones along Main Street higher up – still low and joined to one another, and across from them a series of small gardens, some with sheds, sprang up between us and the wide pink beach.

From down here I could see the beach itself was huge, a curve at least two miles long with dunes that rose like hills behind it, casting shadows on the shore. A narrow white wood footbridge spanned the shallow gully of the stream to where those dunes began, but even as I paused and looked at it and wondered if I might have time to go across, Jane said with satisfaction, 'There's the path,' and shepherded me past the bridge and round to where a wide and slushy pathway veered up from the street to climb a good-sized hill. Ward Hill, the woman at the post office had called it.

It was a headland, high and rounded, thrusting out above the sea, and as I came up to the top I looked behind and saw I'd climbed above the level of the dunes and had a view not only of the beach, but of the distant houses and the hills beyond. And turning back again I saw, towards the north, the blood-red ruin of Slains castle clear against cliffs of the next headland.

I felt a small thrill. 'Oh, how perfect.'

'I don't know,' Jane said, slowly. 'It looks rather dismal.' She was looking at the cottage, standing all alone here on the hill. It had been rubble-built, with plain square white-washed walls beneath a roof of old grey slates that dripped with dampness from the melting snow. The windows were small, with their frames peeling paint and the worn blinds inside were pulled down like closed eyelids, as if the small cottage had wearied of watching the endless approach and retreat of the sea.

I reached out to knock at the door. 'It's just lonely.'

'So will you be, if you live up here. Perhaps this wasn't such a good idea.'

'It was your idea.'

'Yes, but what I had in mind was more a cosy little place right in the village, near the shops . . .'

'This suits me fine.' I knocked again. 'I guess he isn't here yet.'

'Try the bell.'

I hadn't seen the doorbell, buried deep within the tangle of a stubborn climbing vine with tiny leaves that shivered every time the wind blew from the sea. I stretched my hand to press it, but a man's voice from the path behind me warned, 'It winna dee ye ony good, it disna ring. The salt fae the sea ruins the wiring, fast as I fix it. Besides,' said the man, as he came up to join us, 'I'm nae in the hoose tae be hearin ye, am I?' His smile made his rough, almost ugly face instantly likeable. He'd have been well into his sixties, with whitening hair and the fit build and ruddy complexion of someone who'd worked hard outdoors all his life. The woman at the post office had seemed sure I'd like him, although she had warned me I might have some trouble understanding him.

'He speaks the Doric,' she had said. 'The language of this area. You'll likely find it difficult to follow what he says.'

I didn't, actually. His speech was broad and quick, and if I'd had to translate every word I might have had a problem, but it wasn't hard to catch the general sense of what he meant when he was talking.

Holding my hand out, I said, 'Mr Keith? Thanks for coming. I'm Carrie McClelland.'

'A pleasure tae meet ye.' His handshake was sure. 'But

I'm nae Mr Keith. Ma dad was Mr Keith, and he's been deid and beeried twenty years. Ye ca' me Jimmy.'

'Jimmy, then.'

Jane introduced herself, never content to be out of the action for long. She didn't exactly nudge me to one side, but she was an agent, after all, and though she likely didn't even notice it herself, she liked to take control whenever somebody was bargaining.

She wasn't pushy, really, but she led the conversation, and I hid my smile and let her lead, content to follow after them as Jimmy Keith fitted his key in the lock of the low cottage door, and then with a jiggle and thump of the latch made it swing inwards, scraping the tiles of the floor.

My first impression was one of general dimness, but when the blinds were raised with a rattle and the faded curtains pushed back, I could see the place, although not large, was comfortable – a sitting room, with thinning Persian carpets on the floor, two cushioned armchairs and a sofa, and a long scrubbed wooden table pushed against the farther wall, with wooden kitchen chairs around it. The kitchen had been fitted at the one end of the cottage with the snugness of a galley on a ship. Not many cupboards, nor much worktop, but everything was in its place and useful, from the one sink with its built-in stainless-steel draining board to the small-sized electric cooker that had, I guessed, been meant to take the place of the old coal-fired Aga standing solid in its chimney alcove on the back wall.

The Aga, so Jimmy assured me, still worked. 'It's a bit contermacious – that's difficult, like – but it aye heats the room, and ye'll save on the electric.'

Jane, standing by the front door looking up, made a pointed remark about that being handy. 'Do you know,' she said, 'I haven't seen one of these since I rented my first flat.'

I came to gaze up, with Jane, at the little black metal box fixed to the top of the doorjamb, with the glassed-in meter and assorted gauges set above it. I had heard of such contraptions, but I'd never seen or used one.

Jimmy Keith looked up as well. 'Michty aye,' he agreed. 'Ye dinna see those ony mair.'

It took 50p coins, he explained, and was fed like a parking meter – run out of coins and the power went off. 'But nae bother,' he promised. He'd sell me a roll of the coins and, when I'd used them all, he'd come open the meter and take them back out and just sell me the coins back again.

Jane gave the box one final doubtful look and turned to carry on with her inspection. There wasn't much left, just a bedroom, not large, at the back, and an unexpectedly roomy bathroom across from it, complete with footed bath and what the British called an 'airing cupboard,' open shelves set round a yellow water heater, good for storing towels and drying clothes.

Jane moved to stand beside me. 'Well?'

'I like it.'

'Not much to it.'

'I don't need much when I'm working.'

She considered this, then turned to Jimmy Keith. 'What sort of rent would you be asking?'

Which was my cue, I knew, to leave them to it. Jane had often told me how inept I was at making deals, and she was right. The cost of things had never much concerned me. Someone told me the price, and if I could afford it, I paid it, and didn't waste time wondering if I could have had the thing for less. I had other things to occupy my mind.

I wandered through again into the sitting room, and stood a moment looking out the window at the headland reaching out into the sea, and dark along its length the ruined castle walls of Slains.

Watching, I could feel again the stirrings of my characters – the faint, as yet inaudible, suggestion of their voices, and their movements close around me, in the way someone can sense another's presence in a darkened room. I didn't need to shut my eyes. They were already fixed, not truly seeing, on the window glass, in that strange writer's trance that stole upon me when my characters began to speak, and I tried hard to listen.

I'd expected that Nathaniel Hooke would have the most to say, and that his voice would be the strongest and the first that I would hear, but in the end the words I heard came not from him, but from a woman, and the words themselves were unexpected.

'So, you see, my heart is held for ever by this place,' she said. 'I cannot leave.'

I cannot leave.

That's all she said, the voice was gone, but still that phrase stayed with me and repeated like a litany, so urgently that when the deal was done and Jane and Jimmy Keith had settled things and I was asked when I would like to take possession, I said, 'Could I have it now? Tonight?'

They looked at me, the two of them, as though I'd lost my mind.